Katy Regnery's

# a modern fairytale
## Collection

*The Vixen and the Vet*

(Beauty & the Beast)

*Never Let You Go*

(Hansel & Gretel)

*Ginger's Heart*

(Little Red Riding Hood)

*Dark Sexy Knight*

(Camelot)

*Don't Speak*

(The Little Mermaid)

*Swan Song*

(The Ugly Duckling)
*Coming 2017*

# Don't Speak

a modern fairytale

Katy Regnery

Dear Michele,
Love hard. And believe in fairytales!
Katy xoxo

DON'T SPEAK

Please visit my website at www.katyregnery.com
First Edition: February 2017

Katy Regnery
Don't Speak: a novel / by Katy Regnery — 1st ed.
ISBN: 978-1-944810-08-5

# Part One

# Chapter 1

"Stay still or I'll stick you again!"

With three pins held between her lips, Laire garbled the words, but her older sister Kyrstin understood her meaning and stopped wiggling.

"You're so nasty when you're workin'."

Laire shrugged, pulling a pin from her mouth and securing the hemline she'd just painstakingly folded. The white satin was slippery under her nimble fingers, but the pins held it in place.

"Laire, when you goin' to make me somethin' pretty?" asked Isolde, Laire's other sister, who, at forty-something weeks pregnant, sat like a beached whale on their father's couch, flipping through a bridal magazine.

Laire turned to Isolde, giving her belly a dry look before raising her eyes to her sister's face, a fair facsimile of her own. "When Junior's finally here."

"I'm sick of bein' pregnant," said Isolde, flipping a page. "I want to be hot again."

Kyrstin looked down at Laire, and both girls snickered softly, prompting a dirty look from Isolde.

"Just you wait, Kyrstin," she said, slapping her magazine down on the coffee table, which had been improvised from an old wooden crab trap with a piece of oval glass set on top. "I bet Remy knocks you up within a month."

"No way," said Kyrstin, puffing up the sleeves that Laire had copied from one of the dozens of magazines they'd bought at the Walmart in Jacksonville two months ago. "No offense, but I'm smarter than that, Issy. I got a prescription for the pill. And I'm usin' it. I'm not ready to be a mom yet. No way."

"Humph," grunted Isolde, sitting up and placing her hands on her knees. "Then you'll be an old mom with saggy boobs. See how you like that."

"Speaking of boobs," said Laire, standing up to check the bustline of the white dress. "Did yours grow a size since last month?"

Kyrstin narrowed her eyes. "Plannin' a weddin' is stressful. Remy's mama is an out-and-out witch, and y'all know it."

"That's what you get for marryin' a dingbatter," said Isolde, hefting herself off the couch with a sigh. "Daddy got any tea, Laire?"

"In the fridge," said Laire, plucking a pin from a plush tomato that she'd found in her mother's abandoned sewing basket. She liked remembering her mother—who'd passed away ten years ago, when Laire was only eight—holding the tomato in her hands as she pinned Laire's Halloween costume. *You're going to be the prettiest mermaid Corey Island ever saw, little Laire.* She blinked back sudden tears and shouted over her shoulder to her oldest sister: "Don't drink it all. Daddy'll be home soon, and tired."

Kyrstin pulled at the bodice of the dress as Isolde waddled to the kitchen. "Ain't fair callin' Remy a dingbatter. He and his been here for ten years or more."

Laire laughed softly, shaking her head. Anyone who hadn't lived on Corey for more than three or four generations was likely to be called a dingbatter or a woodser, and her sister knew it.

"Don't listen to Issy," said Laire, who loved her sisters

despite their constant bickering. "She's just big and ornery right now."

"Please, Lord, let the baby come soon."

"She's due tomorrow," said Laire. She tried to slip two fingers into the bodice, but it was too tight against her sister's skin. "You want me to let this out or you want to lose a few pounds before July?"

"Only three weeks till the weddin'," griped Kyrstin. "Best let it out."

Laire nodded. "Take it off, then. Can't pin it so close without makin' you bleed, and there's no time for more fabric if you stain it."

Kyrstin huffed softly, stepping down from the milk crate she'd been standing on in the center of their father's living room, and heading for the back hallway. Just before she disappeared, she turned to look at her little sister. "It's a beautiful dress, Laire. Like a princess dress. You did a good job. Mama . . ." Her voice slid away, but she cleared her throat to find it again. "She woulda been real proud."

The tears Laire had just fought back returned with a vengeance, and Laire swiped at her eyes, grateful for her sister's kindness. "Think so?"

"*Know* so," said Kyrstin with a sad smile. "I'll be right back."

Laire watched her go, leaning down to pick up the crate and put it in the closet beside the front door. The grit of salt and sand under her bare feet reminded her that she still needed to vacuum the house before her father returned home from a long day of crabbing. She pulled the old Electrolux from the closet and dragged the fabric-wrapped cord to the wall, plugging it in. She attached the nozzle to the hose and turned it on, pushing it back and forth over the frayed, faded welcome mat just inside the door as she pondered whether or not Remy and his family should still be called dingbatters after a decade on the island.

As a tenth-generation Corey Islander, Laire Cornish was about as "old Corey" as they came, and she had the accent to prove it. Her mother, who'd taken some classes in hospitality and tourism at Carteret Community College, had made certain her girls were aware of the Corey brogue, and took steps to mitigate it in their speech with non-islanders. Islands like Corey, Harkers, and Ocracoke in the Outer Banks of North Carolina, had been settled by the English hundreds of years ago, but had remained largely isolated thereafter, which meant that the accent and speech patterns had never really changed from what one might have heard from sailors in the 1700s. Laire couldn't count the number of times tourists had asked her if she was Australian or Scottish. She wasn't, of course. But her accent, a mix of Elizabethan English and American Southern, made for a highly unusual combination that wasn't always understandable by dingbatters and woodsers.

As the gravelly sound of vacuumed-up sand and salt faded away, she finished the carpet quickly and turned off the old machine.

"You're good to Daddy, Laire," said Isolde, who stood in the kitchen doorway holding a glass of sweet tea on top of her rounded belly. "How's he feelin' lately?"

Their father, who had suffered a mild heart attack just after Christmas, was back at work again, crabbing with his brother and nephew, just like nine generations of Cornishes before them.

"Okay, I guess," she said. "I make him eat oatmeal every morning."

"He hates it?"

Laire smiled. "Of course."

"He eats it?"

"With grumbles."

"Mama would've . . ."

Just like Kyrstin, Isolde's voice trailed off, like talking

about their mother was something they shouldn't do. *Or maybe*, thought Laire, *it just hurt too much.*

Isolde, who was twenty-four, had gotten married to her high school sweetheart, Paul Hyde, last summer and discovered she was pregnant three months later. It was the way on Corey Island to marry and have kids young, but Laire suspected it was extra hard for her sister to be without a mother now.

Laire put the vacuum away and turned to her sister. "It's okay to talk about her, Issy."

"What good is it?" asked Isolde, sniffling before taking another sip of tea. "Won't bring her back."

"I miss her too," said Laire, holding her sister's familiar green eyes, feeling jealous of her sister's memories and wishing she would open up and talk about their mother more.

"Here it is!" said Kyrstin, holding the wedding dress carefully across her forearms as she reentered the living room.

Laire took the dress and sat down on the brown plaid couch, shaking out the bodice to figure out where to open the seams as Kyrstin took the tea from Isolde's hands and finished it up.

"You know what I think, Issy?"

"Tell me, Kyrs."

Laire looked up at the pair of them and rolled her eyes. From the singsong tones of their voices, she knew what was coming.

"Now that our little Laire is a high school graduate, I think it's finally time for her to figure out when she's gonna let Brodie into her shorts."

"Poor Brodie," said Isolde with a snicker.

Kyrstin giggled. "You holdin' out on us, Laire? You got someone else in the wings?"

Laire pulled on the left side seam harder than she should, making several beads scatter to the carpet, then looked up at them. "You're a couple of jackasses, is all I know."

"Ooo! Testy!" said Isolde, turning to Kyrstin. "Go get me more tea. You drunk all of mine."

"Get it yourself," said Kyrstin. "I want to know when Laire's settlin' down."

*Never*, she thought, leaning forward to open the sewing box on the coffee table and pull out a seam ripper to help her finish the job.

*Never, never, never, never, never.*

The word circled around and around in Laire's head like a promise, like a vow.

*I am never "settlin' down" on Corey Island and having half a dozen kids with a local boy before I hit thirty. There's a whole wide world out there, away from here, away from Corey, away from the Outer Banks, and I intend to see it.*

". . . touch your boobies, huh, Laire?"

She looked up from the dress in her lap. "*What*?"

"Brodie told Remy you let him touch your boobies. After the prom."

Laire's face flushed with heat as she blinked at her sister. "That's a lie!"

Yes, she had gone to the high school prom with Brodie Walsh, but that was it! The second he'd tried to kiss her, she'd clocked him in the nose and run home. Touched her boobies? Hell, no! They'd never even kissed!

Kyrstin shrugged, but her eyes were merry. "Why would he make it up?"

*To trap me*, thought Laire, shoving the white fabric off her lap and standing up. She turned away from her sisters, looking out the picture window over the couch. Their father's one-story, two-bedroom house was directly on the water, and she looked out at the harbor, seething. Fishing boats, coming in from a long day of catching or crabbing, pointed toward Corey Island. One of those boats was her father's. Had he heard this rumor that she'd let Brodie touch her intimately? She sucked in a horrified breath.

Her father was a strict, religious, old-school islander. He loved his girls more than anything, but he was proud and he wouldn't stand for that sort of loose talk unless it included some sort of respectable commitment between the participants—a commitment Laire didn't want from Brodie or any other island boy.

"It's a lie," she said again.

It wouldn't be the first time a local boy had compromised the reputation of an island girl to push her into a relationship. But damned if Laire would let it happen to her.

"Well, I think Brodie's cute. Filled out *real* nice. And his daddy's boat is newer than most of the—"

"No!" growled Laire, still staring out the window. *I don't want to be trapped here forever!*

"Little Laire better get off her high horse," advised Isolde, her voice taking on an edge. "Eighteen years old and never had a boyfriend. You could do a lot worse'n Brodie."

*Damn Brodie Walsh to hell and back!*

With twenty-one kids in the entire high school and only six in Laire's graduating class, the pickings for a prom date had been slim. Not to mention, she mostly looked at the island boys, whom she'd known since infancy, like a bunch of jerky brothers. At least Brodie, whose mama was the daughter of the pastor, seemed to have some manners. At the time, she had considered him the least disgusting of her choices, but now? Gyah! She could just kill him for spreading rumors about her when she'd kept her reputation lily-white for eighteen long years.

Laire looked over her shoulder, shooting her oldest sister a dark look. "I didn't let him touch me. There's no understanding between us. It's a lie and that's that."

"Hope Daddy don't catch wind of it then," said Kyrstin, giving Laire a shit-eating smile over the rim of her tea.

*They don't understand*, thought Laire, crossing to the front closet to grab a hanger for the dress. *They think it's a game.*

She hung the dress carefully on the bar, at the back of the closet, behind Mama's old winter coat, and closed the door. She'd work on it later. She didn't trust herself with the delicate material and beadwork right now. Her hands were shaking with fury.

She loved her sisters, but they were both content to marry local boys and be fishermen's wives. They'd have a bunch of kids—the eleventh generation of Cornishes—who would grow up together here on Corey, which had a static population of just under nine hundred souls. Isolde and Kyrstin would end up running Bingo Night at the United Methodist Church and rope the altar with fir greens at Christmastime. On their tenth anniversaries, their husbands would take them on a big weekend to Raleigh or Myrtle Beach, and they'd talk about it for decades after.

*Remy took us on down to Myrtle, but I felt fair quamished by all the lights and smells.*

*You want t'talk smells?* she imagined Isolde exclaiming. *It's right yethy in Raleigh with all the bus fumes!*

And all the other women organizing bins of clothes at the village secondhand shop for the annual sale would tut and nod in agreement: Off-island might be interesting for a visit, but Corey was home.

And the thing is?

It was a good life. A respectable life. A fulfilling life. Hell, it had been her mother's life, and Laire loved her mother more than anyone else in the world, living or dead.

But it just wasn't the life Laire wanted.

She had a very different plan for her future, and it included being part of the off-island world. Specifically, the world of fashion.

Not only had Laire made Kyrstin's wedding dress from scratch, but last summer she'd made Isolde's as well. Her passion for clothes had started when she was nine or ten, after her mother had passed. Her sisters had had no interest in their mother's old Singer sewing machine, but Laire, who'd spent many happy hours listening to it hum, had found profound comfort in teaching herself how to use it. She imagined her mother's fingers on the bobbin, threading the needle, lining up the presser foot on a seam, and felt her presence keenly.

By age twelve, she was making shorts and blouses for herself and her sisters. And by fifteen, she was being asked to help classmates with prom and graduation dresses. Now, at eighteen, she had as many as five or six jobs at a time, making dresses, shorts, pants, and blouses for friends and family on the island, in addition to outfitting herself, Kyrstin, and all of her sister's bridesmaids for the July wedding.

And one day? Well, one day she wanted to make it up north to the Parsons School in New York City or RISD in Rhode Island. She wanted to go to college for fashion design and learn from the best. She wanted to start her own line of clothes, inspired by the greens and blues of the water and sky on Corey. She wanted her own house that didn't smell like crabs, with carpets that weren't perpetually covered in a gritty dust of dried salt and sand. She wanted a different life than Corey Island could ever hope to offer.

That said, college didn't come cheap. She figured she had three or four years of clothesmaking to go before she'd be able to swing the first-year tuition, even with financial assistance. And working on free jobs, like her sister's wedding, did nothing to further her cause.

She looked up to find her sisters staring at her.

"So?" asked Isolde. "What're you goin' to do about Brodie?"

"I'll march over to his house, and I'll stand there in his

driveway, and I'll call him out as a liar for the whole island to hear," she said, raising her chin.

Isolde gasped. "You will *not* make a scene, Laire Maiden Cornish."

"Oh, yes, I . . . I goddamn *fucking* will!"

Laire's use of the word *fuck* made her sister's eyes wider than a full moon over the Sound. They were not the sort of family who used curse words beyond an occasional *damn, ass,* or *hell.*

"Better not kiss Daddy with that mouth!" exclaimed Kyrstin, shaking her head in disapproval.

Isolde shoved the tea at Kyrstin and placed her hand over her belly as she took an angry step toward Laire. "I don't want my baby hearin' that kind of filthy talk. I'm goin' home."

"Good." Laire put her hands on her hips. "Don't let the door hit you in the ass on the way out!"

Isolde had just gotten to the front door as it swung open, and there, taking up the entirety of the doorway with his maple-tree strength and brawn was their father, Howard "Hook" Cornish, the best crabber in the Outer Banks.

"Where y'all off to now, Issy girl?"

Isolde leaned up on tiptoe and kissed her father's whiskered cheek. "Laire's in a mood, and Kyrstin drank all your sweet tea. See you tomorrow for services."

"Amen," said Hook, calling after her. "Take care, now. Y'all keep my grandbaby safe, hear?"

"I hear!" came Isolde's muffled reply as she stomped out of the house and started her car.

Hook turned to his remaining daughters, giving Kyrstin an annoyed look. "Y'all drank all my sweet tea, huh?"

"I'll go make more, Daddy," said Kyrstin with a sheepish smile, taking her empty glass into the kitchen.

"Yeah," he drawled to himself, "but it'll be from powder, I

s'pose." He turned to Laire, scanning her face with his sharp blue eyes. "And you're in a mood? What for?"

Laire shrugged. "Issy's the one in a mood."

He looked out the window as she pulled out of the driveway, kicking up gravel with her tires. "Might be. But she's big as a house, Laire. Cut her some slack."

He was right. She *was* big as a house, with a mother-in-law who was loving but demanding, and no mother of her own to lead her through the terrifying mystery of childbirth.

"I'll do that," she said. "You mommucked, Daddy?"

*Mommucked* was an islander word meaning "dead tired." It was the sort of word her mother would have reminded her not to use off-island, but here, at home, it was the right word.

"Aye-up. Went through a thousand pounds of bait, and I cracked my back hookin' a buoy. Long day." He had taken off his knee-high rubber boots and yellow all-weather coveralls on the porch, but his jeans were filthy and he smelled strongly of fish and the sea. Right yethy.

As though he could read her mind, he chucked her under the chin and grinned. "Best shower before that tea." He turned toward the hallway that led to the bathroom and two bedrooms, then pivoted back around with a low groan. "Ah. Shoot. Almost forgot. Got a delivery to make over in Buxton." His lips pursed after a long sigh. "But my tired's got tired."

"Buxton?" said Laire, perking up as she pictured the castle-like summer homes of the superwealthy who lived a short ways up the coast.

Buxton, like Frisco, Avon, Rodanthe, and Nags Head, was where millionaires from Raleigh, Charlotte, and even faraway places like New York City, spent their summers. It wasn't an area that Laire had gotten to see up close very often, but the few times her father had taken her on a delivery, she'd been fascinated by a totally different world so close to home.

"Aye-up." He put one hand on his hip and rubbed his

forehead with the other. "Guess I'll shower later. Gotta take six crates of blues to a house up there."

"You're tired," said Laire. "I could help. I don't mind doin' it for you."

Her father looked up. "You're a girl. How're you goin' to haul six packed coolers from the dock up to the house?"

"Daddy," she said, crossing her arms over her chest and fixing him with a no-nonsense glare. "I been hoistin' crates o'blues since I was littler'n the one inside Issy."

Her father cocked his head to the side and took a long look at her, then chuckled. "Fair enough. I guess you have, at that." He checked his watch. "It's three now. Promised delivery for four thirty."

"Then I'll get going," said Laire, her heart thumping with urgency and excitement. "Sound side or ocean side?"

"Sound. Place called Utopia Manor," said her father, who explained the exact location of the house and that the blue crabs he'd caught today had been promised for a party that evening.

From his instructions, she knew approximately where she'd find the house. "Dock the boat and walk around to the front door?"

Her father shook his head. "There's a kitchen entrance on the left side of the house. Caterer's from the Pamlico House. Lady named Judith Sebastian in charge. Find her first, then bring up the coolers. They prepaid." He raised his chin and looked stern. "No takin' tips, now."

"No, Daddy," she said. "Anythin' else?"

"That's it." He grinned at her, his tanned, weathered face handsome, even after a long day and covered all over with salt-and-pepper whiskers. "You're a good girl, li'l Laire."

"You take a nice hot shower and don't worry about a thing. I've got it covered."

Racing to the room she still shared with Kyrstin, Laire

tugged off her white shorts and pulled on a pair of jeans. Earlier, she'd twisted her strawberry blonde hair into a messy bun, but now she brushed it out and secured it into a neat ponytail. She swapped her gray Corey HS T-shirt for a black, long-sleeved, button-up shirt she'd made for herself, and paired it with a black patent-leather belt. Plucking her shiny black Wellies from the back of her closet, she pulled them on over her jeans, up to her knees. Checking out her reflection in the mirror, she decided that she looked as fashion-forward as possible for someone hauling crates of fresh crab, and ran back down the hall.

Sparing a moment to wave good-bye to Kyrstin, she grabbed the spare boat keys from the hook in the kitchen and sailed out the door.

## Chapter 2

Laire stood at the wheel of her father's boat with the wind in her hair and six coolers of blue crab on ice behind her. Her father had been lean on details, but she gathered that the folks up in Buxton were having a fancy party and had requested fresh catch delivered same-day.

Blue crabs.

For as long as she could remember, blue crabs had been her family's livelihood.

Both of her grandfathers had crabbed the Pamlico Sound.

Her father and his brother, Laire's uncle Franklin, called Fox by friends and family, had been crabbing since they were old enough to walk.

But Uncle Fox had also been blessed with business savvy, and about ten years ago, he and Laire's father had opened King Triton Seafood, a commercial fish house on Corey Island that sold fresh catch to restaurants, caterers, hotels, and locals. Because they were commercial fishermen themselves, they were trusted by local fishermen *and* outside buyers, and had built up a reputable business in short order. Most of their stock came directly from fishing boats every afternoon, and they were picky about what they sold, making them a favorite purveyor for posh hotels and inns in the mid Banks and even a few folks who came out from the mainland.

The Pamlico Sound, the largest lagoon in the Eastern United States, was the name of the body of water between the Outer Banks and the mainland of North Carolina. Three inlets, at Bodie Island, Hatteras, and Ocracoke, fed the Sound salt water from the Atlantic Ocean, and two rivers from the west, the Neuse and Pamlico, fed it fresh water, which meant that the Sound was a mix of both: water from the sea and water from the land.

Dotted along the eastern shoreline of the Sound were the towns of the Outer Banks: in the south, Ocracoke and Corey, which were close-set islands; then, moving north, Hatteras, Buxton, and Avon; the cluster of Salvo, Waves, and Rodanthe; and finally, up on the northern Banks, Nags Head, a crummy name for the crowning jewel of the Outer Banks.

From Hatteras north, tourism had been prevalent since the Civil War, though Millionaire's Row in Nags Head had seen a vacation-home-building boom between the 1920s and 1950s. That boom had never really included the southern islands of Ocracoke and Corey, where commercial fishing was still a way of life and tourism had only started in earnest about twenty years ago. It was a growing industry still dwarfed by the northern towns', and Ocracoke, five times the size of Corey, with a regular ferry from Hatteras, saw about ten times the business as small and hard-to-reach Corey.

Laire zipped past the bustling town of Hatteras, spying a pair of dolphins playing in her wake off the portside and giggling at their antics. From Hatteras, she zoomed past Frisco, then slowed down as she neared Buxton, anxious that she not miss the house expecting her father's delivery. Checking her watch, she was gratified to see she'd made good time. It was almost four o'clock, which meant she didn't need to rush.

She cleared Brooks Point, hugging the Buxton shoreline at

Brigand Bay, careful that her arrival so close to shore was wakeless. The first house she saw had the four-story rectangular tower she recognized from her father's instructions. Beside it was another large house, then another. Then, sitting slightly apart from the other three mansions and bigger than them combined, she recognized her destination: Utopia Manor.

Three stories high, with five pronounced gables on the roofline, a green lawn, a pool, and a long boardwalk that led directly from the house to the Sound, she couldn't have missed it if she tried. It was the most beautiful house she'd ever seen.

On the lawn between the house and the pool, she could see hired help setting up tables in the late-afternoon sunshine, unfolding chairs and scurrying about with linens and china. Her father hadn't filled her in on what festivities were taking place at Utopia Manor tonight, but one look at the preparations told her that whatever it was, it *must* be a big deal.

Throwing the buoys over the side, she slowed to a crawl, cutting the engine to drift in alongside the pristine dock made of new lumber. Leaping from the bow with a line in her hand, she knotted it to a shiny chrome cleat, then jumped back on board to shimmy aft and do the same for the stern. Once she was securely tethered to the dock, she reached for the paperwork in her hip pocket, unfolding the invoices as she hopped back onto the dock. She ran a quick hand through her windblown hair and straightened her shirt before heading up to the house.

It wasn't a short walk on the winding boardwalk, over the shallows and sand dunes, and included several sets of stairs up from the water's edge to the house. Suddenly Laire wondered how smart it had been to insist she could carry the six packed coolers on her own.

Good thing she was early. She could take her time if she needed to.

She sighed with pleasure as she walked past the perfectly

manicured rolling lawn and around the beautifully landscaped pool area, heading around the house as her father had instructed.

"Hey!"

She heard his voice before she saw him.

Had she known the ultimate cost of that simple glance heavenward, maybe she wouldn't have stopped. Maybe she would have just kept on walking with her head down. But fate held no warnings for Laire Maiden Cornish.

Shielding her eyes, she looked up at a deck wrapped around the second floor of the mansion, waiting a moment for her eyes to adjust as he came into view.

There, in the glittering sunlight . . . a boy.

No, a *man*.

A young man, a little older than she, tall and muscular, with jet-black hair and a square jaw, dark brown eyes, and a deep tan. He wore a robin's-egg blue bathing suit with Kelly green palm fronds in a small repeat and a pair of sunglasses buried in his thick hair. In one hand, he held a phone up to his ear, and in the other, he slowly swirled a glass filled with ice and clear liquid. He stared out at the sound, concentrating on his call.

"Hey!" he yelled. "Can you hear me now?" He huffed with annoyance, pulling the phone away from his ear and squinting at it before trying again. "Pete? It's Erik. Can you hear me?" He set the glass down on the balcony's wooden railing and gave his phone his full attention. Staring down at it, he muttered, "Shit. No reception."

*It's Erik.*

*Erik.*

*His name is Erik.*

Feeling a sharp burn in her lungs, Laire realized she'd been holding her breath and sucked in a huge gulp of air as she stared up at him, frozen in the moment, utterly mesmerized.

She had never seen a more perfect, more handsome person in her entire life.

The sun glinted off his dark hair and wrapped his body in gold, making him appear godlike so very far above her. Were she the type to swoon, Laire imagined she would have been a puddle of goopy longing on the ground below him, content to sacrifice her pride for a glimpse at his beauty.

"Erik, honey? Can you come down here please?"

The voice was loud near her ear and startled Laire, who whipped her head around to find a woman standing directly behind her, looking up at Erik. She was tall and elegant, with very dark brown hair in a tidy chignon. Wearing a chic black bathing suit and a patterned sarong, she could have walked out of a magazine.

"Mom, there's no reception here!"

"We're in the wilds," she said, taking off her sunglasses to reveal deep brown eyes fringed with dark lashes. "I need to know where you want me to put you, Hillary, Peter, and Vanessa tonight. Please come down for a moment, won't you?"

Erik's mother turned back toward the lawn, the shiny gold bracelets on her wrist clinking as she walked away.

Looking down at her dull black boots, which had a sheen of dried salt on them from the trip over, Laire realized how incredibly out of place she was, and her cheeks flushed. She had no business mooning over *Prince* Erik. Keeping her head down, she started walking toward the side of the house, but his voice stopped her once again.

"Hey!"

She leaned her head back, shielding her eyes, her feet unwilling to keep walking away if there was the slightest chance he was speaking to her.

*And the miracle of it all?*

He was.

"Hey," he said again, resting his elbows on the deck railing and grinning down at her.

"M-me?"

"Yeah. You," he said, nodding at her. "Hey."

"H-hey," she squeaked, shocked she was able to respond at all.

"You workin' the party?"

"Um . . ." *He's talking to me. He's talking to me.* "N-no. I've got crabs."

*I've got crabs.*

*Oh my God.*

*I did* not *just say that.*

His eyebrows shot up, and his grin widened into a full-blown smile, accompanied by a soft chuckle. "You do, huh? Well, that's too bad."

*Please, earth, open up and swallow me whole.*

Sadly, it didn't.

"N-no! I mean . . . I mean, I'm *delivering* crabs. I don't *have* them! I don't have crabs!"

He laughed again, this time a rich, warm belly laugh that made her insides turn to goo.

"Glad to hear it, Freckles," he said, picking up his glass and taking a sip.

Said freckles burned so hot, she was certain her cheeks were maroon. "I have to go."

"Where to?" he asked.

She pointed to the corner of the house. "Kitchen."

"Wait, where?" He cocked his head to the side as though he was having trouble hearing her.

. . . or *understanding* her.

Her accent. It was strong because she was so nervous.

"The kitchen," she articulated carefully.

"Ahhhhh. Right. To give them crabs?" He was barely able to finish his question because he started laughing again.

She took a deep breath and shook her head, willing this entire situation to be somehow banished from the fabric of time.

Except . . .

*Except no.*

She wouldn't trade it. Not a second of it, crabs and all.

Glancing back up at him, she allowed herself—just for a moment—to trace the perfect lines of his face, to memorize it, to keep it safe inside her heart so she could pull out the memory and gaze at it like a picture whenever she wanted to: beautiful Erik, the black-haired prince of Utopia Manor, smiling down at her.

"Bye," she murmured, forcing her feet to start moving again.

Flustered by a combination of humiliation, bewilderment, and lust, once she rounded the corner of the house, she stopped and leaned her head against the clapboard, closing her eyes and pressing her hands to her cheeks. She sighed, immediately conjuring the memory of Erik's smile again and savoring it before tucking it safely away.

And then, a proud realist, she opened her eyes and reminded herself who she was: Laire Cornish from Corey Island, delivering crabs to a mansion for a posh party. A delivery girl. A fisherman's daughter. Nothing less. But certainly nothing more to someone as rich and beautiful as the young man on the balcony.

They had shared a moment, sure. But that's all it was: a moment that was already gone.

Thus grounded, she stepped away from the house and walked purposefully through the open door of the kitchen to find the catering manager and make her father's delivery.

\*\*\*

Erik Rexford chuckled as he watched the cute redhead disappear from sight, headed to the "*keet*-chin." He'd noticed her when his mother had called up to him—her trim little body angled away from him and strawberry blonde ponytail long and straight

26

against her black shirt. She didn't fit in, wearing a long-sleeved, dark-colored shirt, jeans, and high, rubber boots on a hot and sunny day. But it made him feel curious about her. *Very* curious. In fact, he'd felt a fierce and sudden compulsion to see her face.

And when she'd turned around? It had almost knocked the wind out of him.

She was pretty.

Man, she was pretty, with her red lips open in surprise and a sprinkle of angel kisses across her nose. He'd always been partial to the clean-scrubbed-girl-next-door look, and this chick had it going on in spades. Except she didn't live next door. He doubted she even lived in Buxton. Guessing by her accent, she probably came from one of the islands down south, where they still fished for a living. Maybe even a fisherman's daughter. *A little mermaid,* he thought with a chuckle, *from a totally different world than mine.*

Turning away from the balcony, he stepped back into his bedroom, throwing his useless phone on the bed and picking up a green polo shirt from the floor. As he slipped it over his head, he remembered the appalled look on her pretty face when she'd yelled, "I don't have crabs!" and started laughing again.

"I read that laughin' at nothin' is the first sign of insanity."

Erik turned around to see his little sister, Hillary, standing in his doorway. At almost seventeen years old, she was four years younger than Erik, but one of his closest friends.

"I guess you'd know, psycho." He reached for his phone, holding it up. "You gettin' any reception out here?"

"Why, yes, I am," she said, pulling her own phone, the latest iPhone model, from her hip pocket.

"Send a message to Pete, would you? Ask him what time he and Van are gettin' here?"

Hillary dropped his eyes quickly. Her voice was soft when she answered. "No. Just . . . walk around the house. You'll get service somewhere."

Erik's shoulders slumped. "Come on, Hills. Just send him a message."

She glanced up at him, her blue eyes wary. "It's awkward."

"Only because you *make* it awkward, which is ree-dick-you-lus!"

Erik's little sister had had a crush on his best friend, Pete. Didn't matter that Pete was four years older and uninterested. Hillary had always liked him, regardless of the fact that her affection was unrequited and likely to remain that way.

In fairness, it probably didn't help her unrealistic expectations that she and Pete had shared a quick New Year's Eve kiss six months ago. It seemed to encourage her false hopes. But then again, Pete hadn't promised her anything, and it was only a peck on the lips, after all. He had also given Vanessa a peck. So had Erik, in fact, and it hadn't changed their friendship at all. It was just New Year's fun. Nothing more. And Hillary was foolish to try to make more out of it.

Hillary raised her chin and gave him a sour look, then started typing out a message on her phone. "'Erik wants to know when you and Van are gettin' here.'" The phone whooshed as she sent the message, and she looked up at her brother. "Happy now, birthday boy?"

"Ecstatic," he said, leaving his room.

Hillary followed behind him. "Who's comin' to this thing tonight?"

"You know Fancy," said Erik, calling their mother by her first name, as he always did when he and Hillary talked about her. "Won't be anybody there under the age of forty 'cept you, me, Pete, and Van."

"A twenty-first birthday for the crown prince of North Carolina isn't an occasion for the young'uns," added Hillary, with a thick dose of sarcasm.

"Or the riffraff."

"Or anyone remotely . . . *fun.*"

Erik stopped at the foot of the stairs and turned to his sister, slapping a palm over his chest. "Fun? Did you say *fun*? Perish the thought, Hillary Anne Rexford! There will be no fun at this party, daughter! There will be ample opportunity for networkin', but under no circumstances are you to have any *fun*!"

"Right." Hillary nodded, unable to hold back a small grin, which she quickly straightened. "Everythin' will be perfect . . ."

". . . and delicious . . .," he said.

"The most expensive wines . . ."

". . . the most succulent crabs," he said, grinning to himself.

"Simply," she said, "the best of everything."

"No room for second best," said Erik. "Losers need not apply."

Suddenly they were out of banter, and they regarded each other for a long moment: their father's blue eyes staring into their mother's dark brown.

"We joke, but it's true," said Hillary with a sigh. "Thank God for Pete and Van."

"Donaldsons and Osborns are *always* acceptable guests at Rexford events," said Erik, referring to Pete and Vanessa's old-money, highly influential families. Their parents would also be in attendance, of course.

Hillary glanced at her watch. "I have a hair appointment in town with Mama. I best get goin'." She turned to go back upstairs, then stopped. "Hey, Erik."

He was headed for the kitchen, but he looked at her over his shoulder. "Huh?"

"You ever wish things were different?"

"What? That we *weren't* the children of Governor Brady Rexford and former debutante Ursula "Fancy" Rexford, the de facto king and queen of North Carolina?" He shrugged. "What's the point of wishin'? Things *are* what they *are*."

Hillary ran a hand through her almost-black hair. "I don't know. But wouldn't you just like to go to a bar in jeans and a T-shirt and get drunk on your twenty-first birthday? Like every other normal person in the world?"

He turned to face her, his voice gentle. "We're *not* normal, Hills. Never have been. We're Rexfords."

"Yeah," she said, forcing a smile, though her eyes remained troubled. "I know."

He reached for arm and squeezed it. "It's a party, sis. Buck up."

"Sure."

"Catch you later?"

"Yeah," she said, giving him a thoughtful look before climbing the stairs.

He watched her for a moment before sailing through the mansion's entry hall, continuing through the west sitting room, to the dining room, then through the swinging doors and into the kitchen. Inside, it was a flurry of activity: twelve vases were lined up on the table as a florist created a dozen matching arrangements; caterers arranged baskets of rolls and manned the twin ovens. When Erik's mother had inherited this house from her parents, it had been half the size, and equipped for the needs of a single family on vacation. But after his father had been elected to the state legislature, Fancy had renovated it into a showplace, complete with an industrial kitchen that could handle catering for huge events.

*Good thing too*, Erik thought dryly. Since his father's ascension to governor, last November, Fancy's entertaining efforts had gone on steroids. Seemed like she was hosting some sort of celebration or fund-raiser every other week. His birthday party tonight, for instance, had nothing to do with him. It was just a vehicle for his parents to schmooze and network. With a possibility of two terms in office before he was ineligible for reelection, Erik knew, his father was casting his eye at the White House eight years from now, and that would take a lot of support. President of the United States. Brady Rexford's lifelong dream.

Erik scanned the heads of the catering staff for a strawberry blonde ponytail. Finding none, he was about to leave, when he was distracted by a loud voice, exclaiming over the hum of activity, "Honey, those look heavy! Let me get one of these fellas to help you!"

Whipping back around, he caught sight of the freckled fisherman's daughter just inside the kitchen door, holding a white Styrofoam cooler that was wider than she was.

"Oh, no, ma'am," she said, her voice breathless as she set down her burden. "Only four left. No big deal." Though she was red-cheeked and sweating, she smiled. "It's good exercise."

"You islanders sure are hearty," noted the woman, who wore a white chef's jacket. "You ever need a job, you come find me."

The girl grinned, her green eyes sparkling. "Thank you, ma'am. I'll go get the rest now."

She disappeared back through the door, and Erik surged blindly across the kitchen to catch up with her, running outside and rounding the house.

"Hey! Wait up!"

She stopped in her tracks and turned, her eyes widening as she looked at him. "You."

"Me," he said. "From the balcony scene, remember?"

She nodded slowly, then turned away from him, gesturing to the boardwalk. "I have to . . ."

"Deliver crabs. I know."

Glancing back at him, she scanned his face, and he got his first really good look at her . . . and quickly realized that his little mermaid wasn't just pretty. She was a knockout.

Her pale, peachy skin was dusted with freckles, and her

sea-green eyes were even greener up close: the color of the Sound in the sun. Her hair, pulled back in a neat ponytail, was reddish-blonde, and soft, straight wisps escaped from behind her ears to frame her face. She was small—maybe five foot four— but he could tell she was athletic and strong, which he liked. His gaze dropped her to chest, which rose and fell under her black shirt. The white button between her tits pulled just a little, and Erik's mouth watered as he tugged his bottom lip between his teeth, unable to look away.

"I . . .," she said, her voice breathy. "I have to . . ."

He looked up, and his eyes slammed into hers.

For a second, he had a wild notion that he should kiss her.

It came on him like a freight train, and he couldn't ever remember having to fight so hard against an impulse. His gaze flicked madly from her eyes to her lips and back to her eyes, which seemed as mesmerized with him as his were with her.

"I'll help you," he murmured.

She shook her head. "Nope."

"Sure. If we each carry one, it'll only be two more trips."

"Nope," she said again, turning away from him to speed-walk around the pool, back toward the boardwalk.

Erik stood frozen, confounded by her reaction.

Unaccustomed to being refused anything by anyone, this situation was especially puzzling because he was just trying to give her a hand. Did she think he had ulterior motives? He tilted his head to the side, checking out her perky ass in too-tight jeans that somehow managed to stay on the safe side of trashy because they were paired with clunky rubber boots. He shook his head and grinned. Damn, but she was the cutest fucking thing he'd seen in a long, long time.

So, sure, maybe he did have ulterior motives, but he was young. She was, too . . . Was that so wrong?

This was his last summer of freedom: the summer between

his junior and senior years at college, his last hurrah. Next summer, he'd be a gainful member of the Raleigh workforce, clerking for a law firm of his father's choice while he worked his ass off in law school at Chapel Hill. But this summer? This summer, he was still free.

And that girl walking so purposefully toward a shabby old fishing boat? With her windblown hair, big green eyes, and freckles? Somehow she felt like freedom.

"Erik!" called his mother, from a cluster of tables in the center of the lawn. "*Please* don't keep me waiting!"

Duty called.

And Erik Rexford, who knew his place, turned away from his sweet little redheaded mermaid, and answered it.

# Chapter 3

Laire heard Erik's mother calling and walked back to her father's boat as a mix of relief and disappointment flooded her heart. Relief, because no matter how he made her heart thunder, smart island girls didn't go near summer dingbatters. And disappointed, because she didn't feel like being smart. She felt like staring into Erik Rexford's dark brown eyes forever.

Rexford. Erik . . . *Rexford.*

She'd almost fallen over when she realized whose kitchen she was standing in. It belonged to Brady Rexford. *Governor* Brady Rexford.

She'd had to sign something called a confidentiality agreement before stepping foot into the Rexford kitchen. Judith Sebastian, the catering manager, explained the gist of it: Laire was forbidden to take pictures while she was on the Rexfords' property or post about the premises on social media, which really wasn't a problem since Laire didn't have a cell phone or a Facebook account anyway.

Scrambling to recall what she knew about the new governor's oldest child, she came up mostly dry, except for a memory of Kyrstin exclaiming that he was hot, and a dim recollection that he attended Duke University, which made him at least two or three years older than she.

Older, and even more out of her league than he was when he was just a hot guy in a big house grinning at her from a balcony.

Erik Rexford was North Carolina royalty.

Grabbing the third cooler by the handles, she hefted it out of the boat and onto the dock with a thud. Stepping up onto the wood planks, she picked up the cooler and walked slowly and carefully along the boardwalk, her back aching and hands burning from the heavy load.

*Let me get one of these fellas to help you!*

No.

Absolutely not.

Cornishes did not accept help (or tips, for that matter) from summer folks.

*We do our work. We do it proud. We keep to ourselves.*

She could hear her father's words in her head.

This was how, her mother had explained a long time ago, islanders were able to hold on to their dignity, despite the ups and downs of a life built within the sometimes-unreliable commercial fishing industry. They welcomed the summer folks, worked for them, fished for them, and sold to them, but they didn't pander to them. They took money for a decent product or a job well done, but islanders looked to their friends and family when they ran into trouble and needed help. *And we certainly don't take no handouts from dingbatters.*

Besides the physical barrier—ten nautical miles—that kept Corey separate from the other islands, and the Corey brogue, which, especially when laid on thick, was difficult for outsiders to understand, an insulated islander mentality kept the rest of the world at arm's length.

And though Laire longed for more than island life, she wondered if she'd ever be able to unlearn such deeply ingrained ways. Until she experienced something substantially different about the world, what she *knew* would likely trump what she *wanted*.

Still, she couldn't help giving Erik Rexford a wistful glance as she trudged by, her cheeks growing instantly hot when he looked up at exactly the right moment to find her gawking at him, and winked.

*Gyah!* She snapped her neck away, facing forward. *Make the delivery and get out of here!*

When she reached the house, she found Ms. Sebastian waiting for her outside the kitchen door with a glass of ice-cold water.

"It's just water," said Ms. Sebastian, holding out the sweating glass. "Nothing special."

Laire placed the cooler down inside the kitchen and accepted the glass gratefully, taking a huge gulp before backhanding her lips and handing the glass back.

"Thank you, ma'am."

"I'm guessing you're sixth—no, *seventh*-generation Corey?"

"Tenth, ma'am."

"Tenth! My goodness."

Laire grinned. "You been to Corey?"

"Several times. I'm from New Bern."

"Up the Neuse?" asked Laire, referring to the estuary that fed the Pamlico Sound, and identifying the placement of other human beings on God's earth, as she always did, by the body of water closest to them.

"My husband was Marine Corps at Cherry Point."

This told Laire two things about Ms. Sebastian: one, she was local, but a woodser; from the mainland, not the islands. And two, she was from a working family; she wasn't a summer dingbatter.

"*Was*, ma'am?"

"He passed a few years ago."

"I'm sorry."

"Thank you." Ms. Sebastian tilted her head to the side. "You're a real hard worker."

"Yes, ma'am."

"You know, I meant what I said before about you comin' to work for me. Any interest?"

She dropped Ms. Sebastian's eyes. "I don't—"

"Don't say no. Think it over first," she said, swirling the ice in the glass, which reminded Laire of Erik up on the balcony, and made her heart ache from the quick flash of memory. "I work at the Pamlico House restaurant here in Buxton. You know it?"

Laire nodded. They were sometime customers of King Triton Seafood.

"If you decide you want a job, come find me. I could use a hard worker this summer to bus tables, maybe work up to waitress. I'd pay you ten dollars an hour to start."

She gasped quietly. Ten dollars *an hour*? If she worked from four until midnight at a party, that would be eighty dollars some nights. Almost one hundred dollars in one day.

Not to mention, the idea of being able to come and go freely in *this* world: to see the clothes that the ladies were wearing for their summer vacations at the inn and learn how people like Erik Rexford lived . . . it was the stuff of fantasy. Almost outlandish in its scope and possibilities.

"I'd have to ask my daddy, ma'am."

"Then ask him." Ms. Sebastian tilted her head to the side. "How old are you?"

"Eighteen just."

"Good." She tilted her head to the side, looking closely at Laire's face. "You're very pretty, Miss . . ."

"Cornish. Laire Cornish, ma'am."

"Laire," she repeated. She offered a small smile. "I hope

your father says yes." Then she turned and walked back into the kitchen.

A job.

A *real* job, in the *real* world.

Not like helping her daddy on the boat, or working behind the register for Uncle Fox in the shop. Not even like making clothes for the women on the island, but a job off Corey Island, with a real paycheck.

She worked out some figures in her head, wondering how much faster she could get to Parsons or RISD if she started working as a waitress during the busy summer season. It hadn't really occurred to her before now—to seek out a proper job off Corey—but now it did, and as she walked back to the boat to get cooler number four, her head was spinning with the promise of it.

*But my father.*

Her heart sank. Her father would never allow it. He wouldn't like her leaving Corey every day. He'd insist that she could work in one of the cafés or restaurants on their island, or, if she pushed him, over on Ocracoke. She took a deep breath as her boots hit the boardwalk. How could she convince him?

"Hey!"

This time, she didn't stop. She kept walking. She had important matters to think about.

"Hey!"

His flip-flops thwacked against the planking as he caught up to her.

"I'm working," she said, without sparing him a glance. If she looked at him, she'd get all moony and distracted again, and right now she had to finish up her delivery and figure out a way to convince her daddy to let her take a job with Ms. Sebastian so she could start earning more money.

"You're makin' me think you don't like me, Freckles!"

*Freckles.*

*Oh, my heart.*

She stopped dead in her tracks and jerked her head to face him. "Not *like* you?" *As if that was even a possibility.* "No! I just . . ."

She had her back to the railing, and suddenly the boardwalk felt very narrow as he took two steps toward her, closing the distance between them and stopping directly opposite her. He leaned his elbows on the opposite railing, which pushed his chest out toward her and left no more than a few inches separating them.

"Just *what*?"

"I don't know you," she whispered, staring up into his black-coffee eyes.

They widened, flicking to her lips, as they had when he'd talked to her outside the kitchen a few minutes ago. "But we could remedy that."

"Why?" she murmured, her chest rising and falling rapidly for reasons that had nothing to do with hauling coolers.

"Why not?" he asked, his perfect lips tilting up in a grin. "Unless you're married. Are you married?"

Her lips twitched. "I'm only eighteen."

"So . . . is that a yes or a no?"

She shook her head. "No. I'm not married."

"Hmm." His eyes dropped to her left hand. "No engagement ring either."

She crossed her arms over her chest. "Are we done here?"

"Not even close," he said, his voice gravelly and low. "Are you about to enter a convent?"

"F-for nuns?" She chortled softly. "No!"

"Are you about to move away to a distant land where it would be impossible for me to find you?"

"No."

"Not married. Not engaged. Not entering a convent. Not

"Laire, like hair?"

She nodded.

"Laire what?" he asked.

She rounded the pool, relieved beyond belief that the side of the house was in sight now. *Laire Who Shouldn't Be Talking to You.* "Laire Cornish."

"Well . . . it's sure nice to . . . meet you, Laire . . . Cornish."

He sounded breathless behind her, which was fairly flattering, considering her name was pretty ordinary on Corey.

"You too, Erik Rexford."

She rounded the corner of the house and almost ran to the kitchen entrance, dropping the heavy cooler just inside the door with a grunt of satisfaction. Resting her hands on her knees for a moment, she took big gulps of air.

"Ahem," said Erik from behind her. "You mind?"

Straightening and putting her hands on her hips, she turned around to face him, and found him standing behind her, a huge grin on his way-too-beautiful face, and the last two coolers in his strong arms.

\*\*\*

That was the moment Erik Rexford knew, beyond a shadow of a doubt, that he couldn't allow this to be their one and only meeting. Her eyes widened, her lips parted, and his dirty mind went straight to the gutter, wondering if that's how Laire Cornish would look when he made her come with his cock or his tongue.

*And I'd sooner die right here and now than never find out*, he thought, grinning down at her.

"I didn't . . . I didn't ask for your help," she said softly to his back as he brushed past her and placed the last two coolers on top of hers.

"I figured you wouldn't. But, sometimes, Freckles?

Sometimes you just lend a hand because you *can*, not because there's a gun to your head."

He wasn't certain where that sentence had come from, because the filthy, fantastic images in his head were a lot less lofty than the words that came out of his mouth. But he found that he meant them—there was room to want her *and* to help her. Both objectives cohabited together in the front of his consciousness.

"These sumbitch coolers are heavy," he said. "I don't know how you did the first four."

"For starters," she said, "I didn't carry two at once."

"Impressed?" he asked, winking at her.

The half smile on her lips said she was, but the way she shook her head, like he was incorrigible, said that she wouldn't allow herself to admit it.

"You *could* say thank you," he said, raising his eyebrows at her, "if you wanted."

"Thank you," she said softly.

"You finished quick, Laire," said an older woman. He was fairly certain she was the head catering lady, and she looked at Laire with admiration. "I guess that ties up our business for today, honey. I'd offer you a tip, but . . ."

"No, thank you, ma'am."

The woman nodded as though they had an understanding, but Erik, to save his life, couldn't understand why they weren't tipping the little mermaid for her work. In a world where everyone was tipped for everything, she'd actually sweated through a job, and she'd get nothing extra for it? Huh. Didn't seem fair, but one look at Laire's face told him that she didn't share his feelings so he remained silent.

"You remember my offer, Laire?" asked the woman.

"Yes, ma'am."

"Hope to see you at the Pamlico House real soon now."

"Thank you, ma'am."

"Get on home now before your father gets worried, okay?"

"Yes, ma'am."

The woman nodded at Laire, her eyes warm, then turned to Erik, all business. "Can I help you with anything, Mr. Rexford?" He frowned at her. Yes, he was accustomed to people working for his parents calling him "Mr." but it sounded way too formal in front of Laire . . . which, he suspected, was partially the point.

Dismissed, Laire waved a hand at the woman, then turned, walking away from the kitchen with her hands in her back pockets, more of a stroll than the serious march she'd employed back and forth between the house and her father's boat. He watched her go, enjoying the way the sun caught the gold and copper strands of her hair.

"Mr. Rexford?"

"Uhhh . . . no. No, thank you."

"Mr. Rexford," she said again, this time trying to get his attention with a bit more urgency in her tone. He turned away from Laire to face her, finding her eyes a lot less warm than they'd been a moment ago. "She's an island girl."

"Yes. I know."

"You don't have any business with an island girl, now, do you?"

He narrowed his eyes at her. He didn't especially appreciate the not-so-subtle warning in her voice. "What if I do?"

Her lips tightened, and he expected her tone when she next spoke to be harsh or judgmental. It surprised him that it wasn't. In fact, it was soft and beseeching. "Let her go, son."

She gave him a sad smile, then turned and walked back into the kitchen, letting the service door close slowly behind her.

*Let her go.*

Why? Why should he?

*Let her go.*

He turned back to watch Laire, who, with each step, moved farther and farther away from him.

*Let her go.*

She was at the lawn now. A few more steps and she'd be on the boardwalk.

*Damn it. He* couldn't *let her go.*

He took off at a sprint, losing his flip-flops on the decorative footbridge between the pool deck and the lawn, and catching up with her halfway down the boardwalk.

"Hey!"

He heard her sigh before she slowed down and turned to face him. "You don't give up easy."

"No, miss, I don't."

"You should."

"I won't," he said.

She kept walking, but he fell into step beside her, his arm occasionally brushing hers and sending lightning bolts up his arm every time.

He cleared his throat. *Concentrate.*

"Give me your number."

"So you can call my house and start a ruckus? No way."

"How about your cell?"

She glanced up at him just before stepping onto the dock. "Don't have one."

"How is that possible?"

"No need for it," she said as she leaned down to uncleat the bow line.

Completely taken aback, he froze, staring at the back of her head as she bent down. He'd never met anyone who didn't have a cell phone. It was *beyond* strange.

And totally fascinating.

She stood up and made her way to the stern line.

*Shift gears, Erik. Figure out another way to find her or you'll lose her.*

"Your name's Laire Cornish, and you're from Corey Island."

"That's right."

"So, even if you refuse to go out with me, I know where to find you."

She was bending down to uncleat the rope at the back of her boat, but she jerked upright to look at him, all humor wiped clean from her face. "You wouldn't!"

He crossed his arms over his chest. "Wouldn't I?"

"*Please* don't come looking for me," she said.

"Why not?"

She shook her head, looking exasperated as she reached down and unknotted the rope. "It'll make trouble."

"Trouble? I'm the governor's son! I'm not *allowed* to get into trouble. You'll be safe as a baby lamb with . . . with . . ."

"A wolf," she muttered, tossing the line onto the boat and giving him a look as she walked around him and bent over the bow cleat.

"If you say no," he said, the unfamiliar taste of desperation making his voice edgier than usual, "you'll leave me no choice. I'll be *forced* to come lookin' for you."

"Please don't," she said again, her eyes worried.

She frowned at him, then threw the line onto the bow and jumped onto the boat.

"I'll start at the post office," he said, stepping closer to her boat, "because they've got everyone's address. And if they don't have yours for some reason, I'll go to the—"

"Don't," she said, plucking a key from a compartment by the wheel and turning over the engine.

He felt almost frantic. *This cannot be the end. No. Absolutely not.* He wanted to hear her voice again—the strange, lovely lilt of her unusual accent. He wanted to know more about her: who she was, what her life was like. He wanted to figure out why he felt so drawn to her. He wanted to touch her, make her smile, make her laugh. There was too much he wanted, and without her digits, how could he get in contact with her? *Fuck!* He *couldn't* just let her go.

"I *will* find you!" he cried over the roar of the engine. "That's a promise, Laire Cornish!"

"Damn it to hell and back!" she yelled. "Fine! You win!"

He stepped closer, reaching out to grab the salt-stained chrome railing on the side of the boat. "Wait, that's a yes?"

"Tomorrow night," she said, frowning at him. "I'll be at the Pamlico House. Eight o'clock."

"Ha! Yes!" he yelled, a triumphant fist raised high. "Okay, then!"

He couldn't help the smile that widened his lips to the point of aching until he stood there chuckling. This wasn't the last time he'd ever see her. The boat started leaning away, and he let go of the railing just before it pulled him into the water. He raised his hand to wave to her, excitement making him feel uncharacteristically giddy.

"See you tomorrow, Freckles!"

She nodded, her eyes both annoyed and troubled as she backed the boat away from the dock without waving good-bye.

## Chapter 4

Laire's father had two boats: the commercial fishing boat and a smaller, prettier leisure boat they used for the occasional cruise on a Sunday afternoon when Hook wasn't working, or for the trip to Ocracoke for a nice supper at one of the cafés over there. And while borrowing either for a good reason had never been an issue, borrowing one to go to the Pamlico House Bed & Breakfast to meet Erik Rexford and accept a summer job wasn't exactly going to be a walk in the park.

That said? Laire had two good reasons to figure out a way to make it work:

One, she wanted the job Ms. Sebastian was offering. If she worked every day from now until Labor Day, she'd amass a small fortune by the end of the summer. And if she was able to keep the job through the end of *next* summer? She should have enough money saved to start college that September.

And two, Erik's threat was real. She could tell by the crazy glint in his eyes. If she didn't show up at the Pamlico House at eight o'clock tonight as promised, she had no doubt he'd arrive at Corey bright and early on Monday morning, as soon as the post office opened for business. And the last thing she needed was the rumor mill—which already had a false story about her and Brodie for fodder—to explode with the news that Laire Cornish was dating a dingbatter. No, thank you.

Her father wouldn't be home until late afternoon, which left most of the day for her to figure out the best possible argument for her cause. She emptied her father's ashtray beside the reclining chair and put his two empty beer bottles in the recycling bin. She made a chicken and rice casserole for his dinner, then scrubbed the kitchen floor, sink, and countertops until the old Formica gleamed. With vinegar and newspaper, she shined the kitchen and oven windows, the same way her mother had done so many years before.

"You got coffee on?" asked a sleepy Kyrstin, shuffling into the small kitchen around eleven and taking a seat at the four-person table by the newly cleaned window. Their mother had made the cheerful oilcloth curtains when her daughters were little, and though they were discolored with age, none of the Cornish girls had the heart to replace them.

"Three hours ago, yes. Now, no." Laire glanced at her watch. "It's almost noon!"

"Make me a cup?"

"Make your own."

"My head throbs like the devil," said her sister. "What time did I get in last night?"

"Heard you banging around at about two."

"Remy and his brother made a bonfire on the beach," said Kyrstin. "You could've joined us, Laire."

"Was Brodie there?"

"Course."

"Then it's good I wasn't."

"Maddie Dunlop was all over him like a cheap shirt."

"Maddie Dunlop is more than welcome to him. He isn't mine."

"You say that like you don't love him!" teased Kyrstin. Laughing to herself for a moment, she sobered when she looked up and caught the expression on her younger sister's face. "Okay. Okay. Make me a cup of coffee and I'll quit teasin'."

Part of her wanted to tell Kyrstin to go to hell, but she needed her sister's opinion, and possibly her help. It wasn't the time to pick a fight or be petty.

Laire turned to the counter and slid the coffeemaker out from the wall. She opened the cabinet, took out the grounds, filled the once-white plastic basket, then filled the well with water and pressed the on switch, pivoting back around to face her sister.

"I need something."

Kyrstin looked up and narrowed her eyes, pushing a rat's nest of hair from her face. "Is that right?"

Laire nodded. "Uh-huh."

"What is it?"

She sat down at the table, folding her hands next to a butter dish shaped like a crab shell. "What do you think Daddy would say about me getting a job?"

"You have jobs," said Kyrstin. "You take care of the house and help out at the shop. Plus, you make pin money with your designs."

"I mean a steady job," clarified Laire. "A *real* job."

"Like at the Hen's Nest? I heard they're hirin'."

The Hen's Nest was the local day care for island children that was especially busy in the summer, when islanders took on seasonal work.

"No. I mean . . ." She winced. There was no good way to back into it. "In Buxton. At the Pamlico House B & B."

Kyrstin raised her eyebrows, sitting back in her chair. "Off-island?"

Laire nodded, standing up to grab a clean coffee cup from the drying rack beside the sink, keeping her back to her older sister. "Yeah. You know that delivery last night? Met a lady there who does the hiring for the restaurant at the B and B. She offered me a job."

"Just like that?"

Laire poured the coffee into the cup real quick, listening as the coffee pitter-pattered into the ceramic bottom. "Aye-up."

Kyrstin eyed her sister with suspicion. "You trust her?"

"She's a woodser from Cherry Point."

"Hmm," she hummed, her posture relaxing. "How much she offerin'?"

"Ten an hour."

"Damn." Kyrstin whistled low, nodding her head in understanding. "That's a lot."

Laire turned to her sister, setting the mug of steaming coffee on the table before her. "Tell me about it."

Krystin looked at her thoughtfully. "How much you remember 'bout Mama goin' for the college courses down at Carteret?"

"Not a whole lot," admitted Laire, who, nonetheless, desperately admired her mother for being one of the few islanders at the time with a partial college education under her belt.

"Yeah, you were real little. But *I* remember. She fought daddy tooth and nail over it."

Laire nodded. She wasn't surprised.

Carteret was a three-hour journey from Corey Island, first by ferry to Cedar Island, then via highway along the fringe of the mainland. She couldn't imagine her daddy was a big fan of his wife being away all day, first of all, let alone traveling such a long distance back and forth all on her own with three small children at home.

"But she still went, didn't she?" asked Laire. "For two years?"

Kyrstin nodded. "She did. And if you want my honest opinion? Uncle Fox took a lot of her advice when he and daddy set up King Triton Seafood. She knew a lot about the summer tourists, settin' the prices, gettin' the word out to the hotels and restaurants all along the Banks. She was a smart lady, our mama."

"I remember she was smart," said Laire wistfully, aching from how much she missed her mother.

"What do you need that kind of money for, Laire?"

"You can't tell Daddy."

Kyrstin gave her a look. "Maybe I will and maybe I won't."

Laire rolled her eyes. Kyrstin talked big, but she wouldn't tell if Laire asked her not to. "I want to go to college like Mama. I want to learn something."

"Yeah. But I've seen the brochures, Laire," said Kyrstin, crossing her arms over her chest, her eyes disapproving. "You're not lookin' at Carteret or Beaufort or even some fancy four-year college like UNC. You want to go up North."

Laire sighed deeply, nodding at her sister. "Is that so wrong?"

Kyrstin shrugged, her voice hopeful. "Brodie's real nice. You've both graduated now. He'd help set you up with a nice little boutique—maybe even over on Ocracoke, by the ferry, where they've got more and more tourists comin' in every summer. You could sell your fashions. He and his daddy make a damn good livin'. You could have a few kids. Live nearby . . ."

Her words were crushing Laire's soul, and Kyrstin must have known it because her voice tapered off.

"No," she said, sipping her coffee thoughtfully. "I guess not. You were always more like Mama than the rest of us."

"Kyrstin," she said, reaching out to lay her palm across her sister's arm. "I love Corey Island. I love you and Issy and Daddy. But I . . . I can't stay here forever. I want to see more. I want to know more. There's a huge world out there, and I want to be a part of it." She looked down at her freckled hand on Kyrstin's freckled arm. So alike, it was hard to tell where her sister's skin ended and hers began. "I'll *always* be your sister. But . . . I feel like this is my chance. The first stepping-stone toward my dream. And since you work at a café on Ocracoke, I thought maybe . . ."

"I might put in a good word?"

Laire nodded, trying for a hopeful smile. "If we talked to him together. Maybe we could explain that my working in Buxton isn't so very different than you working in Ocracoke. Just a summer job for extra money."

"Buxton *ain't* Ocracoke, Laire, and you know it," Kyrstin reminded her dryly.

"Please," said Laire softly.

As she watched her sister's face soften, she thought of Erik Rexford, and her heart pinched with guilt. When Kyrstin helped her sway their father this afternoon, she'd also be unknowingly complicit in helping Laire make her date with the governor's son—a fact that would have affected Kyrstin's willingness to help. A job was one thing. Dating a dingbatter was another, and there's no way on God's green earth that Kyrstin, who was happy on Corey, would approve.

"I'll do it," said Kyrstin, surprising Laire with her quick and sudden alliance, "on one condition."

Laire held her breath. *Here it comes . . .*

"You make me somethin' supersexy for my weddin' night."

Throwing her arms around her older sister, Laire promised to make something so dirty, it would bring Remiel Poisson to his knees.

\*\*\*

*Too bright.*

The sun was *way* too bright.

Erik groaned and flipped onto his stomach, staring down at

the concrete pool deck though the plastic slats of the lounger and wishing his head would stop pounding.

"Anyone have an Advil?" he muttered.

Hillary laughed from two chairs down. "Poor Erik."

"Don't joke," said Vanessa from beside him. A soft, warm hand landed on his back, rubbing soothingly, and he knew it was hers. It was the type of thing she was always doing—rubbing his back or holding on to his arm. Van was super touchy-feely and always had been. It didn't mean anything. Besides, it felt nice. "Birthday boy here drank his weight in Champagne! I'm not surprised if his poor head is achin' a little."

Pete, who lounged on Erik's other side, asked, "Where's *my* sympathy, Van? My head's achin' too!"

"Are you the birthday boy, Peter Donaldson? No, I didn't think so. You'll just have to fend."

"Damn!" exclaimed Pete, chuckling ruefully. "Cold woman!"

"You need someone to rub your back?" Hillary asked Pete, her tone trying for kidding but sounding too hopeful to stick the landing.

"Why? You offerin'? Ha-ha. No, thanks, Hills," said Pete, still laughing. "I think I'll go sit in the hot tub a spell and warm up from the chill over here."

"By all means," said Vanessa, her fingers still sliding up and down Erik's back. "Go sit in your own warm filth."

"Ha! Like Fancy Rexford would allow any *filth* at Utopia Manor."

"She allows *you*," said Vanessa under her breath.

"I heard that, Van," said Pete. "But, honey, we both know the Donaldsons have been in North Carolina longer than the Osborns, so you can stuff it."

"*Stuff it*," muttered Vanessa in a cultured Southern accent. "Such a gentleman. You *are* crude, Peter Donaldson."

"Aw, Van, you can kiss my crude . . ."

The word *ass* was swallowed by the splash of a body entering the hot tub.

"He's so antagonistic," said Van with a humph, her fingers massaging the kinks in Erik's lower back.

Erik, Pete, and Vanessa had met in preschool at Saint Paul's Lutheran in Raleigh, attended the Branchbrook Academy for lower school, and completed middle and upper school together at the Asheville Christian School, a boarding school that had educated at least one of the parents of each. They'd essentially known one another from the cradle: Three Musketeers who'd historically had each other's backs while bickering like siblings.

But over the past three years, since they'd headed off to college, their relationships with one another had changed a little, becoming more nuanced and complicated. First of all, for the first time in their lives, they lived apart. Erik attended undergrad at Duke, while Vanessa was at Wake Forest, and Pete was at UNC–Chapel Hill. They still saw each other during holiday breaks and spent time together on the Outer Banks every summer, but something indefinable had changed between them.

Vanessa, who'd always been a pretty, blue-eyed brunette, had blossomed into a beauty. She had phenomenal tits and a rounded ass, but was also slim and tall, willowy and elegant.

Pete, who was blond, blue-eyed, and as burly as a linebacker, still argued with Vanessa every chance he got, but the way he looked at her had changed, and even Erik had noticed. Pete had always had a soft spot for Van growing up, but that soft spot had changed into something bigger and more possessive in the past year or two.

Erik had noticed that Van had filled out, of course, but his feelings for her had never deepened from friendship. He still saw her as a pseudo-sister. A really pretty sister, yeah, but still . . . a sister. He had zero sexual attraction to her. She was just . . . Van, his lifelong friend.

"You need an Advil, honey?" asked Van, close to his ear. "I can go grab you one."

"You don't mind?"

"Not a bit," she said, caressing his back a final time. "I'll be back in a jiff."

He sighed, wondering what time it was and assuming it was around twelve. Fuck, but today was crawling by when all he wanted was for eight o'clock to get here sooner so he could clap eyes on the little mermaid again and confirm that she was as cute in person as she'd been in his dreams last night.

The sound of rustling interrupted his pleasant thoughts, and suddenly Hillary's voice was close to his ear. "You're leadin' her on, Erik."

"Who?" *The little mermaid?*

"Van. That's who."

He leaned up on one elbow, squinting to look up at his little sister's face. Hillary was sitting on the edge of Pete's abandoned lounger, a black floppy hat shielding her pale skin from the sun as she stared down at him with pursed lips.

"Never in a million," he said, rolling his eyes. "Van and me aren't like that."

"My butt. Even if *you're* not, *she* is." She put her sunglasses back on and swung her feet, up, leaning back with a sigh. "You're in hot water, and you don't even feel the burn."

Erik shook his head, which made it ache all the more, souring his precarious mood. "We've been friends forever, Hills. You're makin' up a situation where none exists." He decided to hit her a little below the belt in an effort to get her to shut up. "Like you did on New Year's, actin' like some li'l ole kiss with Pete meant somethin' more than it did."

She gasped lightly beside him, then hid it by clearing her throat. "Low blow."

He loved his sister and heard the pain in her voice, which made him feel instant remorse. "Sorry, sis. I'm an asshole."

"*And* a dumbass if you don't see what's right under your nose."

He settled himself back into the chair with a grunt of satisfaction, letting his forehead drop back onto the warm vinyl. "Why can't you just let us be friends? Why does it have to be more?"

"Because it *is* more. To her. And you know it."

"Even if that's so—and I'm *not* sayin' it is—it's not my fault that I don't feel the same. We can't always get what we want, no matter how hard we want it." His voice was gentle when he added. "You know that better'n anyone."

"I guess I do," she said, all the sass gone from her tone now. "But I also know exactly how she's thinkin', Erik. I can see it all over her face. She's thinkin', If I just hang in there, one day, he'll see me. And he'll know what I've known all along: that we're meant to be."

The wistfulness in her voice made him cringe.

Hillary was talking about Pete when it was clear as day that Pete wasn't interested in Hillary. Never had been. Pete wanted Van. And Erik respected that. Hell, in his mind, Van was Pete's girl, whether she wanted to be or not.

Fuck, but this situation was all screwed up. How were they supposed to get through the whole summer together with Hills liking Pete, Pete liking Van, Van liking him, and him liking . . .

His thoughts of a strawberry-haired beauty were cut off by the sound of the slider opening and closing again.

"I only had Tylenol," Vanessa called, her sandals thwacking on the pool deck. "Will that do?"

He leaned up to find her approaching with a red and white bottle in one hand and a glass of ice water in the other.

"You're an angel of mercy," he called.

Her eyes, deep blue and wide, softened instantly as she

approached, and Erik looked away fast, Hillary's warning fresh in his head.

"Told you," his sister muttered under her breath from beside him, watching their interaction over the rims of her sunglasses.

Erik swung his body around and sat up on the edge of the chair as Vanessa sidled over. She gave him the glass and two tablets, which he swallowed quickly.

"Thanks, honey," he said, blinking up at her.

"Anythin' for you. You know that," she answered, her tone heavy with unspoken meaning. Suddenly she smiled sweetly, reaching down beside her lounger for a bottle of sunscreen. "Get my back?"

He looked at the bottle, then up at Van.

"Pete!" he yelled, still holding her eyes so that *his* meaning was as clear as could be. "Can you give Van a hand with some suntan lotion? I think I'll go inside and catch some zzz's."

Vanessa flinched, her cheeks coloring with embarrassment, but she plastered a smile on her frosty face as Pete leaped eagerly out of the hot tub and rounded the pool deck to be of service.

"Sure thing," he said, reaching for the bottle with his beefy linebacker fingers as soon as he reached the chairs.

"I'll catch y'all later, huh?" said Erik, standing up and heading for the house.

"Erik!"

He turned back to face Vanessa, who looked at him longingly.

"We're all goin' out together tonight, right?" she asked, sitting primly on the edge of the lounger as Pete squeezed some cream on his palms.

Erik shook his head as a sudden image of Laire Cornish made him *feel* the same sharp longing he saw in Vanessa's eyes.

Hillary was right. This situation was stickier than he'd noticed before today. Maybe he should stop hanging out with Van so much . . . and tonight was the perfect time to start.

"Sorry, honey," he said gently. "Y'all are on your own. I've got plans."

Vanessa's face fell as Pete suggested they go to a movie together, and Hillary, who may or may not have been intentionally included in his invitation, enthusiastically agreed.

## Chapter 5

In mid-June, the sun didn't set over the Pamlico Sound until almost 8:30pm, which meant that Laire had a beautiful, golden ride to Buxton that evening.

*There are moments*, she mused as the wind swept her hair back and the spray of salt water landed on her skin, *when the whole world feels perfect*. And right now, right here—zooming north toward Buxton, where she was about to accept a lucrative summer job *and* meet up with a young man who made her heart quiver like Jell-O—she was determined to savor such a moment.

Not that her conversation with her father had been chocolates and cherries.

When she'd first asked to use his boat, he told her yes, and for a moment, she almost thought she'd get away with borrowing it without accounting for her destination. But then, as he popped open a beer and sat down in his chair, he casually asked where she was planning to go.

She shot a worried look at Kyrstin, who had sat down on the footrest by their father and reminded him of his initial objections to her working on Ocracoke. He listened, nodding his head, before turning his eyes and asking Laire if she wanted to work with her sister over at the Ocracoke Bistro.

"What if I did?" asked Laire.

"Can't say I'd love it, with all them tourists playing grabass with the local girls, but you'd have your big sister here to look out for you, and Bernard Mathers has been a fair boss to Kyrs. I guess . . ." He rubbed the scruff on his chin. "I don't love it to pieces, Laire, but if you want to make a little extra money this summer, I won't stand in your way."

He took a long sip of beer. "But come think of it, why d'ya need the Stingray? Can't you get a ride over to Ocracoke with Kyrs and Remy?"

About to tell her father that she had no intention of working on Ocracoke, Kyrstin interrupted her. "The problem is that Bernie needs Laire on the six-to-midnight shift. And my hours is switchin' to eight to two."

"Huh. Why's that?"

"Well, I was sort of offered a promotion," said Kyrstin, her attention fixed totally on her father.

Laire nudged her sister in the back with her knee. *What are you doing? What about Buxton?*

Kyrstin leaned forward, ignoring Laire. "I'm goin' to do some bartendin', and Laire's goin' to take over my shift."

Their father's eyes widened, and he set his beer down on the table. "Bartendin'?"

Kyrstin nodded. "Pays better, Daddy. Way more tips."

"Slingin' drinks?"

Laire finally understood what was happening here and why Kyrstin had been so quick to "help" Laire: she had her own agenda. She needed an excuse to take a different position at the Ocracoke Bistro, and Laire getting a job there was a good reason.

"Don't like the thought of one of my gals behind a bar."

"What's wrong with it?" Kyrstin asked defensively.

"Seems base."

"You're old-fashioned. My tips'll be double."

Their father shook his head, looking troubled. "Nothin' wrong with bein' old-fashioned, gal. You think this is a good example for your little sister?"

"Hard work and honest money?" said Kyrstin, raising her chin. "Yes, sir, I believe it *is* a good example."

"All this talk about money. You need money? Seems like Remy is doin' fine. Thought maybe you'd quit waitressin' when you settled down, not work *more* hours."

Kyrstin placed her hand on her father's knee. "Daddy? You know the old Carver house?'

The Carver house was a centuries-old mansion close to the harbor on Corey Island. It had been a sea captain's house in the 1800s, then an inn, then a restaurant, but for a good fifteen years, it had been uninhabited, battered by the elements, and given only minimal care by a local real estate office.

"Course," said their father, wrinkling his eyebrows. "What of it?"

"We're buyin' it," said Kyrstin. "Me and Remy. We're goin' to renovate it and reopen it as a bed-and-breakfast."

"A what?"

"An inn."

"For who? Ain't nobody on Corey need an inn."

"For tourists, Daddy."

"Tourists on Corey?" he humphed. "Leave that to the Ocracoke folks. Don't need tourists here."

"It's what me and Remy want. Our own business."

And that was the moment Laire knew that she couldn't say another word and would need to be a complicit vehicle in her sister's small deception. They all had dreams, it seemed, and this one belonged to Kyrstin. Laire would do whatever she had to do to ensure it came true for her.

Her father's eyes shifted to her. "What do you think of all this?"

"I really want the waitressin' job," said Laire.

"I mean, about the Carver house."

"Château le Poisson," said Kyrstin quietly, her cheeks coloring. "Means Fish House . . . in French."

"Ch-Château le Poisson." Laire nodded. "It's a fine idea, Daddy. 'Bout time we had an inn on Corey. Ocracoke's got at least six or seven now." She added quietly, mostly for Kyrstin's benefit, "And I think it'd make Mama real proud."

Kyrstin snapped her head around to look at her little sister, mouthing "thank you" as she swiped at her eyes.

Hook Cornish knew defeat when it sat green-eyed in front of him.

"Fine. You make some extra change for your Fish House," he said to Kyrstin. Turning to Laire, he added, "Want that I have a word with Mathers before you start? Ask him to keep an eye on you?"

"No!" cried Laire.

"No," said Kyrstin, a little more smoothly. "I'll do that, Daddy. And besides, I'll be there to look out for her. She'll be just fine."

"Well, then," he sighed, looking up at Laire in defeat. "I guess you can use the Stingray. Keep it gassed up, Laire. And if I need it from time to time, you be sure to hitch a ride with your sister and Remy, yeah?"

Laire nodded. "Course, Daddy."

"Now leave me be a while, girls," he said, closing his eyes and leaning back into his chair. "I'm mommucked."

Laire confronted her sister later, in their shared room, while she changed into an outfit for her secret date.

"Why didn't you tell me?" she demanded. "About the bartending, and the Carver house, and . . . and all of it?"

"The house was a secret. And I only got the idea about bartendin' this mornin', after I talked to you. Bernie's been grousin' about Monica quittin'. I called him and offered to take over the bar. He said yes, and with the extra money, Remy and I decided we could finally place a bid on the Carver property."

"Is that really what you want to do? Open an inn?"

Kyrstin nodded. "You know it was always Mama's dream, right? I read it in one of her school workbooks." Her smile was wistful as she shrugged. "You ain't the only one with dreams, Laire."

"Mama's dream was to open an inn?"

Kyrstin nodded. "She outlined the whole plan: buy the Carver house, renovate it, add a restaurant. It was all there. I showed it to Remy, and he just about fell over—he was just as excited as me. We can do it, Laire. We can make Mama's dream happen." She grinned. "And you just helped us. A lot."

Kyrstin kissed Laire on the cheek and ran to tell Remy the good news.

And Laire took such satisfaction in helping her sister, and, by proxy, her mother, that it assuaged all of her immediate guilt about lying to her father.

But now, as she zoomed toward Buxton, she had misgivings.

What if her father showed up at the Ocracoke Bistro to check on her? What if Bernie Mathers showed up at King Triton to place a special order and her father happened to be there? Surely he'd ask how his *daughters* were getting on. She sighed. This wasn't the sort of lie that could remain out there forever. She and Kyrstin would have to find a way to wiggle out of it.

But not yet.

For now, her sister should have the right to follow her dream, Laire could take the job at the Pamlico House, and someday soon, they'd come clean.

She smiled into the wind, letting herself be excited for Kyrstin—and for herself. *We're making our dreams come true!* It felt so good . . . and somehow it mitigated her nerves over seeing Erik Rexford again tonight.

With all the jockeying it had taken to make tonight happen, she hadn't been able to keep Erik Rexford in the forefront of her mind, but now? Knowing she'd see him again so soon? Her heart started fluttering, and she wondered—for the thousandth time—what a boy like him wanted with a girl like her. She couldn't answer that question to save her life, nor could she refuse herself the opportunity to find out.

Keeping herself off-limits to the island boys had given Laire a reputation for being cold and uptight, but that was just a persona that she employed to ensure her name was never tangled up with someone else's. Inside, she was just as hot and curious as any other teenage girl who got quivers below her belly when she walked in on Kyrstin and Remy making out half naked, or saw a movie where a boy and girl fell madly in love and moved against each other, skin to skin, moaning and writhing with need and passion.

Like the parents of three other girls in her class, her father had pulled her out of school on the one day in sixth grade that they taught sex ed, instead asking Isolde to have a word with Laire "at some point." But even though Isolde, a senior in high school at the time, had been dating Paul for years, she'd colored as red as an apple and never broached the subject with her little sister. There'd been no official talk. Whatever information Laire had about boys and sex had come from her sisters talking about their boyfriends and whatever she could glean from TV shows and movies. In short, she *knew* the facts about the facts of life, but she figured that was a hell of a lot different from firsthand experience.

For the first time in her life, she *wanted* that experience. Last night, she'd dreamed that she was in one of those movie sex scenes with Erik Rexford, skin to skin, with his body moving over hers, creating an ache deep inside her that had lingered all day and told her something very important: she *wanted* Erik

Rexford to smile at her, to touch her, maybe even—in her wildest dreams only, of course—to do the things that Brodie Walsh had bragged about them doing. But *most of all* . . .

. . . she wanted him to kiss her.

She just wasn't totally sure how to go about making that happen.

By off-island standards, Laire knew, she was woefully inexperienced, but up until this moment, that hadn't been an issue, because she had no interest in any of the boys she'd grown up with. Now she bit her bottom lip, wishing she knew more or had a little more experience. For a moment, she remembered Erik Rexford staring at her mouth with such raw hunger, it had set her entire body on fire. Did that mean he wanted to kiss her too? It had to mean *something*, right?

She released her lip with a determined pop.

No matter what else happened tonight, Laire wanted her first kiss, and she wanted it from Erik Rexford, the closest she would ever come to her own Prince Charming. And then, no matter what else happened in her life, she'd have the memory of Erik's kiss. She'd know, for the remainder of her days, how it felt to be wanted by someone like him.

Ignoring the swarm of butterflies invading her belly, she pushed down on the throttle and raced the rest of the way to Buxton.

Tilting her wrist to check the time as she tied up at the Pamlico House, Laire found that it was seven forty, and she quickly changed into the cream suede mules she'd bought brand-new for Kyrstin's wedding. They were the best shoes she had, but she'd have to be careful not to scuff them, or her sister would surely complain.

They were so new and pretty, wearing them gave her the little boost of confidence she desperately needed. She wore them with cream-colored skinny jeans and a silk blouse. The blouse was the piece she was most proud of. She had shamelessly copied it from a design by Foundrae. It was a deep-plum, layered-silk, fringed tank top that showed off her collarbone and the slight swells of her breasts to perfection. It was, by far, the most sophisticated piece she owned, made even more so by the crepey peekaboo silk that showed the faint outline of her belly button just over the low-slung light denim on her hips.

She'd washed her hair after her talk with Kyrstin in the kitchen, blow-dried it, then twisted it carefully into a bun for some curl. As she walked up the dock to the Pamlico House, she took out the pins that held it and shook out her pinkish-orange locks, feeling the soft curls bounce around her shoulders before settling.

At the top of the gangplank, she found a sidewalk, but she came to an abrupt stop, her mules still on the concrete. She stared up at the beautiful inn and took a deep breath, having a moment of panic about the job and Ms. Sebastian . . . and Erik Rexford. Suddenly it all felt like too much for sheltered li'l Laire, who barely knew anything about the world beyond Corey Island. Was she crazy for taking this job? For meeting this man? Who did she think she—

"I worried you might not come."

Turning to her left, she gasped as a smile exploded across her face.

"Hi," she said breathlessly, putting one of her hands in her back pocket and running the other though her hair.

"Hi," he said, laughing softly as his smile grew quickly to match hers. "I have a confession. I've been here since six."

"Six? But I said—"

"I know," he said, reaching for her free hand and lacing his fingers through hers without permission. "You said eight. I guess I just . . ." He shrugged. "I didn't want to miss you."

Holding his hand was scrambling her brain and making all the air in her lungs slip through her lips until she was light-headed and had to remind herself to breathe.

"I'm here now," she said, her voice soft and thin.

He took a step closer to her, so close that his chest brushed into hers with every deep breath he took. His dark eyes seized and held hers.

"I can't stop thinkin' about you. I couldn't wait to see you again," he said.

His glance slid to her lips as it had last night, and she heard the words in her head: *A first kiss. You want him to be your first, don't you?*

Laire tilted her head back to look up into his face, which was backlit with the pink, gold, and lavender swirls of the dying sun, and her heart filled with so much tenderness, there was no way for one organ to hold it all. It spilled over into her chest, and she breathed it in, keeping her face upturned, reluctant to miss even a moment with him.

Her heart raced with awareness—of herself, of him, of being alone with him, away from her island.

*Go ahead. Kiss him. Kiss the boy.*

"Laire . . .," he whispered, his breath falling softly on her lips as she leaned up on tiptoe and pressed her virgin mouth to his.

His fingers untwined from hers, and he wound both arms around her waist, pulling her close, until her chest was pressed flush against his, the buttons of his crisp gingham dress shirt pushing into the thin silk of her tank top.

The hand she'd hidden in her back pocket slid free, tracing the warm, hard skin of his forearm to his elbow, over the folds of his rolled cuff to the starched cotton of his bicep, which flexed beneath her fingers. His lips were brushing hers gently, almost tentatively, and for a moment she panicked, wondering if he was just being nice, if maybe the way he'd looked at her mouth hadn't signaled interest after all.

But when her fingertips, which slipped soundlessly over the ridge of his shoulder, came into contact with the bare skin of his throat, the kiss changed. Stepping closer to her, his knee parted her legs, and she leaned forward, into him, cupping the back of his neck with her palm and holding on tight as his tongue swept the seam of her lips. They parted for him, inviting him inside.

He groaned, his hot length of tongue sliding erotically over hers as he held her tighter. Her free hand slid up the other side of his throat, her fingers lacing and locking behind his neck to keep his face close to hers, his lips affixed to hers, his body flush and hot and close.

Timidly, she touched the tip of her tongue to the soft, wet, ridged side of his, and she flinched with the intense clench-and-release in her pelvis, the sudden warmth that flooded her white cotton panties as Eric pushed his thigh between her legs. As he supported her against him with strong arms around her back, Laire lost herself in the sensation of their tongues tangling and dancing, teasing each other with hot touches and languorous slides.

*More. More. More, please,* she thought. *More for now, and for later, and for the years that I waited, and for the years up ahead, when we won't know each other anymore. More.*

His chest pushed into hers violently as his fingers curled into fists against her lower back, the knuckles kneading the silk that separated his skin from hers. Her nipples, beaded into sensitive points, met a wall of elegant muscle behind his shirt. The rosy nubs were exquisitely tight under her cotton bra, aching with a yearning she'd never experienced and had no clue how to make better—only instinctively certain that kissing Erik was the key to her relief.

"Laire, Laire, Laire. Baby, we're in public," he whispered against her lips before thrusting his tongue back into her mouth again, as helpless as she to cool the heat between them.

She whimpered, slipping her hands from his neck to his cheeks and tilting his head for a better angle, sighing with pleasure when his mouth sealed over hers, invading once again with a hungry growl.

The hands on her lower back slipped under her blouse, his palms flattening on the skin of her back, and pushing her pelvis flush against his, where a long, rock-hard ridge of muscle throbbed against the apex of her thighs.

And it felt so good . . . so good . . . so, so, so . . .

*W-wait!*

Her eyes widened, and her tongue, which was sliding against his, stilled.

*Oh, God. That's his . . .*

Her lips went slack, and the hands clutching his face loosened their hold.

*It means he wants to . . .*

"Laire? You okay?"

These words were soft and sweet near her ear, the shell of which he licked, sending a thrill straight to her groin and making her sigh with desperation as she forced her eyes open.

"I, um . . . I don't want to . . ."

He nibbled the skin of her neck, and his voice sounded a little drunk. "Don't want to . . . what?"

She leaned back just enough to break contact, to make him raise his head so she could see his eyes, which appeared to be black, the dark brown irises obliterated by the wideness of his pupils.

"You want to have sex with me," she stated bluntly, staring into his eyes.

His lips parted in surprise, and he blinked at her, taking a deep breath that made his chest push against hers again.

"What are you . . ." His eyebrows furrowed. "I mean . . ."

"I can feel it," she said curtly. "I know you want to. Don't deny it."

"I don't . . ." He cleared his throat. "I mean, I wasn't tryin' to—"

"We're *not* having sex," she said adamantly. His arms loosened a little, and she stepped away from him, ending their intimate groin-to-groin contact.

"I didn't think we were." His words were said slowly and carefully, speaking the way you would to a startled or frightened child.

"You sure about that?" Giving his waist a meaningful glance before looking back up at his face, she added, "Because part of you seems to think we are."

He stared at her like he was trying very hard to figure out something important and stay calm while he did so. "Yes, I'm sure I'm not tryin' to have sex with you. We were just kissin'."

She raised her chin. No, she wasn't the most experienced person on the planet, but she knew full well they were doing a lot more than "just" kissing because she'd felt his . . . his *thing* pushing against her, and, unlike Kyrstin, she wasn't on birth control. Not to mention, she wasn't the kind of girl who did more than kiss. Once you moved on from kissing, things got serious fast. She knew that for a fact, and it made her heart race with panic.

"I'm not getting married and . . . and making babies!" she blurted out. "I'm too young!"

"Whoa! What?" he said, releasing her to raise his palms defensively. He took a step back, staring at her in shock. "What the hell are you talkin' about?"

"I have plans for my life!" she said, covering her chest with crossed arms as she stared up at him.

"Well, hell." Looking utterly baffled, Erik wiped his lips, then put his hands on his hips. "Me too!"

## Chapter 6

Damn it, but she was confusing the hell out of him.

They'd said hello, he took her hand, and before he knew it, she was kissing him. Then, out of nowhere, she tells him that she's not going to have sex, get married, and make babies with him.

*What the hell?!*

What exactly did she think was happening between them? Had he somehow led her to believe that they were making some commitment to each other by meeting for dinner tonight? Not to mention, damn it, but *she* had kissed *him*, not the other way around.

Aside from his overwhelming confusion about how and why she'd jumped from a passionate kiss to telling him she wasn't having sex with him—and *Christ!* he certainly wasn't looking to get married and have babies at twenty-one years old!—part of him felt offended. No matter how out of control he might have *felt*, Erik Rexford was, first and foremost, a gentleman. Though some of his peers were aggressive assholes with willing *and unwilling* women, Erik was not. He certainly wasn't going to throw her down on the sidewalk in front of the Pamlico House and have his way with her, if that's what she was implying.

Her expression was awfully dark, though her lips, which had tasted sweeter than any he'd ever known, were slick and bee-stung from his attentions. And fuck, but she was beyond beautiful, standing there uncertainly in the brand-new moonlight. His attraction to her, from the very first second he'd seen her, was fierce, and he wanted to unravel this hiccup between them before it turned into anything significant.

"Can we, um . . . can we back up a little? Maybe sit down for a second and talk this out?" he asked, gesturing to an empty group of Adirondack chairs on a green lawn that overlooked the Sound.

She nodded curtly, preceding him with that no-nonsense march she'd used to take the coolers up to the kitchen yesterday. But this time she wasn't wearing clunky black boots. She was wearing little white-heeled shoes that made her ass sway back and forth like something out of a fucking daydream.

His cock, which was still as hard as a rock, twitched behind his khaki shorts, and he cleared his throat, desperately trying to think of hockey—taking a puck to the nuts. It worked a little, and he'd lost some of the hardness by the time they reached the chairs.

"Let's just . . . sit," he said, still confused about what had just happened.

Her posture was rigid as she sat on the edge of the brightly painted chair that the inn had placed on the lawn for guests seeking a quiet moment and a beautiful view. Erik sat down beside her, staring at her profile, blown away—even in this incredibly awkward moment—by how pretty she was. Her strawberry-blonde hair curled around her shoulders and looked so fucking soft and inviting, he had to force himself not to reach out and touch it. Why hadn't he run his fingers through her hair when he was kissing her? When he'd had the chance? He flinched, silently praying that he'd have another opportunity, because, fuck, if that was somehow their first and last kiss, he'd just as soon die.

He *needed* to touch her again, the absoluteness of the instinct almost blinding.

*Don't do it*, he thought, staring at her stony face. *Now isn't the time.*

He cleared his throat. "I got the feeling you *wanted* to kiss me, Freckles."

She turned to him, her eyes wide and honest. "I did."

"Sure about that?" he asked, trying to keep his voice light.

"Yes," she said, her tone free of guile or uncertainty.

"Good," he said. "Because I wanted to kiss you too."

"But that's *all* I wanted," she quickly added, looking at him squarely.

The overwhelming spike of disappointment he felt at the prospect of never getting further with her than a kiss was tempered by the comforting notion that kissing her was pretty fucking spectacular.

"Was it a good kiss?" she asked, her voice much softer and more uncertain than it had been a second ago.

"Yeah," he said, nodding at her. "Top ten, for sure."

Her lips twitched and her eyebrows furrowed. "Nine better, huh?"

"No, actually," he said, his surprised laugh tapering off as he stared at her. "I revise my answer: *none* better. Top one."

Her smile was sudden and blinding. "Really? It was?"

"Yeah, really. Best kiss I've ever had," he admitted with a soft chuckle, delighted by her smile, delighted that he was the one who'd made her look so happy. "How about for you?"

"Best for me too." She pulled her bottom lip between her teeth, her smile hanging on, though the color in her cheeks deepened. "*Only* for me, actually. I never kissed anyone before you."

*Wait. Fuck! What?*

"Wait. That was . . ." His voice trailed off as he processed what she was saying. "That was your *first kiss*?"

She looked up at him and nodded, her sea-green eyes unapologetic, no excuses issuing from her lips.

He'd been taken aback yesterday, when she said she didn't have a cell phone, but this admission was the first *real* insight Erik Rexford had into exactly how sheltered she was. By eighteen, Erik had lost track of the number of women he'd kissed in his life, but Laire, at eighteen, had saved her first kiss . . . for him.

"I was your first," he murmured.

"Uh-huh."

"Why me?" he asked softly, surprised by the words.

"I don't know. I just . . . I wanted it to be you." She laughed, shaking her head as she looked away from him. "Maybe because you're so different."

This confession, made with zero pretense or attempt at flirtation, made him so happy, he couldn't actually remember when he'd last felt so honored by anything. His life was full of affectation and insincerity: a birthday party attended by important people he didn't know, ceremonies recognizing his father for whatever legislation appealed to the special interests of certain groups, invitations to galas and soirees where everyone tried to outtalk the person beside them with grand ideas and impress the person on the other side with vacation plans and name-dropping.

It was all bullshit.

But this was real. *Real.*

For no good reason at all, this girl he barely knew had given him something priceless.

And shit, what had he done? He'd pulled her flush against his cock like he'd die if they didn't fuck. He cringed. No wonder she had freaked out.

"I didn't know, Freckles. Sorry I got so . . . excited."

She flicked a glance at him, and two spots of bright pink appeared in her cheeks, but she didn't say anything.

He sighed, letting his breath out long and low as he ran a hand through his hair. "Did it, uh . . . did it meet your, uh, expectations? The kiss?"

"Yes," she said, but she was still staring down at her hands, which were folded primly in her lap. "Except . . ."

He tensed. "Except . . . ?"

"I thought it would just be mouths. And, well, tongues, maybe. Like in the movies. I didn't know about the hands. Or your, um, chest pushing against my, um . . . you know. Or, um, your . . ." She glanced at his groin, and her cheeks blazed red as she pulled her bottom lip between her teeth. "I know what happens between men and women, in bed. I just . . . I didn't know it all happened so fast once you started kissing."

"Not every kiss is like that one," he said, hoping to Christ it wouldn't be the last they ever shared. "That one was . . . *really* good."

"You know so much more than I do." She groaned, looking up at him. "You must think I'm really stupid."

"No!" he said, his voice low and serious. "No. I don't think you're stupid." He finally risked touching her again, reaching for her hand and holding it gently between his. "Not at all."

*But you're the most inexperienced girl I've ever met, and I'm not sure how I feel about that.*

She took a deep breath but didn't pull her hand away, and he was profoundly grateful to be allowed to hold her hand, which quickly and firmly settled his feelings about her inexperience: he didn't care. She was like no one he'd ever met before. In a world where he felt like he'd seen it all, she felt fresh and new, and a fierce surge of protectiveness swelled within him for all that she hadn't seen and didn't know.

She chuckled softly. "I thought you needed to kiss for a real long time before you wanted to have sex."

"Laire," he said, waiting until she looked up at him, "can I be brutally honest with you?"

Her eyes widened nervously, but she nodded.

"Sometimes you don't even need to kiss before wanting someone." He grinned, threading his fingers through hers. "The truth is . . . I wanted you the second I laid eyes on you."

Her sharp gasp made his balls tighten. "You did?"

"Yeah. Of course."

"But . . . I didn't even . . . I wasn't trying to—"

"You didn't *have* to do anything." His grin grew into a wide smile, and he tilted his head to the side, utterly captivated by her innocence. With his free hand, he reached for a lock of her hair and pushed it behind her ear, cupping her cheek when she leaned into him. "You think *I'm* different? *You're* different, darlin'. You're beautiful and honest and interestin', and you want to know the truth? The way you made me chase you down for a date was . . . I don't know. I liked it. I'm attracted to you. *Really* attracted to you."

"Yes." Her face grew instantly grim again and leaned away from his touch. "I know."

"Hold on now. That's not a bad thing. It doesn't mean . . ." Damn, but this was awkward. Didn't she have a mother to explain these things to her? That kissing someone made you feel certain things, but that those things didn't always lead to sex. Not immediately, anyway. He cleared his throat. "Laire, I can't help it that I'm attracted to you. But that doesn't mean I expect to have sex with you or that I'll ever pressure you for more than you want to give. And to be clear, I'm not lookin' for a wife or family. That's not on my agenda right now. Hell, I'm in college. I'm *years* away from anythin' like that."

Her eyes nailed his as her lips parted in wonder. "*Years*?"

"Uh-huh."

She grinned at him, all gloominess flying away from her face as quickly as it had landed there. "*Years.*"

"At least," he said. "I need to go to college, then law school, find a job, work for a few years to establish myself. *Then* I'll think about settlin' down. I mean, someday, yes, I'd like to have a wife and family. But certainly not *now.*"

"But you're twenty-one," she said matter-of-factly, like everyone she knew thought about settling down at twenty-one, which was, well, weird.

"Where I come from, most people don't get married right out of college. I doubt I'll get married until my late twenties. Maybe even my thirties."

"Wow. *Ten years,*" she murmured with wonder, leaning away from his hand to look up into his eyes. Her eyes sparkled with excitement when she added, "Because you have dreams for your life, and you want to make them come true first, before you settle down, right?"

*Dreams? I don't know about that.* Erik had never really had his own dreams; his future had, more or less, been decided *for* him.

"Plans, more like. There are lots of plans for me."

"That's how I feel too!" she said, looking happy and relieved. Then she winced, her eyes flicking to his groin and back. "But I felt your . . ."

"Sure you did. If we kissed again, you'd feel it again. It means I'm turned-on. It means—"

"You want sex."

"Yeah. No. I mean . . .," he said, squirming a little and wondering how in the hell they'd ended up here. "We just met, you know? That? Sex? It comes later."

"But you said you already want it."

Damn, this was like being back in one of his prelaw classes at Duke. She wasn't going to let a single loophole go unexamined.

"Okay. That's true. But first, I want to get to know you. And we definitely wouldn't do *it* unless *you* wanted to."

"But if we did, what about our futures? What about your plans and my dreams?"

"What about them?"

Her shoulders slumped. "If we had sex, we'd have to get married."

*What. The. Fuck?*

How his eyeballs didn't pop out of his head and land on the grass between them was a fucking miracle.

*Okay. Okay. Breathe, Erik. Breathe.*

Her values were coming into clearer focus—and from what he could gather, they were old-fashioned and incredibly conservative, almost like a throwback to the 1950s. He'd never known anyone remotely like her, like this fisherman's daughter from a world that was somehow frozen in time.

He tried to remember what he knew about the more remote islands on the Outer Banks, but he'd spent his summers in posh Buxton, mostly oblivious to the year-round islanders. His knowledge of their ways was painfully thin. He knew from her accent that she'd been raised in a pretty isolated place. She wouldn't let him come to her island to visit her, for fear he'd "make trouble." She didn't have a cell phone, and frankly, he wouldn't be surprised if she didn't have the internet either, which meant that his world—the *modern* world, as he knew it— wasn't exactly her comfort zone.

Her world was alien to him . . . which meant that his was alien to her too.

His mind flitted back to the catering manager last night, telling him to "let her go." He was starting to understand why she'd said that, and why she'd warned Erik that he didn't have "any business with an island girl."

But one look at Laire told him he did.

It didn't matter if one hundred people warned him away from her because this particular island girl held him rapt. Since meeting her, he couldn't think of anything but her—finding a way to see her again, getting to know her. And now? After a kiss that tilted the axis of his world after a million that hadn't? He wanted more. He *needed* more.

Erik was a student of law, not building, but he was ready to roll up his sleeves and start bridge-building between their worlds if that's what it took to get to know her. And to do that, he'd need to treat her words and ideas with respect, even though they felt foreign and antiquated to him.

*If we had sex, we'd have to get married.*

"Um. No, Laire. To be honest with you, I don't . . . I mean, I wouldn't marry a woman just because I slept with her," he said. "One has nothin' to do with the other. In the world I come from, people can just . . . *enjoy* each other if they want to . . . without, you know, makin' a lifetime commitment." He scanned her face, hoping that his words wouldn't scare her away. "Put it this way: I would sleep with someone I loved and wanted to marry. But I would *also* sleep with someone I didn't love and might not want to marry . . . as long as she wanted it too."

"You've done that?" she asked, her forehead creased, her voice a whisper. "*Slept* with someone?"

He hated it that he had to nod yes, but there was no point in lying to her. He was in the middle of the weirdest conversation he'd ever had with anyone, but in for a penny, in for a pound. He was determined to see it through.

"Oh," she said, her cheeks flushing with a new wave of color. "Nice girls don't do that where I come from. If you let a boy touch your body, you eventually settle down together. That's the way it is. Everyone knows what you're doing, but they don't care as long as you got plans to make it right."

*Make it right. Which, apparently, meant marriage. Whoa.*

He exhaled a shaky breath he didn't realize he'd been holding. "Okay, I got it. Nice girls don't have sex before they're married, or, um, engaged."

"They *shouldn't,*" she said. "And if they do, they deserve the reputation they get."

"They *deserve* it?"

She nodded her head gravely. "Yes. They knew the consequences and made their choices anyway."

"And what exactly are the consequences?"

She looked away from him, out at the Sound, mulling this over for a moment before turning her eyes back to his. "A girl like that might be more comfortable moving away from Corey, I guess."

"Wow." He nodded, a chill passing through him at the unapologetic absoluteness of her suggestion. "I see."

"But you don't agree." She tilted her head to the side, scanning his face with curiosity. "You think a girl can give herself to someone and *not* marry him and still be . . . *good*?"

"Yeah. I think . . . I mean, I think . . ."

Damn it, what *did* he think?

In the real world, in *his* world, he didn't consider sex that big a deal. He wasn't some herpes-spreading manwhore, but Erik had lost his virginity when he was sixteen, like most of his friends. And he'd been with several girls since, most notably his college girlfriend of two years, Alexa, with whom he'd broken up in March.

But—here and now—he and Laire weren't in *his* world. Here, sitting on Adirondack chairs, looking out at the Pamlico Sound in Buxton, neither on her island nor at his mansion, it somehow felt like they both had a foot in each world. Did he think a girl who slept with a man before marriage was "bad"? No. He didn't. Nor, however, did he want to disrespect her values by touting his own as more right.

He sighed, tightening his fingers through hers, looking at

her lovely face and wondering what it was about her that had so quickly and firmly ensnared him. This conversation was awkward—much more so than he'd usually tolerate—and yet it somehow felt worth it. In fact, it felt unthinkable to abandon it and walk away from her. He could feel his feelings for her taking root in his heart—protectiveness and tenderness developing within him in tandem, made only more potent by his almost-blinding lust for her.

Concentrating on his feelings instead of his attraction to her helped him to choose his words carefully. "I think that we come from different places and see the world differently."

"Or maybe you're just a man," she said, her tone on the cusp of defensive. "Men's urges make them want more than a girl should give."

He narrowed his eyes at her. There was some truth to what she was saying, but he'd spent half an hour trying to understand where she was coming from and help her understand him. He'd be damned if he let her boil it down to some bullshit refrain about gender inequality. Her words weren't fair, and he wasn't going to let her get away with them.

"I'm a *person*," he said, raising his chin. "And I believe that if two people *care* about each other and want to *be* with each other, it's nobody else's business what they do when they're alone together. It's private. It's up to them to make up their *own* rules."

Her eyes widened again, and she searched his face with such heartbreaking solemnity, it made his guts clench with something indefinable and unfathomable. Had he understood the scope and force of what started between them in that moment, of what was now alive and growing deep within him, he might have run from her.

But he didn't know and he didn't run. And like stepping from life to eternity, or over a bridge to a place of no return, he faced her, waiting for her to respond, waiting to know if there was a future for them, or merely a farewell.

"I like that, Erik," she said, her lips tilted upward with wonder, her eyes soft and welcoming.

The way she looked at him. *Fuck.*

He felt his breathing hitch with the power of it, with the power it had to make everything feel—no, *be*—okay. He leaned forward and pressed his forehead to hers, closing his eyes as the darkness shielded them from the rest of the world in a little bubble of their own making.

"We can make our *own* rules," she whispered against his lips. "I like that so much."

He felt his heart open like a story, like a song, like the wings of a gull or the clouds that rain or the soft sweet place between her legs that he may—*or may not*, in all likelihood— ever know. Like doors and windows and spirit and the heavens and tightly locked doors that are portals to somewhere a man might want to spend his forever.

His heart opened wide, and he leaned forward to brush her lips with his, a profound sense of *someday* catching his breath with the same wonder he'd read in her eyes.

"Me too, Laire. I like it so much too."

***

Seated across from Erik at a shiny wooden table by the windows, Laire looked at the menu with approval. The Pamlico House didn't buy their seafood from her father and uncle, but they had a good selection of local catch, and with a quick peek at the back of the menu, she recognized the purveyor as someone over on Ocracoke about whom her father had spoken with respect.

She felt a sharp squeeze in the pit of her stomach as she thought about her father. She was betraying his trust by sitting at this fancy candlelit table with Erik Rexford, but to save her life, she couldn't imagine leaving.

At one point during their talk, Erik had said that he was "turned-on" by her, and in a very real way, Laire felt that something deep inside her had been turned on tonight when she kissed him. Like a light switch, or an on button, she felt alive in a way she'd never felt before—connected to him in a way she couldn't have imagined before tonight. It made her feel scared and breathless in one moment, but excited and invincible the next, like she was starting an unknown adventure with the perfect person—and she never, ever wanted that feeling to end.

"Anythin' good?" he asked, glancing at her over the top of his menu.

"Lots," she said. "Want a recommendation?"

He looked surprised but nodded. "Sure."

"It's late June. End of spring, early summer," she explained. "Blue crab is in season both spring and summer, so you can't go wrong whether it's caught in wire pots or trawlnets. But see the bluefish here?" He nodded. "Spring catch. Same with the sea trout. You'd be better off with mackerel because it's a—"

"Summer catch?"

She nodded. "Young but fresh."

He placed his menu flat on the table. "What's the best winter catch?"

"Gill net fishing's good on the ocean side in the winter," she said. "Bluefish, croakers, sea trout, striped bass. Any of those."

"I don't fish much, but when I do, it's off a dock with a fishin' pole and some worms."

"Aw," she said, tilting her head to the side and giving him a saccharine smile. "That's cuuuute."

He chuckled softly. "Why do I suddenly feel like a five-year-old?"

"Cause that's how a five-year-old fishes?" she suggested

with a giggle. "Naw. I'm kidding. Hook and line gear is fine. You can catch seven or eight at a time when they're moving."

"Seven or eight? How's that?" he asked.

"Commercial fishing. One line, eight hooks," she said. "Catch 'em fast, you can have a good day."

"You know a lot about this," he said.

She nodded. "Everyone on Corey knows about fish. It's a lifestyle."

"So why don't you order for us?"

She shook her head. As much as she knew all there was to know about the fish on the meu, the side dishes were all foreign-sounding to her. *Braising reduction? Edamame? Raisin smear?* Were these items actually food?

"I don't think that's a good idea," she said, feeling her cheeks heat up as she kept her eyes glued to the strange-sounding words.

"Why not?"

She leaned forward, looking up at him. "I don't know what half of these things are."

"Like what?"

"Braising reduction?"

"A sauce."

"Edamame?"

"Japanese peapods."

"Raisin *smear*?" she asked.

He chuckled. "Got me there. I have no idea. Maybe smushed-up raisins?"

She laughed along with him, then nodded. "Let's do this: I'll order the fish; you order the rest. Deal?"

He nodded at her. "Deal. We make our own rules, Freckles."

His words went straight to her heart with a wild shot of something that felt so wonderful, her whole body flushed in response, and suddenly she was remembering their kiss—the way he'd pressed his private place against hers, the way his tongue had felt sliding against hers.

"Whatever you're thinkin' about, I wish I was thinkin' about it too," he said softly, his eyes dark and serious when she looked up at him.

"I'm thinking about you," she admitted breathlessly.

He shifted in his seat. "And what *exactly* are you thinkin', darlin'?"

"How much I want to kiss you again," she whispered.

"Me too," he said, his voice low and intense, sending shivers of yearning down her spine.

She darted a glance around the restaurant quickly. Well-dressed couples chatted softly with each other, their faces bathed in candlelight. The ladies wore pearl necklaces and upscale collared shirts by Ralph Lauren and Izod, and the men spoke softly, laughed without much sound. This was not the Corey Fish Pot, where Remy regularly hauled Kyrstin up against his chest and kissed her lustily at the bar. This was a nice and proper place, and she needed to stop looking at Erik Rexford like she wanted to eat him with a fork and spoon.

Maybe splashing some cold water on her cheeks would help.

Folding her napkin carefully, she placed it on the table. "I'll be back in a second."

"Laire," he said, and her eyes slid to his, captivated by the hungry look in them. "Are you askin' me to follow you?"

"To the ladies' room?" she asked, feeling her eyes widen in surprise. "N-no!"

"Oh," he said, leaning back in his chair and picking up his glass of red wine. "Sorry. I guess I . . ." He shook his head and took a sip of wine.

"Do people *do* that?" she whispered, leaning toward him. "Meet in the ladies' room to kiss?"

He grinned at her as he placed his glass back on the table. "Yes, ma'am. Sometimes they do."

"Naughty," she said, smiling back at him as she stood up. "Can you wait until after dinner to kiss me again?"

"If I have to," he said, though his eyes made a leisurely sweep down her body, making her feel hot and eager and impatient.

She sighed with longing, ruefully wondering if nice restaurants ever packed dinners to go. "I'll be right back."

In the restroom, she washed her hands with the coldest possible water and reminded herself to behave. As she exited, she bumped into Ms. Sebastian, who was headed for the kitchen.

"Laire!"

"Ms. Sebastian!"

The older woman reached for Laire, hugging her like a long-lost friend, and though Laire was surprised by the gesture, it felt so good to be hugged, she leaned into the embrace for a moment before pulling away.

"I'm glad to see you again so soon."

"I came to say I want the job," said Laire.

"Really? Your father said yes?"

Laire took a deep breath. "Sort of. He thinks I'm working at a place on Ocracoke for now."

Ms. Sebastian's face lost some of its warmth. "You lied to him?"

"My sister did," she said. "She needs him to think I'm taking her job so she could take a promotion to bartender."

"You sure it's wise to deceive him like that?"

Laire shook her head. "No, ma'am. But I love my sister, and she has her reasons. I'll come clean soon."

"Promise me?"

Laire nodded. "Yes, ma'am. Kyrstin's getting married the week after next. Then she can do what she wants, and I'll tell him the truth."

Ms. Sebastian's face relaxed, and she nodded. "That sounds okay with me. Can you come on back to my office and fill out some paperwork?"

"Oh," said Laire, glancing back at the dining room. "Can I fill out the papers tomorrow night when I come to work? I'm . . ."

"You're . . .," prompted Ms. Sebastian.

"I'm sort of on a date tonight."

Ms. Sebastian's eyes cooled, and she looked over Laire's shoulder, her eyes landing effortlessly on Erik, who sat alone at a far table by the windows. When she looked at Laire again, her expression was set somewhere between disapproving and worried. "That's Erik Rexford."

"Yes, ma'am."

"You're on a date with the governor's son."

*We make our own rules.* Laire lifted her chin. "Yes, ma'am."

"I guess you know what you're doin', huh?"

"I guess so," she said, wishing she felt more conviction behind her words.

"Then it's none of my business." Ms. Sebastian nodded crisply. "Do you have black pants and a white T-shirt?"

"Yes, ma'am."

"Fine. Wear them tomorrow. See you at four."

"Four, ma'am?"

Ms. Sebastian nodded. "For table setup before the dinner crowd. Is that a problem, Laire?"

"No, ma'am. And when will I be finished?"

"Kitchen closes at nine. Last tables bused by ten."

Four to ten. Sixty dollars a night. It was a small fortune.

She grinned at her new boss. "Thank you, ma'am. I won't let you down."

With one last grim glance at Erik, Ms. Sebastian turned

toward the kitchen. "See you tomorrow."

*I got the job!*

She watched Ms. Sebastian go, then headed back for her date with Erik with a spring in her step, hoping to sweet Jesus that their date would end with another toe-curling kiss and a lot less talking.

## Chapter 7

Almost a week into Laire's new job at the Pamlico House restaurant, Erik had kissed her at least a dozen more times—always outside the restaurant, under the stars, usually around ten, when she was finally finished with her shift and about to head home.

He arrived every evening between nine and ten and sat at the bar drinking red wine or beer, waiting for her to finish her shift, after which he would meet her behind the restaurant, walk her down to the dock, kiss her senseless for as long as she let him, then wave good-bye as she stepped onto her boat and drove herself home. He stayed out of her way as she worked, catching her eye as she bused a table nearby, or giving her a wink when she picked up a drink order for a busy waiter.

In public, he was her secret admirer.

In private, he was her passion.

When she woke up every morning to clean the house, fix her father's dinner, and work on a new idea for a blouse or a skirt, she thought of him constantly. Of the way he cupped her cheeks as he kissed her, of how it felt to have that long ridge of muscle pushing against her soft, wet places through his shorts and her pants every night. She'd smile, remembering the sweet, low rumble of his voice close to her ear, or the way his tongue tasted after he finished his glass of wine.

If she finished early and they had a little extra time, sometimes they'd walk slowly, from the back door of the kitchen to the Adirondack chairs where they'd talked the first night. She'd sit on his lap, and he'd hold her tight, his lips brushing her ear and neck as he told her about his day. Other times, they would sit on the dock beside her boat, his arm around her shoulders, their legs dangling in the brackish water as they stole a few extra minutes to kiss or talk.

Laire became familiar with the major players in Erik's life: his mother and father, his sister, Hillary, and good friends Pete and Van, who each had a summer home on the northern Banks. She imagined they were a happy foursome playing at the beach or lounging by the pool, lucky Hillary the only girl with three handsome boys who'd met in kindergarten and graduated from high school together. Laire didn't know a ton about Pete, and even less about Van, whom Erik mentioned only in the context of the whole group, but that was probably her fault, as she focused her questions primarily on his family.

His father, the governor, was ambitious and demanding, his expectations of Erik far more onerous than her own father's of her. And his mother, Ursula, whom he called Fancy, seemed much more concerned with her social engagements and furthering her "reach" (whatever the hell that was!) than her son's happiness. Piecing together the unspoken parts of his narrative, she gathered that Erik didn't really want to be a lawyer and didn't have strong political aspirations like his father. What he seemed to enjoy most was sports—playing hockey and lacrosse, tennis and golf, sailing and swimming. She had yet to learn what he wanted from life; she only knew that following his father into government service wasn't his dream.

But these snippets of conversation happened between soul-shaking kisses that stole her breath and her heart, making her long for things that nice girls weren't supposed to want without a wedding ring. She often found herself reconsidering Erik's words from the night of their first kiss: *If two people care about each other, it's up to them to make up their* own *rules*. More and more, Laire wondered if the all-consuming, first-thing-in-the-morning, final-thing-before-sleeping feelings she had for Erik Rexford were, indeed, love. How else could she explain the waves of aching longing she felt whenever she was away from him, and the sharp, sweet relief when he finally held her in his arms? If they did fall in love, what rules would she and Erik make for themselves? And would she be able to reconcile those choices against the person she'd been raised to be? Because she wanted more from him. Oh, God, every day, she wanted more.

On Friday night, Erik sat at the bar with a single red rose before him, and as he met her outside after her shift, he presented it to her with a grin.

Never having received a flower from a beau before, Laire raised it to her nose and inhaled deeply as he walked them over to their favorite chairs and pulled her onto his lap with a happy sigh.

"What's this for?" she asked, looking up into his dark eyes with a shy grin.

He dropped his lips to hers in a sweet kiss. "It's our one-week anniversary. We met a week ago today."

She giggled, nodding her head. "I guess we did."

"You had crabs, remember?"

"Oh, Lord," she groaned. "You ever gonna let me live that down?"

"Unlikely," he said, nuzzling her nose with his. "Though I am curious how you knew about that kind of crabs."

"Ha," she said. "Can't live in a town that catches blues and not hear jokes about crabs from the cradle."

He chuckled, brushing his lips against hers. "Makes sense,

I guess." He leaned his head on the back of the chair and looked at her. "So! I have somethin' to ask you."

"What?"

"Well, this is nice, you know? Meetin' you after work every night . . ."

"Mm-hm," she murmured, shifting in his lap to press her chest against his and thread her fingers through his hair. "It is."

His lips were so close to her ear, they brushed her skin with every word. "But it's not enough, Freckles. Not for me. I know you work most nights, but I was wonderin' how you'd feel about spendin' the day with me sometime."

She froze. "The day?"

"Yeah. The whole day, until you have to be here for work. You and me. Kissin' and sunnin' and swimmin' and . . . whatever else we felt like doin'."

"Hmm," she said, pursing her lips and looking down.

This was a problem, of course, that she was *scared* to fix, and *dying* to fix at the same time. Being with Erik for only a few stolen minutes every night before she made the trek home wasn't enough for her either, but the structure of their relationship— meeting in the shadows of Buxton, where no one knew her—had given her a false sense of security. They learned a little more about each other, they held hands, they flirted, they kissed, they fell harder and harder every night . . . all without having to mesh their worlds.

But going out on a date during the day could be risky. Where would they go? Who might see them? How in the world would she explain what she was doing with Erik Rexford if she was caught? And what if her father or sisters somehow found out?

He slipped his fingers under her chin and tipped her head up so he could look into her eyes.

"Laire, I just want more time with you."

"I know." *Me too.*

"Well, let's make it happen. What days are you free?"

Most any day worked, honestly. She was free every day from nine until three, occasionally helping her sister with wedding plans or working for a few hours at King Triton. Carving out the time to meet Erik wouldn't be a problem. Where and how she met him were much more worrisome matters.

"I have to help my sister a little this week," she said, evading the question.

"Kyrstin, right? The one gettin' married?"

She nodded. "In a week."

"Well, is there a day that's better than the rest? Whatever it is, I'll make it work. I'll come pick you up at your house, say hello to your father and sisters so they know you're in good hands, and then we'll go spend the day together."

Her blood went cold and her breath caught. Her father and sisters? Out of the question. They would forbid her to see him again, and she'd be forced to quit her job immediately. Pick her up? No. Absolutely not. He could *not* pick her up in his fancy antique all-wood speedboat. Even if her father was working and her sisters weren't around, *someone* would see them. Questions would be asked. Rumors would be started.

"No."

She slid her fingers from his hair and leaned away from him, picking up the rose on the arm of the chair.

"No?" His voice was gentle but confused. "What do you mean? I thought—"

"No. You can't come to Corey," she said, leaning away a little more, concentrating on the delicate red petals and ignoring the sting of the thorns.

"Of course I can."

"No," she insisted, looking up at him, one of the rose's thorns biting into her skin as she clutched it tighter in her fist. "You don't understand. You *can't*, Erik. There would be qquestions and rumors and—"

"Hey! Hey, hey, hey," he said gently, cupping her cheeks and forcing her eyes to look into his. "I like you. I *really* like you. I know we've only known each other for a week, but I only want to *be with you* this summer. No one else."

Even though this conversation was tricky and upsetting, she allowed herself a moment of pleasure that he wanted to be with her only because she couldn't imagine being with anyone but him.

"Do you *want* to spend time with me, Laire?"

"Yes," she whispered, unable to look up at him.

"Then why can't I come to Corey and pick you up for a date?"

"Because it's . . . it's complicated."

"Wait a second," said Erik. "Does your family know about me? Do they know we're seein' each other?"

She gulped, forcing herself to look up at him as she shook her head.

"Oh," he said softly. He sighed, and she heard a hint of hurt in his voice when he said, "I'm a secret, huh?"

"Yes," she said, her heart racing, her fingers tightening around the thorny stem. *One of many.*

She still hadn't had a chance to tell her father that she was working in Hatteras, not Ocracoke, although Kyrstin, who was happily waiting bar, was turning out to be a master of deception, lying to their father with a finesse that should have scared Laire. But they'd have to come clean sooner or later, wouldn't they? She'd more or less promised herself to tell him right after Kyrstin and Remy's wedding next weekend. He'd be good and mad, but maybe she could convince him to let her keep her job when he understood the kind of money she was making.

That said, more and more, keeping her job was the least of her worries.

He would blow a gasket if he found out she was dating a

dingbatter . . . and kissing him every chance she got, pushing the envelope between what was allowed and what was indecent. Not to mention, a dingbatter was bad enough, but a dingbatter who also happened to be the governor's son? Her father was a man of few words, but none of those words were especially fond of big government and the way rules were made in Raleigh that affected folks minding their business in the Outer Banks.

Her heart started racing as she thought about her father's reaction to her dating Erik Rexford. It would be a disaster of epic proportions.

". . . not sure how I feel about being a secret," he was saying, his voice thoughtful, with an unmistakably sour edge. "It makes me feel like we're doin' somethin' wrong when we're not."

Except, by her way of thinking and the values with which she'd grown up, *they were*. They were doing something *very* wrong. It's just . . . she couldn't seem to help herself. Her feelings for Erik were deeper and more intense every day.

"I'm sorry," she said, wiggling to disengage from his arms, the rose losing petals as she pushed against his chest. She perched on the tip of his knee, her back ramrod straight, facing away from him, staring out at the black Pamlico. "It won't work."

"The date?" he bit out. "Or . . . us?"

She shrugged miserably as a trickle of blood ran down the length of her thumb.

"You're bleedin'," said Erik, putting his hands on her waist and swiveling her effortlessly to face him again. His expression was stony, his voice hurt. He reached for her hand and gently unfurled her fingers. Taking the rose from her grip, he threw it to the ground beside them, then lifted her palm to his mouth, sealing his lips over the puncture and sucking.

His tongue swirled around the small hole as he tenderly

tried to kiss away her pain, to no avail. Finally he looked up at her, his thumb sealing the small puncture as he searched her eyes and spoke gently.

"Darlin', I come here every night to be near you. I live for sunset like a vampire because that's when my heart starts beatin' each day, when I grab the keys to the car or boat and race over here to be with you. It makes me crazy all day to be away from you because I want more. I want to talk for hours and kiss you and find out what makes you laugh and . . . Damn it, Laire, this isn't enough."

A moment of panic swept through her, and she wondered, for a heart-stopping moment, if he was about to tell her that he wouldn't be coming by anymore. And in that moment, she knew that, no matter how much it scared her to imagine her family finding out that she was seeing Erik Rexford, she would risk it. She couldn't lose him. She wouldn't let that happen, and if it meant she had to bend, had to take a chance that frightened her, she'd take it.

Their stolen moments every evening weren't enough for her either. She wanted more time just as much as he did. *Our own rules.* They could figure this out together, right?

Before she lost her nerve, she leaned into him, pressing her aching breasts against his chest and reaching up to caress his cheek. "I could meet you Sunday after work. I'm only working the brunch shift, from seven to one. I'll be free for the rest of the day, and my father won't expect me back until eleven."

"I have a car," he said, his eyes lighting up with happiness, and her heart clutched, then sang, with the knowledge that her words, her actions, had made him smile like that. "I'll drive you wherever you want to go."

"I'll have to move the boat to Hatteras Landing," she said, her mind racing, trying to figure out the best way to cover their tracks. "I can't leave it here all day."

"I'll arrange for a slip and pay for it," he offered.

She raised her chin. "No, you will not."

"Laire, I asked *you* on a date. I intend to pay."

"Date starts when you pick me up at the marina at one thirty."

"You drive a hard bargain, darlin'," he said, leaning down to kiss her. "But I'll take what I can get."

"Okay, then," she sighed, her eyes flitting hungrily to his lips.

"Thank God," he murmured.

She wound her arms around his neck and let him pull her flush against his body, melting into a hot kiss and reveling in the feeling of his chest pushing into hers with every ragged breath he took. Her nipples beaded as though at his command, and she arched her back to get as close to him as possible. Plunging her fingers back into his thick dark hair, she moaned as he sucked on her tongue before changing the angle of their heads and resealing his lips over hers.

Her stomach filled with flutters as his hands moved down her back, his palms landing on her ass and squeezing gently as his tongue slid slowly against hers before he nipped her top lip between his. She was breathless when she suddenly realized his lips weren't moving on hers anymore.

Opening her eyes slowly, she blinked up at his smiling face, feeling hot and bothered and needy.

"More," she murmured, nuzzling his nose with hers.

"Open your eyes, Freckles," he said, his breath ragged against her skin. She did, and his eyes, dark and wide, met hers. "Don't tell me this won't work. Don't ever say that to me again."

Her breath caught, but she nodded. "I won't."

His eyes fluttered closed, and he reached up to cup her cheeks. "Our rules, Laire."

She rested her forehead against his. "Our rules, Erik."

"Our rules," he whispered again, then smiled, laughing softly with happiness, and she smiled with him, vibrating with wonder, leaning forward to press her lips to his and seal their promise.

***

Freshly showered and shaved and dressed in pressed red Nantucket shorts, a blue and white striped dress shirt with rolled cuffs, and Top-Siders, Erik hopped down the last two steps with a spring in his step. It was one o'clock on a bright sunny day, and he was going to spend the rest of it with his favorite girl.

"Well, my goodness, Mr. Handsome! You're up late today!"

He pivoted around in the front vestibule to find his mother approaching from the living room, a huge vase of blue and white flowers in her hands.

"'Mornin', Mother."

She offered him her cheek, and he kissed it.

"It's afternoon."

"Slept in."

"Makes your father see red, you know."

"Good thing he's spendin' most of the summer in Raleigh, then."

She smiled indulgently. "Looked over those law books he left for you?"

*No.* "Took a peek."

"Better take more than a peek by the time he gets here next weekend," she said, an edge in her cultured voice. "One more year at Duke, and then you'll be in law school. Wouldn't hurt to be a little prepared, now, would it?"

Hiding a grimace, he turned away from her, plucking his car keys from a bowl on the sideboard by the stairs.

"Headed somewhere?" she asked.

"Yep. Plans."

"Where to?" He turned to grin at her, and she nodded

knowingly. "I'd wager there's a girl involved."

"You'd win that bet, Mother."

"Secret plans every night. Now today too," she hummed. "Makes a mother wonder."

He gave her a look. "Wonder what, exactly?"

"Who my handsome boy is headed off to meet at all hours of the day and night." She giggled like a teenage girl. "I can only hope that it's . . . Van?"

"Van?" he asked, so taken aback, he said her name like he *hadn't* known her his whole life. His mother thought he was dating *Van*?

"Miss Vanessa Osborn, you scamp."

"Oh."

"You courtin' her, Erik? I hope you're bein' a gentleman. Tillie and Reginald are old friends."

She used an old, formal word like *courting* to be charming, but the reminder of their lifelong friendship with the Osborns held a warning. *Shoot.* She'd really been giving this some thought. Best nip it in the bud before it got out of control.

"No, mother, I'm *not* seein' Van. I'm . . ."

As he stared at her expectant dark brown eyes, his voice trailed off, and he finished up this conversation in his head quickly. . . . *dating a local fisherman's daughter who I met while she was delivering crabs to my birthday party.*

His chest pinched with misgivings.

*Fuck. No.*

What a scene she'd make. She'd forbid Erik to see Laire ever again. She'd lecture him about his place in the world and his parents' expectations of him. She'd tell him in no uncertain terms that the governor's son didn't bed the local help. And yeah, all that would hurt his ears and suck in general, but he could handle his mother. That's not what worried him.

What made his blood suddenly run cold was the thought

that Fancy would figure out a way to invade Laire's privacy and discretion, hunt her down on her little island and make a scene, embarrass and shame her. An overwhelming protective instinct—no doubt left over from his Neanderthal ancestors—rose up within him, hot and urgent. No matter what, he would never, ever subject Laire to his mother's judgment and scorn.

*Hell* no.

"Well?" she prompted, her expression wary but still curious. "If it's not Van, who is it? Katie Healy? Stephanie Reynolds-Jones?"

Two other well-heeled daughters of North Carolina who had houses in the Banks. *Fuck.* She was staring up at him, waiting for an answer, and since he couldn't come up with anything better on such short notice, he said, "Promise you won't say anythin'?"

To protect Laire, he'd have to let his mother think he was dating Van, but the last thing he needed was for Van to find out he'd told his mother they were dating. She didn't need that kind of encouragement, and trying to explain to her that he'd used her as an excuse wouldn't go over very well.

"I'll be as silent as the grave," his mother promised, her eyes sparkling with anticipation.

He leaned forward and kissed her cheek, speaking softly as though sharing a confidence with her. "It's Vanessa. You guessed it. But we want to keep it a secret for now and see how things go."

"Oh, I just knew it!"

He cringed inside at her enthusiasm but plastered a smile on his face. "We're takin' things slow, Mother. Now, don't wreck everythin' by talkin' about it, you hear?"

"I hear," she said, grinning at him like the cat that got the cream.

Stepping back, he gave her a stern look. "Remember your promise, now."

"I won't say a word . . . but, Erik!" She reached out and touched his arm. "She's perfect for you. Vanessa Osborn and Erik Rexford," she said, her eyes taking on a dreamy look as she headed toward the kitchen to water her flowers. "Absolute perfection."

"I'm a lucky man, Mother," he called after her, finally allowing himself to wince.

"Yes, you are." She sighed happily. "You treat that gal nice, now!"

The kitchen door swung shut, and Erik turned around to find Hillary standing on the stairs behind him.

"What gal?"

*Shoot.* "No one."

"Well, I'm not deaf, and if I'm not mistaken, our mother just exclaimed your name with Vanessa's and said the words "absolute perfection," which it would be, I suppose, for Fancy Rexford. But I happen to know you're *not* datin' Vanessa Osborn."

"Shh."

"Why?" she asked, raising her voice a touch. "Don't want Fancy to know you're lyin'?"

"Maybe I'm not," he snapped.

"Yes, Erik dear, you most definitely are. Because while you're MIA, doin' God-knows-what every night around nine o'clock, my heart is being ripped out at various parties and beach bonfires with our friends."

"Huh? What do you mean?"

"You're off having a jolly time while I watch Pete make cow eyes at Van and listen to Van gripe about my brother's disappearin' act." Hillary took another step down, placing her hands on her hips as she stood in the vestibule across from him. "So . . . who is she?"

He was torn between his loyalty to Laire and his

surprisingly strong desperation to share his happiness with his sister.

"You can't tell anyone."

"Huh. This is intriguin'."

"I mean it, Hills."

She nodded slowly, her eyes locked on his. "Okay. I promise."

"All right. Come on, then. Not here."

He gestured for her to follow him and slipped out the front door, with his sister trailing behind, until they reached the safety of the garage. He pressed in the code to open the door and watched as it rose slowly.

Walking around to the driver's side, he slipped into the seat of his Mercedes convertible, and Hillary sat down beside him. He turned over the motor, creating a nice hum of white noise before turning to her.

"You don't know her. She's a local girl."

"She's a—are you nuts?"

Erik braced his hands on the steering wheel and sighed. "No. I just . . . I like her."

"Where the hell did you *meet* her?"

"She delivered seafood for my birthday party."

"She's a seafood delivery girl?" Hillary snorted. "Oh, Erik, Fancy is goin' to shit a brick over this."

His eyes widened. "You swore you wouldn't tell!"

Hillary took a deep breath. "Calm down. I won't. But she's goin' to find out."

"How?"

She shrugged. "I don't know. Somehow. Don't you watch movies? These things never work out well. And you just used *Vanessa* as your cover? Erik, Erik, Erik. This is no good."

"Maybe I'll just introduce her to Fancy and hope for the best."

"*Her*? The local girl?" Hillary gave him a look. "The best

bein' a merciful death?"

"Then I'll keep it a secret."

"Good luck with that. Especially since she talks to Tillie Osborn every other day. How long you think she'll keep your happy news to herself?"

"She promised."

"Oh! And Fancy Rexford has never, ever broken a promise," said Hillary, sarcasm so thick, he could almost smell it.

"I'm not breakin' it off with Laire. I like her. This is *my* summer, and I want to spend it with her."

"Laire? What kind of name is that?"

"Scottish."

Hillary blew out a long breath, looking at him with worry in her eyes. "I'll do what I can to run interference."

He chucked her under the chin with a relieved grin. "Thanks, sis."

"But, Erik, you know you can't get serious with her, right?" His sister gulped softly. "One more year at Duke. Three at Chapel Hill. Another settin' up your law practice. State senate. Congress. Governor. Daddy's just warmin' the seat for you on his way up." She paused for a moment, her voice soft and sorry when she continued. "A fisherman's daughter can't be a part of that plan. You can't—"

"Fuck! I don't . . ." He huffed, banging his fist on the steering wheel. "Fuck!"

They sat in silence for a while until Hillary turned to him. "Sorry, Erik."

He sighed, turning to face her. "Remember last week? When you asked me if I ever wished that things were different?"

She nodded.

"I do. Sometimes I wish things were different."

"Like what? What things?"

"Like, I'm not interested in politics!" he blurted out. And man, it felt good to finally say it.

"You say that like it's an option," she muttered.

"And I don't want to date Van, let alone marry her!"

"Somethin' that should be made clear to *her* at some point," Hillary said.

"I just . . . God! I like this girl."

"Laire, the local fisherman's daughter who delivers seafood?"

"She's also a waitress."

"Christ."

He sneered at her. "Why is that bad? Why are we such fuckin' snobs?"

"*We're* not. I don't care if your new girlfriend is a waitress or a seafood delivery girl. I'm sure she's a nice person, but Fancy—"

"She's a lot more than a nice person, Hills. She's interestin'and fun, and she's different, really different, than anyone we know. And she's smokin' hot and—"

"I get it," said Hillary. "You genuinely like her."

"A lot."

Hillary reached for his arm. "Then keep her a secret. Ironclad. Don't take any chances. Because if Fancy finds out? It's over."

He took a deep breath and nodded at his sister. "Will do. Thanks, Hills."

She gave him a small smile, reaching for the door handle.

"Hey," he said, reaching for her arm before she could leave. "Fuck Pete. Forget about him. Find someone else. If he doesn't see how awesome you are, Hills, he doesn't deserve you."

She gave him a sad smile. "I wish I could. I wish I could forget about him and move on."

"But you can't."

She sighed. "Not a chance."

"Then you're going to have to do somethin' at some point. You know that, right? Pete's about as thick as they come. I mean, awesome and fun and loyal, but he's not goin' to see you if you don't speak up."

"Van casts a long shadow," said Hillary. "I know."

Erik grinned at her. "Thanks for the talk."

She left the car and closed the door, keeping her hands on the frame before looking down at him, a curious expression in her eyes.

"Exactly how long have you known that you didn't want to go into politics? And *when* exactly are you plannin' to share that delicious nugget of news with Fancy and Daddy? I want to be sure I don't miss the fireworks."

"Forever," said Erik on a long sigh. "I have no fuckin' interest in it."

"What about the law?" she asked.

"I don't mind it," said Erik. "But all things equal, I'd just as soon go into entertainment law and work with a professional sports team."

"A sports team. Oh, Lord!" said Hillary, giving him one last look as she left the garage, muttering under her breath. "This is shapin' up to be *quite* a summer."

## Chapter 8

"Hey!" called Erik, waving at her from the top of the gangplank, a beaming smile making her heart—and most of her worries—take flight.

Laire had checked out all the boats in the marina when she got there, relieved to see none that she recognized, but she was still wary of being seen, so she'd chosen to wear a floppy beach hat and sunglasses for their date. Both had been her mother's, once upon a time, which gave her a little extra courage as she walked toward her beau . . . in the middle of the day . . . in public.

Her daddy's Stingray didn't have a forward cabin where she could change, so she'd gotten ready in the ladies' room at the Pamlico House, brushing out her hair and swiping on a little makeup. By cutting off some old jeans, she'd made herself a pair of cute and trendy denim shorts. She paired them with a hot-pink polo-style shirt, made from leftover material she'd used to make a maternity dress for Issy.

Flip-flops purchased at the Pamlico House gift shop with a hot pink and Kelly green grosgrain ribbon and a matching D-loop belt, rounded out her outfit. All those ladies she noticed the first night she and Erik had dined there passed through her mind as she approached him: she was preppy enough to fit in with any of them now. She just hoped Erik liked the way she looked too, which, judging from the grin on his face, was already a done deal.

"Hey," she said, pulling off her sunglasses as she got to the top.

"Damn, woman. You look good enough to eat," he said, reaching for her and pulling her into his arms. He brushed her lips with a kiss. "I can't decide if I want to show you off or take you to a secluded spot and hide you for the rest of the day!"

"I can't believe we *have* the whole day," she said, breathless from excitement and being so close to Erik again.

"I brought my chariot," he said, glancing toward the parking lot. "Want to see my kingdom?"

"*Your* kingdom?" she said. "The Banks is more mine than yours!"

He chuckled. "Fair enough, but we're not allowed in your part."

*True.* "So where did you have in mind?"

"Ever been to the Elizabethan Gardens up in Manteo?"

"Never even heard of it!" she said, grinning at him with genuine delight. As long as he planned to go north instead of south, she could relax. King Triton didn't deliver north of Avon and Manteo was a fair ways north of there. She'd know absolutely no one there, and more importantly, no one would know her.

"Well," he said, glancing at his watch, "it'll take an hour and a half to drive up. Want to stop in Rodanthe for lunch first?"

She nodded eagerly. She'd never been to Rodanthe either.

"I know a decent spot called the Good Winds Café, and I checked the menu online; they have mahi-mahi, crabs, and oysters today."

"Online, like, you checked the menu on the internet?" she asked, touched by his thoughtfulness.

He nodded. "Please tell me you know what the internet is."

She chuckled, slapping him on the arm. "I'm not *that* backward! There's a computer at King Triton, and I know how to use it."

"Then promise not to Google me."

She screwed up her nose at him. To be honest, she didn't know what Googling was, so she changed the subject. "The mahi will be fresh, but the oysters will be farm raised, not fresh catch."

"Then mahi it is!"

A wave of unbridled, unadulterated happiness swept through her being, and she leaned up on tiptoe, her eyes closing when her lips came into contact with his. She arched her back, pressing her chest to his and winding her arms around his neck. She'd learned how to kiss him, how to elicit that soft groan of pleasure that made him hold her tighter, his muscles—all of them—hardening into stone against her. Her breath hitched as her tongue found his and a million butterflies took flight in her belly. But he suddenly drew away, and she looked up at him, opening her eyes in confusion.

"I'm goin' to embarrass myself," he said, licking his lips, looking like he would kiss her all day if they weren't in public on full view.

She could feel the way he prodded into her and looked down to find his shorts dramatically tented outward.

"Oh," she said, giggling up at him. "Sorry."

He shook his head, his lips pursed and sour. "*Now* she says she's sorry . . . when I'm so turned-on, I could practically change the tides by pivotin' back and forth."

Her shoulders shook as she laughed silently. "I'll turn around and give you a minute to . . ."

"To what? Look at your gorgeous ass? Won't help." He looked down at his erection and sighed. "Let's just make a run for it."

Taking her hand, he ran for the parking lot, pulling her behind him until they reached a shiny black car. He opened her door, and she sat down on the supple tan leather seats with a sigh, fastening her seat belt as he rounded the car and sat down beside her.

She'd never been in a convertible, let alone a car this clean and fancy, and she turned to face him. "This is *your* car?"

He nodded. "My twenty-first birthday gift."

Laire's eighteenth birthday was last month, and she'd been given a parcel of new fabric, spools of thread, and replacement bobbins from her father and all the latest fashion magazines from Kyrstin. With a homemade cake from Issy to round out the festivities, she'd felt like the luckiest girl alive.

She could barely fathom a world where someone was given a luxury car as a birthday gift. And yet, here she was— experiencing that world for herself.

"It's very beautiful."

"*You're* very beautiful." He pressed a button, then leaned across the bolster to kiss her as the car started without a key.

She was too distracted to kiss him back and stared, slack jawed, at the car's console.

"How did your car just start?"

He leaned away, pointing to a plastic thing in the cupholder between them. "As long as this is in the car, I can just press a button to start the ignition."

"Well!" She looked up at him, shaking her head with wonder. "That's amazing!"

He chuckled softly, shifting the car into reverse. "*You're* amazin'."

"*You're* a broken record," she said. "I'm *not* that beautiful or that amazing."

The car jerked to a halt and he stared at her, all kidding wiped free from his face, his lips turned down. "Yes, you are."

"Erik," she said gently, "don't put me up on a pedestal just because I'm different from you. I'm just a girl from a small island. I know who I am, and I'm not special. I know my place in the world."

"Your *place*, right now," he said, his face still dark, "is sittin' next to me. And I say you're the most beautiful girl I've ever seen—"

"Erik—"

"—*and* amazin'. *And* special."

She tilted her head to the side. "The higher you put me, the steeper I'll fall."

"Just for today," he said, his voice deep and thick with longing, "you're mine. And to me, Laire, you're perfect."

Laire took a deep breath, shaking her head with disapproval as her lips tilted up of their own volition. "Fine. I won't argue with you if you're going to be stubborn."

"Excellent. Glad we got that settled," he said, pushing his sunglasses onto his nose and backing up the car again. "Now tell me all about you. Every detail, and don't leave anythin' out, you hear?"

"Yes," she said. "But first, how was dinner with Pete and Van last night? We got sidetracked when you picked me up, and I didn't get to ask."

He cleared his throat, pulling out of the Hatteras Landing parking lot and onto Route 12 north. "Good. Van sure does give ole Pete a hard time."

"How so?" she asked.

"Pete has a thing for Van, but it's not goin' anywhere."

Laire thought this over for a second, trying to figure out Erik's meaning, then suddenly a light bulb went off in her head. "Oh, gosh! I didn't know that Pete was a homosexual!"

Erik almost swerved off the road as he looked over at her. "What?"

"My cousin's girlfriend's brother was a homosexual too,

but honestly we don't have many on Corey."

"Wha—Why do you think Pete's gay?"

"Because he has a thing for Van."

"Riiiiight . . . and . . .?"

She certainly hadn't expected to have to explain this to Erik, who was so much more worldly than she. "When one man has a thing for another man, that's called homosexuality."

"But Van's not—"

"Into Pete?" She shrugged. "Poor guy. I guess Pete can't help who he likes."

"Hold up. You think that Van's a . . . Oh, God. I think I get it now." Erik tugged his bottom lip between his teeth. "Can I ask you somethin'?"

"Sure."

"Would it bother you if I hung out a lot with another girl?"

Laire swallowed, a surge of jealousy making her feel downright jittery for a second. "Yes."

"Even if she was just a friend?"

She looked at him—at his profile, which was so handsome, it made her stomach flutter like crazy. How could any woman have Erik Rexford for a friend? She would eventually fall in love with him, wouldn't she? Of course. He was everything a woman could ever want—handsome, thoughtful, sweet, wonderful. Yes, it would bother her. Very much. Because she knew something Erik didn't: he'd never be able to have a woman friend who didn't want him the way she did. As far as Laire was concerned, it was impossible.

"Yes," she admitted.

He nodded slowly. "Okay."

"Okay . . . what?"

"Okay, Pete is gay and he's really into Van," he said quickly.

"Yeah, I know. I figured that out." Something felt off, but

she couldn't put her finger on it. "So why'd you ask me about other girls?"

"Because I wasn't sure if my little mermaid had a jealous streak or not."

A jealous streak. Hmm. Suddenly she wondered if Erik had one too, and she squirmed in her seat, thinking about Brodie and the goddamned rumors he'd started. "Would it bother *you*? To hear I was spending time with another man?"

Erik's neck whipped around to face her so fast, she wondered his head didn't snap off. "Are you?"

"No!"

His eyes were wide and dark as he turned them back to the road, adjusting and readjusting his fingers on the steering wheel. "Yes. It would bother me, Laire. It would fuckin' gut me, darlin'."

Growing up around fishermen, Laire wasn't a stranger to such profanity. She'd even used the f-word a time or two to shock her sisters, but she'd never heard Erik use it before. She reached over and touched his arm. "I'm not. I'm not seeing anyone else. I promise."

He took a deep breath and sighed, cracking his neck as he stretched it, touching each ear to his shoulder before relaxing again. His voice was tender when he said, "I meant what I said last night, Freckles. I only want to be with you."

"And I only want to be with you," she reassured him gently.

He sighed, looking over at her with a happy grin. "*Now* tell me everythin' about you."

"Why? You looking to be bored to tears for a while?"

"Trust me, darlin'. I won't be bored."

"You asked for it," she said, taking off her mother's hat and letting the wind rush through her hair as she started talking.

***

Erik listened carefully as they drove up to Rodanthe, as they ate fresh mahi-mahi over grilled vegetables, and got back in the car headed for Manteo.

Her voice was musical as she spun tales about her corner of the world, telling him rumors about pirates' gold buried somewhere on Corey and describing the cast of characters that called her island home. Populated almost exclusively by fishermen and their families, most of the islanders had lived on Corey for generations. Laire's family had been there for *ten* generations, since sailing over from Scotland in 1685.

Erik, who appreciated history in general, could barely fathom that sort of certainty about his own heritage, which was a blurry mix of upper-class Southern stock, originating in England on his father's side and Germany on his mother's. Hard-pressed, he remembered something about a cotton plantation from the 1800s on his father's side and lauded university folk from Greensboro on his mother's, but these weren't really facts, just impressions. Laire's family history was easily traceable, vibrant and living, with a thread still intact that started in Edinburgh and existed, in her, this very day.

She explained to him that, unlike Ocracoke, another remote island in the southern Outer Banks, Corey didn't have any ferry service, which made it very difficult to reach. And because it didn't have ferry service, Corey didn't have the sort of tourist amenities—a public marina, restaurants, shops, inns—that the other islands, including Ocracoke, offered. The influx of tourist dollars into the Banks had fueled the surrounding economies, which had, to some extent, given up on commercial fishing as a livelihood and lifestyle. But not Corey. Corey was still fueled by the same traditional work, and work ethic, that had existed for over three hundred years. Virtually untouched by time, like some remote communities he'd heard of in the mountains of Appalachia, the Corey Islanders had grudgingly invited some modernity onto their island—telephone, television, and even the internet (dial-up, for Chrissake!)—but by and large, they still managed to maintain an extremely traditional culture, not completely unlike whatever culture would have been found there twenty or forty or even sixty years before.

Laire spoke respectfully of her father, of whom she was clearly in awe, explaining that he and his brother (Uncle *Fox*, unless he'd misunderstood her) had started their own business on Corey, selling fresh catch to the surrounding towns, including Ocracoke, Hatteras, Buxton, and Avon. This was, he gathered, the mark of some local social standing—that they'd managed to figure out a way to sell their fish off-island—and he grinned at the pride he heard in her voice and saw on her face as she explained that they had their own dock and shop and even a website where nearby restaurants could place daily orders.

She spoke affectionately, though not without a little bit of eye rolling, about her two older sisters: overprotective Isolde, whom she called Issy, and Kyrstin, who was getting married next weekend to an island boy named Remy.

But her voice was markedly different—warm, wistful, and a little heartbroken, if he wasn't mistaken—when she spoke of her mother, who'd passed away when Laire was very young. He sensed an active ache of loss, and it made his heart thrum with sympathy and tenderness. But her mother had done something quite shocking, apparently, by Corey standards: she'd attended college. Time and again, Laire inserted this fact into conversation about her mother, her eyes shining with pride. And he sensed, though she didn't articulate it, that Laire wanted to be like her, and he wondered how that longing would eventually manifest itself.

And somewhere along the way, between Rodanthe and Manteo, between fresh mahi-mahi and the Elizabethan Gardens, Erik Rexford, the prince of North Carolina, started to wonder if Laire Cornish, the commercial fishing princess of Corey Island, could love him someday—because everything about being with her felt awesome, felt predestined, felt so fucking *right*. With her sitting beside him, zooming up the Carolina coast on the most beautiful early-summer afternoon he could ever remember, he made a wish that he'd never, ever live another day of his life without her. He made a wish that she would, somehow, someway, be his forever.

He took that wish and he buried it deep inside and freed it from his mind, to nestle safely and grow on its own, left only with a lingering hope that someday the children of wildly different neighboring kingdoms might create a whole new world of their own.

"Lord, I've been going on all afternoon," she said, plucking her pop bottle from the cupholder, unscrewing the cap, and taking a sip. "It's almost four. You should've told me to shut up an hour ago."

"No way! I think your life is interestin'."

She chuckled. "Like watchin' paint dry."

"A lot better'n that. I promise."

"You know what?"

"Nope. Tell me," he said, glancing over at her pink cheeks and tan freckles, falling wildly for her with every second they spent together.

"It's your turn to answer some questions for me."

"Is that right?"

"Yes, sir, it is."

"Or else?"

"Hmm." She tapped her index finger on her lips in thought. "I've got it!"

"Tell me," she said.

"I get a kiss for every question I answer."

Her eyes widened and she giggled happily, nodding her head. "Can I get thirty questions in before we get there?"

"I'll drive slower," he said, passing a sign saying that they were eight miles from the Washington Baum Bridge, which would take them across the Roanoke Sound to Manteo.

"Fire away, woman! Time's a-wastin'."

"Okay, okay! Let's see. Um. Oh! One, what's it like bein' the governor's son?"

"Mostly I hate it," he blurted out. "I mean, there are times I enjoy the perks—end zone tickets for a Panthers game or ice time with the Hurricanes—"

"You ice-skate?"

"That's question two, and yes, I do. I'm a Duke Blue Devil, darlin'!"

"Devil sounds right enough," she shot back with a grin. "I didn't know people ice-skate in North Carolina."

"We have an NHL team, Laire." She stared at him blankly. "The National Hockey League?"

"Oh!" she said, grinning at him. "I don't know much about hockey. Mostly they just watch NASCAR on Corey. At the Fish Pot."

"The Fish Pot?"

"The local bar." She giggled softly. "They call it the Piss Pot when they're drunk."

Erik chuckled, then asked, "Ever been to the NASCAR Hall of Fame in Charlotte?"

She shook her head, feeling her cheeks flush. "I've never been that far inland."

They stopped at a red light, and he turned to stare at her for a second. "You are a rare thing."

"Is that bad?"

"That's question number three, and the answer is no. It's amazin'. It keeps me wonderin' about you . . . every minute, all the time. I never know what you're goin' to say next to blow my mind."

Warmed from his compliment, she grinned, thinking of another question. "Why do you hate being the governor's son?"

He seemed to mull this over for a second before the light changed and he laid on the gas. "I don't have much privacy. Everythin' I do at Duke is reported on: which girl I'm dating, if I screw up a game play, if I—"

"*Are* you datin' someone?"

"That's five. And yes, ma'am, I sure am."

Laire's breath caught. "You are? Who is . . . I mean—"

"You," he said, darting a glance to her. "I'm datin' *you*, Laire."

Feeling like a complete idiot, she took a deep, somewhat ragged, breath and nodded. "Oh, I . . ."

"There's that jealous streak again."

"Don't play with me, Erik," she said softly. "I don't know enough about boys to know when you're kidding."

"I didn't mean to mislead you, and I'm *not* kiddin'," he said. "You're the only girl I'm with right now."

Which only made her wonder . . .

"How many have come before?"

He cringed, then huffed softly. "I don't want to answer that question, Freckles. Next."

"Is it a long list?"

"That's question six. And no, in my world, it's not. But in yours . . ."

"How many?" she asked softly. "How many who meant something?"

He was silent for a while, staring out the windshield as they crossed the bridge to Roanoke Island. Finally he sighed. "I've had about six girlfriends."

"And how many have you slept with?"

"Laire, come on."

"I need to know," she said softly.

She didn't know she was going to say those four words before they came tumbling out of her mouth, but she knew the truth of them right away. Since meeting Erik and learning about his less conservative views on intimacy and sex, Laire couldn't stop wondering how many women he'd bedded, and her imagination was starting to get the best of her. What if the number was ten or fifty or—*goddamn it!*—one hundred? How many was a few? How many was a lot? She had no idea. And for whatever reason she couldn't articulate, she needed an idea.

"Five," he said, his voice low.

She gasped softly.

Five.

*Five.*

Five women had lain naked with him, feeling the heat of his skin flush against theirs.

Five women had spread their legs and felt the fullness of Erik Rexford inside them and looked into his eyes when he reached his climax.

Five women had known—had experienced—the most intimate, private, sacred part of Erik.

*My* Erik.

Five.

There was never such a hateful number on the face of creation.

No, it wasn't one hundred or fifty or even ten, but Lord, how a spike of white-hot jealousy skewered her heart, making it race with fury and disappointment and ridiculous, unrealistic regret. *Why wasn't I one, two, three, four, and five? Why couldn't I have been there instead of someone else?*

"Laire?"

She'd been holding her breath, but now she exhaled and breathed in quickly, the air brackish and dirty as they continued west on Roanoke Island, traffic rushing at them and by them, tall grasses and marshland to her right, and beach houses in the distance.

"I wish you hadn't asked me," he muttered.

"Did you love them all?" she asked, watching the scenery slip by, unable to look at him.

"No."

"Did you love *any* of them?"

"I thought I did at the time. Now I don't know for sure."

"How many of them did you love?"

"Please—"

"How many?"

"Two."

She gulped. Lord, she wanted to hate those two girls, but hate didn't come quickly. She ached with the knowledge that he'd given his heart to them, but she was strangely comforted to know that he'd cared for them before sharing himself.

"Laire," he said, interrupting the miserable silence between them, "I'm sittin' here feeling like I should apologize for somethin', but frankly that's bullshit." He cleared his throat. "I don't come from a place where sleepin' with someone before marriage is wrong. And I know you do, and I respect that, darlin', but I'm not going to say I'm sorry for playin' by the rules of the world I live in." He paused again, as though waiting for her to say something, but she couldn't. She didn't trust her voice. "I will say this: I treated all five girls—*women*—with kindness and respect." Again he paused, adjusting his hands on the steering wheel. "Maybe you wish I'd say that I regretted sleepin' with them, but I won't say that, even for you. Every experience I've had, every person I've known, every step I've taken, eventually led me here, to this car, sittin' next to you. And I wouldn't trade that for anythin', Laire. So it is what it is. And if knowin' that I slept with five women means that you don't want to know me anymore, I'll be sorry. But it'll tell me that we're too different to meet in the middle. It'll tell me that this wouldn't have worked out anyhow."

"Shut up," she blurted out in a whisper.

"I'm just tryin' to—"

"That was beautiful," she said, blinking her eyes furiously but unable to keep tears from slipping down her cheeks.

She didn't love it that he'd slept with other women.

But his words.

Oh, God, his sweet, careful, candid, heartfelt words about his past determining his future made her want to embrace those women and thank them for helping to make him the man sitting beside her today. And then she knew: that's how she would live with it. That's how she would accept his experience—as a gift, not a curse—because this man sitting beside her was her first love, and he wouldn't be who he was today without all the days that had come before.

"*You're* beautiful," he murmured, reaching blindly over the bolster to hold her hand.

She took his hand and anchored it between hers, raising it to her lips to press a sweet kiss between the strong grooves of bone and vein.

"And you just about gave me a heart attack, darlin'."

She kissed his hand again, then settled it on her lap, cradling it between her palms like a treasure. "Me? How?"

"That's questions twelve and thirteen," he said, turning right at a green sign that read "Fort Raleigh National Historic Site" and below that, "The Elizabethan Gardens." "I was more than half afraid you were going to make me turn this car around and drive you back to Hatteras."

"You think I could give you up so easily, Erik?"

"That's fourteen. And darlin', I'm still learnin' who you are. But, my heart . . ." He paused. "It fuckin' hurt to think you might."

"I'm . . ." She gulped, swiping at her damp cheeks as she took a deep breath. "I'm already in too deep, Erik."

He turned into a parking space, pressed a button to shut off the engine, and turned to look at her. He reached for her face, cupping her cheek, his dark eyes searching hers.

"Laire," he whispered. "I'm falling in love with you."

Her heart lurched with the sweetness of it.

"Erik . . ."

"Madly."

She reached for his face, and their lips met hungrily, sealing their new bond, their new love, with a passionate, furious kiss.

## Chapter 9

The last time Erik had been to the Elizabethan Gardens in Manteo, it had been as an escort to Vanessa for her parents' thirtieth-anniversary party, three years ago. Eighteen at the time, they weren't old enough to drink, but Pete had managed to swipe a bottle of Champagne, and they'd hidden in a corner of the Woodland Garden, passing it around until it was empty.

Erik's mother had drunk too much that night, loudly sharing the costs to upgrade Utopia Manor with a small pack of groupies by the fountain in the Sunken Garden, which embarrassed his father. As retribution, about halfway through the festivities, his father disappeared for longer than seemly with one of those groupies, adjusting his pants when he finally reemerged from the little copse that held a Virginia Dare statue.

And Erik had seen it all.

Since his childhood, he'd seen too much.

Too much excess. Too much self-centeredness. Too much hypocrisy. Too much disloyalty.

But this time, as he passed through the gates of the sunlit gardens, Laire Cornish's fingers were threaded through his, the softness of her palm pressed flush against his. Unhappy memories were no match for the bloom of love within him, and he squeezed her hand, looking down at her smiling, upturned

face and feeling the full bounty of his fortune in meeting her—
someone real, someone genuine, someone modest.

"It's so beautiful here. I feel like I should whisper," she
said, her sea-green eyes wide and sparkling.

He leaned down and kissed the tip of her nose. "You don't
have to whisper."

"I wish I'd brought a sketchbook," she said with a sigh,
stepping forward onto the carefully manicured brick path.

"I didn't know you sketched," he said.

"Mm-hm." She nodded, stopping to admire a massive light
blue hydrangea. "This blue is . . . unbelievable."

With his free hand, Erik took his phone from his hip
pocket. "Want a photo?"

"I'd love one!"

"Well, stand next to it."

She did and he took a quick picture. "You want to hold the
camera? Then you can take all the pictures you want. Just press
the black circle on the bottom."

Shyly, she took the phone from him and dropped his hand,
squatting down beside the puffy blooms to take several more
pictures. "I have no idea if it'll capture the color right, but I can
try."

In the distance, Erik heard the low rumble of thunder and
grimaced. Flash summer storms rolling off the Atlantic weren't
unusual.

"Sounds like a squall," noted Laire, straightening up to grin at
him.

"You don't mind?"

"A little rain?" She giggled, shaking her head. "I'm not
sugar."

She offered him her hand, and he took it, joining her down
a wide path with flowers and shrubs on both sides.

"Lilies. Hibiscus. Ahhh. Roses," she hummed.

Dropping his hand again, she leaned closer and took several more pictures, and Erik watched her, his heart swelling with tenderness for her—for the care she took in observing everything around her, for the way she lived totally in the moment.

"What do you sketch?" he asked. "Flowers?"

"No," she answered, sidestepping up the path a bit to get a close-up of an especially vibrant pink rose. "Um, clothes. Blouses, mostly, but dresses too. Skirts, pants. Ladies' things." She turned and looked up at him. "Dark cloud up there. We're in for it."

Before he could ask her more about her interest in fashion, his attention was stolen by a young couple with two children hustling along the path toward them. The mother pushed a stroller single-mindedly toward the exit, and the father was a little ways behind, trying to grab the hand of an escaping toddler.

"Ava! Ava Grace, you need to hold my hand!"

The stroller whooshed by, shadowed by the toddler, in a rainbow dress, who screamed, "I wanna walk with Maaa-maaaa!"

As she reached Erik and Laire, she looked up at them and lost her balance, stumbling onto the brick path in a colorful heap. Laire rushed forward before he could totally register the spill, falling to her knees beside the child and gathering her into her arms. By the time the father caught up, the little girl was bellowing her misery into Laire's neck, but Laire sat nonplussed on the path, looking up at the men.

"Sorry I didn't catch her in time," said Laire with an apologetic wince.

"My fault, not yours. She darted away." He shrugged, looking tired. "She's going through a phase. Only wants her mama, but the baby's getting over a cold, and Cindy didn't want him in the rain."

Erik looked over his shoulder, but the mother and stroller were no longer in sight. They'd taken cover in the gatehouse that led to the parking lot. *Good thing too*, he thought, as the sun slipped behind a storm cloud.

"Ava Grace," said Laire in her soft brogue. "That's a *real* pretty name."

In response, Ava Grace raised her head and sniffled loudly, her sobs subsiding.

"You ready to go with your daddy now?"

"My knee is huuuurted!" she cried, her lips tilted downward in a perfect upside-down U.

"But I bet your daddy can take you to the bathroom and patch you right up, one-two-three."

"One-two-three?" repeated Ava Grace, unconvinced.

"Mamas are good for so many things," said Laire, gently detaching the clingy child and setting her on her feet. "But Daddy's are good for fixing things."

"Like what?"

"Oh," said Laire, kneeling back on her heels as she chatted with Ava Grace, "like toys, and bicycle chains, and bloody knees."

"My daddy never fixed my knee afore."

"Tsk," said Laire. "You ever given him a chance?"

The toddler shook her head, a impish smile suddenly making her lips tilt up. "You look like a princess."

"I do, huh?" asked Laire.

"Uh-huh," said Ava Grace, reaching out to touch Laire's strawberry blonde hair. "You're pretty like a princess."

"That's real nice, Ava Grace," said Laire, standing up and dusting off her shorts. "Now, how about you go with your daddy and get cleaned up, huh?"

Ava Grace looked up at Laire with something akin to hero worship, then turned around and took her father's hand just as the first raindrops began to fall.

"Thanks," said the dad, looking grateful. "You've got a way with kids."

"Oh, I don't know." Laire shrugged, but her cheeks colored, a sign of pleasure. "Just got a lot of little cousins."

"Can you say good-bye, Ava Grace?" he prompted.

"Bye, princess lady," she called, staring at Laire over her shoulder until they stepped inside the gatehouse.

Erik's experience with children was minimal, but like the child's father, he couldn't help but note that Laire had a special way with the little girl, and though he wasn't anxious to be a father just yet, he tucked the memory of Laire and Ava Grace away. Who knew? Someday he might want to take a look at it again.

He almost told her she was amazing, but remembered her warning not to place her on a pedestal and switched gears.

"You *do* look like a princess," he said, reaching for a lock of her hair and tucking it behind her ear.

Her cheeks, already pink, deepened to red. "You're making me blush."

"Yes, I am," he said, pulling her into his arms.

His lips found hers effortlessly, and he counted off in his head. *Kiss number two. I get twelve more today, and I'm not wasting any.* Tracing his tongue along the seam of her lips, she opened for him like the flowers she'd been photographing, and he sucked her tongue gently into his mouth, inviting it to play with his.

The rain fell harder on the back of his bent neck and slid down his forearms, which held her tightly against his body. He could taste the warm summer sweetness of the drops as they slipped between their lips and heard them interspersed between their light moans, landing in gentle pitter-patters on their hair.

When she leaned away and opened her eyes, there were droplets in her eyelashes. She was smiling, her lips rosy and slick. Suddenly he had an idea. "Come with me!"

Taking her hand, he ran down the path, past the statue of Queen Elizabeth I and the Sunken Garden, mentally crossing his fingers that the little gazebo was still there in the north corner of the gardens, hidden and private.

They were soaked by the time they raced up the steps of the small, six-sided structure, which had three little benches inside and was covered with a cone-shaped thatched roof. Laire's arms glistened with rainwater, and her once silky curls lay damp and flat around her shoulders. He ran his hands through his own wet hair, slicking it back, staring at her with a feverish intensity as he realized that they were alone. Very. Much. Alone.

*Finally. At last.*

Her eyes, now more black than green, stared back at him as her chest, covered with her wet, skintight top, heaved with exertion.

"Laire," he murmured, the sound of her name breathless with want.

"Yes," she whispered.

\*\*\*

They launched themselves at each other, their lips colliding. Erik's hand reached for her cheek, holding her face firmly as his fingers plunged deep into her hair. Kissing her madly, he walked her backward into a corner of the small structure, her shoulder blades hitting the walls behind her. She leaned her head back into the void as he wrapped his arms around her, the heat of his lips forging a furious path from her mouth to her throat, resting for a moment on her throbbing pulse, licking the droplets of water from her skin with his silken tongue. The hands around her back slipped beneath her shirt, quickly unsnapping the clasp of her bra as she buried her hands in his hair, demanding his lips again.

Their teeth collided as she arched against him, her hands
flush against his cheeks as she directed their kiss, aware of a
sudden, welcome warmth on her breasts, protecting her sensitive
skin from the cold wet of her bra and shirt. Her breath hitched as
she felt a quickening, a ripeness, a realization, and then—like
the blinding shock of white lightning against a dark sky—she
felt a streak of lust rip through her entire body as his fingers
gently rolled her nipples.

She whimpered with surprise and desire, the word *more*
circling endlessly as he kneaded the delicate, virgin skin of her
breasts and his tongue mated relentlessly with hers. Rubbing the
straining points, the pad of his thumb brushed over the aching
buds as she shamelessly pushed her breasts flush against the
warmth of his hands.

*This is wrong. This is too far.*

She heard the voice in her head but was helpless to stop
him because she wanted this so desperately. She *wanted* his
hands on her secret places. She *needed* the heat of his flesh
pressed intimately against hers, learning the peaks and valleys of
her body just as certainly as she wanted to know his. His touch,
gentle yet searing, sent shivers of longing down her spine and
warm waves of desire just south of her belly, where they pooled.
High tide, building higher and higher.

His kiss grew more urgent, and she trembled in his arms,
her eyes rolling back in her head as she tried to catch her breath.
With his palms cupping the fullness of her breasts and his
thumbs still massaging the tender tips, she shuddered in his
arms, her body tensing for one glorious moment. And then . . .
she felt something within her give way, break apart, collide, and
shatter, exploding into a million pieces that rocked her being
from the core outward. Vinelike tendrils of passion unfurled
through every limb of her body, stretching her from within as
she convulsed in his arms and her panties flooded with wet
warmth. His lips were gentle against hers—the eye of her body's

storm—nipping softly, brushing tenderly. His hands still covered her breasts, but his skin rested easy against hers, organically now, not erotically, like it was simply meant to be there, like his flesh was born to seek hers, and, once together, like they should never again be apart.

Her head rested against the wall of the gazebo as she panted through the final shudders of her first orgasm, feeling alive and limp and gloriously loved.

\*\*\*

At some point, instinct had taken over: an almost blinding lust that had urged him forward. His fingers had unclasped her bra without permission or forethought. His hands had spanned her waist, then skimmed over the silky skin of her belly, moving upward. By the time his palms reached her breasts, cradling the warm, soft skin with reverence, he'd journeyed way too far to consider retreat. He wanted to touch her. He desperately wanted to be the first to touch her.

Because what he said in the car—that he was falling in love with her—wasn't a line or a lie. It was truly how he felt: like the world would fucking end and the planet stop spinning if he couldn't be with her. She was an unlikely obsession, this girl he'd known for such a small amount of time. Were he asked under fire, he couldn't possibly account for the depth and certainty of his feelings for her. It was like being swept away on a current he couldn't fight. He could either move with it, or he could drown.

Without replacing the cold, damp cups of her bra, he slipped his hands from her breasts and immediately pressed his chest against hers to warm her through the dampness of their clothes. The rigid peaks of her nipples pushed against him, and he gathered her into his arms, maneuvering slightly to sit down on a bench behind him and cradle her on his lap. She rested her cheek on his shoulder, her drying hair tickling the skin of his throat as she took a ragged breath and exhaled softly. Now and then he felt the aftershocks of his ministrations, the way she shuddered or sighed, the way she nestled against him like she wanted to burrow into his soul for all eternity. She didn't know, but she was already there.

"Laire?" he asked softly, his voice competing with the rain falling on the thatch above.

"Mmm?" she murmured, pressing her lips to his throat.

"You okay, darlin'?"

"Mm-hm," she hummed, her voice low and sleepy.

He smiled to himself, holding her closer. "Sure?"

"Yeah," she sighed.

"First time?"

"You know it was."

"I love that it was."

She took another deep breath, kissing him again. "Is it always like that? When . . . when a man touches a woman? On her breasts?"

"Not every woman's as sensitive, I imagine."

"And when you touch a woman . . ." She wiggled on his lap, and he knew that her clit was likely as taut as her nipples, aching for his touch. ". . . on her below-parts? That happens again?"

His cock, which was semi-erect against her ass, twitched. "Even more, darlin'."

"My God," she murmured, sitting up. "I can barely imagine."

And if Erik thought she was stunning before, now . . . now she belonged to him. The sated look on her face, the softness in her dark eyes, the slack bee-stung pink of her lips. It was his. It was his because he'd put it there, and he felt such a wave of protectiveness, of devotion, of crazy forever-style love, he couldn't stare at her anymore without blinking back an unexpected burn in his eyes.

Placing his hand on the back of her head, he pushed her face into his neck and held it there while he made himself breathe in, clean and deep, and let the power of those feelings settle in him and around him. They were a part of him now. He owned them just as much as they owned him. And thankfully his tears receded before falling.

"Rain's stopping," said Laire, her voice sweet.

"Hmm," he murmured. "But I thought we'd just live here in this little house forever, Freckles."

"Cozy," she said, pressing her lips to his throat again, the gesture comforting and distracting at once. "Erik?"

"Yeah?"

"On Corey, what I just let you do would be bad."

He clenched his jaw against the notion that anything they'd just shared could be bad. "We're not on Corey."

She swallowed, then laid her cheek on his shoulder again, her warm breath kissing his neck. "I know."

"You feel bad, Laire? I mean, do you feel like it was wrong?"

She was quiet for a moment before lifting her head to look into his eyes. "It was too beautiful to be wrong."

"Our own rules," he reminded her. "Our rules say what we did was beautiful."

Her lips tilted up, and she nodded at him. "Our rules are the best."

"Yes, they are," he said, chuckling softly at her happy, satisfied face.

He looked over her shoulder at the path. Beams of sunlight were starting to make their way through the trees. Tourists would start looking around the gardens again. Anyone could wander by them, and while being caught making out wasn't a big deal in his eyes, he imagined she might not feel the same.

"Want me to hook you up?" he asked, patting the

unfastened halves of her bra through her shirt.

She sat up and reached under her shirt to quickly latch and adjust her bra. "Nope. All good."

He cupped her cheeks tenderly as he rested his forehead against hers. "Thank you."

"For what?" she asked, holding his forearms gently with her fingers.

"For trustin' me. For lettin' me be with you."

She nodded, grinning at him. "I'm glad it was you."

He brushed his lips against hers and sighed. "Want to go see more of the gardens, darlin'?"

She hopped up, sliding one hand down his forearm to his hand, which she clasped in hers. "Yes, Erik, I do."

\*\*\*

At the gift shop he bought her a sketchbook and a silver pendant etched with a heart. When he put the necklace around her neck, the silver charm lay between her breasts, heavy and warm, and she blushed, remembering their passionate time in the gazebo.

She'd have to hide the necklace before she went home tonight, but it was hers, and she'd cherish it, and it would always—*always*—remind her of the perfect day with her love.

As they drove away from the gardens and back across the bridge from Roanoke Island to the Banks, Laire had the first pangs of sadness. It was only seven, but their beautiful date was coming to an end. Sooner than later, they'd have to drive back down to Hatteras and say good-bye. And it wasn't that they couldn't have another date again, but just for today, she'd actually freed herself from Corey for a few hours. She wasn't frightened of being found out. She wasn't worried about being seen with Erik. She had embraced her time with him with a fullness and gratitude that felt so wonderful, she hated the idea of going back to sneaking around. She wished every day could be like today.

Erik held her hand across the bolster as they turned south

on Route 12.

"You know," he said, oblivious to her heavy ruminations, "you never did tell me about your sketches."

"I make my own clothes. And my sisters'. And for lots of other women on the island."

"I didn't know. But you always look great."

"Thanks. Remember how I mentioned that my mother went to college?"

"Uh-huh. You were proud of her."

She nodded. "I want to go too."

"To college? Away from Corey?"

She glanced at him and answered tartly, "Since there's no college there, yes."

"But . . . I can't imagine you leavin' your home."

*I can.* "I've looked into it. The two best fashion design schools on the East Coast are in New York and Rhode Island."

"N-New York? Laire! *New York City?*"

His voice was so shocked, she felt defensive. "I can go anywhere I want to."

"Says the girl who hasn't been farther inland than Jacksonville."

"Just because I haven't doesn't mean I can't," she said, releasing his hand and crossing her arms over her chest.

"Well, of course you *can*. I just . . . What does your father think?"

Her lips twitched. "He doesn't know."

Erik took a deep breath and sighed. "So you like designin' clothes?"

"I love it. I've been designing them since my mama passed."

"The shirt you have on?"

"Mine," she said.

"That hot blouse you were wearing the first night you met

me on Buxton? The maroon one that made my mind go blank?"

She grinned. "Mine again."

"Those little shorts that keep teasin' me today?"

"Mine."

He looked over at her and nodded. "You're talented."

"You think so?"

"Yes, I do." He paused. "So how does this plan work exactly? Laire going to college?"

She sighed. "Laire works for two summers at the Pamlico House and saves every dime. Little by little, she tells her father about her plans until he stops forbidding her to go. And then, when she's twenty, she applies. With any luck, she'll be accepted, and . . ."

"And she'll go to New York and become a big-time designer."

"In a nutshell."

"And I'll be able to say, 'I knew her when,'" he said wistfully.

Reaching for his hand, she pulled it to her lips and kissed it as the sun drew closer and closer to the sea.

*Hopefully,* she thought, *you'll still know me then.*

# Chapter 10

Laire leaned her elbows on the countertop at King Triton Seafood on Wednesday morning, staring out the front window and dreamily remembering every detail of last night with Erik.

He'd been back at the bar on Monday night during her shift, but after Sunday's date, she felt a new closeness to him, a new intimacy with him that made her heart thrum with love every time she looked over and saw him. She refilled her water pitcher at the bar so many times, the bartender began to joke with her about the patrons floating away. He didn't know she'd fill two or three glasses, dump the rest in the kitchen, then return to the bar to fill it again ten minutes later. Any excuse to lock eyes with Erik.

When he pulled her into his arms on Monday and Tuesday nights after work, they'd kissed hungrily, like their lips touching and tongues entwining was the only sustenance they craved and needed. Last night, holding her close on the dock in the dim moonlight, he'd told her again that he was falling in love with her and asked her for another date on Sunday.

Unfortunately, however, Laire had to say no.

She wasn't working on Friday, Saturday, or Sunday brunch, though she'd picked up some hours on Sunday night to make up a bit of the loss. This weekend, she was attending Kyrstin's rehearsal dinner, wedding, and wedding brunch. After Thursday night, she wouldn't see Erik again until Sunday night at the earliest, and her heart ached at the thought. It seemed like an eternity.

"Laire, all good?" asked Uncle Fox, who peeked into the storefront from the back of the shop, where they had butcher and prep counters and freezers.

"Aye-up," she answered, looking at him over her shoulder.

"Lookin' forward to Kyrstin's festivities this weekend, huh?"

"Yes, sir," she answered, swiveling on the stool to face him.

Her uncle was only two years older than her father, though he'd worked a lifetime on fishing boats and it showed in the weathered creases on his face. His two sons—her cousins Roland and Harlan—were out working his boat today.

"First Issy. Then Kyrstin, Ro's weddin' is comin' up in September." He scratched his salt-and-pepper beard. "Just leaves you and Harlan outta the five Cornish cousins."

She nodded. "Guess so."

Her uncle cocked his head to the side. "What about, uh, Brodie Walsh for you, Laire? Preacher's grandson. Nice boy, good family."

Laire's heart sped up, her cheeks flushing with heat. "I don't know Brodie that well."

"That so? Hmm. I think I mighta heard different on that count."

Shit, fuck, and damn it. Her uncle knew. He knew what that snake Brodie Walsh had been saying. She could see it on his face.

"You heard *wrong*, Uncle Fox, and I will call out *anyone* who says I have an understanding with Brodie Walsh!"

He raised his eyebrows, an irritating grin hanging on the

edges of his mouth. "Well, well. Lover's spat, I guess."

*Lovers? Gyah!* "Whatever Brodie says about me is a filthy lie!"

"Okay, okay, li'l Laire. Don't get yourself in a snit, now. Ole Brodie's prolly just tryin' to win you over with a little—"

The bell over the door jingled, and her uncle stopped midsentence, his posture changing from relaxed to professional. His arms, which had been crossed over his chest, fell to his sides, and he cleared his throat, using his proper business voice when he asked, "Can we help you, sir?"

Swiveling back around on her stool, Laire gasped, her eyes widening, no doubt, to saucers, even as her heart leaped with sudden and unexpected delight . . .

*Erik Rexford.*

. . . and disbelief . . .

*In my uncle's goddamn fish shop.*

. . . and terror . . .

*What. The ever-loving. Hell?*

"Laire, honey," said her uncle cajolingly. "Can you help out this fine gentleman?" Her uncle stepped up to the counter beside her and nudged her with his elbow. "My niece ain't used to tourists."

Erik's lips turned up just slightly as he looked from her uncle to her. "I'm not a tourist. I'm Erik Rexford. I live over in Buxton."

"Huh," grunted her uncle. "Rexford. Like the governor?"

"His son," said Erik, keeping his eyes trained on her uncle. "Heard y'all have the best seafood in the Banks."

"You hear that, li'l Laire? The best."

"Yes, sir," she murmured, barely daring to breathe as she searched Erik's eyes, which were still fixed on Uncle Fox.

"You need some fresh catch, son?"

"I thought I'd pick some up. I was huggin' the shore on my

way back to Buxton from Ocracoke and saw your sign on the dock."

She had no idea why he was here, and she was terrified of being found out, but seeing his handsome face and windblown hair still made her sigh with pleasure. Swallowing, she took an order form from under the cash register and tried to smile at him like she wasn't about to have a heart attack.

"Can I take your order, um, sir?"

"What do you recommend?" he asked, his voice deep and warm, and God, but her whole body was reacting to seeing him so unexpectedly—her nipples tightening, her mouth watering. She wanted to reach out and touch him, to grab him by his navy blue Ralph Lauren collared shirt and drag his lips across the counter to hers.

"Well," said her uncle, assuming he was speaking to him, "got some blues came in yesterday . . . sea trout—"

"Sea trout's a spring catch," said Erik, flicking a teasing glance to Laire. "How about mackerel? That should be more in season now, right? Young, but fresh?"

"I'll be damned." Uncle Fox nodded, obviously impressed. "A dingbatter what knows his fish."

"Come again?"

Laire couldn't contain a small grin and stared down at the counter, hoping to God her uncle wouldn't catch her smiling at his expense.

"Just a li'l island speak," said her uncle. "Sure. I've got some mackerel."

"Actually," said Erik, his eyes flitting to Laire's for a moment. "I need somethin' that'll travel well."

"How d'ya mean?" asked her uncle.

Erik looked at her again, his smile disappearing, before raising his glance over her shoulder to her uncle. "I'm headed up to Raleigh for a few days. Leavin' today. Family business. I'd like to bring somethin' for my mother. Somethin' that'll keep on the car ride."

Her lips parted as her uncle started talking about blues keeping nice on ice. Now she understood. He was here to tell her that he wouldn't be around tonight or tomorrow night. He had no other way to tell her that he wouldn't be sitting at his regular seat at the bar, to explain his absence, and so he'd risked coming here to tell her in the only way he could.

She raised her head, and her eyes slammed into his for confirmation. He nodded slowly at her while speaking to her uncle. "Yes, sir. I'd appreciate it if you could pack some up for me on ice."

"Laire," said her uncle, "I'll go get 'em and pack 'em in back. You charge him for three dozen, hear?"

"Yes, sir," she said, still staring at Erik.

As soon as her uncle was out of earshot, she whispered, "You came to tell me? That you were leavin' for a few days?"

He nodded. "I hoped you were workin' this mornin'. I couldn't think of another way to get word to you. I'll be in Raleigh until Sunday. I didn't want you to think I was standin' you up or that my feelin's had changed or . . ."

She smiled at him, then looked down at the counter, blinking back tears as she wrote up his order.

"Erik," she whispered.

"Hmm?"

She chanced a glance at him. "I'm falling in love with you too."

They held each other's eyes for an intense moment. Though Erik had said these words to her twice, it was the first time Laire returned them, and she could see the sudden surge of tenderness in his eyes as he gazed back at her. He leaned toward her, and it took every ounce of her strength not to leap across the goddamned counter that separated them.

Before one of them did something stupid, she drew back

and cleared her throat. "That'll be eighteen fifty, Mr. Rexford."

He reached into his back pocket, opened his wallet, and slid a credit card across the counter to her.

"Want that I tape up the cooler?" yelled her uncle from the back room.

"Sure! Thanks!" called Erik.

She took the card, still warm from his body, and ran it through the machine. When she returned it to him, his index finger brushed hers, and she shivered with longing.

"I'm workin' Sunday night."

"I'll see you then," he whispered.

"I'll miss you," she mouthed as she handed him a pen.

He nodded at her and signed the receipt, sliding both back across the counter.

"Here we go!" said her uncle, hefting a cooler onto the counter. "Now you got crabs!"

Laire couldn't help the way her mind returned seamlessly to their first meeting, nor the way her shoulders suddenly started shaking with glee.

"Enj-joy them," she managed to choke out, grateful to her uncle for inadvertently adding a bit of levity to the moment.

"I will," he said, taking the cooler and tucking it under his arm. "Thank you, sir."

"Our pleasure, Mr. Rexford."

"Thanks, miss," he said to Laire, his eyes telling her everything his lips couldn't.

"Our pleasure, Mr. Rexford," she said softly, hating the moment he turned around and walked out of the shop.

The little bell tinkled again as the door shut behind him, and she watched him walk the length of the dock, back to his pretty little boat. It was as though her heart stretched from her chest to his, aching with the exercise, longing to go with him, unsatisfied to stay within Laire when, more and more, it belonged to Erik.

"The goddamn governor's son!" her uncle cried, rapping his knuckles on the countertop. "Your daddy won't believe it!"

"He was nice," she said hopefully, turning to look at her uncle.

"Nice. Pshaw." He screwed up his face at her. "He's just another rich dingbatter. Nothin' more, nothin' less."

She lifted her chin. "Wouldn't be the worst thing in the world for him to tell a few folks about those blues if he likes 'em."

"I figure we do well enough with the *hoi polloi*," her uncle shot back, using an old island term for "regular folks."

Laire shrugged. "I guess we do."

"Well, Laire," he said, "I'll be off now. Got a few deliveries over on Ocracoke. Let me know if the president's daughter stops in for some mackerel, eh?" he asked, chuckling as he turned and headed for the back room.

She looked up in time to see Erik's boat zoom away.

Four nights without him.

She hated the very thought.

Reaching into her pocket, she massaged the warm metal of her Elizabethan Gardens pendant, braced her elbows back on the counter, and sighed.

\*\*\*

Erik had no interest in the soiree at the Governor's Mansion tonight, but this morning his mother had called from Raleigh and insisted that he and Hillary be there. First Family pictures including handsome Erik and pretty Hillary always got more media attention. Plus, Fancy liked the wholesome image of them all together.

He thought about refusing to go.

Being so far away from Laire wasn't something he wanted when he treasured every stolen moment with her. But altercations with Fancy never went well—his mother was adept at getting revenge later, and with his lies about Vanessa hovering between them, he didn't need more trouble. So he'd grudgingly said yes and agreed to drive himself and Hillary back to the city.

It was over four hours from Buxton to Raleigh, which meant he needed to leave by noon at the latest. As he hung up with his mother, he'd been frantic at the notion that after showing up at the Pamlico House every night to see Laire, he'd suddenly be a no-show without any explanation. Remembering that she sometimes worked in her father and uncle's fish shop gave him the idea of trying to catch her there, and thank God it had worked.

His decision to stay in Raleigh until Sunday was solely based on Laire's unavailability this weekend. Since she was going to be busy with her sister's wedding, he figured it was easier to stay away for a few extra days. It would be torture to know she was so close if he wasn't allowed to see her.

After speaking with her, he sped home from Corey to Buxton, making the drive in a cool forty minutes. But he was so preoccupied reliving their short conversation, including the sweetest declaration his ears had ever heard—*I'm falling in love with you too*—he didn't notice Vanessa standing on the dock until he was pulling up alongside.

"Hey, stranger!" she called. "Throw me the line and I'll cleat you!"

*Huh. What's Van doing here?*

"Yeah, um, okay." Remembering his manners, he waved in greeting. "Hey, Van! What's up, honey?"

"Your mama called and invited me up to Raleigh with y'all for the weekend," she said, flashing him a million-dollar smile. "Couldn't say no to the governor's wife."

Fuck.

He sighed, feeling annoyed.

He liked Van as a friend. Truly he did. But his lie had just gotten a whole lot stickier. His mother probably thought she was doing him a favor, but actually she was making his life far more difficult. He didn't want to spend the weekend with Vanessa and how the hell was he going to be convincing about dating her in front of his mother when the only person he wanted to be with was Laire?

"Oh," he said. "Great."

She put her hands on her hips. "Such enthusiasm! I didn't tell you that you needed a root canal, Erik!"

"Of course not," he said, forcing a grin. "Glad you're comin'."

"Without Pete taggin' along," she said quickly. "Just you and me."

"And me!" chirped Hillary, suddenly appearing on the dock behind Vanessa. "And I call shotgun."

Erik forced himself not to smile, but damn, he loved his little sister.

"That's not very gracious," noted Vanessa, a sour expression puckering her lips as she turned to glare at Hillary.

"She gets carsick," said Erik.

"Since when?" demanded Vanessa.

"Just started this summer," said Hillary. "Wouldn't want me to puke, now, would you?"

"Of course not," said Vanessa magnanimously, turning back to Erik. "Well, I guess we'll have plenty of time to catch up in the city."

"Can't wait," added Hillary.

"You're not twenty-one yet," said Vanessa, giving Hillary dagger eyes. "My mama invited y'all for dinner on Friday night, and I was hopin' Erik would take me out on Saturday night to a few of Raleigh's hot spots!"

Erik sighed, forcing himself not to roll his eyes. Seemed like Van had the whole weekend planned for them. He glanced up at Hillary, who shrugged her shoulders at Erik. *I tried.*

"Hot spots, huh? I guess we'll figure it all out once we get there," he said, dreading the four-hour drive, the party tonight, and the prospect of Vanessa trying to get alone time with him all weekend. But what could he do? He'd have to put her off as gently as possible when they were alone but make sure his arm was around her every time Fancy looked over. What a fucking mess.

He turned to his sister and his fake girlfriend, concealing a grimace with a plastic smile.

"Well, pretty girls, I guess we all better get ready to go."

\*\*\*

Back at work on Sunday evening, her eyes sliding to the restaurant door every five minutes, Laire couldn't help mentally reviewing her weekend as she bused tables, refilled water glasses, and impatiently waited, after what felt like an eternity, to see Erik's face again.

Whether intentional or an oversight, the fact that Laire was seated beside Brodie Walsh at her sister's wedding reception yesterday turned out to be a blessing in disguise, because she'd finally had a chance to confront him in a public way without making a big scene.

"Hey, sweet Lairey," he'd greeted her, his eyes skimming greedily down the dusty-rose pink of her bridesmaid gown.

"Hey, snake," she'd said amicably, appreciating the way all conversation at the table had suddenly ceased, six pairs of surprised eyes turning to Laire and Brodie.

"Now, baby—"

She stood behind her chair with her fingers biting into the back. "Don't ya dare call me baby like we have an understandin', ya yethy lout," she hissed, her accent all the stronger for her anger.

"Come on, now. Y'all were singin' a different tune on prom night," he said, looking around the table uneasily at her sister Isolde; brother-in-law Paul; cousins Roland and Harlan; Roland's fiancée, Maura; and Kyrstin's best friend, Rachel. Brodie was on *her* turf right now, and he knew it.

She raised her chin. "I'm surprised ya *remember* prom night, since ya got mommucked drunk."

"I waren't that—"

"Yeah, ya ware," said Laire. "So drunk, ya tried to kiss me all sloppy 'n' prolly don't remember me sluggin' ya. But that's how ya woke up wi' a black eye."

"Nah. That ware a fishin'—"

"Accident?" she finished for him. "No, it waren't. 'N' we both know it."

He stared down at the table, knowing that he'd been bested and it was time to shut up.

"Ya *never* kissed me 'n' ya *never, ever* touched m' body, Brodie Walsh. Now, ya go on 'n' admit that 'n' we can let this go as friends. If not . . ."

He raised his head, nailing her with his eyes.

The thing about living on a small island? Everyone had a little dirt on everyone else. Brodie didn't know what Laire had on him, but she could tell from his expression, he'd just as soon she keep it to herself.

"Fine. We din't do nothin'," he said, looking around the table at her kinfolk. He turned back to her and sneered at her as he bit out, "Happy now?"

"Overjoyed," she answered acidly. "'N' you *will* stop spreadin' lies 'bout me."

"Don't matter nohow," he said, looking across the church fellowship hall at Maddie Dunlop. He folded up his napkin, which he plopped on the table before him. "I got juicier fish t' fry." He stood up to his full six feet, two inches, and looked down his nose at Laire.

"Well, go fry 'em then, 'n' let me 'n' mine be." Not one to

back away, she looked up at him squarely in the eyes. "Give Maddie my regrets."

"Cold bitch," murmured Brodie as he pushed back his chair and sauntered away in Maddie's direction.

Laire took a deep breath, pulled out her chair, and sat down, looking up at her sister, who stared at her in disapproval.

"He was a good catch," said Isolde. "Shouldn't have done that, Laire."

"Nice enough kid," added Roland. "Just a little wild. Ya could've tamed him."

"Can't just refuse everyone. You two would've made real pretty babies," said Rachel, who wasn't the prettiest or youngest girl on Corey and would likely be stuck marrying one of the Masterson twins.

Rachel grinned at Harlan, who averted his glance quickly so as not to encourage her. Single like Laire and only a year older, he winked at her. "Good on ya, Laire. He's a jackass, all gassed up 'bout hisself. Not half good 'nough for m'cousin."

"Thanks, Harlan," she said, sitting down beside him and grateful for his camaraderie. Issy's husband, Paul, mercifully changed the subject to summer tourists on Ocracoke and Kyrstin and Remy's plan to open an inn on Corey, which kept them all busy for the rest of the reception.

"Water over here, miss?"

Laire was jolted back to the present and sighed, refilling a patron's water glass with a polite smile, though she was still fuming about Brodie inside.

Since Laire's uncle had already found out about Brodie's comments, she could only assume her father had too, and she just hoped that the small scene that played out at the wedding would get back to him. She didn't want him thinking she and Brodie had an understanding or, worse, that she'd let him touch her and then changed her mind. Nice girls didn't do things like that. It occurred to her to say something directly to her father, but she shivered with embarrassment. She couldn't imagine, even in her wildest nightmares, discussing something so awkward with her daddy. Maybe it would all just blow over now. She hoped so.

And just as that comforting thought passed through her head, Erik Rexford rounded the corner of the barroom and sat down in his regular seat, his eyes seeking and meeting hers with a twinkle and a smile. Her heart burst with happiness, and she held her hand up in greeting.

Yes, everything would be just fine now.

\*\*\*

Erik nursed his beer, stealing glances at Laire whenever she passed by the bar. He had been jumpy this morning, eager to get back to the Banks and see her, but even more anxious to get away from his mother and Vanessa, who had been anything but subtle over the long, annoying weekend.

From Vanessa surprising him with a unwanted peck on the lips for the photographers at his mother's gala on Wednesday evening, to an intimate dinner with both sets of parents on Friday, followed by Van's whiny insistence that he accompany her to her sorority sister's birthday party at a swanky downtown restaurant on Saturday, it felt like she and his mother had been plotting up a storm. Even though his mother had promised not to say anything about Erik and Vanessa dating, Van was acting like they were a bona fide couple, and her actions had Fancy's stamp of approval all over them.

And he was sending Vanessa wildly different signals: near his mother, he kept his arm around her waist or shoulders, but when Fancy wasn't in play, he was careful not to touch Van at all, because every time he did, he felt like he was betraying Laire's trust.

Not to mention, it wasn't fair to Vanessa. He knew it wasn't fair, but he just wasn't sure what to do about it. He didn't want Fancy digging into where he was spending all his time this summer. He needed her to *think* he was spending time with Van so she would leave him alone.

They were halfway through the summer now, with only five more weeks until he had to return to Duke, and he felt—keenly—the way time was winding down. Maybe he could try to avoid Vanessa as much as possible. Lord knew he wanted to spend every waking moment with Laire, not Van.

. . . which was why tonight was so important to him.

Hillary, who was attending dressage camp for a week, stayed behind in Raleigh. His mother was going to a ladies' tea on Monday afternoon, which meant that she wouldn't return to the Banks until Monday night at the earliest. And his father had state business that would keep him in town until next weekend.

It all added up to one glorious conclusion: for tonight, at least, Utopia Manor was all his, and if tonight's dinner crowd was typical of a sluggish Sunday with folks leaving the 'Banks to return to the mainland, he and Laire might actually have more than an hour together before she had to head back to Corey Island.

With fingers crossed, he took another sip of his beer.

Sure enough, by nine o'clock, he watched her wipe down the last of the dinner tables, his eyes flicking impatiently to one last couple who were canoodling over their candlelit dessert like they had hours to kill.

Laire had hardly spoken to him, or even given him more than a smile or a nod, while she was working, but when the bartender asked her to take his place for a moment while he used the bathroom, she stepped behind the mahogany bar and stood before Erik with a shy grin.

"Hi."

"Hey, darlin'," he said, pushing his empty beer glass to the side and smiling back at her. "I missed you. I hated bein' away from you."

"Me too," she said, biting her bottom lip for a second before releasing it. "It felt like a long time."

He gestured with his chin toward the canoodlers. "As soon as those two leave, you're finished, right?"

She nodded, watching as the man fed the woman a forkful of pie. "But they sure are takin' their time."

"Laire," he said.

She turned back to him, eyes expectant.

"My house is empty tonight. Everyone's still in Raleigh. Come over."

He watched the play of emotions on her face: excitement, wariness, worry, and finally, as she raised her eyes to his, determination.

She nodded. "Okay. Just for a little while. Then I have to head home."

Some insane part of him, accustomed to looser, more modern girls, had actually fantasized that they'd figure out a way for her to spend the whole night, but instead of being disappointed, he found himself profoundly grateful that she was willing to come over to his house at all.

He beamed at her, "Damn, you make me happy."

She giggled, plucking a rag from under the bar and running it along the shiny wood of the bar. "You make me happy too."

"Laire!" Erik looked up to see the bartender walking back. "Ms. Sebastian says you can go. She'll finish up tonight."

"Really? Great!" she said, bunching her shoulders together and grinning at Erik.

"Meet me at my car," he mumbled, leaving a twenty under his half-finished beer and heading quickly for the exit.

\*\*\*

Laire ran back to her locker to grab her purse and check her face, her heart racing with excitement. She'd never been inside Erik's house, so she was excited to see it up close, but more than anything, she was desperate to have him all to herself. It would be a short ride to his house, which meant they'd have over an hour together before he had to drive her back to the Pamlico House dock. Grinning at herself in the break room mirror, she gasped when she saw Ms. Sebastian's face join hers.

"You startled me!" she exclaimed, pressing a hand to her heart as she turned around to face her boss.

"Last week, when he didn't show, I was worried and relieved at the same time," Ms. Sebastian said. "And tonight, when he showed up, I was worried and relieved again."

"You don't need to worry, Ms. Sebastian," said Laire. "He's good to me."

The older woman nodded. "I can see he's very smitten, but, Laire, how does this work? Where does it go from here?"

"Anywhere we want it to," she said softly, though her voice lacked conviction.

"So your father will be okay with you datin' a dingbatter? And his father? The governor? He'll be delighted with his Duke University son datin' a fisherman's daughter?"

"He's not just a dingbatter, and I'm not just an islander," she protested, taking a step away from Ms. Sebastian, and crossing her arms. "There's more to us."

"Of course there is," said Ms. Sebastian, her face concerned, her eyes soft. "But he's got a handful of weeks before he heads back to school, Laire. And then what? Where does that leave you?"

To be honest, Laire hadn't thought that far into the future. It hadn't even occurred to her that Erik would be leaving one day soon, and not just for four or five days, but for much longer. She winced, her heart hurting as she processed what Ms. Sebastian was saying.

As though she realized the pain her words were causing, the older woman reached out and placed her hand gently on Laire's shoulder. "I'm just worried about you, honey. Tread softly. Be careful."

Laire swallowed, looking up at Ms. Sebastian and nodding.

"He's waitin' for you," she said, giving Laire a small smile before dropping her hand and heading back to the kitchen.

# Chapter 11

On the ride to his house, Laire didn't say much, staring out her side of the car. Her mood had changed between leaving the bar and joining him in the parking lot, though he had no idea why. When she got in the car, she smiled at him but didn't lean over the bolster to kiss him as he'd expected. She seemed less excited and more contemplative too.

*Hmm. Maybe it's just nerves about being alone together.*

Last Sunday, even though they'd managed to find a private moment during the rainstorm at the gardens, they'd actually been in public the entire time. Maybe she wasn't entirely comfortable going to his empty house with him.

"Laire," he said, looking up at the sign that welcomed them to Buxton as they zoomed past, "I'd never pressure you to do somethin' you didn't want to do. You know that, right?"

"Of course," she said, turning to look at him, her eyes wide and trusting.

*Hmm. Maybe she's worried about getting caught.*

"I promise my family isn't there. They're all in Raleigh."

"Yes. That's what you said."

*Huh. What's going on with her?*

"I missed you somethin' awful, darlin'."

"I missed you too."

"I'm not plannin' to leave again," he said quickly.

"What do you mean by that?"

"I mean I'm stayin' put, here on the Banks, until the end of the summer."

"Oh," she murmured, her shoulders slumping as she turned away from him.

*God damn it.* He wasn't good at this. Never had been. He didn't know how to read a woman's mind, for heaven's sake. If she was upset about something, she was going to have to go ahead and tell him.

He pulled into his driveway, cut the engine, and faced her. "Spit it out."

"Spit *what* out?"

"Why're you so upset?"

She took a breath and opened her mouth like she was about to say something, then closed it with a loud sigh.

Obviously there was *something* on her mind.

"Laire? You're killin' me. Please just tell me what's goin' on in your head."

She pivoted her whole body in the seat to face him, and she was so fucking beautiful in the moonlight, he trembled, forcing himself not to reach for her until she'd told him what was wrong and he'd had a chance to clear it up.

"You hated being away from me," she said, as though confirming it.

He nodded. "Yeah, I did, Freckles. A hundred percent. It sucked."

"For me too," she whispered. "But at the end of the summer, you're leaving, Erik. For a lot longer than five days."

"End of the summer's not for weeks yet."

"*Five* weeks. That's nothing! That's less than nothing! It'll slip by in the blink of an eye."

"But it's five weeks *together*! It's five weeks of kissin' and huggin' and talkin' and . . . Laire, it's not nothin'. It's everythin'!"

"But at the end, you leave," she said softly, and for the first time, he noticed the tears brimming in her eyes.

He reached for her cheek, cupping it gently. "I do. I have to go back to college."

She pulled away from his touch for the first time he could remember, and it hurt.

"And how far away is Duke from Hatteras?" she asked.

"Five hours. Maybe six," he said softly.

"And that's for a person who actually has a car!" she exclaimed. "Which I do *not*."

"I *do*," he said, but he heard the uncertainty in his own voice. The truth was, he hadn't really thought about what came next. He'd been living in the moment and enjoying the here and now way too much.

"Oh. And I'm *so sure* that once you're back at your fancy school, you're going to want to drop everything and come visit your summer fling on the Outer Banks." She took a ragged breath, looking away from him as she swiped at her tears.

"Summer fling!" he yelled.

*Fuck, no! She is so much more than that to me!*

He opened his car door and walked around to her side, swinging open her door and offering her his hand which she, thank God, took, allowing him to help her out of the car. Pushing the door closed with his foot, he pulled her into his arms, sighing with relief to finally feel her pressed against his body, where she fucking belonged.

"You are *not* a fling to me," he whispered passionately in her ear. "Not even close. I've never . . . I've *never* felt this way about anyone."

"Erik," she sobbed.

He held her as close as he could. "Laire, darlin', please don't cry."

She rested her cheek on his shoulder. "It hurts to fall in love with someone. It hurts awful."

"Fuck," he whispered. "I don't want to hurt you."

"But where does this go?"

"I don't know," he said. "But we still have five weeks to figure it out."

"Either way," she said, sniffling softly near his ear. "I stay here and you leave."

"Wait a second," he said, leaning away from her. "Our rules, remember?"

She nodded, looking up at him.

"So maybe I come back once a month. And maybe you work up the courage to tell your father we're datin' and you come spend a weekend with me at Duke."

"No, I can't!"

"You *can*, Laire," he said, putting an edge in his voice. "You're eighteen. You're an adult. He can't tell you what to do."

"I live under his roof."

"Still, you need to stop bein' afraid of him and be yourself. Hell, Laire! You want to go to college in New York City! You don't think he's goin' to object to that?"

She took a deep breath, and her breasts pushed into his chest, making his cock stir behind his shorts. He wanted to kiss her and hold her and make out with her in the quiet darkness of his parents' beach house. He didn't want to stand in his driveway wasting these precious minutes together quarreling over inevitabilities.

"How about this?" he said, putting his arm around her shoulders and walking them both toward the house. "I promise we'll figure out a way to make it work. I know this, darlin'. When we say good-bye in August, that's just 'good-bye,' not 'the end.' I don't want to date anyone else . . . at Duke or otherwise. And I don't want you to be with anyone else on

Corey. I want us to stay together."

She gasped softly. "You mean it, Erik?"

He did. One hundred and fifty percent. "Of course. I'm crazy about you, Laire."

Suddenly her arms were around his neck, and she was leaning into him, her face tilted back, her lips waiting for his. And he obliged her, sealing his mouth over hers and groaning with relief to finally be touching her intimately again. On the front steps of Utopia Manor, they kissed in the moonlight for ten minutes or more, her whimpers mixing with his moans, his hands under her shirt and hers under his. Hot and wanting, both of them panting for more. When he drew away from her, he was rock-hard and aching.

"Let's take this inside?" he breathed."I don't want to give the neighbors a show."

She looked up at him and grinned, then her eyes rose higher. His gaze followed hers, to the millions of stars in the inky night sky.

"We're just two tiny specks of dust in a big, wide world," she murmured. "But I feel so much, Erik. I feel so much, it's like the whole universe couldn't hold it even if it tried."

He looked back down at her, at the stars reflected in her eyes. "I know exactly how you feel, darlin'."

\*\*\*

After a tour of the three-story mansion, they turned and walked back down the grand staircase, to the living room on the ground floor, which had floor-to-ceiling windows and sliding glass doors that led to the pool deck. Laire stood at the windows, looking out at the pool and the lawn and, way beyond, the reflection of the moon on the Sound.

"I've never seen a house this beautiful," she said.

His hands landed on her shoulders, and he pushed her hair aside, his lips landing softly on her neck. She tilted her head to the side to give him better access, sighing when his tongue flicked out over the sensitive skin.

She was still unsettled about her conversation with Ms. Sebastian, and though Erik had done his best to reassure her that he wanted to figure out a way to continue their relationship after the summer, she couldn't deny the worry in her heart. She hoped they'd come up with a more concrete plan in the weeks before he left for Duke, but she didn't want her worries to spoil tonight, so she leaned back, into his body, closing her eyes as he kissed the skin of her throat.

"I've never seen a *woman* this beautiful," he said, putting his hands on her waist and turning her around so that she faced him.

His lips landed on hers at the same moment he started backing away from the windows, pulling her with him to the plush blue and white checkered couch behind them. As the cushions hit the back of Laire's knees, she lowered herself to a sitting position, letting Erik reach for her legs and pull them up onto the couch. She lay back, and before she knew it, she felt the heavenly weight of his body pressed against hers as he bracketed her head with his elbows and continued kissing her.

Lying on her back, she could feel every hard muscle, every swell and cove of his body over hers, pressing into hers. As their tongues slid and sucked, she tried arching her hips into his and was rewarded with a low groan of pleasure as he thrust his pelvis against hers, the rigid line of his erection pressing into the apex of her thighs.

"Can I see you?" he asked, kissing her neck as his fingers slid to the top button of her blouse.

"See me?" she panted.

"Remember in the gazebo?" he asked. "You let me touch you. I want to see you too."

"Oh." He was asking if he could see her breasts, and the idea was so erotic to her that she felt muscles deep, deep inside her body flex and release. "Yes."

His fingers carefully unbuttoned her shirt as he kissed a path from the base of her neck to the simple lace border of her white cotton bra. Leaning up just slightly, he parted her blouse. She felt the cool air kiss her skin and shivered.

"Are you cold?" he asked, nuzzling his nose against the erect tip of her cotton-covered nipple.

"N-no, I'm . . ." She gulped. "Maybe it's bad, but I want more."

One hand covered the swell of her breast, but with the other he cupped her face. "Nothin' we do is bad. Nothin'. I care so much for you, Laire. So much."

"Me too," she said, taking a deep breath and smiling at him. "Our rules. I want you to touch me there."

Dipping his head to kiss her lips, she felt his fingers unhook her front-clasp bra and gently spread the cotton cups. He lifted his head, looking into her eyes with such profound tenderness, Laire's own eyes burned with tears as she watched him lower his gaze to her breasts.

He winced, as she would were she in pain, then seized her eyes again. "I've never seen anything as perfect as you."

"Touch me, Erik," she murmured, closing her eyes and letting her head fall back onto a throw pillow.

One of his hands landed softly on her right breast, his palm a gentle friction on the distended nipple. The other hand cupped her left breast, his thumb brushing the sensitive tip for a moment before she felt the soft, wet heat of his lips suck the aching nub into his mouth.

She gasped from the sharp sweetness of the sensation, her eyes rolling back in her head as her hips lifted from the couch, seeking, demanding more from the source of her pleasure. His tongue swirled around one nipple as his thumb and forefinger gently rolled the other to a peak. Covering her damp skin with the warmth of his palm, he skimmed his lips across her chest and licked a circle around the tip of her other breast. When he sucked the erect bud into his mouth, she writhed beneath him, her pelvis pressing into his chest with urgency.

She rested her forearm across her eyes, listening to her quick and choppy breathing. "Erik," she sobbed, "I need . . . I need . . ."

*More.*

*So much more.*

"Tell me," he whispered, his breath hot then cold over her glistening skin.

But she didn't know what to ask for. She didn't know how to put it into words. She only knew that he was the only one who'd provided the relief she'd found in the gazebo. He knew how to take care of her.

"Please," she whispered.

He raised his head, and a thick lock of dark hair fell across his forehead. "I can make it better, darlin'. You want me to make it better?"

"Uh-huh," she murmured, biting down on her lower lip as she moved her hips in frustration.

His fingers trailed down the naked skin of her belly, skimming and tickling her soft skin until he reached the button of her black skirt. He popped it open, then reached for her zipper. As the teeth opened slowly, she had a moment of panic, and her eyes popped open. She lurched up, resting her hands over his.

"I can't—"

"Shhh," he said. "It's okay."

"No, I . . . Erik, I can't be . . ."

"What?" he asked, a small smile softening his face.

"Naked," she whispered, feeling her cheeks flush.

His smile widened, though she sensed he was trying to control it. He swallowed slowly, then cleared his throat, adjusting his hand under hers. He rested it, flat and still, on her skirt, over the place that throbbed for him. "Is this okay?"

She nodded. "Mm-hm."

Holding her eyes, he slowly shifted his hand, slipping it under the waistband of her panties and flattening it on the warm flesh of her lower belly. "Is this okay?"

She imagined that the tips of his fingers were touching the tight strawberry blonde curls that no human fingers had ever touched except hers and her doctor's. But this was Erik. And Erik loved her. She was certain of it.

"Mm-hm," she sighed, sliding her own hands away and letting them rest on the couch beside her hips. She closed her eyes as his fingers dipped lower, spreading the soft folds of skin that hid the aching little button of nerves beneath.

She gasped sharply as his finger came into contact with that part of her, whimpering with pleasure and just a little bit of fear that had nothing to do with trusting Erik and everything to do with the feelings, the changes, the symphony of sensations pulling her head and her heart and her very soul in too many new directions to follow.

"It's okay," he whispered close to her ear, sucking the lobe between his lips as his finger slid against that hidden place once again.

"Errriiiik," she murmured, pulling her bottom lip between her teeth.

His finger dipped lower for a moment, and when it returned to slide between her silky folds, it was wet and slick, the digit slipping back and forth across the aching nub with increasing speed and pressure.

He trailed gentle kisses along the column of her throat, resting his lips against her throbbing pulse as she started breaking apart. Her fingers twisted into the couch cushions as her head strained back against the pillow, her hips flexed up to meet his every touch and slide. Breathing faster and faster, she felt the convulsions start deep, deep within her body, radiating out until her entire body was shuddering with pleasure so intense, she felt tears roll from the corners of her eyes.

"I love you," Erik whispered. "I've never felt like this for anyone before."

"I . . . I love . . . y-you too," she panted.

His lips claimed hers hungrily as he slipped his fingers from her panties. Gathering her into his arms, he shifted them both to their sides, facing one another and holding her as her body shuddered and shook from the aftershocks of bliss. She rested in his arms, limp and sated as he wiped tears into her hair with the pad of his thumb. And she knew—in that moment she knew—how it felt to be utterly loved, and she trusted him, this man so different from her in every way, with a depth and width and breadth that she never could have imagined was possible.

When she could finally open her eyes, she looked directly into his.

"Erik . . . that was . . ."

"Beautiful," he murmured, pressing his lips lightly to hers.

"But what about you?" she asked, feeling the stony ridge of his erection pushing against her.

"Do you . . . do you want to touch it?" he asked, searching her eyes.

It felt wrong to say no, because she sensed he needed the same relief she'd just enjoyed, but she wasn't ready; it felt more wrong to say yes.

"Will you hate me if I tell you I'm not ready yet?"

"One," he said, kissing her forehead, "I could never hate you. And two," he said, kissing the tip of her nose, "we go at your pace. *Always* at your pace. No matter what." She arched her back and rubbed her breasts against his chest, feeling languorous and lucky, but he gently pushed her away. "That said? I need to excuse myself for a few minutes. I'll be right back, okay?"

It took her a moment to realize why he needed to leave, but then it occurred to her: if she couldn't give him relief, he'd have to give it to himself. Oh. She took a deep breath as he stood up. His footsteps retreated up the stairs, and she heard a door close. He was . . . he was . . .

She gasped as her heart sped up. She imagined his hands on that part of himself, and her recently spent muscles spasmed one last, unexpected time as she pictured his face in the throes of pleasure. She wanted to see it. God, how she wanted to see what he looked like when he experienced the same waves of bliss she'd just felt within her own body.

*Not yet*, whispered her heart as she sat up and gazed at the stairs he'd disappeared up. *Maybe someday, but not yet. Wait until you have a plan.*

She swung her legs over the side of the couch and reached for the clasps of her bra, which she fastened before pulling the halves of her blouse closed. As she buttoned it, she stood, tucking it back into her black miniskirt, which had bunched up around her waist. She straightened the skirt, running her palms over the black twill, then paused for a moment to listen, to see if she could hear Erik. But no. The house was completely silent.

Sighing, she reached for a lamp and turned it on, walking around the dimly lit room slowly, gently fingering a blue and white ceramic elephant sitting on the top of the shiny black grand piano. Just beyond the figurine was a collection of framed photos, many of Erik. Little peeks into his life before her.

She picked up a photo of him wearing a cap and gown, no doubt his high school graduation picture, and smiled back at the look of triumph on his handsome face. As her gaze widened, she was distracted by the two people flanking him: a burly, blond young man, and a stunning young woman with jet-black hair and blue eyes. Erik had his arms around their shoulders, and they all laughed at the camera.

*Old friends.* Her heart pinched as she stared at the beautiful girl whose head was resting on Erik's shoulder, even as she faced forward. *I wonder who she is.*

Relieved that the photo was taken several years ago, which meant the girl was part of his past, she set the frame back on the piano and picked up another: this one of Erik beside a girl who had blonde hair and blue eyes and was the spitting image of Governor Rexford. Surely this was his little sister, Hillary, and Laire smiled at the photo, hoping that one day, in the very far-off future, that she and Hillary Rexford might be friends.

She heard footsteps coming down the stairs and turned to see Erik, wearing a big smile, his shorts no longer tented uncomfortably.

"All good?" she asked, still grinning from the photos.

He crossed the room and drew her into his arms. "Much better now."

"I was looking at your pictures." She pointed to the photo of him and Hillary. "Your sister?"

He nodded. "That's Hills."

"You look nothing alike."

He steered her away from the pictures on the piano, toward the windows. Opening one of the doors for her, she preceded him out onto the pool deck. "Everyone says that. She looks like our dad. I favor my mom."

Laire's shoes were still inside, so she walked barefoot to the edge of the pool and sat down, dangling her legs in the aqua blue water. "I look like my mother too. She was a redhead."

"And your sisters?"

"Both gingers, like me. You'd recognize them as my family on sight."

Erik sat down beside her, putting his feet in the water. "You know, I was thinkin'. My family comes out here for Thanksgivin' every year. What would you think about spendin' it here with us?"

"Erik—" she started, coming up with a million reasons to refuse him.

"Will you just think about it?" he asked. "It could be, like, a goal for us—to tell our families about our relationship and introduce them to each other. After you came here, I could go back to Corey with you and meet your father and sisters."

Her promise to herself to tell her father about her job in Hatteras after Kyrstin's wedding had already been broken. She couldn't even risk telling her father about her job, for fear he'd make her quit, destroying the ease with which she saw Erik every night. But the hope in Erik's eyes made it impossible for her to say no, though she felt certain she would be unable to do as he requested. It would take years for her to prepare her father for the reality of Erik Rexford in her life. And even after years, he still wouldn't like it.

"I'll think about it," she said, resting her head on his shoulder.

"That's better than nothin', I guess," he said, putting his arm around her.

"Hey," she said, hoping to lift his mood. "I had an idea for next Sunday!"

"What's next Sunday?" he asked.

Her cheeks flared with heat. She'd just assumed they'd do something together next Sunday, as they had last week. *Oh, shoot.* Had she presumed too much?

"Well, I'm free for the day after brunch again," she said softly.

"And you're askin' me out on a date?"

She took a deep breath. That sounded so forward. Is that what she was doing? Yes. Yes, it was.

*My goodness*, she thought, *how much I've changed in a handful of weeks, asking a man out on a date.* It's something she wouldn't have dreamed of doing before meeting Erik.

"Our rules," he murmured softly, as if somehow knowing

she needed a little encouragement.

"Yes," she said, grateful for the semidarkness, which hid her red cheeks. "Yes, I am asking you out on a date, Erik Rexford."

He chuckled happily, raising her hand to his lips and kissing the back of it. "I accept! What did you have in mind?"

With a heart lighter than air, she told him about the haunted lighthouse of Currituck Beach, the fishing pier up in Duck, the wild horses in Corolla, and a play called *The Lost Colony* over on Roanoke Island. She'd researched these previously unknown attractions on the computer at King Triton after Erik's Wednesday visit, she told him proudly, and he kissed her tenderly for her ingenuity and bravery.

"That's dates for every Sunday until the end of the summer," he said, grinning down at her. "I really might start to think you're into me, Laire Cornish."

"Oh, I am," she said softly, winding her arms around his neck and pulling his lips down to hers. "I am completely into you, Erik Rexford."

# Chapter 12

The problem with a handful of stolen Sundays, Erik learned, was that they went way too quickly.

By August ninth, he had spent almost every summer night at the Pamlico House and every Sunday sweeping Laire away to another Outer Banks destination.

They managed to find places to park in the dark where they could reach for each other with ever-increasing hunger, and once or twice, when Utopia Manor was empty, she had joined him there for a few hours too. His fingers had touched every peak and valley of her gorgeous body at this point, and somewhere along the way, she'd mustered up the courage to touch him back—her fingers tentative as they brushed against the tip of his cock, the gesture all the more erotic because of her inexperience and his sharp desire.

They still hadn't been completely naked together, and Erik had no hopes for sex, but he loved her desperately, and being with her was worth it, no matter how blue his balls were when they said good-bye at the end of the night.

But the unfortunate and unavoidable reality was that summer was winding down, which meant that his time with Laire was coming to a close. And no matter how often he asked her about joining his family for Thanksgiving, she demurred every time with a "maybe" or an "I'll think about it."

He began to understand that having her visit him at Duke was never going to happen, and when he received his courses over e-mail, he realized that coming down to the Banks with any regularity was going to be almost impossible. Besides his aggressive senior-year course load, he had been given a starting position with the Devils, an honor that he couldn't turn down but that would mean weekend practices and Saturday games up and down the East Coast.

If she wouldn't commit to Thanksgiving, he didn't know with any certainty when he would see her again. But if they could just get over that hurdle together and commit to sharing their relationship with their families, he hoped the Cornishes would accept him and that she'd be able to come and see him when she wanted to, e-mail without fear of getting caught. Hell, he'd buy her a cell phone and a set up a hot spot so they could call and text too. He'd do whatever he had to, to keep her in his life. Maybe their families wouldn't be happy about the relationship initially, but at least it wouldn't be a secret anymore. When he was feeling especially hopeful, Erik even imagined their parents being so understanding that maybe Laire could spend the entirety of Christmas break with him in Raleigh. He had several thousand dollars saved up in his bank account from birthday and Christmas gifts—he could even buy her a used car so she could come and go as she pleased.

They just had to choose to make their relationship a priority and agree on the way to share it with their friends and families. And as far as Erik was concerned, Thanksgiving was not only ideal, but the first possible opportunity once their time this summer was over.

He refused to think in terms of saying good-bye to her or ending their relationship in any way. For starters, he couldn't bear it—the thought of her with someone else made him physically ill—but also, Erik Rexford wasn't a quitter. He believed in the strength of the feelings they shared. He believed they could go the distance—marriage, children, forever—if they could just hold on to one another. And he couldn't imagine ever loving or trusting another woman the way he did Laire. Everything about her was genuine, and he wanted—no, he *needed*—her in his life to give it perspective and meaning and foundation.

So when his parents decided to drive Hillary back to the Asheville Christian School together on August tenth, tomorrow, leaving Utopia Manor empty for two whole days, he also knew it was his last major chance to convince her of his plans for them before he returned to school the following weekend. He had to get her to agree to spend some real time with him so he could sell her on Thanksgiving once and for all.

"'Evenin', Erik," said Ms. Sebastian, who'd finally stopped giving him the stink eye about three weeks ago.

"Hey, Ms. Sebastian," he said, giving her a warm smile.

He knew that Laire not only looked up to Ms. Sebastian as a boss, but he sensed that she felt the sort of affection for the older woman that she had on reserve for the mother she'd lost. And although it had taken him most of the summer to win her over, he respected Ms. Sebastian. He appreciated the way she looked after Laire. In fact, part of him was counting on her to keep looking after Laire even after he'd returned to Duke.

"Headed back to school soon?"

He nodded grimly. "Next weekend."

The older woman's eyes flicked over to Laire, who was taking an order in the dining room. "She's done well here this summer."

She *had* done well. She'd stayed a busser for only a couple of weeks before her promotion to waitress, and he had it on good authority that she was Ms. Sebastian's star employee.

"You've been good to her, ma'am."

Her eyes nailed his. "She'll miss you awful."

"I'll miss her too," he said, a lump making his throat tight. "Any chance you could let her off early tomorrow?"

"What's tomorrow?"

"My folks are leavin' to take my sister back to school in Asheville. I'll have the house to myself."

"And you want her to . . .?"

He ran a hand through his hair. "I just want time with her, ma'am. Nothin' else."

Ms. Sebastian searched his face, then nodded once. "If she wants to leave early, I won't stand in her way."

"Thank you," said Erik.

She turned to leave, then pivoted back around. "Good luck at school, Erik."

"Thank you, ma'am," he said.

"You'll come back?" she asked quickly. "To the Banks?"

He nodded. "At Thanksgivin'. I'm hopin' Laire will . . ."

"Will . . .?" She raised her eyebrows in question.

"I hope she'll be ready to tell her father about us by then so we can . . . spend the holiday together. Move forward."

"Ah," said Ms. Sebastian, grimacing. She took a deep breath and sighed, her eyes heavy with concern. "Well, good luck," she said again softly before heading back to the kitchen.

*Not exactly a ringing endorsement*, he thought.

Laire approached the bar with a tray and set it on the busing counter at the corner. "I'm almost done."

He took a twenty out of his wallet and slipped it under his glass. "Meet me at the chairs?"

She grinned at him and nodded. "See you there!"

*** 

Usually, after making out with Erik for an hour after work, the wind on her face felt like a blessing, cooling the heat of her body and bringing her back down to earth before she arrived home.

But not tonight.

Tonight her cheeks burned with longing and guilt, want and shame—and more than anything else, the sharpest frustration she'd ever felt.

Erik's house would be empty tomorrow night.

And he'd invited her to stay the night.

After her initial wave of sharp desire to spend a whole night in his arms, she'd gotten angry—at him and at herself.

Why would he invite her to do something she wasn't able to do? The only reason her double life had lasted this long was because they'd followed a strict set of rules. On weekdays and Saturdays, she left her father's dock at three o'clock in the afternoon and returned by eleven o'clock at night. On Sundays she left at nine in the morning and returned by eleven in the evening. As long as she didn't deviate from that plan, he didn't ask questions, aside from an occasional "How's work, li'l Laire?" which she always answered with a chipper "Just fine, Daddy." And somehow—she chose to believe it was grace—she hadn't been given away by either Mr. Mathers over on Ocracoke or Kyrstin, who covered for her regularly with little comments about how well she was doing at work.

But with such a carefully constructed web of deception, how in the world was she supposed to leave at three in the afternoon per usual and not return until *the next day*? It wasn't possible. It just wasn't possible. Her father would notice if she wasn't at home the next morning, and her sisters, who knew nothing about Erik, wouldn't cover that big a lie for her. No. She couldn't do it.

But it wasn't fair how desperately she *wanted* to.

She wanted a night in Erik's arms.

She wanted the memory of falling asleep beside him.

She wanted to know what it felt like to see him when her eyes opened first thing in the morning.

As their time wound down, he talked constantly about

seeing her over Thanksgiving break, but he didn't seem to understand that she still couldn't conceive of telling her father about their relationship. With Buxton and the Pamlico House, Sundays with Erik, and being intimate with a dingbatter, there were too many lies.

For her to ever introduce Erik to her father, she'd need about a year to lay the groundwork.

First of all, after Erik went back to school, she would tell her father she'd found a year-round job on Buxton. He'd hem and haw, but she thought he might be okay with it after letting her work all summer, and plus, he'd regard it differently since it was off-season work. Jobs off-season were hard to come by— she didn't think he'd stand in the way of her making money over the long, hard, cold months of fall and winter.

She could, perhaps, meet Erik for the first time over Thanksgiving break, and again over Christmas break, casually mentioning in front of her uncle that the governor's son had recognized her waitressing at the Pamlico House and asked her out on a date.

Once or twice over the spring, she could mention Erik's name again, and maybe, *maybe by next summer*, she could tell her father that she'd gone out with him a couple of times. By then, he'd be accustomed to her working away from Corey, and he'd have had time to let Erik's name, however unwanted, become a part of her life. He still wouldn't like it. He'd still raise the roof, but it would be better—so much better—than telling him at Thanksgiving, when he'd know she got involved with Erik while lying all summer.

She wanted Erik to understand, but every time she tried to tell him *her* plan, he circled back around to Thanksgiving again, insisting it was the best way. But she didn't agree. Erik didn't seem to understand that "pulling off the Band-Aid" wasn't the way to communicate with Hook Cornish. And if she did, her father would stonewall her for sure.

With a heavy heart, she cut the engine close to home, floating softly up to the dock by her house and jumping soundlessly onto the dock. She tied up the boat, surprised to see the orange glow of her father's pipe in the screened porch. *Hmm.* He was rarely up at this hour.

"Daddy?" she called through the screen as she walked up the flagstones.

"'Evenin', Laire," he said, his words garbled from the pipe he held between his teeth. "Waited up for you."

"Everything okay?" she asked, trying to control the sudden bolt of panic that made her heart race and her hands go clammy.

"Aye-up. Issy came by with the baby for a spell. He's a nice little thing, but he's got his days and nights reversed." He grinned at her. "Like you."

"Me?" she asked, breathing easy as she sat down in her mother's rocker.

He looked out at the water, nodding. "You. Up all night screamin' like a banshee. Sleepin' like a lamb all day. Put yore mama through the ringer. Fair mommucked every mornin', she was."

Laire chuckled softly. Her father didn't speak of their mother much, so it was music to her ears to hear this little piece of information.

"I miss her," she said.

He nodded. "Aye-up. She was a good'un."

For several moments they sat in silence before her father spoke again. "Brodie Walsh come into Triton today. Had some early yellowfin. Nice." Laire clenched her jaw hard, staring down at her knees. Her father cleared his throat. "You ever think you might like a li'l'un like Issy's got?"

She sucked in a sharp breath. "Not with Brodie Walsh."

Her father looked at her askance. "Been some talk about you and him this summer."

"Lies," she said firmly.

"Maybe," said her father, sighing. "Heard you told him off at Kyrstin's weddin'."

"I did. And he admitted he lied about me."

Her father puffed on his pipe. "Still and all, talk is talk. Yore name be wrapped up w' his now, Laire."

"I don't want Brodie Walsh. He's full of himself. He lies. He's immature. He drinks. He's not . . ." *Erik.*

"Just wants a nice gal like you to make his life sweet."

He wasn't hearing her at all.

Staring straight ahead, at the Sound, her eyes burned with frustration and injustice, with longing for Erik, hatred for Brodie, and a sharp desperation for the mother who might have understood her better.

"You got yore nice fashions. Done a little waitressin'. Time to think about settlin' in, li'l Laire. Find a nice boy. Let him court you for a spell."

She felt bile rising in her throat.

"I'm mommucked, Daddy," she said, standing up. "Think I'll go to bed."

She reached for the door when his voice stopped her.

"Oh, Laire! One other thing. Me and yore uncle's headed out tomorrow afternoon to Harkers Island. Crabbin's strong down there this year. We'll stay the night on the boat and be back Friday afternoon."

*Wait!* "W-what?"

"No need to make my dinner for tomorrow. Nor breakfast for Friday."

"You'll be . . ." She cleared her throat and tried desperately to remove any blatant enthusiasm from her voice. "You'll be gone until Friday afternoon?"

He shrugged. "Might be back afore you head out to work Friday, might not. Hopin' for a decent haul."

Standing behind him, Laire clenched her fists by her sides as a wave of pure, unbridled, unadulterated joy swept through her. She was free. *For a whole night.* She could have a whole night with Erik.

"Yes, sir," she said softly as tears of happiness pricked her eyes. "Take care now."

"Aye-up," he said. "Night, Laire. Consider what I said. 'Bout Brodie Walsh and you."

"Yes, sir," she murmured, letting the door shut behind her as she raced into her room, her cheeks wet from tears of silent celebration.

\*\*\*

Laire was as mad as Erik had ever seen her when they parted ways yesterday.

They'd been cuddling on the Adirondack chairs—she was sitting cradled in his lap—when he asked her if there was any way she could spend the night with him tonight. He knew it was a bold request, but damn, he just wanted the time with her, and he'd been quick to add that sex was definitely *off* the table. He wasn't looking for *that*. He just wanted hours and hours with her.

Suffice it to say, it hadn't gone well at all. With a mix of anger and frustration, she'd leaped off his lap and stared down at him, hands on her hips, lecturing him about how staying overnight wasn't an option and how could he—knowing her precarious situation—ask it of her? He'd tried to calm her down before she left, and they'd kissed and hugged good night, but he could tell she was still upset.

And now? As he zoomed over to the Pamlico House at six o'clock, he wondered if he'd pushed her too hard last night, and his heart clutched with misgivings. He felt like he'd fucking die if she was still mad and wouldn't come over at all tonight, when it was their last, best chance to be alone before he had to go back to school.

Everything was winding down around him—Hillary had already gone back to school in Asheville. Pete, who was expected for three weeks of football camp before classes, had left for Chapel Hill this morning, giving Vanessa a ride back to Raleigh. She was chairing her sorority rush and would meet some of her sisters for preplanning at Wake Forest next week.

It had been an awkward couple of weeks dodging Van after the party at his parents' house in July. He'd been beyond grateful when she left for a four-week tour of England and Scotland with her aunt and uncle. When he'd seen her last Saturday afternoon for an end-of-season BBQ at Utopia Manor, she didn't seem nearly as pushy as she'd been before leaving, and even mentioned some guy in England whom she was "seeing." Whether or not this was true, Erik breathed a sigh of relief. His mother still had some vague idea that he and Van were together, but if Van had moved on to this new guy, at least he could stop feeling bad about leading her on for a spell.

Erik's biggest problem was time. He had a week at most before he had to leave the Banks. He could maybe push his departure to next Thursday, but his parents would insist on seeing him in Raleigh for a weekend before he left for Duke.

There was no time left.

No fucking time.

And it was killing him to leave Laire behind without a plan in place to pick up where they were leaving off.

They needed to talk. They needed to figure out how to keep this good thing going during the one hundred days they'd be apart between now and Thanksgiving. And Erik felt an urgency to figure it out tonight, even if he had to fight her for the time.

Pulling into a parking spot by the inn, he strode inside, a man on a mission.

But the moment he saw her, he knew something was up. As he sat down in the bar, two hours earlier than usual, she came right over to him, something she'd never done before.

"We need to talk," she whispered near his ear.

He sucked in a tight breath as his heart sank. Those four words were possibly the most dreaded combination in the English language.

*Fuck.*

*Fuck. Fuck. Fuck.*

*Why did you push her so hard yesterday?*

He swallowed, grinding his jaw once. "Okay."

"Follow me," she said, walking briskly from the bar to the reception area. Without looking back or stopping, she continued up the stairs, to the second floor, and then up more stairs, to the third. At the third floor, she opened a door that led to a steep, dark staircase and she continued up with him following behind. At the top, she opened another door, and Erik quickly realized that it led directly outside.

Erik had never been upstairs at the Pamlico House, but suddenly he found himself alone with Laire on a widow's walk four stories high and almost two hundred years old.

With new planking and enough room for four lounge chairs, it was a beautiful spot for guests to sun themselves, except he couldn't shake the feeling that she was about to break up with him, so he couldn't possibly enjoy it. He stopped just inside the door and waited to hear what she had to say, his insides turning with a fear that made him feel nauseous.

When she turned around, her face was split with a smile that surprised him, and he relaxed a little, stepping forward.

"I can come!" she said, her eyes alive with excitement. "Tonight. I can stay with you."

He'd been holding his breath, but now he exhaled in a loud whoosh, reaching for her and pulling her roughly into his arms.

"Fuck, Laire," he muttered into her hair. "I thought you brought me up here to break it off."

"To break things off with you?" she asked in a rush.

"I fuckin' pressured you last night when I promised I never would."

"You didn't really. You just asked. I shouldn't have gotten mad. I just . . . I wanted to stay over, but I couldn't figure out how!"

His heart was finally returning to normal as he leaned away and looked down at her face. "I love you."

"I love you too," she answered, leaning up on tiptoe to kiss him.

And he wanted to kiss her—and goddamnit, he planned to kiss her all night long—but right now he needed to understand. "How? How did you manage it?"

"My daddy's going crabbing down by Harkers Island tonight. Just told me yesterday. Won't be back until tomorrow afternoon."

He cupped her face, feeling a burst of laughter bubble up from deep inside. "Just like that?"

She nodded, grinning up at him. "Just like that."

He bent to kiss her softly. "All night."

"All night," she murmured against his lips. "But . . . Erik . . ."

"What, darlin'?"

"We can't . . . I mean, we can't . . ."

"I know," he groaned softly, nuzzling her nose. "I meant what I said last night. I just want time with you. We go at your pace, remember? Always."

"But what if . . .?"

Her voice trailed off, and he drew back, putting his index finger under her chin to lift her eyes to his.

"What?"

"What if I say I want to?" she asked in a rush.

He swallowed. "To have sex?"

She nodded, her eyes wide and fraught.

"Are you ready for that?" he asked, searching her face.

Her shoulders lifted just a little. "When I'm with you, it's like I can't stop. I don't want to stop. I want to do everything, experience everything, with you." She sobbed softly. "I need your help to be good."

"You want me to put the brakes on?" he asked. "Is that what you're askin'?"

Her lips trembled before she nodded. "Yes."

He took a deep breath and let it out slowly, feeling the way it tickled the insides of his lips as he exhaled. Could he make this promise? Could he promise her that he would stop them, even if she was begging him for more?

He wanted to believe that he could. He desperately wanted to believe that, for Laire, he could do anything.

"Okay," he said, pulling her against him again. "Okay. I promise."

She threw her arms around his neck and kissed him like the world would end if she didn't, then nuzzled his nose with hers. "But anything else we want to do is up to us."

"Being . . . naked?" he asked, grinning at her because she could barely say the word *naked* a few weeks ago.

She giggled softly. "Uh-huh."

"Touchin' you . . ." He cleared his throat. "Down there? With my tongue?"

She leaned back, her eyes wide and shocked. "Do people do that?"

He grinned at her expression. "Hell, yes, darlin'."

She dropped his glance, thinking for a moment. "Can I do that to you too?"

"Ahh," he groaned, all the blood in his head racing to his cock at the mere thought of her lips sucking him. "Yeah. You can."

With a soft whimper, she reached for his face and kissed him again. "Ms. Sebastian said I can leave early. Said you asked last night."

"I did," he admitted. "I hoped."

"Then I'll see you at eight?"

"At eight. And then you're all mine."

She kissed him again, giggling against his lips as she wiggled from his arms, ran back to the door, and disappeared.

Two hours.

His cocked strained against his shorts in anticipation.

*Lord, it felt like an eternity.*

# Chapter 13

If every other drive to Utopia Manor had felt exciting, tonight's was making Laire breathless.

For the first time since she'd met Erik, they weren't going to have an hour of making out at the Pamlico House dock, or even two hours at his house, or even a half day together visiting some landmark on the upper Banks. No. Tonight was totally different. Tonight she was going to sleep beside him. In his bed.

Her breath hitched.

My, how she'd changed this summer, from a teenager who could barely utter the word *naked* to a woman who reached for her man with new confidence and sanctioned passion. She had grown up this summer in so many ways, and now, tonight, felt like the apex of that growth—her reward for leaving childhood behind.

His fingers curled around hers, and he raised her hand to his lips.

"You nervous?"

"A little," she answered honestly. "But excited too."

"What time do you have to be home tomorrow?"

"Ms. Sebastian said I could leave my boat overnight, but I'm thinking I should be home by midmorning, just in case my daddy gets home early."

"He said he'd be gone until afternoon, though," said Erik his forehead creasing.

"I know," she said. "But better not to risk being found out."

"Humph."

"We have all night, Erik. Let's just enjoy it."

He sighed and kissed her hand again before releasing it and putting his hands back on the wheel. "You're right. I just hate to think about sayin' good-bye."

She knew that their farewell and subsequent months-long separation were weighing on his mind. The thought weighed heavy on hers too. And it had led her to a decision that had surprised her in its intensity and certainty.

"You know how you keep talking about Thanksgiving?" she asked.

"Uh-huh."

"Well, I'm *not* going to be ready to introduce you to my family yet. I'm sorry."

"Laire—"

"You have to understand. I'm going to need time to explain this, to set it up for them. I'm thinking I won't actually be able to introduce you to them until next summer. I'm sorry, Erik, but that's the way things have to be."

He huffed softly, clenching his jaw in frustration as he pulled into his driveway and hit the button on his visor for the garage door.

"But," she said softly as he pulled into the garage and cut the engine, "I will come here and spend the day with you and your family. I'll say I'm working. I can meet your folks and sister at Thanksgiving. Maybe again at Christmas. They can get to know me a little—"

"Laire!" He turned to her, his eyes wide. "You'd do that?"

She gulped, nodding her head. "I would."

A small smile tilted up his lips, growing bigger and surer as he stared at her. "You'll come for Thanksgivin'. You promise?"

She smiled back at him, tears biting at her eyes as she understood how much it meant to him. "I promise."

Leaning across the bolster in the dark garage, he reached for her face, pulling it to his and kissing her. It lasted only for a second before he rested his forehead on hers. "I'm relieved. I just needed some sort of definite plan in place. Somethin' to look forward to."

"So did I," she admitted.

"Come inside?" he asked, nuzzling her nose. "I know you don't drink much, but my parents always keep a bottle of Champagne cold, and I want to celebrate. One glass?"

Laire had never had Champagne before, and the idea was too tempting to refuse.

Ten minutes later, standing at Erik's kitchen counter as the cold bubbles sluiced down her throat, she learned what all the fuss was about. It was delicious.

"You like it?" he asked, already knowing the answer.

She nodded, marveling at the delicate flute in her fingers. So many times she'd served Champagne to patrons at the Pamlico House, but she'd never actually imagined herself tilting one of those flutes back into her own mouth. Sighing happily, she took another sip and giggled. "It tickles."

He grinned at her. "Can I ask you somethin'?"

"Course. Anything," she said, leaning over the marble counter, looking up at his handsome face.

"Do you have an e-mail account?"

She laughed in a short burst because his question came out of nowhere and surprised her. "I do. You have to have e-mail to order things. Not that I order a lot of things, but every now and then, I do."

"Well, how about we exchange e-mail addresses, and then we can keep in touch while I'm away at school?"

It was something Laire hadn't considered, and her heart

leaped at the notion of them still being in contact. Sure, she'd only be able to check her e-mail quickly, when it was quiet at King Triton, which wasn't often, but even if she checked in once a week, it would lessen her longing for him, wouldn't it?

She looked up at him, a smile on her face, when something occurred to her and made her look back down at the counter with misgivings.

Wait. *Would* it make her miss him less? Or would it heighten her yearning to an almost unbearable level? Not only for Erik, but for the wonderful world he inhabited while she was still stuck on Corey. He'd tell her about the people he was meeting and places he was going, and what would she share with him? The number of blues her father had caught that day? That she was making a new blouse for someone he'd never heard of? That Ms. Sebastian had added grouper to the winter menu?

In a blinding moment of self-realization, she understood that what she offered him—an eighteen-year-old fisherman's daughter from the Banks—was charming *now*, while he was close to her, but might not hold such allure from a distance. And she needed for him to long for her just as much as she longed for him. She needed it to guarantee his return, and weekly updates about her less-than-fascinating life wouldn't help her cause when he was surrounded by sophisticated college girls.

Taking another sip of the Champagne, she looked up at him and shrugged. "I don't think so. I don't have a computer at home. Only at work, and I can't risk Daddy or Uncle Fox catching me writing to you."

The sudden disappointment on his face made her heart clench.

"Oh," he said. "Then I suppose phone calls are out too?"

"It's just not a good idea for them to see Duke come up repeatedly on the ID. They'll get suspicious. And if I call you, it'd show up on the bill."

"So we really won't talk to each other until I get back for Thanksgivin'," he said softly, his voice low and sad as the realization hit home.

"Unless you can come out for a weekend?" she asked hopefully.

He grimaced. "I got my hockey schedule. Every weekend's accounted for."

"Oh," she said, finishing the last of her Champagne and realizing, in that moment, how much she'd hoped to see him for a weekend between August and November. It hurt to know that she wouldn't.

"Yeah," he said, refilling their glasses. "It's crazy."

"Sounds like it."

"Laire?" he said, clinking her glass. "You want to stop talkin' about this?"

She didn't trust speaking over the lump in her throat so she took a sip of bubbly and nodded.

"Want to go lie on my bed and just . . . I don't know. We can watch TV or take a nap or talk about nothin'?"

Her breathing hitched when he said "lie on my bed," but she felt her whole body react in protest to his suggestions. She wanted to be in his bed, yes. She had no interest, however, in TV, napping, or talking.

"No," she said.

"No what?"

"No TV," she said, tipping back her Champagne flute and finishing it. "No napping. And limited talking."

His eyes were dark as he stared at her over the rim of his glass, quickly downing the rest of his wine too. "Then . . .?"

She rounded the corner of the counter, a mix of nerves and want, and took his hand. "Take me to bed, darlin'," she said, using his nickname for her, hungry for the weight of his body on hers, the glorious touch of his hot mouth to her nipples, to her . . .

.

"With pleasure," he growled, leaning down to kiss her once, hard, before leading her up the stairs.

\*\*\*

Erik's bedroom, which, like the rest of the house, his mother had decorated in a nautical theme, had a queen-size bed with a navy and white striped duvet. Facing the bed were a fireplace and two leather wingback chairs, and in the corner, his bathroom. Straight across the room were sliding doors that led to the balcony from which he'd first glimpsed Laire. The furnishings were top-notch, but because Erik spent so little time in the room, it looked more like a posh hotel room than his bedroom back in Raleigh, with ACS and Duke pennants on the walls, and framed pictures of his family and friends on the bureau.

As they entered the room, he closed the door behind them out of habit, then dropped her hand. He walked to the windows and pulled the gauzy curtains aside so they could see the moon on the Sound. The room was instantly flooded with soft gray moonlight, and Erik sighed, giving himself a pep talk: reminding himself not to pressure her, not to go too fast, to be aware of her body language. His body was taut with want, his cock hard as a rock. *Fuck*, she was finally *here*, in his bedroom. But he forced himself to take a deep, calming breath, promising himself he'd behave, before he turned around to face her . . .

. . . and found her naked, her pale body bathed in moonlight, her clothes in a small pile on the floor behind her.

He gasped softly, his breath catching as he stared at her. The breasts he had touched and kissed so lovingly were high and pert, the deep pink nipples standing at attention. Her arms were at her sides, and his eyes dropped lower, to her pussy, which was covered with a triangle of curls. Taking a ragged, gasping breath, he caressed the swell of her hips and perfect legs with his eyes before letting his searing glance travel slowly back up her body to her face.

"Tell me what to do," she murmured, her voice so soft, it was barely audible.

"L-Laire," he whispered, striding across the room to pull her into his arms.

Her fingers reached for the buttons of his shirt, dispatching them quickly as they kissed hungrily. He shrugged out of the cotton material, releasing her only to tug the cuffs from his wrists. She reached for his belt and unbuckled it as she leaned up on tiptoe to kiss him again, and Erik, impatient to feel her skin pressed against his, hooked his thumbs into the waistband of his khakis and boxers, and forced both over his hips without unzipping, grateful for the whoosh of fabric against his legs.

Finally naked.

Bare to each other.

He reached for her, pulling her against his tingling, impatient skin, which melted into the satiny warmth of hers, his rigid cock cradled against the soft V of her thighs. With his arms around her, he backed her gently to the bed, leaning into her until she lay on her back.

"Scoot up," he mumbled before joining her, lowering one knee to either side of her perfect legs and bending his head to kiss the soft, virgin skin of her stomach.

"Erik," she murmured, reaching for his head, her voice heavy with lust but edged with a hint of panic.

"I want to kiss you here," he said, covering the rosy thatch of curls over her clit with the palm of his hand.

She gasped, her breath hitching as her fingers curled into his scalp.

"Let me," he whispered, parting her with his fingers and stroking her clit tenderly as he wedged his knees gently between her legs.

"Oh, God . . . okay," she murmured breathlessly.

Kneeling before her, he put his hands under her hips, cupping her ass to draw her body closer to his face. Bending his head, he closed his eyes and let his tongue glide gently against her nether lips, first up one side and then down the other.

She mewled softly, arching her back and pressing her head into his pillow as he lapped at her already-swollen clit, then flicked the tender bud with his tongue, feeling his own erection harden in response to her whimpers and moans. She reached for his forearms, curling her fingers into his muscle as he took the throbbing nub between his lips and kissed her, sucking lightly, caressing her aching place with his tongue before letting her go. Her hips bucked, and she pushed against his face, her fingernails digging into his flesh as she cried out in pleasure.

"I want to feel you," she sobbed through panted breaths, her hips still gyrating against his comforter rhythmically. "I want to feel you inside me."

He slid up the bed to lie beside her on his side, leaning over her to kiss her lips and look into her heavy, half-closed eyes.

He wanted to. Oh, fuck, but he wanted to.

*I need your help to be good.*

Her words resonated in his head as she reached for his neck, curling her fingers just under the base of his skull and demanding his lips. Rolling on top of her, his cock throbbed against her damp curls. She was wet and ready for him, aching for him just as he was aching for her.

"Please," she moaned beneath him, wiggling her hips, trying to get closer. "Please. We don't have to . . . have sex. I just want to know how it feels."

He kissed her again, long and hard, his tongue mating with hers, thrusting and sliding the way he wished his cock could, and it wasn't enough. It just wasn't e-fucking-nough.

"Laire," he whispered against her lips, thrusting lightly against her, frustrated that she was warm against him but not wet and enveloping, not sucking him forward, not surrounding him with contracting, quivering muscle.

"Do it," she said, biting his lower lip. "Just for a minute."

*Just for a minute.*

Fuck.

So fucking tempting.

He panted over her, bracing his weight on his elbows.

"I'd still be takin' your virginity, darlin', even if we didn't . . . finish."

She nodded urgently, a whimpering, pleading noise slipping through her lips. "I know. It's okay. I want you to."

Cupping her face with his hands, he forced her to look at him. "Laire, you made me promise."

"I release you from your promise," she breathed. "I love you."

Reaching down between their bodies, he positioned himself at the entrance of her sex, holding himself there, wincing from the strength it took not to slide forward.

"I love you. I don't . . . I don't want you to regret this," he said.

Her hands skated down his back, finally resting on his ass. As though she knew instinctively how to urge him forward, she squeezed his cheeks at the same time she arched her back and raised her knees. And with a gasp of defeat and relief, Erik slid into her welcoming warmth, into the tight, hot sheath of her sex, bursting through the light barrier of flesh until he was buried within her to the hilt.

She cried out—an "unh-ah!" sound of pain—wincing and panting loudly beneath him, her eyes clenched shut, her body rigid.

"Baby," he gasped, keeping his body as still as possible, resisting every urge to move within her. Her muscles clamped around his thickness, and for a moment his breath hitched and his eyes rolled back in his head, his arms shaking on either side of her head as he fought for self-control. He'd never felt anything like the exquisite fist of Laire's pussy squeezing him—

the heat of her, the wetness, the perfect fit of her body wrapped around his.

"I'm okay . . . I'm okay . . .," she panted, her breath hot on his lips as a tear rolled from the corner of her eye into her hair. "I knew it would . . . I knew it would hurt a little."

"Are you okay?" he asked, his voice thready and husky at the same time.

Want.

Worry.

She licked her lips and nodded, finally opening her eyes to look up at him. They were deep and sea-green, glistening with tears but shining with love, and though five women had come before Laire in his bed, none had ever owned his heart as she did. And suddenly it didn't hurt to remain still, letting her accustom herself to his invasion. It felt right. It felt good. It felt . . . *beautiful*.

He nuzzled her nose, kissing her gently. When he drew back, she was smiling at him, her face soft and dreamy. "We're one right now, Erik."

"We're one, darlin'."

He pulled his hips back a millimeter, then let himself fall forward again, watching the play of emotion, of deep pleasure, across her face.

"More," she murmured. "Do it again."

He gulped. He didn't have long before he'd come. It had been a wonderful summer with Laire, but while helping her uncover her own sexuality, his needs had been somewhat neglected. He wouldn't have much longer before he'd need to come. And while she was a virgin and he hadn't been intimate with anyone in months, without a condom between them, he definitely didn't want to get her pregnant.

"One last time," he said. "Then I'll pull out."

She nodded. "One last time. Please."

Pulling his pelvis back, he withdrew from her almost entirely, then, holding her eyes, he thrust forward again, once, twice, three times, her hips meeting his every time.

"I have to . . . stop," he said, out of breath, his arms taut beside her head. "We have to . . ."

"Okay," she said, but her hips flexed again, taking him deeper, and he groaned, feeling his balls tighten in warning.

Pulling out of her with a desperate jerk, he slid his cock into the soaked valley he'd loved with his tongue, thrusting his silken shaft relentlessly against her clit. She whimpered loudly, grabbing his cheeks and kissing him as their teeth clashed together violently. His body slapped against hers, their voices a chorus of grunts and moans, whimpers and gasps, louder and faster. until she tensed beneath him, crying his name, and he came on her clit and her stomach in hot, wet spurts of white.

"IloveyouIloveyouIloveyou," she repeated over and over again as she rode out her orgasm, their foreheads touching, their panted breaths mingling.

Sucking in a deep, ragged breath, he rolled to his side, taking her with him, holding her flush against him, with her head tucked into his throat, as he entwined his legs with hers. She shuddered in his arms, her eyes still closed, her breathing shallow.

"Are you okay?" he finally whispered, pressing his lips to her head and wondering how she'd feel about showering together and hoping she'd want to.

She nodded, the hair on the top of her head tickling his chin. "I've never . . . I mean . . ."

Her voice broke off, and he squeezed her body against his. "I know. Me neither."

"What?" She leaned her head back just a little so she could see his face. "You've been with other women."

"But I never loved any of them the way I love you."

She sniffled softly, and a tear snaked down her face.

"Thank you for keeping your promise."

His conscience twisted a touch. Had he kept his promise to her?

"Did I?"

She nodded, cuddling back against him. "The best you could."

"Is that enough?" he asked.

She nodded again. "For me it is."

"Thank you for trustin' me," he said, sliding his hands along the sweet, soft skin of her back and hoping that one day they'd be able to have sex to fruition—that he'd come inside her, make babies with her, keep this sweet woman by his side for life.

"I love you," she said again. "No matter what."

"Me too," he promised. "No matter what."

And then, because some moments are too perfect for anything else, they found their rhythm—hearts and lungs working in perfect harmony—and fell asleep in each other's arms.

\*\*\*

Though they planned to have one final Sunday date before Erik returned to school, Laire couldn't help a sharp feeling of melancholy as they said good-bye at the Pamlico House dock the following morning. It had been heaven to spend the night with him, and now that she was fully dressed and headed home, she deeply regretted not having sex with him to fruition. Though she knew it was best that he "pulled out," as he called it—and no, she wasn't anywhere near ready to be a mother, God forbid— she grieved not knowing what it would have felt to orgasm together and to feel his hot seed flood and fill her. She only hoped that one day, when the timing was right, she'd have another chance. A million more chances.

"Get home safe," he said, using his thumbs to swipe away

her tears as he kissed her tenderly. "I'll be here tonight at the bar."

It wasn't enough, but it was still comforting.

She sniffled, then nodded. "I know."

He cupped her cheeks with his palms. "We're goin' to make it, Laire. We're goin' to be okay until Thanksgivin'. And then there's only a short wait until Christmas. Even if you can't get to Raleigh, I have three weeks off and no hockey. I can get out here at least twice to see you. We'll make it work, darlin'. I promise you."

She covered his hands with hers. "I'm not worried. I trust you."

He nodded, but his eyes were unsettled. "Think about e-mailin' me?"

"I just don't—"

"Think about it," he insisted softly.

She nodded, leaning up on tiptoe to kiss him. "Okay. I will."

He'd stood on the dock, waving good-bye as she drove away. And even after he was a small speck in the distance, she could still see him, hand raised, standing at the edge of the dock. She let her tears flow freely for the next fifteen minutes of the ride, then dried them, reminding herself that between now and next Thursday were five more nights and one glorious Sunday. She'd ruin their final days together if she cried all over him every time they were together. Was it poignant? Yes. Did it hurt? Like hell. But she needed to have more faith in them.

Taking a deep breath, she turned into the cove that led to Corey Harbor and slowed down as she passed a friend of her father's, who yelled something at her that she couldn't hear so she just waved in response. Continuing into the bay, she skimmed the shoreline to her house.

The first thing she noticed was her father's fishing boat.

The second thing she noticed was her father himself,

emerging from the house to greet the devil.

The third thing she noticed was Issy and Kyrstin scurrying at his heels.

*Why is he home? Why is he home? Why is he already home?*

Her heart was beating so fast, she could barely breathe, but she pulled in alongside the dock as her father stepped onto the planking, demanding, "Throw me the line."

Scrambling to the bow, she threw him the rope, watching, with increasing horror, as he cleated the boat to the dock without a word, his face drawn, his eyes furious.

Flicking her eyes to Kyrstin's, she found them wide and severe.

*Shit.* She was in trouble. *Big, huge, mammoth* trouble.

"Get on in the house now," growled her father, his blue eyes flinty.

Looking over her father's shoulder she found Issy, who held baby Kyle against her chest and looked at Laire like she'd like to spit and roast her.

"Get. In. The. House," she whispered angrily, snarling at her youngest sister.

Laire scurried off the boat, past her father and sisters, head down, beelining for the porch door. She slipped inside, turning into the living room and perching on the edge of the couch as her mind tried to figure out what was going on and how the hell to explain her absence.

Her father, preceded by her sisters, entered the living room, his huge presence taking up most of the room, his eyes angry and tired.

"Where you been?" he asked, looming over her, cracking his knuckles against his palms.

She darted a glance to Kyrstin, the only one in the room who knew that Laire had been working in Buxton. Kyrstin shook her head almost imperceptibly to signal Laire that she hadn't said anything.

"I . . . I, um . . ."

She didn't know what to say. Should she admit to working at the Pamlico House? What about Erik? No. No! She couldn't mention Erik, or her father would forbid her to ever see him again.

Her father took a step toward her, hands on his hips. "Issy come by last night to check on ya. The li'l'n keeps her up so she comes by regular."

"You weren't here, Laire. Not at nine, not at ten, not at two in the mornin'!" cried Issy. Laire blinked at the panic in her sister's voice, understanding, for the first time, that she wasn't just angry, but scared. "I waited for you, but as the hours went by, I got worried, so I called Kyrstin. She hadn't seen you all night. Said you never came into work. We called Brodie to see if you was with him, but he said he hadn't seen you in weeks. I was scared. So I radioed Daddy."

. . . at three o'clock in the morning.

Fuck.

Laire put a hand to her chest, which felt tight with her racing heartbeat and the horrible adrenaline rush of being found out. She needed a story. And fast.

"So where you been at, gal?" asked her father again. "And who you been with all night because he's goin' ta need to make it right w' you."

Make it right.

No.

No. No. No.

Marriage.

Her father was talking about a shotgun marriage.

She had to say something fast, to distance herself from the island men her father would suspect.

"I . . .," she started again, glancing at Kyrstin before

continuing. "I haven't been workin' on Ocracoke. I've been workin' over in Buxton."

"You *what*?!"Her father recoiled, stepping back as if she'd slapped him. He looked over at Kyrstin.

"You knew 'bout this?"

Kyrstin nodded, giving Laire dagger eyes before dropping her head in shame.

"Since when?" her father demanded.

"I n-never worked on Ocracoke. I just . . . Kyrs wanted a bar job, and so I let her—"

Kyrstin's head snapped up. "Don't you *dare* blame this on me, Laire!"

"I'm not *blamin'* you!" she cried. "But—"

"So two of my girls been lyin' to me all summer." Her father took a deep breath and exhaled long and hard, reaching up to press his palm to his chest. "Lyin' like snakes."

"No, Daddy," said Laire, even though it was true. She *had* been lying all summer. She'd been living in a fantasy world with Erik Rexford, and it was all crashing down around her.

"Yes, Laire! YOU BE A LIAR!" he boomed.

"Daddy, please, calm—"

"Don't you *dare* tell me to calm down! Where you been all night?"

Kyle started crying. and Laire looked up at her sister, whose pinched expression was traded for a mother's tenderness, jostling her baby in her arms. "Don't cry, li'l'un."

At some point, tears had started falling from Laire's eyes too. "I'm sorry. I'm so s-s-sorry."

"So you been in Buxton. All summer," her father said, his voice resigned, heavy and deeply disappointed, which gutted her. "But you still come home every night by 'leven. 'Cept for last night."

She gulped, the memory of Erik's body sliding inside hers

still so sharp, she could *feel* him. She could feel his beautiful fullness, and it made her want to weep for what was happening now—for the price she was going to have to pay for those cherished hours spent with him last night and this morning.

"Daddy . . ."

He shook his head, his face a mask of disappointment and shame. "I thank t'Lord your mama's gone and can't see this disgrace! Would've killed her if she waren't already dead!"

His words hurt worse than any physical punch, kick, or hit to any tender part of her body, and she felt herself reeling from them, wanting to curl up in a tight ball until she could wake up from this nightmare.

"Don't . . . say . . . that . . .," she sobbed. "Please . . ."

"IT BE THE TRUTH!" he cried. "You *shame* her memory, Laire!"

"Please," she begged him, hugging herself as tears fell down her cheeks in ceaseless streams. "Please don't—"

"I know . . ." He started in a softer voice, then stopped, rubbing his chest with the heel of his palm. When he started speaking again, his voice was softer and more breathless. "I know you been with s-someone . . . so you best tell me who. Now. Right now, Laire! I'll . . . I'll h-head up to Buxton and I'll force h-him to . . . to do right by you. If he's a man with any . . . p-principle, he'll . . . he'll do right . . . he'll . . ."

*Don't speak.*

She shook her head back and forth, her tears falling in rivulets. She couldn't speak. She wouldn't. She would never, ever give up Erik's name. No matter what.

"GOD DAMN IT, LAIRE!" he bellowed. "You speak to me! Who you . . . b-been with? First that . . . t-talk about . . . Brodie Walsh! Now this! You tell me . . . y-you tell me . . . where you b-been, you . . . lyin' little . . . you lyin' . . ."

His voice wheezed and cut off, and Laire looked up as he clutched at his chest desperately, his knuckles white as his fingers dug into the bib of his overalls.

"Daddy?" said Kyrstin in a panic, lurching forward to reach for him.

He stumbled backward, hitting a lampshade and knocking the lamp to the ground with a clatter. Grasping for the wall behind it, he knocked three framed pictures to the ground, shattering the glass. His eyes were wide and scared, his face paler by the second.

"Daddy? Daddy!!" screamed Issy, rocking her baby helplessly as their father slumped to his knees. "Call 911. LAIRE! CALL 911!"

But Laire couldn't move, frozen with terror, sobbing silent tears as she watched her father—her *beloved* father—her *only living parent*—fall onto his side, hitting the floor with a loud thump that shook the little house.

"KYRSTIN, CALL 911!" screamed Issy, and Kyrstin, who was kneeling by their father, crawled to the end table, grappling for the phone.

Their father lay motionless on the floor.

And if he was dead, Laire had wielded the knife.

As that despicable thought flashed like white lightning across her consciousness, Laire fainted, smashing her forehead on the glass coffee table on the way down.

## Chapter 14

When Laire didn't show up to work on Friday night, Erik was disappointed to miss seeing her, especially after the mind-blowing night they'd spent together. But after reminding himself that they couldn't easily get in touch with each other should she have to miss an evening of work, he decided not to indulge his worry and headed home early to spend some time with his mother, pack up for school, and get some sleep.

They certainly hadn't gotten much last night, he thought, letting happy memories take over as he drove himself home.

After an hour-long nap, they had gotten up and showered together, touching each other, soaping and rinsing, their fingers sliding over each other's bodies as they bathed and toweled off. Laire borrowed a shirt of his that just covered her, and Erik threw on some jeans before making a fire in his bedroom fireplace and lying down next to her. They talked and kissed, sharing plans for Thanksgiving and Christmas as a balm against their imminent separation.

When dawn lightened the skies, they stripped and climbed into his bed together, falling asleep for a few hours facing each other. Waking up with Laire in his arms was both miraculous and heartbreaking. Knowing that he would see her in November helped, but it seemed like an eternity. And yet, he wouldn't trade a second of their sweet time together and promised her silently, in those sacred minutes of holding her quietly, that he would never love another as he loved her.

Still glowing, he picked up a bouquet of roses on the way to the restaurant on Saturday night, eager to see her. When she wasn't at work again, he felt true misgivings and went to the kitchen to see Ms. Sebastian, politely asking her why Laire wasn't working. With worried eyes, she told him that she hadn't heard from Laire since she left early on Thursday.

That's when Erik first felt icy panic seep into his blood.

What was going on? She'd left with plenty of time to get home, right? He doubted they'd been caught. Her father had said he wouldn't be home until late afternoon, and she'd arrived home before noon, for sure. Unless she'd never arrived home?

His parents were back at the house entertaining friends, but he skipped polite greetings and beelined to his room, searching the Coast Guard website for any accidents in the Sound on Friday. When he didn't see any, he called the local station to be sure, but they had no reports of a young woman in distress.

So where was she? Was she sick? Was she regretting their night together and avoiding him? Without speaking to her directly, he didn't know.

He didn't bother heading to the Pamlico House on Sunday morning to see if she'd turned up for the brunch shift. Instead, he called King Triton Seafood at precisely 10:01 and asked to speak with Laire.

"Who's this?" asked a man's voice.

"I, uh, I came in and bought some blue crab last week. I said I'd be back, um, for more today, but the girl there said to call before I came in again to be sure you had more in stock." It was a lie, but he hoped it was a believable one.

"Huh. Well, Laire ain't here today, but she knows better'n anyone that we always got blues."

"Felt like she had a good eye for 'em," said Erik, trying to disguise his voice to sound more local, more like Laire. "Will she be in later?"

"Negative," said the man, his voice terse. "Her daddy had a heart attack."

"Wait! What did you say?"

"Her *daddy* had a *heart attack*," he enunciated, "so obviously she can't be *here* while she's sittin' by his *bedside*. You want the blues, you'll just have to let someone else help you. Okay, then?"

*A heart attack.* Fuck! *That's* why she wasn't coming to work. He knew how much she missed her mother—he could hardly imagine how much she was suffering if her father was in danger. His own heart twisted painfully, imagining her fear and sorrow.

"God, I'm . . ." Erik gulped, trying to hold back the emotion he felt and sound more conversational. "I'm sorry to hear that. Is he, uh, is he goin' to be okay?"

"How the fu—I mean, I don't know, sir. He's not dead yet. You wanna send flowers? He's up in Nags Head."

*Nags Head? Laire was in Nags Head?*

"Sir, you want those blues set aside, or what?"

"No, I . . . Thank you. I . . . I have to go."

He hung up the phone and stood up, pacing his room, trying to figure out what to do. Running a hand through his hair, he had a sudden idea and opened a Web browser on his phone.

*Hospital. Outer Banks hospital. Nags Head.*

He punched the address into his map app.

An hour.

It would take only an hour to be there by her side, offering whatever comfort she needed.

Racing down the stairs, he grabbed his keys from the basket in the vestibule and ran out the door to his car.

\*\*\*

Laire woke up at the Hatteras Health Center on Friday night, her head aching something awful. When she opened her eyes, she whimpered from the pain and quickly closed them again.

"You knocked yourself out," said Kyrstin's voice, flat and low. "Needed eight stitches."

Laire opened her eyes slower the second time, focusing on Kyrstin's face. She sat between the two clinic beds on a mint-green stool, looking at Laire over her shoulder.

"Daddy?" Laire gasped, finding her throat dry and scratchy.

"Still out of it."

"But . . .," whispered Laire, "is he . . .?"

"Alive?" she asked. "Yeah. No thanks to you."

Laire gasped from the sudden rush of relief, her eyes instantly burning from tears.

"Awake?"

"In a . . . a coma," Kyrstin whispered, her voice breaking. Then she turned back around to face their father, lying in the opposite bed.

Laire winced in pain, whimpering softly again before closing her heavy eyes and falling back to sleep.

When they moved her father up to Nags Head the next morning, Issy tried to stop Laire from going with him, claiming that seeing her when he woke up would just upset him all over again. But Kyrstin had been a surprising ally, telling Issy that Laire had as much right to go up to Nags Head as they did. She wasn't exactly warm and affectionate, but she stood up to Issy until Issy backed down in a huff.

Laire and Kyrstin called a taxi service from Hatteras and paid a hefty fee to be driven up the coast. It only occurred to Laire as they pulled away from the health center that she could have called Erik and asked him to drive them. But, for the first time since meeting him, the thought of Erik didn't fill her with warmth or excitement or happy tingles. She felt desperately sad and confused as she stared out the taxi window thinking about him, some significant part of her blaming him for what had happened to her father. If she and Erik had been more responsible, if they'd been able to stay away from each other, if he hadn't pursued her so damned doggedly in the beginning, this never would have happened.

So quickly, the magical, secret world she and Erik had built all summer had been toppled—tarnished beyond recognition when her father fell to the ground, clutching at his chest. Laire inhabited a grotesque new world now, in which her beloved father was glad her mother was dead—a world in which he had almost been killed by her irresponsibility.

It made her feelings toward Erik much more complicated than they'd been on Thursday, much less black-and-white. What if loving Erik ended up killing her father? How could that love be right? It couldn't be. Which meant that loving Erik was just a fantasy. A self-serving, self-indulgent, childish fantasy that, left to their wild, unhampered, unchecked desires, had raged out of control, hurting someone she dearly loved. And more than a fantasy, it was wrong. And the worst of it was, on some level or another, she'd known it was wrong all along.

On the interminable ride from Hatteras to Nags Head, with these terrible thoughts swirling, Laire's conscience tidily relegated her worth to the darkest, lowest level of shame, propelling her into a state of guilt—of such profound, profane, breath-catching, terrifying guilt—that her love for Erik felt almost unbearable.

Her father lay prone in a hospital bed, his prognosis still uncertain.

She had no right to happiness or love.

Not now and maybe not ever.

*That* was her new reality.

Their father was settled into a room in the cardiac unit, and in a strange twist of events, Issy, who prided herself on being the most caring and responsible daughter of the three, wasn't able to sit by their father's bedside. She wasn't permitted to bring baby Kyle into the adult wards, due to a breakout of pneumonia. With Paul at the height of his sea-fishing season and her in-laws unable to watch the baby for more than a day, this meant that Issy had had no choice but to return to Corey with her son, leaving her younger sisters with their father.

Kyrstin and Laire, who checked into a motel in Nags Head, took turns sitting beside their father's bedside, hoping against hope that he'd wake up soon.

On Sunday afternoon, with Kyrstin at the motel taking a nap, it was Laire's turn, and she held her father's weathered hand in hers, reading to him from the Bible and praying that she'd have more time with him.

"Laire." She opened her eyes and looked up to see Nurse Patty, assigned to her father's care, peeking into the room. "There's someone here to see you. He's at the nurses' station."

"My cousin? Harlan Cornish?"

"Didn't catch his name. A man, though, with a big bouquet of flowers."

Uncle Fox had called earlier to say that Harlan might be coming up to visit, and she almost cried with relief at the thought of seeing him.

She nodded eagerly. "Sure. Send him in."

"I'll do that." Patty flicked a glance to her patient. "His color's good."

"When do you think he'll come to?"

"Hard to tell," she said. "His body created the coma to protect itself. But his vitals are better and better. Stay hopeful."

Laire's eyes filled with more useless, painful tears, and she nodded, turning back to her father. When she heard the sound of a man's heavy footsteps, she didn't look over her shoulder.

"Hey, Harlan. You can put the flowers anywhere."

"Laire."

The voice wasn't Harlan's, but it was just as familiar—soft and worried, deep and beautiful. It was the voice of her dreams, of her torment, and every space in between. Laire's breath caught with a sudden burst of love she didn't want to feel, but she was in control of herself enough not to turn and face him.

"Laire? How you doing, darlin'?"

"Erik," she murmured. "What are you doing here?"

His hand landed on her shoulder. "I was worried when you didn't show up to work. I called King Triton."

She whipped her head to face him. "You did *what*?"

"I pretended I was a café owner," he said, his eyes registering instant concern as they carefully swept her face. "What . . ." He cringed, reaching up to gently touch the bandage covering her stitches. "What happened to your head?"

She recoiled from his touch, quickly reaching up for his hand and leaving it to hang in the air between them. "Don't touch."

He searched her eyes. "Okay. But what happ—"

"Doesn't matter. You *can't* be here."

"I was worried."

"You. Can. *Not*. Be. Here," she repeated in a grave, urgent whisper, flicking worried eyes to her father, who slept peacefully, before looking back up at Erik. "Go."

"Laire," he said, his eyebrows knitting together in confusion. "I just . . ."

"You *have* to go," she insisted, turning back to her father. "*Now*."

"I'll wait for you—"

"No."

"—in the cafeteria," he said, his voice serious and losing patience. "I'm not leavin' till you come talk to me."

"Don't you *understand*?" she bit out in a furious rush, her eyes flashing, regret and anger rushing to the fore of her confused emotions. "My father almost *died*! Might *still* die! I *can't* talk to you. Go home, Erik. Go back to Raleigh. Go back to Duke. Leave me alone!"

Her words knocked him off-balance. She saw it. She felt it. And it hurt like a sharp knife to a soft place.

"Leave you . . .?"

"Alone. I mean it," she said, keeping her face stony even as goddamn tears trailed down her cheeks, betraying her. "Please leave."

"Darlin', I don't have to go until Thursday. I can be here with you every—"

"No, you *can't*! You're not listening to me!" she cried. "I'm not your darlin'. I'm not your anything. We were just a . . . a fling. A fantasy. I'm an islander; you're a dingbatter. It's over."

He flinched, his face twisting as her words sank in.

Laire looked away, concealing a whimper and ignoring the cracking and breaking of her heart. It had already been torn in half between her father and her lover. Now those halves were splintering into tiny pieces, painful shards, in this hospital room where her father lay unconscious and her lover begged for something she couldn't give him: more time. They'd run out of time in spectacular fashion, and everything that had existed between them didn't feel real—felt like a fantasy, like a sweet dream that had ended in a gruesome nightmare.

"Please go," she begged him.

"I don't understand."

"There's nothing to understand. The summer's over. *We're* over."

He'd been leaning down toward her, but he straightened up, still looking down at her, his eyes fraught and confused as they searched hers. His voice low, but fierce, his face as shattered as her heart, he asked, "Why . . . why're you doin' this? I'm sorry about your father . . . but we *love* each other."

She sucked in a painful breath, the truth of his words biting at her. He *did* love her, and she *did* love him, but Laire Maiden Cornish had gotten a bleak and sudden dose of reality when her father went into cardiac arrest because of her recklessness. She and Erik were an impossibility in the real world. There was no use pretending any differently.

"No," she said, hating herself, hating him, hating her father, lying so still and silent between them, hating her sisters and the Pamlico House and the whole fucking world. "It wasn't *real*, Erik. It wasn't *real*."

He gasped, blinking at her in disbelief as his face blanched to white. White. Like white-hot pain. She could see it. She could feel it, and it burned her inside like nothing she'd ever felt before.

"You can't mean that, dar—"

"Laire? Everythin' okay?" Over Erik's shoulder, Kyrstin came into view, standing with her hands on her hips just behind Erik. "I'm back. I woke up early."

"Kyrs," she murmured, clenching her jaw to try to stanch her tears.

"I'm Kyrstin," she said to Erik. "You are . . .?"

"No one!" said Laire, springing up from the chair beside her father. She shifted her eyes from Kyrstin to Erik. "He's no one. He's just in the wrong room. You were leaving, weren't you?"

Erik's eyes shuddered as if he'd been sucker punched, and when they opened, they were glistening and heavy. He turned to Kyrstin. "Yeah. I'm . . . I'm leavin'."

Kyrstin raised her eyebrows, taking a good look at him before shifting her stare to Laire, who stood with her fists clenched by her side. After a moment, she slid her gaze back to Erik. "Nurses' station can help you find whoever you're lookin' for."

Erik clenched his jaw, then swallowed, nodding at Kyrstin before looking at Laire.

"I'm sorry," he said, and if those shards had any chance of repair, now they were blown to dusty smithereens with the deep sorrow, deep regret, she heard in his voice. "I'm sorry to have bothered you."

He leaned forward to place the flowers on the table at the foot of her father's bed, met her eyes one last time, then turned and left the room.

She watched him go, felt the burn in her lungs and in her eyes and everywhere he'd so lovingly touched. She'd never known pain like this. Not when her mother died. Not ever. And yet she blinked until her tears retreated. Then she lifted her chin and her gaze to her sister.

Laire and Kyrstin stood in silence, facing each other, neither of them saying anything.

Finally, after what felt like an eternity, Kyrstin pulled a chair to the opposite side of their father's bed and sat down, taking their father's right hand, and Laire, who'd made her choice, for better or worse, sat down across from her sister, and took his left.

## Chapter 15

### *Three months later*

Erik Rexford was drinking way too much.

His grades were shit.

He'd been benched from the Devils.

He'd been placed on both academic and social probation.

And the media was having a heyday.

There were rumors about why he'd changed from a golden-boy college athlete to a bad-boy, out-of-control drunk who'd been suspended for the rest of the hockey season after three fights on the ice.

Some attributed the change to his on-again, off-again relationship with Vanessa Osborn, who had been swept off her dainty feet by the British independent filmmaker Phillip Longfellow, known in peerage circles as the fifth Viscount Longfellow, during a summer sojourn in London while Erik remained at his family's summer home in the Outer Banks.

Others wondered why Erik had kept such a low profile all summer. Instead of partying with his fraternity brothers in Durham or making the society pages at posh events in Raleigh, he'd been spied only once: with Vanessa, at a party at the Governor's Mansion in July. Maybe he was depressed? Or on drugs?

There were others who waved his bad behavior aside as healthy college hormones, and still others who called him a spoiled brat who needed a firmer hand.

Only Erik, and his sister, Hillary, knew the true reason for the great change in his disposition:

Erik Rexford's heart had been permanently and irrevocably broken.

*Buzz. Buzz, buzz, buzz.*

*Buzz. Buzz, buzz, buzz.*

"Fuckin' shut up!" yelled Erik, throwing an extra pillow from his bed in the direction of his cell phone, which was probably still in the hip pocket of the jeans he'd worn last night.

*Buzz. Buzz, buzz, buzz.*

"Fuck!"

Squinting from the stream of bright light filtering through his bedroom window, he groaned as he flipped onto his back.

*Buzz. Buzz, buzz, buzz.*

*Buzz. Buzz, buzz, buzz.*

"Fuckin' *fuck*, Hills!"

Scrambling out of bed naked, he grabbed his jeans off the floor and took out the offending phone. Hitting the Talk button, he pressed the phone to his ear.

"*What?*"

"Oh, there it is: the sweet voice of my darlin' brother. Good mornin' to you too."

"It's fuckin' early," he grated out, sitting on the edge of his bed.

"It's noon."

"So fuckin' what."

Hillary sighed, and he imagined her rubbing her forehead with consternation. "So it's also Thanksgivin' on Thursday. My classes end tomorrow. Are you goin' out to Buxton, or what?"

Thanksgiving.

Fuck.

He hated the word. He didn't want to hear it. He definitely didn't want to celebrate it.

"No."

"So you're leavin' me to the wolves."

"Fancy's furious at me. Daddy can't look at me without explodin'. I'm sure they'd both prefer it if I wasn't there."

"I'm sure they'd both prefer it if you got your shit together."

"Hills—"

"I *know* what happened," she said in a rush, "and I know it hurt you. *Bad.* But you have to move on at some point. You can't self-destruct!"

"Why not?" he asked softly, clenching his jaw and swallowing over the giant lump in his throat.

Laire had been so stony, so cold, that day in the hospital, he'd tried going back the following day, hoping she'd softened a little, but she'd told the nurses not to allow him to visit. They'd taken one look at his driver's license and politely asked him to leave. With no other choice, he returned to school that following Thursday, but he called King Triton more times than he could count during the first two or three weeks back at Duke.

The first time she answered, his heart soared at the sound of her voice, and he begged her not to hang up. He could hear her breathing into the phone, ragged and shallow, as he told her he loved her. But no more than two or three seconds passed before he heard the click of the call disconnecting and the drone of the dial tone.

About a week later, she answered again, but this time she spoke first.

"Stop callin' here."

"Laire? Laire, darlin', I need to talk to you. Please, just—"

"It's over, Erik."

"No. I can't accept that."

"You're deluding yourself."

"Tell me what I can do. Please. *Please*, Laire."

"It's over. You need to let me go."

And the line went dead.

He couldn't get his head around it. He didn't understand. Yes, her father had had a heart attack, and he understood that she loved her father, and he even understood that the cold way she'd behaved in the hospital, while incredibly painful for him, made sense. Her sister was coming and going. Her father could wake up at any moment. He was still a secret. The timing was bad.

What he didn't understand was why she hadn't softened by now. Why did she insist that they were over? Why did she think that the love they'd shared was just a fantasy? Why was she closing him out of her life after they'd shared the most amazing summer together?

His mind had returned to that last night over and over again. Had it been a test? To see if he'd keep his word about having sex? And had he let her down—failed the test—by letting things go as far as they did? If that was true, he'd just as soon die that he'd killed their happiness by betraying her . . . except she'd stayed all night after that, waking up in his arms and telling him she loved him.

They'd had a plan in place to see each other over Thanksgiving. And perhaps what he hated the most about himself was that, while he knew, rationally, that she'd broken up with him at the hospital, part of his heart still desperately hoped she'd show.

But if she didn't—if Thanksgiving Day came and went without her—they were really and truly over.

And if that was true, what was he supposed to do with the love he had for her? It was big and wide and real to him, this white-hot, beautiful love that saturated his heart and lived vibrantly in his memories of them. His stupid heart couldn't let go of her. He thought about her, dreamed of her at night, looked at pictures of her on his phone. He drank too much at parties to numb the pain, couldn't concentrate on his studies, and hit too hard against the boards in hockey because he was confused and angry. Angry? No. *Furious*. He was *furious* that she'd turned her back on the best thing he'd ever known.

He loved her.

Fuck, but he loved her more than his own miserable fucking life.

Self-destruction sounded perfect.

"Because I love you," said Hillary gently. "Because I need you. And because if you don't go for Thanksgivin' and she shows up, you won't forgive yourself if you're not there."

Fuck, but his sister knew him too well.

His heart clutched and he bent his head, his voice breaking when he asked, "But what if she doesn't?"

Hillary sighed. "Then it's time to pick up the pieces and finally move on."

*I can't. I can't move on without her. I'll be stuck here in hell, loving her, forever.* Tears pooled in his red, hungover eyes, slipping down his bristly cheeks.

"Fine," he said, softly, hating himself for hoping. "I'll be there."

\*\*\*

Laire wrote up the order she'd just taken over the phone, adjusting her perch on the stool at King Triton and stretching her neck back and forth. With the late-day sun shining through the windows and her uncle and father out making deliveries, the store was quiet, and her eyes grew heavy. She sighed, resting her elbows on the counter and her head on her elbows. This happened every afternoon lately: this drowsy, heavy feeling, like all she wanted to do was take a nap.

Fatigue. The very word scared her. She'd heard it enough times while her mother's health was declining.

Something was wrong with her, and she'd been ignoring the symptoms for a few weeks, but today, since it was quiet, she needed to get on the internet and try to figure out what was going on. Her father had had an iron deficiency after his first heart attack—maybe that was it? She prayed there wasn't something more serious wrong.

Opening her eyes and sitting up, she clicked on the mouse and waited for a search page to come up.

In addition to daily fatigue, the smell of certain kinds of fish, which had never bothered her before, now turned her stomach. Not to mention, she had this out-of-control appetite suddenly. As a result, she'd gotten a little liberal with the comfort food this fall, and her jeans bit into her abdomen uncomfortably. She was overweight and constantly tired and had occasional nausea.

She was also sad.

So fucking sad all the time.

A sad shell of her former self.

She was sad that she had caused her father's heart attack and worked, every day, to win back his trust and love. But it was an uphill battle, and more and more, she suspected that something had changed—or been destroyed—between them. He could barely look her in the eyes. There was no teasing, no asking about her day. And when he did look at her, his shame was so apparent, so sharp and thick, it made her cringe with self-loathing. She didn't know how, but she needed to redeem herself. She desperately needed to win back her father's love.

And it wasn't just her father either. She was sad that Kyrstin and Issy looked at her differently now: not like their beloved little sister, but someone tarnished, someone a little dirty, someone who didn't follow the rules and had gotten herself in trouble. They didn't know where she'd been that night, but they studied her with shrewd eyes, trying to figure out if she was still pure. She wasn't, of course. She was spoiled now. And though it had felt worth it in the heat of the moment to open her legs for Erik Rexford, she didn't know if it was worth it now that she was paying the price for her lust and hedonism.

She was sad that the rest of Corey Island had found out about her night away, when her father had searched frantically for her that evening. And now they speculated in whispers that cut off abruptly, about where she'd been, and with whom. She had been the highlight of the Corey gossip mill for months now, the subject of low-toned rumors and haughty, knowing looks. It would be a long time before the islanders forgot about her missing night. In fact, it was an episode that would follow her around for the rest of her life, changing the way people saw her and interacted with her. She was a little less worthy now. A little too worldly.

She was so sad, she hadn't designed a blouse or a dress in months, not that anyone had asked. But her fingers weren't interested in creating something beautiful. Not for herself or someone else. It was like all her creative energy had been siphoned away when she watched Erik walk out of her father's hospital room with a broken heart. It was like she had killed the best part of herself when she ripped out his heart and stomped on it.

She was so sad that she forbade herself to think about Erik because she worried for her sanity if she did. When she dreamed of him, she woke up crying uncontrollably and had even woken up her father once or twice.

The love she bore for him was ceaseless and throbbing, an open wound on her heart that made her feel like she was dying inside. Unlike his life, which had certainly sped up with his move back to college, hers had slowed down. Unable to use her father's boat, she was trapped on Corey, working every day at King Triton, where her father and uncle were constantly in and out and could keep an eye on her. Since barely anyone spoke to her anymore, she was left for quiet hours alone with her thoughts, and she tortured herself, second-guessing her decision to force Erik from her life. But what had been her alternative? Her decision to be with Erik had almost killed her father. No matter how much she loved Erik, she loved her father more, didn't she? Yes, of course she did. She *should*, right? A good daughter would choose her father's health over the love of her life, wouldn't she?

And yet her love for Erik hadn't died, as she'd hoped. It lived, strong and aching, within her, hoping for a day when it might be allowed to thrive again.

She sighed, feeling mentally exhausted as she looked back down at the computer.

The cursor was blinking.

She typed "weight gain, fatigue, nausea" and pressed Enter. WebMD came up with a list of possible health concerns:

Depression. Well, yes. That made sense. But her symptoms were physical, not just mental. She felt it in her gut—something more significant was going on.

Type 2 diabetes. Hmm. She bit her bottom lip, trying to remember if there was diabetes on either side of her family, but she came up dry. Still, she ripped a piece of paper from a notepad under the counter and wrote down the disease.

Congestive heart failure. Her breath hitched. Certainly heart problems ran in her family, considering her father's two heart attacks. She wrote down the three words carefully, frowning at them.

Hypothyroidism. She read the word slowly aloud, "Hypo-thyroid-ism," and her fingers grew instantly cold, withdrawing from the mouse in horror as she stared at the second syllable.

*Thyroid.*

Her breathing hitched as she whispered it again, "*Thyroid.*"

Laire's mother had died of medullary thyroid cancer, a

cancer that might have been treatable had it been discovered before stage 4.

Without waiting another moment, she picked up the phone and dialed the Hatteras Health Center, making an appointment to see the nurse practitioner tomorrow and have some blood tests run on her thyroid.

Because she hadn't been allowed to use her father's boat since the day she'd returned from staying overnight with Erik, she asked Kyrstin if she'd drive her over to Hatteras for her appointment, and after sharing her fears, Kyrstin agreed.

The next afternoon, Laire sat uneasily on the paper-covered examination table while one nurse prepared three plastic vials for a blood draw and another nurse analyzed Laire's urine in a small room beside the bathroom.

A knock at the exam room door made Laire look up.

The nurse doing the urine analysis peeked into the room. "Can I, uh, speak to you for a second?" she asked her colleague. "I'm not sure you need to, um, to do the draw."

"Will you excuse us?"

Laire had spent a few minutes online yesterday, reading through the symptoms for hypothyroidism, and with every additional page of information, she was more and more certain that she was suffering from a precursor to the disease that had killed her mother.

In a strange way, she felt at peace with this realization. If she was sick, it would supersede her transgressions. She would have to undergo surgery in Carteret, like her mother, and maybe even chemotherapy on a weekly basis. Her father and sisters would have to drive her over to the mainland, fuss over her, and worry for her safety and care. And maybe it sounded crazy, but if cancer was what it would take to draw them all back together, Laire was ready to face it. No. More than that. She was ready to *embrace* it.

The nurse reentered the room, taking a deep breath and

cocking her head to the side as she stared at Laire.

"Laire, on your admittance form you said you weren't sexually active."

She stared at the nurse, who held a piece of paper in her hand. "I'm not."

The nurse took another deep breath, her brow knitting as she looked down at the paper. When she looked back up at Laire, her expression was severe. "Not at all?"

Laire's mind skated back to her night with Erik, but he'd barely been inside her for more than a few seconds, and he'd climaxed on her stomach. That didn't count, did it?

"Really, I—"

"Laire, honey," said the nurse, taking a step forward and placing a calming hand on her arm, "are you sure you haven't been with anyone? Sexually? Maybe . . . it wasn't your choice? Did someone . . . force you or—"

"No!" she said, shaking her head as she jerked her arm back. "Nothing like that! I swear."

"Then . . ."

She glanced at the printout in the nurse's hand, her stomach clenching with worry. "What does it say on that paper?"

"Well, it seems that your urine test revealed the presence of . . ." She paused, searching Laire's face. ". . . the pregnancy hormone hCG. In fact, we found 288,000 mIU/ml in your urine. That level is commensurate with a woman who is ten to twelve weeks pregnant."

Laire. Stopped. Breathing.

She stared up at the nurse blankly, in stark horror, trying desperately to get her head around what the nurse was saying.

The nurse smiled gently. "It would also explain your fatigue, increased appetite, and weight gain, especially around the abdomen."

"No."

"Yes, I think—"

"*Pregnant?* You're saying I'm *pregnant*?" she cried.

"It looks that way. Yes."

As the nurse reached for her arm again, Laire shook her head, murmuring, "No. No, no, no, no, no. You're wrong. You're . . . wrong."

"I don't think we are."

"*You are*!" she screamed.

"Calm down, Laire," said the nurse, squeezing her arm gently. "You need to calm down."

"No! This can't be happening! I thought cancer. It's cancer, like my mama!"

"We can still do blood tests if you want, but you have no real symptoms of hypothyroidism that can't be explained by pregnancy. This diagnosis makes more sense, and the urinalysis—"

"I don't care about that! It's *wrong*!"

"It isn't wrong." The nurse looked down at the sheet in her hand again. "It's correct, Laire. You're about three months along."

"Oh, my God, no! This can't be happening!" she shrieked, leaping off the table and backing away from the nurse.

"Dear," said the nurse, standing back and holding up her palms. "It's okay. You need to calm down, or you'll hurt the—"

"Shut up!" she screamed. "It's not okay! It's not! It's not true!"

Tears were streaming down her face as the nurse opened the door, called to the other nurse, spoke to her briefly, then turned back to Laire.

"Laire, there are options."

*Options? On Corey Island? With her father? With her sisters? No. There were no options. There was nothing but rejection and shame and humiliation. Options?!*

She shrieked with a high-pitched laugh that sounded as crazy as she felt.

"Please sit back down, Laire. I just asked the nurse to get your sister."

"What?" gasped Laire, her eyes widening almost impossibly. "No! Noooo! Don't tell her! Don't—"

She lurched forward, pushed the nurse away, and ran from the exam room, trying to reach Kyrstin before she heard the shameful truth, but as she arrived in the waiting room, one look on Kyrstin's face told her she was too late.

"Laire," said Kyrstin, looking over the nurse's shoulder, her voice a whisper, her face white. "What have you done?"

## Chapter 16

Laire and Kyrstin walked down the road, to the Dancing Turtle coffee shop, in silence, the only sound a bottle of prenatal vitamins shaking like a baby rattle in Laire's purse with every step she took.

Sitting at a table by the windows, Kyrstin ordered them two cups of coffee, then folded her hands on the table, waiting to speak until Laire finally looked up and met her eyes.

"So?" asked Kyrstin. "What're you goin' to do?"

Laire sniffled, shaking her head. "I don't know."

"I just thought you were eatin' too many doughnuts."

"Don't joke," said Laire.

"I'm not!" insisted Kyrstin. "You got yourself a little poochie tummy, Laire. Ain't goin' to be long before others notice it too."

"I can't . . . I can't . . ."

"You can't what? Can't have it or can't kill it?"

Laire had been staring at a crack in the tabletop's Formica, but now she snapped her head up and looked at her sister in horror. "I'm *not* killing my baby!"

*Erik's* baby.

For the first time since receiving the devastating news, her heart clenched with the awesomeness of it: *Erik's baby.* Inside her body. She dropped her hands to her belly and rested them over the small swell protectively.

"Great," said Kyrstin, nodding curtly at the waitress who brought their coffee. "Choice one made. You're keepin' it."

"I'm keeping it," whispered Laire, unable to keep her lips from turning up in a tiny smile, as she allowed herself to remember, for the first time since she left him that morning, how beautiful she felt nestled naked in his arms.

"Where, *exactly*, are you raisin' it?" asked Kyrstin, stirring some creamer into the steaming cup and forcing Laire back to earth.

Laire reached for the sugar and overturned the cylinder, letting the white crystals spill into her coffee. They reminded her of sand in an hourglass, moving too quickly when she needed more time.

"I don't—"

"It'll kill Daddy," said Kyrstin, her voice no-nonsense and eyes lethal. "Just so we're clear, li'l Laire, let's review the facts: you runnin' around with some unknown boy gave him a coronary. Knocked up and unmarried? It'll *kill* him." Kyrstin clenched her jaw before sipping her coffee. "So I'm askin' you again: where you gonna raise your baby?"

A chill went through Laire, freezing her brief moment of happiness.

Kyrstin was right.

Finding out his eighteen-year-old, unmarried daughter was pregnant would kill Hook Cornish, so she had a couple of options: one, get married, or two, leave Corey before she really started showing.

"Get . . . married?" she asked Kyrstin timidly.

"Fine. That's an option. Get married, and then you can tell Daddy it was a weddin'-night baby. Everyone will know it wasn't, but nobody'll say anythin' if you're married."

Laire stirred her coffee absentmindedly, allowing her mind, for the first time in over two months, to think—really *think*—about the possibility of a future with Erik Rexford.

"So who you gonna marry?"

"What do you mean, *who*?" Laire cocked her head to the side. "The baby's father, of course."

"And he'll be just thrilled about this, huh?"

Laire dropped her sister's gaze, thinking about Erik's beautiful face, his desperate voice on the phone, the way he'd looked at her, spoken to her, held her. *I love you, Laire.*

"I don't know if he'll be thrilled, but he loves me." She nodded. "I think he'll do what's right."

"Laire," said Kyrstin. "I never asked, but that was *him*, wasn't it? At the hospital that day?"

Laire met her sister's eyes, gulping as she admitted the truth. "Yeah."

"Is he local? From Ocracoke? Or—"

She shook her head. "Summer dingbatter."

"Oh, fuck," whispered Kyrstin. "From where?"

"He has a house in Buxton."

"From *where*?" asked Kyrstin again.

"Raleigh." She took a deep breath before leveling her eyes with Kyrstin's. "His name is Erik Rexford. He's . . ." She gulped again. "He's the governor's son."

Kyrstin stared at her for a moment, her mouth open. "The governor of *what*?"

"N-North Carolina."

"*What?* What the *fuck* are you talkin' about?" She held her coffee cup frozen midway to her lips. "You were datin' the goddamn governor's son all summer? *He* knocked you up?"

Laire nodded, taking a small sip of the coffee but finding it too bitter to enjoy.

"Oh, Laire," said Kyrstin, taking a long sip, her wide eyes over the rim registering complete and utter shock. "Oh, my

God."

"I'll go see him," said Laire quickly. "We had . . . we had a plan . . . to meet at Thanksgiving."

"You had a *plan*?" Kyrstin scoffed. "We don't know how people like that work! Laire, you don't know he'll do right! Oh, my God. This is—"

"He will. I know he will. I know him. He loves me."

"How do you know that?" Kyrstin leaned forward. "I thought you broke it off with him that day at the hospital. It's been months. Long enough for him to move on."

Kyrstin's well-chosen words hit a tender spot, and Laire winced, reaching up to wipe the tears that had started falling.

"I thought I was doing the right thing."

"How's that exactly?"

"Daddy was sick and I was so scared, Kyrs. I thought . . . I needed to be a good daughter. And I . . . I blamed him some. We'd spent the summer together, but *my* father was lying unconscious, while he was heading back to his fairy-tale life at college. It wasn't fair. It was easier to believe that there wasn't any chance for us to—"

"Enough melodrama. You need a plan," said Kyrstin, dabbing at her lips. "You talked to him since?"

"He tried to call me at King Triton in September, but . . ."

"But what?"

"I told him to stop bothering me. Eventually he stopped."

"So you've had no contact with him in two months, but you're gonna walk up to his house, tell him you're pregnant, and ask him to marry you?" She laughed the way Laire had laughed in the doctor's office—high-pitched and a little crazy. "That's *not* a plan."

"What other choice do I have, Kyrstin?"

Kyrstin locked her eyes with her little sister's, her lips thin and white. When she spoke, her voice was low and merciless.

"Forget the governor's son. Find an island boy and fuck him fast."

Laire's eyes widened in horror and she recoiled in her seat. "No."

Kyrstin nodded. "Brodie's still up for grabs. Drinks a lot. You'd just have to seduce him once."

"No!" Laire sobbed. "I don't want Brodie! I love Erik!"

"Who cares?" growled Kyrstin in a furious whisper. "You need a solution and I'm givin' you one."

"I can't do that," she said, weeping.

"Laire!" said Kyrstin fiercely, reaching for her sister's hands. "You gotta get married fast. Fast, you hear? You gotta get married and make this right . . ." She searched Laire's eyes frantically as her grip tightened painfully. ". . . or you can't *never* come home. You know that? You *understand* that? Never, ever. You'd be dead to us. Forever."

Laire clenched her jaw as tears streamed down her cheeks.

Kyrstin continued, her tone and fingers merciless. "So you figure out what you have to do and you do it. You got yourself in this mess. You *need* to make it right."

"I get it," sobbed Laire, wresting her hands free and rubbing the feeling back into them. "I get it."

"I ain't feelin' sorry for you, Laire," said Kyrstin, though her voice, edged with concern, betrayed her. "You don't wanna take a swing at Brodie Walsh? Fine. Then after our Thanksgivin' dinner with Daddy, we'll say you're stayin' the night at my house, and Remy can run you up to Buxton. You can tell your . . . *boyfriend* what's happened, tell him he has to marry you— much good it'll do you."

"Why don't you think he will?" asked Laire, her voice soft and broken. "Why can't you be positive?"

"Because I'm not a goddamned *idiot*. Because those people ain't *our* people. They don't live their lives the same way we do, Laire. They got different values, different priorities. You *know* that. You can't expect nothin'. I certainly don't. When you come on back from Buxton with your heart in tatters, you can choose an island boy and set up a date. Get him drunk. Fuck him. And he'll do right by you."

"I can't seduce someone I don't love just so my baby has a daddy. I can't . . .," she said, reaching up to dry her cheeks again. The very idea chipped away at her soul. Trapped on Corey for the rest of her life with a man she didn't love? It was a fate worse than death for Laire, who wanted so much more than Corey could offer.

"Then get a ring from the governor's son," said Kyrstin acidly, "and good fuckin' luck."

Kyrstin's doubts made Laire wince, made her doubt herself. But Erik had loved her, hadn't he? Yes. Yes, she was sure that he ha d. Then again, fear and anger had caused her to choose her family over Erik. She had rejected him and hurt him, forced him out of her life. What if he *had* stopped loving her? What if he *had* moved on as she'd urged him to do?

"What if he doesn't give me one?" she murmured, stricken. "A ring?"

Kyrstin raised her chin, her face sad for an instant before it frosted over. "Then you know what you have to do. And if you won't do it, don't come home."

***

Laire had made the drive from Corey to Buxton over a hundred times over the summer, but now? In the middle of November with Remy cold and silent at the helm? It was freezing and wet and completely unpleasant. Nothing like the long, warm days of summer, when she loved feeling the wind in her hair and thinking about her blossoming love with Erik Rexford.

Kyrstin explained to Remy what had happened, and Laire felt his disapproval and disgust in the looks he'd given her today. She could barely keep down a bite of turkey, the only glimmer of hope watching Issy with baby Kyle and thinking that she'd have her own little angel to love in six short months.

The most surprising thing about discovering her pregnancy, two days ago, was the speed at which her feelings about motherhood had changed. Laire had always regarded pregnancy as a trap—a way to keep an island girl on Corey forever, whether she wanted to be there or not. But now? With Erik's baby growing inside her? Her entire heart had shifted. Her love for her son or daughter was rivaled only by her love for Erik, and with a hope that edged into desperation, she prayed that Erik would welcome her back into his life. They'd figure out a way to make it work, right? Once they were married, he could return to Duke to graduate, and she could live with Kyrstin and Remy until he had his degree. And okay, her daddy might not love it at first, but a daughter respectably married, with a li'l'un on the way, would eventually bring him around, wouldn't it?

And once Erik finished college, the sky was the limit: she and Erik and their baby could form a new life wherever they wanted. She didn't care where, as long as they were together.

Stepping onto the Rexfords' dock in the darkness, she looked up at Remy, briefly wondering if she'd ever see him again, then banishing the thought from her mind and giving him a weak smile. "I'll see you soon?"

"I'm s'pose to leave you here." Remy shrugged. "And Kyrs said to remind you not to come back 'les you're wearin' a ring."

"I won't," she said. *But I'll get that ring. I know it.*

"Then, uh, good luck, I guess," said Remy, raising a hand in farewell as he pulled away from the dock and turned back into the dark Sound.

She gulped nervously, watching his stern lights get smaller and smaller, until she couldn't see them at all anymore, then she turned and walked up to the boardwalk.

*Go out with me..*

*I can't..*

Voices from the past haunted her as she stepped carefully over the planks in the dark, remembering the first time she'd ever set eyes on Erik Rexford.

*I will find you! That's a promise, Laire Cornish!*
*Damn it to hell and back! Fine! You win!*

As she reached the pool deck, she could see a party going on in the living room, a large group of people holding Champagne glasses as waitresses in black and white passed silver trays of light bites.

*Oh, God, please don't let him hate me*, she prayed silently. *Please let him understand I only pushed him away because I was scared and hurting.*

She walked around the pool, by the chairs where they'd held hands, stargazing and talking about Thanksgiving.

Here she was, after all.

On Thanksgiving.

She stopped a short distance from the glass doors, staring at the party inside, at the pianist playing jaunty carols and the merry ding of crystal against crystal. She didn't see Erik, but he was in there somewhere, and her heart clenched with joy, with hope, and yes, with relief. She had missed him. She had missed him too desperately for words.

Taking a step forward, she raised her chin and—

"Can I help you?" asked a smooth, deep voice, and Laire turned to the right to see Fancy Rexford, the First Lady of North Carolina and Erik's mother, leaning against a porch column in the darkness, a lit cigarette dangling from her fingers, the orange bud bright and beautiful in the darkness.

"Good evening, ma'am," she whispered. She cleared her throat, telling herself to be brave as she walked away from the doors and over to Mrs. Rexford. "Happy Thanksgiving."

"Who are you?" she asked without preamble.

"I've come to see Erik."

"Have you?" she asked. "And . . . does Erik *know* you?"

She nodded. "Yes, ma'am. We're, um . . . we're friends."

"Friends?" she asked, looking at Laire's green blouse and simple black skirt with a sniff. "What *friend*? I've never seen you before."

She had a crystal glass in her other hand, filled with ice cubes and clear liquid, and it clinked as she took a sip, reminding Laire of the first moment she'd ever seen Erik.

Laire wasn't easily intimidated, but Mrs. Rexford was formidable, even in the dark, Maybe especially in the dark. She cleared her throat. "Well, we, um . . . we spent some time together this summer."

"*You*? And Erik?" She laughed, a light tinkling sound like how posh ladies sounded on soap operas or in the movies. "Oh, no. No, dear. I don't think so."

"I swear to you. I know Erik. I need . . . I need to see him. It's urgent." Her hands moved to her belly protectively, and Fancy's eyes dropped to Laire's stomach, narrowing in understanding before sliding slowly back up to her face.

She popped her cigarette between her lips, grabbed Laire's arm, and yanked her into a shadow, searching her eyes.

"Who the *fuck* do you think you are?" she asked in a hiss, her voice fierce with menace.

"Ma'am . . ."

Fancy released Laire's arm and blew a stream of smoke into the sky before looking back at her. "You're trespassin' on my property."

"No, ma'am. I was invited."

"Not by me you weren't."

Laire's heart sped up and her breathing became more shallow. "By Erik."

"I don't believe you," she said, taking another draw on her cigarette. "Probably saw his picture in a magazine."

"Please, ma'am."

"Please what?"

"I need to see him."

"Why?"

"I'm . . . *expecting*."

Fancy's eyes flared with fury, and she stepped forward, forcing Laire to back up toward the pool, farther away from the house. "You're *expecting* an ass whoopin' . . . because you're a liar and an opportunist and a goddamned little gold digger comin' here on Thanksgivin' Day with your disgustin' lies about my son."

"No, ma'am, I swear," she said, taking another step back. "I'm tellin' the truth. Please just let Erik—"

"You're *not*," said Fancy, taking another sip of her drink. "What do you want? Money? You heard that Erik Rexford spent his summers on the Banks, and you came up with a plan to extort money from his family? You wouldn't be the first little bitch to come up with such a clever plan, but you have underestimated your target, girl."

"How . . . What do you mean?"

"My boy? My Erik? He's *taken*. He's been good and taken for a while now, which is how I know he was *never* with you."

"W-what? What do you mean?"

Fancy threw her cigarette to the ground and reached for Laire's arm again, holding it with an iron grip and pulling her toward the sliding doors. It was dark outside so, while they could see in, it wasn't likely that the folks inside eating and drinking could see them.

This time, Laire found Erik immediately, and her heart burst with joy, then clenched in sorrow. His dark hair, thick and unruly, was so familiar, her fingers twitched to touch it. But as she caressed his face, it was impossible not to notice that it was sallow and drawn. He'd lost some weight too. Because of her?

Had he been as lovesick for her as she'd been for him? She took a step toward him, but Fancy's fingers dug painfully into her arm.

"See that stunnin' girl next to my handsome son?"

For the first time, Laire realized that Erik had his arm around a dark-haired beauty, dressed in a couture cream and gold cocktail dress. She held a Champagne flute like she'd been born with it in her hands, smiling at at Erik like he hung the moon. Who was she? And why did she look so familiar?

"That's Vanessa Osborn," said Fancy. "Erik's lifelong love, Van."

*Van. Van.* Her lungs stopped working. *But Van is . . . is . . .*

"Van?" she repeated dumbly, staring at the beautiful girl she'd seen in so many of the pictures in Erik's living room. "No, that's not Van."

"Of course it is," said Fancy, releasing Laire to sip her cocktail. "I've known Van all my life. So has Erik."

With her eyes, Laire traced Erik's arm from his shoulder to where it rested comfortably around Vanessa's shoulders, his hand curved possessively over her shoulder like a cape.

"No. No," she said weakly, her voice cracking as the terrible truth of Fancy's words sank in. "Van's a *man*. He's . . ."

"What in the hell are you *talkin'*—Does that *look* like a man to you?"

"No," sobbed Laire softly, staring at them together—their matching dark heads and perfect, patrician faces. Vanessa would have a deep and cultured voice like Erik's mother, wouldn't she? A beautiful, refined Southern accent to match Erik's. She was perfect for him. She was his match in every way.

. . . which meant . . .

*Oh, God.*

. . . he'd lied to her. He'd allowed her to believe that he was available when he clearly was not. He'd allowed her to think—every time he mentioned Van—that she was a he, when really she was . . . she was his . . .

"Oh, God," whispered Laire as memories she treasured started shattering, recontextualized into terrible lies.

"Why?" she whimpered, her whole body trembling as she stared down at her toes. *Why?*

To get her into bed? To have two girls at once? Was it some sick prank to fuck an island girl? Was she just a challenge? Had he felt anything for her? Had he just used her for a backup fling? *Oh, God, why?*

She looked up again. Van—*Vanessa*—held up her hand, on which she wore a diamond ring. She waggled it in front of Erik and giggled as he shrugged, then chuckled along with her.

Fancy, who had lit another cigarette, leaned closer to Laire, her tone conspiratorial. "See the ring on her finger? My grandmother's ring. Now hers."

The wind was sucked from Laire's lungs, and her stomach turned with the few bites of turkey she'd been able to hold down earlier. *He's engaged. He's engaged to someone else. The ring I need belongs to someone else.*

She sobbed, turning away from Erik's mother and stepping quickly over to the shrubbery that circled the pool deck.

"Aw," said Fancy. "Well, that's just charmin'."

Laire hunched over, retching until her stomach was empty, then turned to face Fancy with tears streaming down her face.

Fancy raised her chin, putting her hands on her hips. She scanned Laire's body with disgust, spending an extra moment on her belly. "I don't know who you are, but my son spent his summer with Vanessa. He's been *with her* for months. Which makes you a liar."

Laire shoulders shook with grief, with the sheer scope and magnitude of his betrayal, and she bent her head, staring down at the pool deck in misery. She'd been so gullible. Such a fool.

"Between you and me?" said Fancy gently. "It was a good

try."

"A good try?" asked Laire, looking up at Mrs. Rexford in confusion.

"A good plan. Simple, local girl. Maybe or maybe not pregnant. Pretty enough. Definitely sympathetic. Shows up at the governor's house on Thanksgivin' Day, when there are plenty of guests, plenty of witnesses. Claims he did the deed. Clever. Devious, but clever."

Laire shook her head as tears coursed down her cheeks, but the lump in her throat made a response impossible.

Fancy's face suddenly hardened, her tone quiet and lethal as she leaned closer to Laire. "But do you know what I hate? Girls who claim they've been touched or raped or toyed with. They drag a boy's name through the mud, splash their dirty lies all over the papers. Then they admit it: 'I just wanted money. I just wanted attention.' Except, that filthy story follows the boy around for life." She dug a finger into Laire's chest. "Well, not *my* boy."

Laire took a step away. "Mrs. Rexford—"

"The jig is up, gal," said Fancy, toeing her cigarette on the deck until the orange light was crushed. "You chose the wrong boy to mess with."

*You chose the wrong boy.*

Laire turned her head, looking over her shoulder to see Erik shake his head indulgently at Vanessa before squeezing her shoulder. Van looked up at him adoringly, saying something that made him laugh, and every hope—every little bit of hope for a happy ending with Erik Rexford—died inside Laire, leaving her cold and empty but for the little, tiny life that deserved far better than him.

*You chose the wrong boy.*

She reached up and dried her tears, lifting her chin as she looked into Fancy Rexford's eyes. "You're right."

Fancy took a deep breath and nodded. "Of course I am. But

as a Thanksgivin' favor to you, I will not call the police and have you arrested for this little ploy. I'm not interested in causin' a scene."

"I chose the wrong boy," said Laire in a daze. "I'm sorry I wasted your time."

"Get along now," said Fancy, finishing her drink. "And don't ever step foot on my property again. If you do, I will be delighted to press charges."

She narrowed her eyes at Laire, then headed back to her party.

Laire watched her slim figure slip through the sliding doors and walk toward Erik, whom she kissed on the cheek, before kissing Van. She took Van's hand in hers, admiring the ring with a wink before turning her glance, briefly, back to the patio. With a victorious grin, she nodded once, then turned back to her son and his fiancée.

And Laire, who was invisible in the darkness, turned away from Fancy, from Erik and his Van, from Utopia Manor, and everything else that could ever connect her with the Rexfords. Around the side of the house, past the kitchen and garage, she ran to the road and just kept running.

*\*\*\**

"I have to give it back to you," said Van to Fancy. "It's just lovely, but I wouldn't forgive myself if I lost it!"

"Aw! It's just a li'l ole cocktail ring. And it looks just perfect on you, darlin'. Go ahead and enjoy it for the party," said Fancy in a singsong voice, her breath reeking of cigarettes and gin. "Maybe someday it'll really be yours."

Van's cheeks colored as she chuckled softly. "Now, Fancy . . ."

"Now, nothin'!" said his mother. "I know you children like your privacy, but whenever you're ready to make it official, Erik, I'm ready to throw the weddin' of the decade!"

Erik rolled his eyes. "Really, Mother . . ."

Fancy leaned forward and kissed his cheek again, clasping his face with uncharacteristic intensity. "You know I'd protect you from anythin', my darlin'. You know that, right?"

Erik was thrown, for a moment, by the sudden fierceness in her voice. "Mother? You okay, now?"

"I'm in my cups," she said, releasing his cheeks with a soft chuckle. She winked at him, grinning like a schoolgirl. "Will y'all excuse me?"

He watched her walk across the room, her gait certain and elegant, though she'd likely had enough alcohol to pickle a horse. "In my cups" was a quaint expression for "drunk," which more than explained her strange behavior.

"She's somethin'," said Van, smiling affectionately.

"That's for sure," said Erik, dropping his arm from her shoulders. He'd gotten used to playing boyfriend with Van over the summer and hadn't broken himself of the habit yet, though the ruse was unnecessary now that he and Laire were over.

"I couldn't believe it when she told me to try it on," said Vanessa, admiring the ring still on her finger. "It was your grandmother's, but she said someday it could be mine."

"I heard her." Erik gave her a sour look. "But we're not even datin', Van."

"I know," she said in a singsong voice, taking a small sip of Champagne. "But we could."

"Didn't I hear you were datin' an earl?" he asked.

"Just a *viscount*," she said, grinning at him, ignoring his mood. She met his eyes, holding them. "Erik, I'm not forward, but you must know . . . I've always had feelin's for you."

"I'm sorry." He looked at her sadly. "I only see you as a friend."

Her face lost some of its hopefulness, but she cocked her head to the side cajolingly. "I'd take my chances that could change. You could take me to the Wake Forest Winter Formal; I could be your date at Duke. We could spend some time together at Christmas break . . . see what happens."

Over Van's shoulder, outside on the pool deck, he saw a shadow move in the darkness, and for a second—for a split second—his heart soared, wondering if Laire had come after all. His heart stopped. His breath caught, and he lurched toward the sliding doors, placing his palms flush on the glass, staring outside at the darkness, his heart thrumming with hope.

"Erik?" asked Van, who'd followed him.

"Did you . . . did you see someone?"

"What? Outside?"

"I think I saw someone! A . . . a girl."

"Are you crazy? It's cold as the North Pole out there!"

Erik whipped open the door and stepped onto the pool deck, looking back and forth, but there was no one there. No boat moored at the dock. No sweet, soft girl telling him she still loved him. Nothing but the faint smell of his mother's cigarette, black and smoky at his feet.

"I thought . . .," he choked out, his insides twisting with disappointment. "I thought I saw . . ."

"There's no one out here," said Van from the doorway. "Come on back inside before you catch your death."

She didn't come.

She didn't come.

It was nine o'clock on Thanksgiving night.

She wasn't coming.

He stared out at the empty pool deck, at the empty dock, getting his ragged breathing under control. She wasn't here and she wasn't coming. They were over—Erik Rexford and Laire Cornish were over—and it was time for him to face the truth.

His heart was broken beyond repair, and he didn't *want* to repair it. He wanted it to stay broken forever. It was the only way to protect it from ever shattering like this again. Reaching up, he pressed the palm of his hand over the broken mess of tissue and blood within, pledging to let it stay broken.

Hillary's words returned to him: *It's time to pick up the pieces and finally move on.*

Okay.

Yes, he'd move on now.

But he would never, ever let himself fall in love again. Never. If he couldn't trust Laire, who'd seemed so earnest, so honest and true, then he couldn't trust anyone. He turned back to the house. Stepping into the living room, he caught sight of his mother across the room, flirting with one of his father's friends, feeling his blood run from hot and hopeful to dead and cold.

Women were deceitful and two-faced, false and dishonest.

They were executioners of hope, assassins of faith.

They could be used, as *he'd* been used by Laire for a summer fling, but that would be the extent of their purpose to him from now on.

From now on, he *hated* women.

That was Laire fucking Cornish's goddamned Thanksgiving gift to him: a legacy of pain and destruction, a future full of hate for and distrust of the opposite sex.

"Erik?" said Van. "Did you hear me before? What do you think? About givin' us a try? A real try?"

"What?" he asked her, looking at her with new eyes that didn't see her as an old family friend, but as an enemy.

"How about givin' us a try?"

"A try," he said softly, as something once soft calcified inexorably within him, unreachable, unfixable, untouchable, dead.

"Erik?" Vanessa whispered. She scanned his face, staring at him warily, her hopeful smile fading.

He looked her body up and down with cold eyes. "No, thanks."

\*\*\*

Laire walked blindly through the night, her tears making the way blurry as the cold wind, hitting her from the Sound and the ocean, bit at her wet cheeks. Making her way to Route 12, she simply walked, aimlessly, trying to process everything she'd just seen and heard.

Even though she'd seen him standing there with his arm around Van—*Vanessa*—part of her still couldn't believe it.

How many times had he told her he loved her? Insisted she was beautiful? Assured her that he wanted her in his life?

How could it have all been lies?

"Rotten, fucking lies," she sobbed, hearing Kyrstin's voice in her head: *Because those people ain't* our *people. They don't live their lives the same way we do, Laire. They got different values, different priorities. You* know *that. You can't expect nothin'.*

She was right. Kyrstin was one hundred percent right. And Laire was a fool of epic proportions. A pregnant fool. A fool who *refused* to go home and trick a local boy into marriage. And *couldn't* go home, because the ring that should have been hers was on another girl's finger.

After twenty minutes of walking, she found herself standing in front of the Pamlico House, blinking in surprise as more tears welled in her eyes. There was only one person in the world she wanted to see, who could—possibly—help her.

She went to the back door of the kitchen and knocked, asking the dishwasher if he could find Ms. Sebastian and send her outside.

She caressed her belly through her black skirt, whispering softly, "We deserve better than him, li'l bean. *You* deserve better."

"Laire?" said Ms. Sebastian, stepping out of the kitchen, smelling of warmth and turkey and cranberries, such a contrast to the bleak cold of the night. "Laire, honey? What a surprise!"

"Ms. Sebastian!" she sobbed, hurtling herself into the older woman's arms and crying torrents on her shoulder.

"Laire! Oh, dear! What's wrong? Are you okay?"

She had no words. The depth of her sorry and fear, worry and exhaustion, were so profound, she couldn't answer.

But thank the Lord for small mercies because Ms. Sebastian, on what was likely the busiest night of the year, held a desperate, distraught Laire close, rubbed her back, and—without knowing anything—promised her that everything was going to be all right.

# INTERLUDE

### *Laire's Christmas Journal*

*The First Christmas*

Dear Erik,

You bought me this journal for sketching on the best day of my life: our perfect day at the Elizabethan Gardens. That was the day you told me you were falling in love with me, and though I didn't say the words, I knew they were true for me too. I said them three days later at my father's fish shop. You came to tell me that you were going up to Raleigh for a few days the only way you knew how.

My God, what an actor you were! What an actor you *are*. I can't stop my tears from falling when I think of those precious days with you, because, whoever you are, you aren't the Erik I fell in love with. *You* are a stranger to me. Wholly. Completely. When I think of you now, I call you the Governor's Son in my mind. I will hate you until the day I die. I promise you that.

But I am not writing to the Governor's Son; I am writing this to *my* Erik—to the man I knew. Even though he doesn't actually exist, I loved him. I still do. It's likely that I always will.

I write these words to him because, no matter how faithless *you* were to me, Governor's Son, I was my truest self with my

Erik.

That day in the hospital when I called us a fantasy, I was lying. I was a frightened girl lying to the boy she loved desperately, hoping that by giving up what she loved most in the world, the trade would assuage God's fury and let her father live.

It worked, to some extent.

My father lived, though in a cruel twist, I still lost him. He never trusted me again and could barely look me in the eyes without shame.

And the Erik I loved turned out to be a fantasy, so I have lost him too.

But I cannot live in a world as brutal and unkind, as faithless and fickle as that of the Governor's Son. I won't allow myself to be hardened. I won't let his poison touch my life. After all, I barely knew him. I can choose to separate him from the Erik I lost.

That Erik, that good, kind, loving, tender man, is preserved in my heart, just as he would be if I had lost him to a tragic accident that terrible Thanksgiving night. That's the Erik I write to here. To the man I knew . . . because, to me, he was real. And I will write to you, my Erik, until I stop grieving your loss. Hopefully, one day, I will have the courage and strength to love again.

I need you to know that I am pregnant with your child.

I found out yesterday that she's a girl, and I plan to name her Ava Grace like the little girl we met that day at the Elizabethan Gardens. I saw her on the ultrasound yesterday, and she has ten fingers and ten toes and I can't wait to see if her hair's dark like yours or red like mine.

Ava Grace is only one of several major changes in my life. Another is that I now live in Boone, far away from the Outer Banks, in the hills of Appalachia. Thanksgiving was Ms. Sebastian's last night of work at the Pamlico House. After I left your house, I ran to her, and when she got off work, we drank tea across from each other at her kitchen table. Surrounded by moving boxes, she invited me to leave the Banks and join her in Boone. I had no other options, so I did.

We live in a little house with views of the mountains. It's near her son, Patrick, who's got shaggy brown hair and kind eyes and is a professor of English at Appalachian State University. Her spare bedroom is my room, and soon it will be Ava Grace's nursery too.

I don't know how I will ever repay Ms. Sebastian's kindness, but if there is ever a chance, I will take it. She is so much more than a friend, sometimes I imagine my own mother sent her to me as an angel to look after me on this journey. I am so thankful for her.

I called my sister Kyrstin the day after Thanksgiving. She wasn't surprised to hear that things didn't work out between me and the Governor's Son. She wished me luck and said she would tell Daddy that I had run away. Believe it or not, Erik, that lie will be much kinder than the reality that I'm unmarried and expecting your child.

I have a job at Harris Teeter, a really nice grocery store in Boone. After I have the baby, I may try to find another waitressing position. My tips at the Pamlico House were good.

Ava Grace wiggles inside me all the time, and I cry myself to sleep, missing you and mourning your loss and dreaming of your face. Those dreams are brutal, reminding me in such minute detail of the way you touched me, Erik—the way you looked at me and told me you loved me. I miss you so much, it eats me up inside, but you are gone, and the only way I can survive your loss is to imagine you are dead.

My tears are smearing the ink so I will close now.

Merry Christmas, my Erik.

*Laire*

\*\*\*

*The Second Christmas*

Dear Erik,

So much has happened in a year, it's hard to imagine it's been that long since I opened the journal and wrote to you, but I will try to fill you in on all that's happened.

We have a daughter, Ava Grace Cornish, who's seven months old and the happiest baby you've ever seen. And why shouldn't she be happy? Ms. Sebastian (aka Nana and Judith) dotes on her like the grandmother she lost so long ago, and Uncle Patrick has probably purchased every stuffed animal to be found in Boone. They cover her nursery (my old room) and my room (the spare room, now mine) and Judith's room (Nana wouldn't have it any other way), and Ava laughs and laughs when we make them dance and squeak.

She laughs all the time, Erik, and she has your smile.

She has your dark eyes too.

And your beautiful, regal nose.

But she lucked out (!) and got my red hair. You can't win 'em all!

She is my shining light and the joy of my life, and no matter what happened with the Governor's Son, I will always be grateful to you, my Erik, for giving her to me.

After I had her, I had some very tough days, missing my father and sisters, and, of course, you. At one point, I had a notion of driving to Duke and presenting Ava Grace to the Governor's Son. But Judith showed me some pictures of him on Google. She showed me a picture of him holding hands with Vanessa Osborn at a Duke formal, and another of him at his sister's graduation from high school in June.

Most painful of all, she showed me a picture of the Governor's Son kissing Vanessa Osborn at a party in Raleigh the same July I was falling in love with you, Erik. It was crushing, of course. It was evidence of everything the Governor's Wife had told me that terrible Thanksgiving: he'd been with Van and me at the same time. And in the end, he'd chosen Van.

After that, I put away foolish notions of driving to Duke or ever reaching out to the Governor's Son. I reminded myself that I never knew him. And I forced myself to move on for Ava's sake.

My Christmas cards to my father and Issy were returned to sender unopened this year, just as they were last year, but Kyrstin's wasn't returned. I hope and pray that someday my father and sisters will forgive me and find space for me and my daughter in their lives again.

I feel like I need to say that I know you're not real, Erik. I know you never existed. I still dream of you all the time, but my memories aren't as sharp as they were a year ago. And that helps. But only a little. Sometimes I feel like I will grieve the loss of you for the rest of my life, Erik. I still long for you—for the man I loved so much—in a constant, aching way, wishing you could see and know our daughter. Her soft coos of pleasure. The way she hums when I feed her smashed yams. How much she loves the pool at the college. The sweet smell of her head when she falls asleep in my arms.

Judith has asked me to set the table, and since Ava is finally napping, I guess I should. But I wanted to write my annual letter to you before the day got away.

I miss you.

I miss you.

Merry Christmas, my Erik.

*Laire*

***

*The Third Christmas*

Dear Erik,

I thought about not writing this year, about tearing up this stupid journal and throwing it in Judith's fireplace. I don't know why I didn't. There are only a couple dozen pages written, and it'll take years to fill them all. Maybe I'm keeping it as a record for Ava Grace. Or maybe knowing this journal exists lets me keep you in a box I only open once a year. For whatever reason, the journal survived. And so here I am, exhausted after a very long and exciting Christmas Day, writing to you, my imaginary boyfriend who never actually existed.

Gyah. It's crazy. I know. I know.

Ava Grace is nineteen months old. Nineteen months. I can't believe it some days.

She said "Mama" at nine months old and "Nana" and "Unca" (for Patrick) at twelve months, and started walking at fourteen months. She zips around so fast now, we all have to be careful what we leave out because she gets into everything. She's tall, and her red hair (which has grown in much darker than mine ever was—your genes) curls around her collar. She says "Me want yoos" for orange juice and "Kitty Found," for Judith's cat, Flounder. Her favorite book character is Biscuit. Her favorite music is by Laurie Berkner.

Now I'm just rambling.

Oh, here's something new!

I started college in September, if you can believe it. Yes, I did. I saved up over $3,000 the summer I worked at the Pamlico House, and another $10,000 working at Harris Teeter. Since Judith refuses to take rent or board (stubborn, beloved Judith), I am quite flush and could easily pay my tuition.

I am four months into my first year, and I'm majoring in fashion design and merchandising. Yes, I wanted to go to up North, but Nana is here and Nana babysits for Ava, so here is where I stay. LOL. Patrick gives me a ride to school every day and brings me home in the afternoons. He has been such a good friend to me, taking me out to meet some of his friends, though I am twelve years younger, and certainly he must feel about me as he would a much younger sister. But his eyes are still kind and his hair is still wild, and when he sings Ava Grace to sleep, my heart clenches a little.

Mostly because I miss you.

Mostly because I wish it was you.

Impossible, I know. Imaginary characters can't sing little girls to sleep.

She points to Patrick sometimes and says, "Dada," and we're all quick to say "No, Ava. Unca!" but it makes me realize that she will ask questions someday, and what will I tell her about you?

Maybe I will say that once upon a time, Mama fell in love with a dark-haired prince who lived in a castle on the beach. That's close to the truth, isn't it? Certainly I can never, ever tell her about the Governor's Son. A lump, half sorrow and half hate, still rises up in my throat when I think about him.

A few months ago, when I opened an account for myself, I searched for him on Facebook. Since we aren't Facebook friends, I couldn't see much of his page, aside from four or five profile pictures: he was just as beautiful as I remembered, with dark, thick hair and brown eyes. But his face was hard and his eyes were cold. I wondered if he'd changed, or if I had. Were his eyes always that cold and I'd never noticed? Because in my memory they are warm and lively. I don't know. I guess I never will. But the overwhelming sadness in my heart made me cry for several nights in a row after Ava was asleep, so I promised myself not to look at his Facebook account again for a long, long time.

My father returned his Christmas card unopened again this year, but Issy and Kyrstin didn't. In fact, Kyrstin called me yesterday, on Christmas Eve, and we spoke for the first time in over two years. It was awkward, of course, but still felt like progress. Issy has a second son now named Konnor. And Kyrstin and Remy have finally opened Château le Poisson. She sounded very proud. I hope it does well.

I miss you.

My memories fade a little, but my feelings don't. My heart can't seem to stop loving you. And when I dream of you, my Erik, I can hear your deep voice, your tender words in my ear . . . *Freckles . . . darlin' . . . I love you, Laire . . . I love you . . . love you . . .*

I wake up with a wet pillow and a heavy heart.

I long for the day when it doesn't hurt anymore.

I fear it too, because then you'll truly be gone and I'll be all alone.

Merry Christmas, my Erik.

*Laire*

\*\*\*

*The Fourth Christmas*

Dear Erik,

I have resigned myself to this annual tradition: sitting down with this journal and writing to you—*you* being the memory of a boyfriend who never actually existed. #Sick. Great, Laire. And I know it's stupid, and probably a psychiatrist would tell me I'm a nutjob, but I can't help it. I want to record my thoughts once a year. You were such a big part of my life, and I want to talk to you, and this is the only way I can.

Without you, I wouldn't have had Ava, wouldn't have left the Banks, wouldn't be in my second year of college. When I pick up this journal, I feel like a widow writing thoughts to her dead husband, and maybe that's wrong, but it's also really, really comforting. And it isn't hurting anyone, after all, is it?

Our Ava is two and a half now, and the terrible twos are no joke. Where did my smiling, laughing, happy baby go? This new Ava bucks ferociously when I try to buckle her car seat, throws her once-beloved yams on the floor, and terrifies Flounder. Just last week, she lay down on the floor at Kohl's and made a ruckus about getting the red velvet party dress instead of the green I'd chosen. She pulled a handful of dresses off the rack and stomped on them to make her point. That got her no dress, a swat on the backside, and an early bedtime.

I adore her, Erik. I love her so much, even her fiery spirt and tantrums, because she's strong. She knows her mind. She asks for what she wants. She is so different from me—from her mother, who was scared to take a job, once upon a time, for fear it would ruffle her father's feathers. I barely recognize that girl anymore. She was so sheltered. So young. So naive.

Judith takes Ava to and from preschool twice a week, and they are the best of friends, Nana and Ava. Up until the end of this past semester, Patrick still drove me to and from school each day, though I should be able to buy my own car after the New Year. I have started designing again in earnest and selling some clothes to my classmates. I've even captured the attention of some of the senior professors, one of whom went to Parsons in New York. She asked if she could send some of my designs to a friend of hers in London—a Madame Scalzo—and I almost died. I'm sure nothing will come of it, but it felt awfully good.

There's been another major development: Patrick asked me to marry him two weeks ago.

I feel like I betray you even by sharing this news, and though I owe you nothing at all, I want you to know that I never slept with Patrick. I did kiss him once or twice, though, more out of loneliness than anything. He's so kind and good to us—he's been the only father figure Ava has ever known. But I found myself comparing his kisses to yours, and I knew I wasn't falling in love with him even though he was, apparently, falling for me. He said that the engagement could just be a promise, and we could grow into our love for each other. He would adopt Ava, and we could move to his larger house near campus. It would have been a good life, Erik, but I . . . I just . . .

Tears were wetting the page so I stopped writing, and now

I'm back.

I couldn't say yes. I couldn't. I hate myself for admitting this, but I'm still in love with you—with the memory of you. And until I feel that sort of forever love with someone again, I don't want to be married. I *know* how it feels to love with every fiber of my being, how it feels to believe, truly believe, that a man loves me as much as I believed you did.

I know it's unlikely that lightning will strike twice.

But I won't marry anyone unless I love him and trust him as much as I did you, my Erik, and I know it's unlikely I shall ever meet with a love that strong again.

After a great deal of thinking, I've decided that I will be a career woman—a good mother to Ava, of course, but also a woman who designs couture fashions for the best houses in New York or Paris or London. I don't how long it will take, but I will make it happen. I will fall in love with *my work*. I will make a good, solid, happy life for my daughter. And it will be enough.

I promised myself I wouldn't, but over the summer, I Googled the Governor's Son. Do you remember, all those years ago, when you asked me not to Google you? I never did. But now I've Googled *him*.

I don't know what to make of what I read and saw.

He is in his third year at law school and being urged to run for state senate next year.

I saw him dressed up for many fashionable events in Raleigh. Always with a different woman. All of them stunning. None of them appearing twice.

I remember, many years ago, when I worked at King Triton, that I could tell when a fish was dead on delivery because its eyes were blank and dull. Your eyes, my Erik, were brown and deep, sparkling with humor and love and tenderness. The Governor's Son has dead eyes.

And I wish it didn't, but it made me sorry to see it.

That said, it didn't make me cry.

Merry Christmas, my Erik.

*Laire*

*** *

*The Fifth Christmas*

Dear Erik,

I write to you from my hotel balcony in Paris.

Yes, Paris.

I have been here for two weeks, and though I have loved every moment, I have missed Ava Grace with an ache that borders on panic, and when I leave tomorrow—Christmas Eve— to fly home, I will be so happy to hold her in my arms once again.

This is the longest I have ever been away from her, but when Madame Scalzo, who taught a one-semester course in European trends, announced she needed an assistant to join her at the annual Noël à Paris fashion show, I put my hat in the ring and was chosen. Once I found out, I almost turned it down, but Judith and Samantha, Patrick's fiancée, insisted that, between the three of them, they could manage Ava Grace's schedule and that I shouldn't pass up a chance like this one.

I have loved Paris. So much. But I have missed North Carolina desperately. My surrogate family, of course, but most of all, our daughter.

How can I describe her to you, Erik?

Let's see . . . she has a fringe of bangs across her forehead and wears her hair in two dark-red braids that Nana fastens every morning with twin rubber bands the same color as the outfit she's wearing. She is tall like you, but slight like me. She still has your grin and your warm, brown eyes. She hasn't lost any teeth yet, though Katie, Ava's best friend at preschool, just lost her first, and Ava is desperate to be next. She's like that— wanting to keep up. Wanting to be first, or at least next. I wonder how that quality will develop? As ambition and drive? I hope so.

She is musical and artistic, and she loves her ballet class more than anything. It was at ballet class, in fact, where Uncle Patrick met Ava's instructor, Miss Samantha. She's Ava's ballet instructor and, now, soon-to-be auntie. They are good together, Patrick and Samantha, and she has become one of my closest friends. Not to mention, Patrick has a dashing new haircut. Turns out, he was very handsome under all that scruff. Maybe I should have married him when he asked! LOL!

My father had a stroke in October, and though I wanted to go see him, Issy and Kyrstin insisted it wasn't time yet. But my card to him wasn't returned this year, so I hope he is softening. Kyrstin, who's made the Château le Poisson into a thriving little getaway inn, says he only works at King Triton now. The stroke stole his upper body strength, which makes it all but impossible for him to crab. Maybe by next summer my sisters will tell me that I've been forgiven and that he's ready to meet Ava and know me again. I pray every night that it will be so. The Sebastians have truly been family to me these past five years, but I miss my father and sisters. I want time with them before time runs out.

And now I'm sad, and Paris, the City of Light, is nowhere to be sad, especially on your last night. I worked hard to lose most of my Corey accent and have been taking French for two years at college. My French isn't good, but passable, and yet I'm constantly asked if I'm from Australia. LOL. I guess that accent isn't totally gone, after all.

This is the first year I didn't look up the Governor's Son.

Not once.

Not at all.

Even my dreams of you, Erik, come less and less frequently, and when they do, I don't wake up crying.

I will always miss you, of course.

But it doesn't hurt as desperately as it did before.

And for that, I am grateful.
Merry Christmas, Erik.
*Laire*

***

*The Sixth Christmas*

Dear Erik,

I have an hour to write—Ava is a sheep in her ballet recital tonight, and Patrick is picking up me and Judith soon.

Judith. My Judith, my surrogate mother, my daughter's only grandparent, has been diagnosed with cancer. It is quite advanced, and the doctor's prognosis was not good. When we first learned of her condition over the summer, I railed and cried, furious at God for letting this happen again. But then I remembered that my mother brought Judith to me when I needed her. She was there for me when I had no one else. So now I will be the strong daughter that Judith needs during these final months. Ava and I will make them as happy as possible.

Ava is in her final year of preschool, bubbly and beautiful, a minx some days, and yet so vulnerable others, she breaks my heart. I love her to the moon and back, though I find myself sorting out which traits are from the Cornish family and which must have come from yours. When she bats her eyes at Uncle Patrick and gets her way, it's you. When she refuses to jump off the diving board because she's "ascared," it's me. And damn, but I won't have my daughter be scared like I was. (Between you and me? I pushed her off that diving board, then jumped in right behind her.)

She finally asked about you in earnest, and Erik, I was so flummoxed for a minute, I just stared at her with my mouth open. But then I told her about the prince with dark hair and dark eyes. I said Mama loved him and he loved Mama. She asked when she could meet you, and tears filled my eyes when I told her that the prince was gone. She asked if he was dead, and internally I had to acknowledge that Ava's biological father, the Governor's Son, is still alive. But I won't ever share her with him. Never, ever. So I lied. I told her I didn't know. And the most amazing thing happened: she nodded her head and went off to play with her LEGOs. I breathed a sigh of relief, knowing I had just dodged a bullet. Oh, Erik, one day she will be eight, or twelve, or fifteen, and what in the world will I say then if she wants to know her father? What will I do when I am certain he will only break her heart as he did mine? I can barely think about it—it makes my chest tight.

I will graduate in June, but I have already received an offer to work with a design firm in New York (remember Madame Scalzo? She offered me a junior designer job at the House of Scalzo!) with a salary I can barely believe. I have accepted the job on the condition that Judith's health is my first priority.

My father's health appears to be stable, from what Issy and Kyrstin tell me, and Kyrs is pregnant with her first child, while Issy is expecting her third. I long to introduce my own daughter to her aunts and cousins. Maybe someday.

If you were real, I would ask you to pray for Judith.

The Governor's Son ran for state senate in November, although he lost to the incumbent. A familiar face was near his on the steps of the capitol when he conceded defeat: Van's. Vanessa Osborn. I haven't seen a picture of them together in years, but there she was, looking beautiful beside him.

I wonder, sometimes, if they are happy together.

And then I think they're probably not, because his eyes still look dead to me.

Not that it matters to me at all. Not anymore.

I miss you, Erik, but there are only ten pages left in this old journal, enough for one more Christmas. I read somewhere that it takes seven years to grieve the loss of a spouse, and for all intents and purposes, that's what I've done. I've grieved your loss. I've dreamed of you. I've missed you.

The memories are fading fast now.

And though a part of me will always miss you, I find I'm almost ready to let you go.

Merry Christmas.

*Laire*

***

*The Seventh Christmas*

Dear Erik,

This will be my last entry in this old journal.

What a long way I've come from the scared eighteen-year-old who arrived in Boone with a woman she barely knew, about to have a baby, her heart utterly broken by the man of her dreams. I wonder if I'd recognize that girl now if I saw her. I don't know. I hope so.

Our Ava is officially a kindergartner and the smartest little girl you've ever seen. She wears two neat pigtails in her auburn hair every day and loves her teacher, Miss Horwath, to death. She will miss her when we move.

In related news, we are moving.

Dear Judith made it until summertime, when she passed away quietly in her sleep after a perfect day in the mountains with me, Ava, Patrick, and Samantha. She knew that Patrick and Samantha were expecting a baby boy they planned to name Jude, and though she deeply grieved not being able to meet her grandson, I know she was comforted by the loving relationship she'd had with Ava.

We buried her on the Fourth of July weekend. July, August, and September were very difficult for me. I even called Madame Scalzo and retracted my acceptance of the position in New York. I told her that the idea of moving to an unknown place was too overwhelming. With her usual pluck, she told me that the job was mine until the New Year, and if I wanted to work remotely from North Carolina for a while, I could.

You see, when Judith passed, she left the house in Boone to Patrick and her condo in Hatteras to me. To be honest, I didn't even realize she still had the condo in Hatteras, but she'd rented it all these years, keeping it, she said, for me. Before she died, she encouraged me to return to the Banks. She said that I should patch things up with my family before it was too late. She said it was time for me to go home. Not forever. Just as long as it would take to make amends.

Throughout the fall, I weighed my options. Patrick insisted I could stay at the house in Boone for however long I wanted to, and I know Samantha was hoping we'd stay indefinitely so that their Jude and my Ava could be cousins. But Judith was ever and always right.

It's time for me to go home and make things right with my father and sisters.

Our things are packed, and my new (used) Jeep Grand Cherokee is bursting at the seams. I have been working (remotely) for Madame Scalzo since September and will continue to do so when Ava and I move to the Banks and sort out Judith's condo. I send up my designs weekly, though I sense she'd prefer to have me in New York full-time.

Ava has cried a million tears about leaving Nana's house, and saying good-bye to Uncle Patrick and Aunt Samantha this evening was a nightmare, but they've promised to come and visit with baby Jude this spring. I will miss them. I will miss them so much.

I don't plan to stay long in Hatteras. In fact, by next summer, I want to move to New York so that Ava and I can start our new life there. But I need to take this time to reconcile with my family. I need Ava to know where her mama grew up, and though I plan to say as little as possible, I need for her to know where her parents spent one remarkable, beautiful summer together, before her mother's beautiful dream came crashing down.

It's time for us to say good-bye, Erik.
It's time for me to move on now.
So here it is:
Good-bye, my Erik.
Good-bye, my love.
*Laire*

Part Two

**Post-Christmas Storm hits OBX**
By Abby O'Shea

December 27—A powerful nor'easter dumped upwards of two feet of snow on the Outer Banks last night, leaving in its wake ocean overwash, ice and wind damage.

Parts of N.C. Highway 12 in Kitty Hawk were closed this morning due to standing water and debris that was pushed up from the beach at high tide.

Heavy overwash and damage to many motels and summer homes have been reported on N.C. 12 on the north end of Buxton.

Strong onshore winds also came across the area Sunday night, with the highest gust—64 mph—reported by the National Weather Service at Hatteras.

A coastal flood warning was set to expire at noon today, but winds on the backside of the storm still haven't subsided. They are blowing in the 20 to 25 mph range, and forecasters believe they won't taper off until Tuesday morning.

Water levels are still running 4 to 5 feet above normal on the oceanside and 3 to 4 feet for the sounds, but are expected to return to normal by Tuesday evening.

West of the sound, parts of northeastern North Carolina woke up Sunday with nearly three inches of snow on the ground.

Damage has been reported as far south as Charleston, S.C., and as far north as Cape Cod.

# Chapter 17

Erik Rexford drew three résumés from the pile and tossed them into the wastebasket under his desk before looking up at his sister, Hillary, and sliding the remaining two résumés to her.

"Follow up with these two."

She gave her brother a hard look before picking up the stapled pages. "Jacob Gilmartin and Edward Wireman."

He nodded curtly.

"The other three were more qualified, and you know it."

*The other three are women.*

He narrowed his eyes and cocked his head to the side. "I like these better."

Hillary, who had come on board as his executive assistant last year, sighed. "I am the single raft of estrogen in this sea of testosterone."

He continued to stare at her without comment. They'd trod this ground before. Many times. He knew what was coming in three . . . two . . . one . . .

"It wouldn't kill you to hire a woman, Erik."

*And yet . . . it might.*

Erik cleared his throat, using a dismissive tone. "Follow up with those two. Anythin' else?"

"Yes, in fact," she said, sitting down in the guest chair

across from his desk as she rested the résumés on her lap. "Fancy called a little while ago."

"And what did our dear mother have to say? Lookin' forward to seein' the ball drop in Times Square?"

"Nope. Amtrak's all messed up from the storm. They're stranded in Boston, and it looks like they'll be snowed in for at least three days, so they've decided to go skiin' with friends in Vermont. They'll spend New Year's in the mountains instead."

"Good for them."

"Erik," she said, her voice gentle but urgent. "She said that Utopia Manor got hit hard with the storm out on the Banks. Mr. McGillicutty called. Power's down. Pool's flooded. Dock got damaged. The repairs are outside of his purview. One of us needs to go out there to meet the insurance company and manage things for a few days."

Like he could give a shit about what happened to Utopia Manor. He hadn't been back in almost six years. He shrugged. "Fine. Take a few days off. I'm sure Pete would enjoy the trip."

His sister and Pete had gotten together two years ago after Hillary had graduated from UNC–Chapel Hill, Pete's alma mater. They lived together in a restored Victorian house in Historic Oakwood, and it was just a matter of time until Pete, who had always been like a brother to Erik, truly *was* his brother by marriage.

He was happy for Hillary. Really and truly happy for her because no one had waited longer or shown more faithfulness of heart than his sister. She was rare among women, and therefore the only woman he allowed to get close to him in any way, shape, or form.

"Can't do it, Erik. Cisco's hostin' the biggest tech conference of the year in two weeks. Pete's up every night until after two gettin' his presentation perfect. He's not goin' anywhere."

"So *you* go."

"First of all, *I* have New Year's plans."

And she knew very well that Erik did not.

"Second of all, I want to be here to support Pete. Get him dinner, be around while he's workin' so hard."

Erik rolled his eyes.

"Not to mention," she continued, giving him a look, "I know, literally, nothin' about architecture and structure damage and all of that sort of stuff. I'd be less than useless." She slumped in her seat. "Come on. You know *you* have to be the one to go."

He clenched his jaw. He hadn't been back to that fucking house in years. Not since the Thanksgiving when *she* didn't show.

*It still hurt. It still fucking hurt, all these years later.*

He looked up at Hillary and growled, "Hire someone and charge it to Daddy."

With his eyes locked with his sister's, he watched hers soften to grief, and she took a halted breath before whispering, "They call you the Ice Man, Erik."

He raised his eyebrows. "Ask me if I give a shit."

"Even if you don't, I do," she said softly. "I want you to be happy."

"You're not the happiness police, Hills," he said, twisting his chair away from her a little.

"You have to *deal* with this," she insisted. "Purge your demons. Say good-bye. Move on. It's been long enough now."

For years Hillary had been saying the same thing: move on. As if moving on from the love of your life, who suddenly and without explanation banished you, then disappeared off the face of the earth, was possible.

It's not that he actually thought about Laire very often. He didn't. He didn't allow it. But she was the truest and realest thing he'd ever known, or so he'd stupidly thought. He'd loved her harder and better than anyone who'd ever come before. And he didn't intend to ever put himself through that misery again as long as he lived. If he didn't love anyone, then no one could hurt him as Laire had.

It had become a challenge of sorts among the most charming, beautiful, successful women of North Carolina: to be the one who finally melted Erik Rexford's frosty heart. But Erik knew something they didn't—his heart was beyond touching, beyond warming, beyond caring. His heart had been crushed into a million pieces, then shoved back into his hands. It wasn't just frozen. It has been broken first. And now it was virtually untouchable.

So they could call him the Ice Man as much as they liked.

It was perfect and he welcomed it.

At least any woman who went out with him knew exactly what to expect.

Not that he dated very often, if you could even call it that. When he needed a date, he had a slew of eager admirers ready to stand up beside him. And there was always Van.

Vanessa Osborn had grown only more beautiful in the years since Laire had shattered his dreams, and she was perpetually in demand. But when she was single, between boyfriends or fiancés or affairs, she was Erik's preferred date to events and dinners, merely because he'd known her for so long. There was an easiness he found in Van's company that owed itself to history and childhood. Maybe he still felt some small bit of warmth toward her since they'd been friends for so long. She was a good companion, funny and interesting. She knew how to drag out a small smile from Erik when no one else could.

And sometimes—sometimes when he was with her and felt an unexpected surge of longing for a home and family of his own—he wondered if she would eventually wear him down . . . and if he and Van would end up together in some affectionate,

passionless arrangement. He knew that she still cared for him—
that she would drop everything in an instant for the chance to be
with him. He fought against the loneliness and weakness that
might lead him down such a path because he knew in his heart
that he'd ultimately destroy Van's chance at happiness, the way
Laire had destroyed his.

The bottom line was this: no matter what Van hoped, his
regard, without his love, wouldn't be enough for her in the long
run. And he would never love Van the way he was, at one time
so long ago, capable of loving a woman. His bitterness and
disappointment would become hers, and ultimately he'd kill the
light inside her that some other man would have cherished.
Staying away from Van as much as possible was the best course
of action. At least until she found someone who loved her.

"Erik?" said Hillary. "Are you listenin' to me? Because I
think you should go spend a few days out there. See the places
where you and . . . and *she* spent time together and say good-bye
to those memories. See if you can't move on now. It's been
years. You need to face your past, or you'll never be able to
move forward. I mean, wouldn't you like to *love* someone? Be
loved by them? Maybe get married and have a baby?"

The problem was, the only time he'd really ever envisioned
himself happily married with children was with Laire, and when
she crushed his heart, she crumpled up that dream and threw it
away.

"Do I *look* like I want a kid?"

Hillary stood up, her patience over, her eyes flashing.
"Well, I'm *not* goin' out there. My plate's full. Either *you* go or
you call Fancy up in Vermont and tell her to figure it out
herself."

"Hills—"

"No! You shut up. You just shut up!" She tucked the
résumés under one arm, then crossed both arms over her chest.
"You want to live in a cold dark place because love stomped on

your heart once upon a time? Fine. Go ahead. But you're *damaged*, Erik. You're *broken*. You let her *break* you. And you're still lettin' her break you every day." She nodded emphatically to make her point before continuing. "You have given the memory of some eighteen-year-old girl this . . . this . . . this *power* over you, and you know what I think?"

Erik narrowed his eyes. "Enlighten me."

"I think you *like* it. I think it makes you still feel connected to her in some sick way. You're like a . . . a male version of Miss Havisham."

*Whatever the fuck* that *means.*

"But one day you're goin' to wake up thirty or forty or seventy, and you're goin' to have nothin' good to show for your life. and you know whose fault that'll be?"

*Hers.*

"Yours!" she cried, as though she could read his mind. "Yours. Because you chose *not* to move on. You chose to wallow in your memories of her. *You* wasted your life. Willfully. And it's such a goddamn shame!"

He stared daggers at his furious little sister, wanting to say something to slap her back into her place, but no words came. His mind was a blank, her words reverberating in his head like pebbles in a tin can and just as annoying. As much as he hated to admit it, she made sense.

Turning around, she marched to the door and yanked it open, then looked back at him, raising her chin and pinning him with a sour look. "I'm *not* goin' out to the Banks, Erik. Furthermore, I'm takin' vacation time until after the New Year!"

The door slammed shut.

"Fine!" he bellowed, leaning back in his chair and spinning it away from the door. He stared out the windows at cold, gray Raleigh. The sun had almost set, and cheerful Christmas lights started to dot the dark and murky cityscape below, which pissed him off.

Christmas was over. Christmas lights after Christmas just looked pathetic, celebrating something that was already long gone.

*Move on. Move on. Move on.*

"Fuck!" he muttered, turning back to his desk and placing his fingers on the keyboard.

***

In a last-minute decision that surprised and delighted his staff, Erik sent out an e-mail advising that the law offices of Rexford & Rexford, LLC would be closed from December 29 through January 2. Then he went home, packed a bag, walked to the Enterprise Rent-A-Car office around the block from his condo, rented a car, and pointed a shiny new Porsche Cayenne SUV east to the Outer Banks.

With downed trees and icy conditions reportedly worse near the coast, the usual four-hour drive would take him twice as long, especially in the dark, but he felt a responsibility to observe and manage the damage to his family's property. Someone had to do it. And truth be told, the week between Christmas and New Year's was an especially quiet time of year. It made sense to check on things, didn't it? Of course it did. It was the sensible thing to do.

He was *not* going back to the Outer Banks to "purge demons" or "say good-bye" to lost loves or anything else so patently ridiculous. Absolutely not. He was merely going as a property agent for his parents, and once his business there was finished, he'd return to Raleigh.

Realizing that he'd have nowhere to stay upon his late arrival prompted him to call the only year-round hotel establishment he knew of in Buxton, the Pamlico House Bed & Breakfast, which also had nothing to do with "facing the past" and everything to do with sleep.

Fuck Hillary's harping.

Fuck Hillary, who was fat and happy in her blissed-out state with Pete.

Fuck anyone who thought he knew what love was, and woe to him who trusted it.

"I thought I knew too," he muttered, pressing harder on the gas.

The first year had been the hardest, of course. Even though his heart had hardened against Laire when she didn't show up at Thanksgiving, by Christmas his resolve to forget her had weakened, and he was desperate to see her face again. His devotion to her, as much as he had fought against it, hadn't died.

The day after Christmas, he'd driven out to the Banks and chartered a boat to take him through the icy Sound from Hatteras to Corey Island. Although he hated her mightily, he needed to see her, and he needed to know why she had pushed him away.

Walking up the dock to King Triton Seafood, his hands sweat, despite the whipping wind of the thirty-three-degree day. When he stepped into the little shop, a redheaded man in his early twenties looked up from the counter.

"Help you?"

He didn't mince words. "Is Laire here?"

The young man, surely a relation of hers, judging by his hair color, had leaned toward Erik, his eyes narrowing. "Who's askin'?"

"I am."

"And you be . . .?"

"Erik Rexford."

Fire leaped into the man's eyes, and his fingers, resting on the counter, curled into tight fists. "You're goin' to want to leave here, sir. Right fuckin' now."

"Come again?" Erik asked, scanning the man's face.

"Laire's gone. And she ain't comin' back."

"What? Why?"

"How do you people sleep at night?" growled the man. "How d'you fuckin' sleep w'the way you treat people?"

"I'm sorry but I don't—"

"Get the fuck out. And never show your face on Corey again, or I swear to Judas, I'll kill you myself."

Erik took several steps back, shocked by the fury in the man's voice, wondering what the hell he was missing.

He quickly reviewed the facts as he knew them:

He and Laire had had an amazing summer.

They'd had an amazing night together.

Her father got sick.

She broke up with him.

*She* broke up with *him*. Not the other way around. She broke up with him without explanation, then stood him up at Thanksgiving. She was not the innocent fucking party in this equation. *He* was. So why the fuck was this punk threatening *him*?

He turned to the door, reaching for the handle, when his confusion and brokenheartedness overcame him. He pivoted back around to face the redheaded man again and cried, "I don't fuckin' understand!"

Vaulting over the countertop with surprising grace for so squat a person, the man lurched at Erik, one fist catching his cheek while the other uppercut him in the chin. *Slam bam*, and Erik stumbled back against the door, pushing it open with the force of his sucker-punched, reeling body. The wind caught the door, and it swung wide open, leaving nothing to break Erik's fall. He tripped backward over the welcome mat and landed on his ass, with the redheaded man looming over him.

"*Now* do you understand, you fuckin' cocksucker?"

Erik looked up at the man—her cousin?—and shook his head. "No."

"Well, that ain't my fuckin' problem. Now git."

Her cousin turned and walked back into the shop, locking

the door, and turning the sign from "Open" to "Closed."

And Erik, who had no more answers than he'd had when he arrived five minutes earlier, had no other option but to walk back to the charter with his bleeding cheek and swollen chin and start making his long way back to Raleigh.

*Laire's gone. And she ain't comin' back.*

Truer words had never been spoken. Laire was gone—his Laire, the girl he'd loved so completely, so passionately, so goddamned much—was gone. And wherever she was, she was lost to Erik, never coming back.

He had mulled over her cousin's words from time to time over the years—the pointed question about how he could sleep at night, as though he'd done her an injustice. Try as he might, he couldn't figure out what that injury was, though it had tormented him for a few years whenever he turned his mind to it. He'd loved her. He would have done anything for her. Perhaps, he'd finally decided, her cousin had been talking about the politics of the Rexford family and his father's administration, which wasn't known for making life easier for the working man. It's the only thing he could come up with because, as far as Erik was concerned, he'd never done anything to hurt or disappoint her.

When he really wanted to torture himself, he sorted through her words at the hospital, trying to wrest from them some meaning, some explanation for the way she'd pushed him out of her life. The last words she'd ever spoken to him were, *I'm not your darlin'. I'm not your anything. We were just a . . . a fling. A fantasy. I'm an islander; you're a dingbatter. It's over. . . . It wasn't* real, *Erik. It wasn't real.*

But it *had* been real. Or at least it had been real for him.

He gasped suddenly, the muscles in his face clenching, and he flinched, growling softly under his breath as if he'd stepped on a rusty nail that punctured the soft skin of his sole. It gaped and oozed, this wound inflicted by Laire Cornish so many years before. It had never healed. It had never been sewn up or doctored. It was as raw and painful now as the day she'd banished him from her life, perhaps all the more so because of the energy he'd expended in trying to ignore it.

Sometimes, lying in his bed alone, late at night, he stared up at the ceiling and wondered what he would say to her if he ever saw her again. And though there was a foolish, masochistic part of him that fantasized about saying nothing, just opening his arms to her and feeling the heaven of her heart pressed against his one last time on this earth, mostly the word "Why?" circled round and round in his head. And sometimes he bargained with God: if he could just find out *why* she'd pushed him away, it would give him the strength to finally let her go.

***

Whatever he expected to feel, or not feel, when he pulled into the well-lit Pamlico House B & B parking lot later that night—anger, sadness, sentimentality—an emotion that he didn't expect to feel was relief. After a perilous nine-hour journey, however, he was exhausted, both physically and emotionally, and whatever he felt about being back at the place where he'd courted Laire so faithfully, it would have to wait for processing until he'd had a good night's sleep.

The drive from Kitty Hawk to Hatteras had been especially shocking. His rental had hydroplaned more times than he could count. He'd gone over and around dead, fallen trees, twice by driving off the road and over the sand. He didn't bother going to Buxton to look at Utopia Manor—it was pitch-black out. There were almost no lights after Rodanthe, so he was better off waiting until morning.

He knew that the Pamlico House had a generator, but the warm lights through the windows were the best greeting he could have asked for. No matter what had happened between him and Laire so many years ago, this little inn was his beacon in the wilderness tonight, and he was grateful for it.

Swinging his body out of the car, he found his muscles stiff from the drive, and doubly stiff from staying alert throughout the dangerous journey. Pulling his phone from the center console, he turned it back on and scrolled for messages using the inn's Wi-Fi. He'd missed a text from Hillary.

*HILLZ: Sorry I stormed out, but you make me piping mad. You know I still love you. Text me when you get there. Drive safe. xoxo*

Erik sighed, his breath a white puff of smoke floating up into the night sky.

*ERIK: I'm here. Pamlico House B & B. Banks are toast. It's good I came. xo*

He slipped his phone into the hip pocket of his jeans, then opened the back door of the rental, pulling his leather duffel bag from the seat and swinging the strap onto his shoulder. On the floor was his laptop bag, and he hesitated for a moment but decided to bring that it too. May as well get some work done tomorrow, before and after meeting the contractor.

Looking up at the inn, his eyes scanned the lighted windows. The reception area was still open, of course, waiting for his arrival, but there were a couple of other lights on as well, in the upstairs guest rooms. Three or four night owls still awake at one o'clock in the morning, he guessed. It wouldn't be a packed house, of course, but it looked like he wouldn't have the inn to himself.

Trudging up the walkway, he stepped into the reception area, suddenly assaulted by the smell of the Pamlico House— oiled floors, old carpets, sea air, and cinnamon. His undammed memories sluiced back, and his breath might have hitched a little as he felt the ghostly weight of her hand in his, the softness of her lips beneath his, the lightness of her step on the shiny hardwood floors.

His eyes scanned the reception area, flicking to the stairs he'd ascended only once, the night Laire took him to the widow's walk and told him she could spend the night. His heart clutched at the memory, and he jerked his glance reflexively to the left. The restaurant was closed for the season, but the old bar where he'd spent almost every night of that summer was aglow with the ambient light of the television, his favorite seat at the corner vacant, as though waiting for him.

"Evenin'. Mr. Rexford, I presume?"

A gray-haired gentleman in jeans and a flannel shirt rounded the corner of the bar area, where he must have been watching the TV, and made his way to the reception desk. He had a mustache and reading glasses, and Erik had a passing notion that if he were casting the role of the Innkeeper for a play, he couldn't get much closer than this guy.

"That's me."

"You made it."

"Barely."

"Roads still bad up north?"

Erik shrugged. "Not so bad north of Rodanthe, but after that . . ."

"Blackout."

"Bad." Erik nodded, looking around the small welcome area. Several lamps set beside antique couches and chairs bathed the room in soft, warm light. Had there always been a fringed Persian rug on the floor and flowers in a vase over the fireplace? He couldn't recall.

"We've got a generator," said the innkeeper, sliding a check-in form and pen across the reception desk. "Fill this out, huh? And include your, uh, your car and license plate info, huh?"

"Sure," said Erik, placing his computer bag on the floor by his feet and letting the duffel slide down his shoulder to join it. He took the pen and started filling out the form. "Got a lot of guests right now?"

The innkeeper shook his head. "Just a few. Let's see . . . We got two couples what come to visit their family over the holiday. They're stayin' until New Year's Day. Got a couple of year-rounders whose gennies got dunked in the storm. They're stayin' until the water gets pumped out and they get their power back. Mother and daughter just come last night. Their place in Hatteras got it bad."

"Huh," said Erik absentmindedly, sliding the completed form back to the innkeeper. "My folks have a house in Buxton."

"Yeah," said the old-timer, nodding at Erik. "I know who you be. Governor's son."

Erik forced a smile he didn't feel and changed the subject. He wasn't in the mood for a political conversation. "You own this place?"

"Aye-up."

"Local?"

"From Ocracoke 'riginally."

"Islander, huh?" Erik asked, trying to keep the bite out of his tone.

"Aye-up." He nodded, offering Erik his hand. "Henshaw Leatham. They call me Shaw."

"That or Grandpa!"

Erik slid his eyes in the direction of the voice and found a young woman coming down the stairs. She was pretty—between eighteen and twenty, he guessed, with blonde wavy hair and a winsome smile. Big tits. Small waist. Bare feet.

Not unlike someone else he used to know.

His face hardened.

"Hi," she said, grinning at him.

"Hi," he answered, not grinning back and looking away from her quickly.

"I'm the granddaughter. Kelsey," she continued, talking to

his profile.

Erik nodded, but he didn't look at her again. He wasn't interested in the flirting smiles of an island girl. Not one bit. Not at all.

The iciness that covered his heart, that had earned him his reputation and nickname, made his next words sound sharp and unfriendly.

"Can I get my key?" he asked Mr. Leatham.

"Can I help you with your bags?" asked Kelsey at his elbow.

Erik wasn't looking at her, but in his peripheral vision, he'd seen her move across the room, from the staircase to the reception desk, and he quickly bent down and picked up the bags, throwing one over his shoulder and gripping the other tightly. "No, thanks."

"Kelsey, honey, ain't it your bedtime?"

"Grandpa," she said, scooting around the reception desk and giving her grandfather a kiss on his bristly cheek, "I think I'm old enough to know when it's time to go to sleep."

"Well, as long as you're still up," said the innkeeper, "how's about takin' Mr. Rexford to room 308?"

"Rexford, like the gov'nor?" asked Kelsey, her blue eyes lighting up with unconcealed interest.

He was forced to look at her. "His son."

"Well, I'll be," she said, twisting a lock of blonde hair around her finger. "Royalty."

"Hardly," said Erik, increasingly more agitated with her flirting. "I don't need you to show me up. I'll find it." He faced Mr. Leatham. "Just the key, please."

The innkeeper nodded, turning to the key slots behind him. He grabbed the key and handed it to Erik. "There's breakfast from seven to nine, and we do a fire pit on the widow's walk from eight to ten at night. In case you don't know, a widow's walk is—"

"I know what it is," he said tightly. *And exactly where it is too.*

"Well, then, I guess you're all set. Need anythin', just come find me or Kelsey."

Still averting his glance from the granddaughter, Erik nodded at the old gentleman. "Thank you."

"Welcome to the Pamlico House, Mr. Rexford!" said Kelsey to his back as he trudged up the stairs. "Enjoy your stay!"

## Chapter 18

Waking up at the Pamlico House Bed & Breakfast for the third morning in a row, Laire stretched her arms over her head and opened her eyes to take a peek at Ava Grace in the bed beside hers. Nestled under a cozy down duvet, her little bug slept soundly, and Laire grinned as she swung her legs over the side of the bed and sighed.

According to Mr. McGillicutty, the contractor retained by her new homeowners' association, it would take about a week to pump the water out of the basement of the condo and address the damage to the boiler and electric panel. Once both had been repaired or replaced, she'd be contacted so that she could move back in. Well, not "back" in, since she'd never actually taken possession of the condo. The storm had gotten progressively worse as she drove out to the Banks on the twenty-seventh. Instead of going to the condo, she and Ava Grace had detoured to the Pamlico House and checked in. It was a good decision. Even with the whipping wind and high waves, they'd been safe and sound, and when the electricity finally went dead, the generator had kicked on to keep them warm.

Yesterday they'd picked their way through waterlogged roads covered with debris to see the condo Judith had left to them. Located on a beach road, it was part of a modest structure—tan terra-cotta with two levels and twenty-two units. Theirs was on the second floor and had two bedrooms and a living room balcony  with Atlantic views. As Ava Grace explored Nana's dark, quiet, fully furnished condo, Laire stepped out on the balcony and breathed deeply.  She could smell the brackishness of the water, and her eyes pricked with requited longing. It had been a long time since she'd smelled the sea. She had no idea if her father and sisters would welcome her back, but it was still good to be home.

Last night, she'd been up until well after one o'clock sketching new ideas for Madame Scalzo, realizing the time only when she heard the guest in the room above hers arrive and unpack. Judging from the heavy sound of his footfalls, he wasn't a small man, though, after she heard his bed squeak with the weight of his body, she hadn't heard another peep. When she finally lay down in her own bed, she imagined him, just for a moment, asleep above her, separated only by a ceiling and floor. She wondered what had brought him to the inn—if he'd been stranded by the storm or if he'd planned to visit Buxton for New Year's. Was he young or old, and why was he alone? Her mind enjoyed the wondering. It brought her a strange, but welcome, sense of intimacy that felt warm and comforting as she fell asleep.

Now, as morning light filtered into the room, she glanced up at the ceiling, imagining him nestled under his comforter, asleep like Ava Grace.

Yesterday the little girl had again asked Laire about her father, and Laire had again used her fairy-tale Prince Charming story, which appeared to satisfy her daughter. But she worried, more and more, about what she would tell Ava Grace someday, when fairy tales and half-truths weren't enough.

Certainly the Rexfords would have no use for her. It hurt Laire's heart to admit it, but she knew it was true. If Ava Grace ever went searching for her father, she'd end up sorely disappointed by people with no character or integrity, no sense of honor or truthfulness or even mercy. Still, she didn't know if she had the right to keep Ava Grace from the man who was, biologically at least, her father.

Though marriage held zero interest for Laire, and plenty of terror, she did sometimes wonder if she owed it to Ava Grace to find someone sweet and stable and get married. Ava Grace so desperately wanted a father figure in her life. But then, consigning herself to a loveless marriage wouldn't help her daughter in the long run, would it? If she were ever to offer the example of marriage to her daughter, she'd want Ava Grace to see her mother well loved and happy. She'd want to model the sort of relationship she hoped her daughter would seek for herself one day.

And if Patrick—sweet, lovely, gentle man that he was— couldn't touch Laire's heart, it was unlikely that anyone else could. Which meant that Erik Rexford had, more or less, spoiled Laire for marriage. She may have moved on from Erik, but she couldn't imagine trusting another man enough to ever fall in love again, or allow her heart to be hurt again.

She sighed, tenderly caressing her child's face with loving eyes. A driven career-woman mother would have to be enough for Ava Grace.

Laire stood up and walked over to the window, pushing away the sheer curtains and looking out at the Sound. She'd thought about paying a little extra for a third-floor room with a balcony, especially since the Pamlico House would be their home for the next week, but she couldn't justify the expense. If she wanted to smell the ocean, all she needed to do was open a window or, better yet, walk outside, which is exactly what she and Ava Grace would do later today.

"Mama?"

She turned around to see her baby sitting up in bed, her

favorite stuffed animal—a penguin named Mr. Mopples, a gift from Uncle Patrick—tucked securely under her arm.

"Morning, baby."

Ava Grace's grin segued into a yawn. "What's for breakfast?"

Laire shrugged as she crossed the room and sat down on the edge of the bed. She pushed a lock of wavy auburn hair from her forehead and leaned forward to kiss her. "I don't know. What do you think Kelsey's making today?"

"Pancakes!" cried Ava Grace, throwing her hands into the air and waggling Mr. Mopples like a flag.

"Pancakes!" said Laire, cupping her daughter's face. She was so beautiful, this perfect little person, with her deep brown eyes and coppery hair. Laire was floored, on a daily basis, that such a perfect little person belonged to her. "Didn't she just make pancakes yesterday?"

"She said she'd make 'em every day for me!"

"I bet that's because you're the best little girl in the world."

"Mr. Mopples doesn't think so," said Ava Grace, giving Laire a very stern look.

"Oh, no?"

She shook her head and sighed. "No. She thinks I'm fourth best."

How *Mr.* Mopples was a she had been beyond Laire's comprehension for years, but when asked, Ava Grace simply answered, "Because that's the way it is."

"Impossible!" cried Laire, pursing her lips in mock annoyance at the battered penguin. "I demand to know who are first, second, and third."

"Katie, Leslie, and Hannah," said Ava Grace, referring to the three little girls in her kindergarten class who had had bigger parts in the Christmas pageant than Ava Grace. "*They're* the best."

"Is that right?"

Ava Grace nodded somberly.

"Well, Mr. Mopples is wrong," she said.

"How do you know?"

Laire turned to the penguin. "Because even if you don't, Mr. Mopples, I see the person sitting here in front of me, and she is *amazing*. She's smart and funny, and she has a huge heart. She's kind and thoughtful. She is loving and brave. Do you know how brave she is, Mr. Mopples?"

"No, Mama," said Ava Grace in Mr. Mopples's voice. "How brave is Ava?"

Laire leaned down on her elbow to look the penguin in the eyes. "Between you and me? She's the bravest kid I ever saw. Katie, Leslie, and Hannah? They still live in their comfy houses in Boone, where they know everybody. But Ava Grace Cornish is having an adventure! She's moved to a whole new world. She's going to start a new school. And you know what?"

"What?" asked Ava Grace in Ava Grace's voice.

"Everyone at that new school is going to love her just as much as I do."

"Are you sure, Mama?"

"One hundred percent positive," said Laire, lifting her eyes to her daughter's. "Don't be afraid, Ava Grace."

Ava Grace took a deep breath. "But I am, a little."

"You don't need to be, baby." Laire tilted her head. "Especially because I found out something yesterday . . . School's not starting until the third. Because of the storm."

Ava Grace's mouth dropped open. "You mean I get an extra day of vacation? At a hotel? With you?"

Laire nodded, grinning at her smart girl. "That is *exactly* what I mean!"

Leaping up from the bed, she jumped up and down with Mr. Mopples, saying, "More vacation! More vacation!"

Laire jumped up beside her, taking one of Mr. Mopples's

flippers and one of Ava Grace's hands and joined them in a happy dance, wishing that every sad day of her daughter's life could be so quickly turned around.

* * *

*More vacation! More vacation!*

He heard the squeaky little voice of a child through the floorboards and groaned as his eyes fluttered open. Erik had purposely pulled the blinds down so he could sleep until eight, and here it was, six thirty, and he was awakened by the people downstairs having a dance party.

"Fuckin' obnoxious," he growled, flipping back over and covering his head with a pillow.

He heard the voice of a woman, likely the kid's mother, shushing her child, and the commotion ceased, though now he was on his guard for more noise, which meant that he was awake. Only five hours of sleep. Fantastic.

Since when did the Pamlico House admit kids anyway?

Picking up his bedside phone, he called down to reception.

"Front Desk."

"Yes. This is Mr. Rexford in room—"

"Three-o-eight," said Mr. Leatham. "What can I do you for?"

"The people in, well, I guess 208—they're pretty loud for six a.m."

"Hum. Yep. That's the young mama with the li'l'un. Remember? I mentioned them? They come over from Hatteras?"

"Right. Well, do you think you could have a word with them about keepin' it down before eight?"

A pause. "You want that I yell at a young lady with a li'l'un?"

"No. I don't want you to *yell* at anyone. Just . . ." The line was quiet as Mr. Leatham waited for instruction or forced Erik to feel petty and withdraw his complaint. Hmm. No, screw that!

He'd paid for a room the same as her. He had every right to a quiet night's sleep. "But if you have a chance to remind her of quiet hours between ten and eight, please do."

"Remind her? I guess I could, but—"

"Wonderful. Then do."

He hung up the phone before Mr. Leatham could work more of his passive-aggressive objections, and whipped the covers from his body. He'd unpacked last night, but now he grumbled as he stood naked in front of the sheer curtains of the balcony doors. Parting the flimsy fabric, he noted the large icicles hanging from the railing and sighed. The sun was out, but the hill from the inn porch to the sidewalk that led to the dock, was white with snow and ice. And around the dock, where the water was brackish from the Atlantic inlets, he could see a fairly thick coating of ice. When seawater froze, it was cold out. Icy cold.

Christ, but winter in the Banks was depressing.

Pulling the curtains closed again, he crossed to the bathroom, took a piss, and turned on the hot water. Stepping into the Victorian bathtub, he let the hot water soothe his still-weary bones, leaning his forehead against the tile wall under the nozzle and sighing deeply.

*You want that I yell at a young lady with a li'l'un?*

He pursed his lips and shook his head in annoyance.

"Yes." Then he paused. "No."

He turned around in the shower, letting the water pelt his back.

*Is that who I am? Who I've become? Someone who yells at women and children for waking up on the right side of the bed while I perpetually wake up on the wrong one?*

He shook his head again and grabbed the tiny tube of shampoo from the soap dish, squeezing a glob into his palm and working it into his hair.

*I wasn't always this way*, he thought sadly, backing up to

rinse out the lather.

He soaped his body, running his hands over the well-defined muscles of his chest and arms. Over the years, especially after he'd been kicked off the Devils in his senior year at Duke, he'd found solace in working out. At home in Raleigh, he had an excellent gym on the roof of his apartment building, complete with an Olympic-size pool, and when he'd moved in, he'd made arrangements for his keycard to work at the health club twenty-four hours a day. Many nights, when he couldn't sleep, he'd make his way to the elevator and up to the thirtieth floor, where he could work out his disappointment and aggression and find the peace to let him go back to sleep.

On autopilot the year after he'd graduated from Duke by the skin of his teeth, he'd allowed his parents to pressure him into law school. He concentrated his studies in public policy as they'd suggested, instead of entertainment law, which had always held his fascination. Locked into a course of study, he graduated three years later and took a job at his father's law firm, as planned. The following year, he launched an unsuccessful campaign for state senator. Though his parents did most of the work and hoped for the best, his icy demeanor and sour expression lost him the vote.

He still had little interest in politics or public policy. He'd allowed his parents to railroad him into a life he didn't truly love. Why? Because most of the time, he simply didn't care.

He had an overwhelming sense of apathy. Work was work. Work made money. Money made life comfortable. But none of it really mattered.

*What matters?* he asked himself.

He paused as the water whooshed the suds from his skin and down the drain.

"What matters?" he whispered, his voice a little desperate when his mind remained a blank.

Hillary mattered, of course. And Pete. His parents annoyed him, but he cared about them. But he had no *great* loves. No sports team he played for. No issues he'd die for. No woman he loved.

And in that instant, Hillary's words revisited him: *You need to face your past, or you'll never be able to move forward. I mean, wouldn't you like to* love *someone? Be loved by them? Maybe get married and have a baby?*

Did he want those things?

He reached for the shower lever and twisted it to Off, reaching for a towel and drying his hair first and then his body.

*Do I want those things?*

He used his forearm to clear a circle of steam from the mirror and looked at his face. *Here you are, back on the Banks, in the place where your dreams began and died. So it's time to answer the question, Erik: do you want more than you have?*

"Yes," he whispered. *I want to move forward. I want to love someone. I want more than I have.*

*Face your past, or you'll never be able to move forward.*

He took a deep breath and exhaled slowly, watching as the steam covered the mirror again, blurring his reflection.

To face his past, he'd need to remember the precious days he spent with Laire. He'd need to look at them and examine them and let them hurt him one last time before letting them go. Without answers. Without explanations. Without anything except the sheer force of his will to have a different life than the cold, lonely, angry, meaningless existence he'd been carving out for himself since her loss.

And he may as well start today.

Pulling on jeans and a sweatshirt, he sat down at the desk in his room and reviewed some e-mails and business correspondence, then closed his laptop, grabbed his coat and keys, and headed downstairs. He'd start at Utopia Manor, where his love affair with Laire had started and ended, and when he was done, maybe he would finally—*finally*—be free.

***

Laire finished the last of her coffee, grinning across the bistro table at Ava Grace, who had just asked for a second helping of pancakes.

"Mama, don't be mad, but Kelsey makes the best pancakes ever."

Laire chuckled at her daughter as Ava Grace dug into another helping.

Looking out the window at the cold expanse of snow covering the lawn, she couldn't help but remember Erik. They'd spent so many nights curled up in those Adirondack chairs together, talking, touching, kissing, sharing their dreams and their hopes and their love.

The ghost of Erik was everywhere she turned at the Pamlico House, where they'd loved each other so desperately. She'd grown so much that summer, changed so much, learned so much. She'd loved so deeply, it hurt. And even though she considered herself over Erik now, being here made it ache again, which she resented.

Not to mention, it had been many years since she'd separated her Erik from the Governor's Son, but here? In this place where she and Erik had been so happy? It was hard to convince herself that the man she'd loved was dead and gone. Somewhere in the world—at an office desk in Raleigh, most likely—Erik Rexford was very much alive.

And her daughter, who had her father's beautiful eyes, was a constant reminder that someday she'd need to tell Ava Grace who he was and how to find him. It scared her breathless to even turn her mind to it.

Her cell phone buzzed on the table, and she flipped it over to find several e-mails delivering at the same time. There was no cell reception, and the Wi-Fi at the inn was coming in fits and spurts. She scrolled through message after message from Madame Scalzo and her assistant and other designers in the New York office. They didn't love the designs she sent last night, which meant a day or two of revising the sketches.

She sighed. "Ava, I have to do some work today. Do you think you could watch a movie on your iPad when we get back up to the room?"

Ava Grace squished up her face and shrugged. "I did that already. It's borin', Mama."

Not only had Ava Grace watched movies and TV shows in the car all the way from Boone to Buxton, but she'd been watching them for two days in their hotel room. She was probably going stir-crazy by now, but that didn't change the fact that Laire needed to do several hours of work and the iPad was the perfect babysitter, unless . . .

Kelsey popped back into the dining room with a heaping platter of pancakes in one hand and a coffee carafe in the other.

"Who wants more pancakes?" she asked.

"Me! Me! Me!" cried Ava Grace.

"Kelsey," asked Laire, "do you do any babysitting?"

Kelsey placed three large pancakes on Ava Grace's plate, then turned to Laire. "Sure. Lots. You need a sitter?"

"Desperately. How about today?"

"Definitely. I can make time. When were you thinkin'? Tonight?"

Laire cringed. "Um, now?"

"*Now* now? Like, *right* now?"

Laire held up her phone. "I just got a dozen messages that're going to keep me busy until late afternoon. I pay well."

"But I still have an hour of breakfast left, and then—"

"Ava wouldn't mind sitting here and eating pancakes, would you, Ava?"

Ava Grace shoved another mouthful between her lips and shook her head.

"And I, well, it's almost seven thirty. Even if you gave me until one. One o'clock," she said, trying to bargain. "Five and a half hours. I could get a ton done."

Kelsey looked at Ava Grace, who grinned up at her. "Well, I guess I could watch her until one. But she'll have to stay here in the dinin' room until nine, and if she's good, she can help me make cookies, and then we'll go outside and make a snowman, and then—"

Laire's phone buzzed again, and she jumped up before Kelsey could reconsider. "That's perfect! Thank you so much!"

Kelsey winked at Ava Grace before refreshing Laire's coffee and heading back into the kitchen.

Laire picked up her cup and turned to Ava Grace. "Promise you'll be good for Kelsey? Mind her? And use your manners?"

"Yes, Mama. Kelsey's my new best friend . . . after you and Mr. Mopples."

Laire chuckled as she stood up, leaning down to press a kiss to her daughter's head. "And you're my beautiful girl."

"Your beautiful *princess*, Mama," said Ava Grace, a drop of maple syrup making a slow descent down her chin.

"Wait a minute." Laire paused, grinning down at her as she wiped the syrup with a napkin. "Are you a princess now?"

"Yes," said Ava Grace nodding, her eyes dead serious. "Daughters of princes are always princesses, Mama."

"Oh." Laire's heart stuttered for a moment, but she kept her smile pasted on her face. *You're going to have to tell her the truth whether you like it or not. Someday she'll need to know.* "Yes. Of course, baby. You're *my* princess. Always."

*Damn you, Erik Rexford.*

As unexpected tears burned her eyes, she turned quickly away and hurried back up the stairs to their room.

\*\*\*

As Erik headed down the stairs with his keys in his hand, the smell of pancakes reminded him that breakfast was served from seven to nine, and lucky for him, it was just after seven thirty. As he reached the reception area, Mr. Leatham, who stood at the reception desk, cleared his throat meaningfully.

Erik stopped on his way to the dining room, looking at the innkeeper with eyebrows raised.

"You just missed her," he said, his expression dour. "The li'l'un's mama."

"Sorry?"

"You could've had words with her, but you just missed her. She just went back upstairs."

Erik sighed, rubbing his forehead. "Look. I don't want to *have words* with anyone. You know what? Forget it. I'll just . . . buy earplugs."

"Whatever you say," said Mr. Leatham with a sniff of disapproval.

It occurred to him that perhaps Mr. Leatham needed to be reminded that Erik was a paying customer, but since he still had a stay of several days ahead, he figured it was better to just let it go and keep the peace. He grimaced at the salty innkeeper and headed into the dining room where he'd had his first date with the girl of his dreams.

As he entered the room, time went backward for a split second, and he paused just inside the doorway. He remembered the soft candlelight on the tables, the way her green eyes had sparkled after the kiss they'd shared at the top of the dock, and the awkward conversation it had started. She was so innocent, so beautiful, so—

"Table for one?"

Erik looked up from his reverie to see Kelsey Leatham standing with her hand on her hip, breasts pushed out. He kept his eyes up.

"Yes, please."

Though there were many unoccupied tables in the room,

she walked him over to a table by the windows beside the only other diner—a little girl, sitting alone with a stuffed penguin on the table, shoveling pancakes into her mouth like there was about to be a world shortage.

The li'l'un. Hmm.

She leaned over her breakfast, a tiny thing with dark red hair, made brilliant by the sunlight streaming in from the window to her right. Not that he was ever around kids, but if he had to guess, he'd put her age right around four years old.

"How about here?" asked Kelsey, and damn if he didn't see a challenge in her pretty blue eyes. Her grandfather must have told her about his objections to the noise, and so she was seating Erik beside his nemesis on purpose.

"Perfect," he said, accepting her challenge by choosing the chair that faced the child.

The little girl looked up at him and waved, her huge, dark brown eyes seizing his. And damn if his breath didn't hitch for a moment, because the only other place he'd ever seen eyes quite *that* dark and wide was, well, in the mirror or the face of his mother. He always thought of kids, especially little girls, as having blue eyes like Hillary's or Vanessa's—vulnerable and light—not almost black. It was extraordinary. And a little unsettling.

After a moment, she stopped waving, fixing him with a glare and saying, "Mr. Mopples says it's rude not to wave back."

Before he could say anything, Kelsey was standing beside his table with a carafe of coffee, and he was gratefully nodding to her to fill his cup.

"Pancakes?" she asked.

"Thanks. Great," said Erik, his eyes flicking back to the little girl, who seemed to be in deep conversation with her penguin.

"Not everyone has good manners, but we still do our best,

don't we? Yes, we do."

Kelsey's lips turned up in a grin, and she shifted to face the little girl. "All good, Ava Grace? Want more pancakes?"

*Ava Grace.*

All the air was suddenly sucked out of the room as Erik's head jerked up to look at Kelsey before dropping his eyes to the dark-eyed little girl—to Ava Grace.

*Ava! Ava Grace, you need to hold my hand!*

*Ava Grace. That's a* real *pretty name.*

*You're pretty like a princess.*

The Elizabethan Gardens.

Six years ago.

With Laire.

The little girl who tripped on the path. Her name was also—

"Mr. Rexford? Um, Mr. Rexford?"

Erik exhaled the breath he'd been holding and glanced up at Kelsey, who was looking at him a little funny.

"Wh—yes?"

"Maple syrup or powdered sugar?"

"Syrup," he murmured, immediately looking back at the little girl who had the same name as the girl who'd tripped on the path, whom Laire had cradled in her arms, who—

"Mr. Mopples says it's *very* rude to stare."

"W-what?"

"Mr. Mopples said so."

"Sorry. Who?"

"You're starin'," the little girl said, her sugar-dusted lips pursed in annoyance.

"Am I?"

She nodded.

"Sorry. Your name is Ava Grace?" he asked.

She nodded again. "Yes."

"My name . . . my name is Erik," he said, trying to regain

his composure. Damn, but he'd been thrown by the mention of that name. There were only a couples of names in the world that could have shaken him that badly, and Ava Grace was, apparently, one of them.

His little nemesis speared a sausage, looked at the beat-up penguin sitting on the tabletop across from her, then offered, through a mouthful of half-eaten food, "Oscar is your name."

"Huh? No. Not Oscar," he said, then enunciated: "Erik."

She chewed a little more, swallowed, then leveled him with her intense eyes. "Oscar."

*Well, this is annoying.* Did the little thing have a hearing problem? He tried again, raising his voice a little. "My name is *Erik,* not Oscar."

"You're yellin'."

"I'm not . . ." He lowered his voice. ". . . yellin'."

"Yes, you did," she said. "Mr. Mopples says your name is Oscar because you are a grouch. Mr. Mopples is always right."

"I'm a . . . *grouch*?"

She nodded matter-of-factly as she reached for her orange juice. "You don't wave, you stare, and you yell. And when Kelsey asked if you wanted syrup or sugar, you a'nored her."

"*Ignored*, not *a'nored*. I *i*gnored her."

"Yes, you did," agreed Ava Grace, replacing her glass after a satisfied slurp. "And Mr. Mopples does *not* approve."

"Who the hell is Mr. Mopples?"

"See? Now you sweared. Your name is *definitely* Oscar."

He counted to three in his head, then asked as politely as possible, "*Who* is Mr. Mopples?"

With her palm open, she gestured delicately to the worn penguin sitting across from her on the table. "Her."

"Him," said Erik.

"No," said Ava Grace. "Her."

"But you said '*Mr.* Mopples.'"

She nodded at him.

"Mr. Mopples is a girl?"

She nodded again. "Do you know why?"

Suddenly, out of nowhere, he was reminded of something Hillary had always said when she was little and people asked why her stuffed elephant, Ella, was a boy.

"Because that's the way it is," he said matter-of-factly, surprised to feel his lips twitch just a touch, remembering his little sister's sass and grateful that it remained intact.

But what happened next was the most surprising thing of all. The little redhead blinked at him, then gasped with delight, her face exploding into the most beautiful smile he'd ever seen, on any child, on any person, in all his living life, and she exclaimed, "Yes! You got it right!"

"Did I?" he asked, chuckling in spite of himself.

"Yes! And no one ever gets it right! Not even Uncle Patrick! Not even *Mama*!" She nodded at him, her grin still huge as she turned the penguin around to face Erik. "*She* is *Mr.* Mopples because that's the way it is."

"Well, Ava Grace," he said, taking a sip of his coffee and feeling more satisfied with this little victory than he'd felt in a long, long time, "it was about time *someone* got it right."

# Chapter 19

Laire had finished most of her designs by noon and managed to forward them to Madame Scalzo by the time one o'clock rolled around and Kelsey knocked on her door to return Ava Grace.

"We had so much fun, Mama!" cried her daughter, racing into the room with snowy boots and leaving little puddles everywhere.

"Ava! Boots off!" She turned to Kelsey. "How'd you do?"

"She's awesome," said Kelsey. "We baked cookies and made snow angels."

"I don't suppose you could sit again tomorrow?"

"I could," said Kelsey, "but mornin's are tough. How about tomorrow evenin'? From five to ten or even later? I can stay up here with Ava Grace, and you can work downstairs in the salon?"

Laire nodded gratefully, taking her wallet off the nightstand and pulling out sixty-five dollars. "Is this good?"

"Great. Thanks." Kelsey took the money and put it in her back pocket. "Did Grandpa say you needed a boat tomorrow, or did I hear wrong?"

"Not tomorrow," said Laire. "Maybe next week, though, when school starts up for Ava Grace. At some point I want to head over to Corey."

"Corey *Island*?" asked Kelsey. "Why the heck do you want to go all the way over there?"

Laire looked down at her bare feet for a moment before meeting the younger woman's eyes. "I'm *from* Corey."

"Nah!"

Laire nodded, unable to hold back her smile. "I am, I swear."

"I thought for sure you were a dingbatter."

"Nope. Islander. Born and bred." Her smile faded. "Left about six years ago."

"And lost your accent." Kelsey flicked a glance to Ava Grace. "Story for another time?"

"And a big glass of wine."

"So you're goin' home to see your folks?"

"Sort of. Maybe." She shrugged, her shoulders brushing her ears and holding for a moment as she considered Kelsey's question. "I left on . . . bad terms. I want to try to make things right before I move to New York this summer."

"Wait! You're movin' to New York?!" asked Kelsey, putting her hands on her hips, her eyes sparkling and impressed. "Got room for one more? As a nanny maybe?"

"What would your grandpa say about that?" asked Laire.

There was only a few years' difference between her and Kelsey, but Laire had lived through a lot of heartache in twenty-four and a half years, and Kelsey felt so much younger than she. The Leathams were originally from Ocracoke, which wasn't anywhere near as conservative as Corey, but many of the values were still the same, and Laire wasn't anxious that her new friend experienced the kind of hardships that she had.

Kelsey shrugged. "Wouldn't love it. Nor my folks."

"Think hard before you make a choice like that, huh, Kelsey?"

The younger woman sighed but nodded her head. "Yeah.

It's hard to leave."

"It's especially hard to come back," said Laire softly, more to herself than Kelsey.

She'd already been back on the Banks for three days, and none of her family was any the wiser. Now that she was here, she found she wasn't in a rush to see them, though they were a huge reason for why she'd decided to move here for a while. Then again, it made sense to settle Ava Grace in at the Hatteras Elementary School and move into Judith's condo first, right? Yes. No sense in jumping the gun. Once they were settled in Hatteras, she'd call Kyrstin and ask for her advice about arranging a visit.

"Mama," said Ava Grace, peeking around the bathroom door, "you know that I have a new friend?"

Grateful for the distraction, Laire grinned at her. "You do?"

"Uh-huh! His name is Oscar!"

She ducked back into the bathroom, and Laire chuckled as she turned to Kelsey. "Oscar? I didn't realize that there was another child staying in the inn."

"Oh," said Kelsey, licking her lips and giving Laire a funny look. "He's not a kid. And, actually, his name isn't Oscar. It's—
"

"Mama!" screamed Ava Grace.

Laire's heart kicked into high gear as she crossed the room in three strides, rushing into the bathroom. "Ava?"

Ava Grace was sitting on the toilet with her snow pants around her ankles, pointing at the shower. As Laire looked around the curtain, she saw a hairy spider the size of her palm resting on the white tile.

"Oh, God," she said, cringing. "Gross."

Kelsey, who had followed her into the bathroom, gasped, then groaned. "Second one this week. I think they got washed in by the storm. They're comin' up through the pipes."

"Mama," wailed Ava Grace. "It's so yucky!"

Laire backed away from the arachnid and handed her daughter some toilet tissue. "Wipe."

"I'll get Grandpa," said Kelsey, backing out of the small room. "Spiders give me the creeps!"

"Me too!"

Ava jumped off the pot and flushed, and Laire helped her take off her boots, snow pants, and parka, settling her in front of the TV with a snack bag of cookies.

It was hours later, after Mr. Leatham had dispatched their hairy friend, and Ava Grace was happily eating order-in pizza for dinner, that Laire realized she'd never gotten the details on her daughter's mysterious new friend, Oscar.

\*\*\*

Erik spent most of the day at Utopia Manor with a local handyman, Charles McGillicutty, assessing the damage to the mansion and coming up with a plan for repair and renovation. The dock had been broken by waves and thrown about twenty yards onto the lawn, which was covered with detritus from the sea. Parts of the boardwalk needed repairs. The pool had been flooded, and the water had leaked through the sliding doors into the living room, destroying the ground-floor hardwood floors, carpets, and furniture. The basement had also flooded, killing the electrical panel. And several third-floor windows had been broken by flying debris, causing damage to the interior and exterior of the house. It was thousands of dollars of damage in landscaping and structure, and Erik needed Hillary to call his parents' insurance agent in Raleigh to come out and make a report right away. He guessed it would a few days for someone to get out to the Banks, so Erik would probably be stuck there until at least the first of January.

Standing on the balcony off his room in the late-afternoon sunshine, he pulled out his phone and texted Hillary, relieved to discover that he had edge service.

*ERIK: Hey. Are you around? At UM.*

While he waited for her to respond, he placed his phone on the railing of the balcony, looking out at the expanse before him: the pool, lawn, boardwalk, and dock. He remembered the first time he ever saw Laire Cornish, standing below him on the pool deck, her green eyes so innocent and lovely as she insisted she didn't have crabs.

For the first time in many years, he chuckled softly about a memory connected with Laire, but his laughter tapered off quickly, and his smile faded. If he'd known that day the heartache that would follow, would he have spoken to her, followed her around like a puppy, carried her coolers to the kitchen, and insisted on a date? Or would he have said hello, then walked back inside, to the safety of his bedroom, and stayed there until she was gone?

Simply put, would he exchange all the wonderful moments that summer for the pain that followed?

It was a difficult question, but Erik sensed that it was at the heart of his success in moving forward with his life.

If he could go back in time and never meet Laire Cornish, would he?

His phone buzzed on the railing, and he picked it up.

*HILLZ: Here. What's up? How's the house?*

*ERIK: In bad shape. Can you call Town & Country Insurance and have an adjuster sent out?*

*HILLZ: Sure. I'll call today.*

*ERIK: I'll stay until they can get here. I'm staying at the Pamlico House. Tell them to call me there. Phone service isn't good out here. I can only get texts out.*

*HILLZ: Will do.*

He stared at the screen waiting for her to say more.

*HILLZ: How are YOU?*

Erik flinched.

As a rule, he wasn't a fan of the sort of soul-searching he was forcing upon himself—one, it felt self-indulgent, and two, staring hard truths in the face wasn't that pleasant—but he couldn't keep living his life as he had been. It was time for a change.

*ERIK: Doing some thinking.*

*HILLZ: And?*

And?

*If you could go back in time and never meet Laire Cornish, would you?*

"No," he said softly to the cold, whistling wind. "I wouldn't."

*I wouldn't trade it. I'd take the good and handle the pain better than I did.*

This was an interesting revelation for Erik because so much of the last six years had been spent feeling like he hated Laire, wishing he'd never met her, wanting to punish her for hurting him as she did. But now? Faced with the ultimate question of whether he'd erase her from his life? He wouldn't. She was the realest thing he'd ever known. She was open and honest, sweet and fresh. No matter how things had ended between them, she'd taught him more about what he ultimately wanted from a life partner than anyone else. How could he reject that knowledge? It was worth more than the pain he'd suffered, wasn't it? Used correctly, it could shape the sort of relationship that might, someday, make him happy again. He knew what to look for, and what not to look for, in a partner. That knowledge was priceless, and he wouldn't have it without her.

*HILLZ: About what?*

*ERIK: I'd like to change.*

*HILLZ: Really?*

*ERIK: Yeah.*

*HILLZ: Tell me more!* ☺ ☺ ☺

He groaned at the smiley faces filling the screen. He could see her setting him up on dates the second he returned to Raleigh.

*ERIK: Chill out. I'm not ready to get married or anything. I'm just figuring some things out.*

*HILLZ: That's good. Really good. That's all I ever wanted you to do.*

*ERIK: Thanks, Hills. Thanks for putting up with me. I've been pretty awful.*

*HILLZ: She did a number on you. But yeah, it's time for you to move on.*

*ERIK: If I never hear the words "move on" again, it'll be too soon.*

*HILLZ: LOL. MOVE ON. MOVE ON. MOVE ON.*

Erik's lips quirked up into a grin, and suddenly he was reminded of the little scamp at breakfast who'd given him such a hard time. He hoped she didn't have a brother, because he was certain to be heckled just as much as Hillary heckled him.

And yet, there was no denying her awesomeness. Four years old and holding her own against a grown man. He chuckled again. If he could have a kid like Ava Grace someday, it might be worth it to try to find the right girl.

Erik sighed, looking away from his phone at the horizon. It was only four thirty, but the sun was low in the sky. It'd be dark soon.

*ERIK: Wench. I have to go. Sun's setting. No heat here and plenty cold.*

*HILLZ: Poor Erik.*

*ERIK: Wiseass. Love you.*

*HILLZ: I'll call the insurance company and be in touch. Love you too.*

He tucked his phone in his pocket and walked back into his bedroom, closing the sliding door and locking it behind him.

There were no lights to turn off as he headed downstairs, walking over the saturated, squishy carpet and water-damaged, buckling hardwood floors on his way to the front door. He locked it behind him, then headed down the steps to his car.

For the first time in a long time, he felt lighter. His *heart* felt lighter, or warmer maybe. He couldn't describe it, only knew that it was changing after a long time of suspended animation. Living in a frozen emotional state might have protected him from further heartbreak, but it hadn't allowed him to heal or grow. The gaping, angry wound that was Laire Cornish's unexplained rejection had festered for long enough. It was a strange and unexpected relief to finally give himself permission to start moving on.

\*\*\*

Laire pulled the covers up to Ava Grace's chin and kissed her on the forehead as she slept. She had no plans for tomorrow, but maybe she would take her daughter somewhere special if the roads were clear enough to drive and it was warm enough to be outdoors. Ava Grace hadn't seen the lighthouse yet, or had a run on the beach. And they should be able to find a place open for lunch in Hatteras, right? They could drive by her new school and maybe look in the windows. Tomorrow would be all about Ava Grace, and tomorrow night she would work for as long as Kelsey agreed to babysit.

As for tonight . . .

One of the things she'd always liked best about the Pamlico House was the widow's walk on the fourth floor. As a waitress at the restaurant, so many years ago, she'd often taken her break up there, staring out at the ocean on one side and the Sound on the other, letting the wind whip her hair around as she daydreamed about a life spent with Erik Rexford. Those dreams had been crushed instead of granted, of course, and maybe that's why she hadn't gone up to the widow's walk yet. It was hardest to face the places where she'd been the happiest.

But she was suddenly reminded that the Leathams lit the fire pit upstairs every night between eight and ten, and Kelsey had encouraged her to go up and relax when she had some free time. She told Laire that they left out warm blankets in the European tradition, and she could stare up at the stars while the fire warmed her face.

Laire had been reluctant to leave Ava Grace alone in the room the first few nights, but she was much more comfortable at the inn now, and—Laire looked down at her daughter's angelic, sleeping face—fast asleep.

Maybe tonight she'd wander upstairs for an hour and relax—sit by the fire with her head tilted back, as Kelsey had suggested, and stare up at the stars. Breathe in the cold, salty air with a heavy wool blanket warming her legs. Just be. Just . . . be.

Life didn't afford a single mother many opportunities to relax, and certainly, once she and Ava Grace were in their new condo, there would be lots of work to be done. While she was here, perhaps she should just enjoy an hour to herself.

Careful not to wake up Ava Grace, she quietly slipped out of her yoga pants and pulled on some jeans and heavy wool socks. Her T-shirt came off next, and she chose a simple black cashmere turtleneck sweater as her top. Her black UGG boots were waiting for her in the closet, and she grabbed her chic black ski jacket and black leather gloves trimmed in gray rabbit fur. She plucked a gray rabbit fur infinity scarf from the top of the bureau and slid it over her unruly hair, which she pulled into a low ponytail against the back of her neck. Checking herself out in the mirror, she noticed that her face looked thin and tired, but at least her threads were fashion-forward.

Giving Ava Grace one last peck on the forehead, she slipped out of the room as quietly as possible, closing the door behind her.

***

With a dozen other guests staying at the inn, Erik hadn't expected to have the fire pit all to himself, and after a long day of facing demons, he was relieved to sink into the plush, comfortable couch on the roof deck and pull a shearling blanket over his legs and chest. The fire warmed his face enough after a few minutes that he leaned his head back, staring up at the stars, and unbidden, he was reminded of Laire's words the first night they'd made out at Utopia Manor: *We're just two tiny specks of dust in a big, wide world. But I feel so much, Erik. I feel so much, it's like the whole universe couldn't hold it even if it tried.*

He winced, closing his eyes against the familiar, yet unexpected, swell of anguish.

How could she have broken up with him like that?

How could she have turned her back on him? Without notice? Without warning?

How could she have let go of something that had made them feel so goddamned much?

And *why*? *Why*, goddamn it?

He would have done anything for her—gone to the ends of the earth—to make her happy.

Borne anything. Tried anything. Waited forever.

He wasn't even given the chance. She turned her back on him and disappeared before he even knew she was gone, and it was So. Fucking. Unfair.

His attention was suddenly drawn to the sound of the door to the roof opening, and Erik opened his eyes, taking a deep breath of icy air and trying to quickly regain his composure. He wasn't in the mood for idle chitchat with another hotel guest, but he was a gentleman, and he'd exchange pleasantries for a moment before heading back downstairs for a glass of bourbon before bed.

He cleared his throat and sat up, looking straight ahead at the person who'd interrupted his starlit silence. Several feet away, she leaned her elbows against the stainless steel railing that ran around the perimeter of the space, her knees pressed against the Plexiglas that separated the railing from the floor, her face, in profile, turned upward as she gazed up at the sky.

She was about five foot four inches tall and slim, dressed in jeans and a black jacket, with some sort of fur scarf around her neck.

As Erik stared at her wordlessly, his lips parted slowly, and his heart sped up, faster and faster, as it always did when he saw a woman with that hair color. It wasn't quite blonde in the moonlight. From where he sat, whether it was a trick of the firelight or real, her hair appeared to be strawberry blonde. Held low against her neck with a simple band, it was straight and long, just like . . . just like . . .

Sitting up straight, Erik didn't feel the blanket fall from his chest, pooling in his lap as he traced the lines of her face in profile, tiny puzzle pieces he'd fiercely longed for finally taking their place before him—the slope of her nose, the pursed bow of her lips, the swanlike grace of her long neck.

"Jesus. It can't be . . .," he murmured breathlessly, rubbing frantically at his eyes. It was only because he was here, where her ghost was everywhere, where he'd been so happy with her. It was a trick. It wasn't real.

But his whispered words, only in competition with the light snap and crackle of the fire pit, had carried in the quiet darkness, and when he dropped his fingers to his lap and focused, he found she wasn't a trick of light.

She was real.

Laire Cornish was facing him.

"Holy shit," he murmured, his chest rising and falling so quickly, he was becoming light-headed. Was this a hallucination? A fucking joke? Without his permission, his feet had planted themselves firmly on the floor, and he was rising, standing, bound by a mutual searing, disbelieving gaze to the woman not ten feet away from him. "Laire?"

Under her puffy little ski jacket, her chest rose and fell as fast as his, and her eyes—her beautiful, beloved, sea-green eyes—stared back at him, wide and shocked, as she nodded her head.

"What the fu—what are . . ...?" he asked, his words barely audible in his ears over the fierce thumping of his heart. He forced his hands, which were sweating and shaking, to land and stay on his hips as he choked out, "Are you . . . are you, um, stayin' here?"

"Y-yeah," she whispered, wincing as she gasped, then sobbed, two mammoth tears slipping down her cheeks like jewels in the moonlight. "E-Erik?"

One gloved hand darted to the railing like she was having trouble standing up, and Erik lurched from the couch to her side, taking her free elbow with a firm hand.

"Breathe," he commanded.

Looking up at him with green, glistening eyes, she sucked in a long, deep breath, filling her chest, which lifted her breasts again.

"Let it go," he said, holding her eyes with his.

Her body relaxed in increments as she released the air, ignoring the stream of gray steam that disappeared over their heads.

"Do it again."

She nodded and breathed deeply again, and he could feel her strength returning. As she filled her lungs, she pulled her elbow away from his grasp and took a step back. Despite the distance she imposed between them, she never looked away, her eyes incomprehensible, storming with too many emotions and not enough light for Erik to decipher their meaning.

"Do you want to sit down?" he asked.

"No," she whispered, crossing her arms over her chest.

Wondering if his proximity was actually doing more harm

than good, he backed away from her as he would a frightened animal. Once there was a good three feet of space between them, he dropped her eyes for a moment, running his hand through his hair as he tried to collect himself.

"I never thought I'd see you again," he said softly. When he looked back up, his hand remained curled around the back of his neck. He needed to hold on to something.

"I know," she said.

His eyes narrowed at her response. "You never *wanted* to see me again."

Because her lips were still parted, he could see her clench her teeth, flexing her jaw and flinching at his words. Finally, she murmured. "No."

His heart clutched with pain at the stark, simple word.

*You never* wanted *to see me again.*

It occurred to him that this was his long-awaited chance to ask her why. Why *didn't you ever want to see me again?* But fuck if a lump the size of the ocean hadn't risen there, making it impossible for him to speak. And his eyes, focused on hers, burned from the prick of tears, making him blink rapidly before looking away from her, out at the Pamlico Sound, which had conveyed them, time and again, to one another.

He cleared his throat, trading pain for anger. "Well, too bad for you, then, because here I am."

A small sobbing noise made him whip his head back to face her, his eyes drawn inexorably to hers, where he found such fathoms of grief, it made the muscles of his face flinch as his heart skipped a beat. His anger took a hike. He knew that look. He'd felt it every day for the six long years he'd been apart from her.

Agony.

"Laire?" he whispered, taking a step nearer to her, his hands reaching up to cradle her cheeks without his permission as his eyes owned hers, searching them for answers: *What is it, darlin'? Why're you so sad?*

She took a step back just before his hands made contact, shaking her head, reaching up with her gloved fingers to swipe the tears from her cheeks. He dropped his hands, letting them fall uselessly, listlessly, to his sides.

"I . . . I have to go," she cried, lurching away from the railing and hurrying toward the door.

"Wait!" he called, turning to follow. "Laire! It's been six years. Please! Just fuckin' wait!"

But the door had already closed behind her.

She was gone.

Again.

# Chapter 20

Laire raced down the stairs, stumbling over her feet in an effort to get as far away from him as quickly as possible. Tears streamed down her face, and her heart—*oh, God, my heart*—throbbed with longing, with memories, with love, with hate, with disappointment and loneliness and the sheer horror of running into him without any preparation.

One moment, she'd been fighting against the memory of stargazing with him at Utopia Manor, and the next, he was standing across from her, staring at her, saying her name, holding her elbow, helping her breathe.

"Oh, God," she sobbed, reaching for the door to her room, only to discover she'd somehow locked it from the inside before leaving. "No!"

She resisted the urge to rattle the knob out of sheer frustration, knowing it might wake up Ava Grace. Out of options, overwrought, and exhausted, she turned her back to the door and slipped slowly down to the floor. As silent sobs racked her shoulders, she compressed her body, pulling her knees up to her chest and leaning her forehead down on them, so her tears could flow freely.

*Erik.*

*Erik Rexford.*

*My Erik.*

*The Governor's Son.*

*Here.*

*Here with me.*

*Here with . . . Ava Grace.*

She shook her head against the sheer insanity of it, reaching up to run her fingers into her hair until they met at the back of head, lacing together.

*We should leave.*

*We should get in the car and go.*

*We could find another place. We could—*

Except there were no other hotels near Hatteras with a working generator. Where would she go? All the up to Nags Head or Kitty Hawk? Were the roads even passable yet?

"*Fuck,*" she muttered, blinking against the watery burn in her eyes and sitting up. She could hear footfalls coming down the stairs, and she prayed it wasn't Erik.

She should have known her prayers would fall on deaf ears.

Four doors down, at the entrance of the hallway that led to the main staircase, Erik Rexford suddenly appeared, looking first to the right, then to the left. His eyes landed easily on her crumpled form, crouched outside her hotel room door at the end of the hall.

"Please go," she murmured, half to him, half to herself, staring up at him through blurry eyes as he walked slowly toward her.

When he reached her, he glanced at the room across the hall from hers. The door read "SUPPLIES," and he leaned against it, slowly letting himself sink to the floor until he was sitting across from her, long legs spread out between them.

His eyes searched her face for a long moment before he raised them to the number on her hotel room door: 208.

She didn't acknowledge this, just averted her eyes, staring at the worn denim on her knee, picking at it with her finger.

"Wait," he said. "Is this your room—208?"

His voice held a slight urgency, and she looked up at him, nodding once.

His lips parted and he blinked at her.

"I'm right upstairs from you. You have a . . . Are you here with a kid?"

Every muscle in her body clenched in reaction to these words, and it took every ounce of her strength not to show it outwardly. She nodded. "Yes."

"Ava Grace," he murmured.

She flinched. "Yes. How do you know that?"

"I met her at breakfast." His face still looked stunned, and his eyes searched hers for answers. "She's *yours*? Your . . . daughter?"

*And yours.*

She heard the words in her head but quickly silenced them. She had no interest or desire in sharing her beautiful, trusting, amazing daughter with the man sitting in front of her; with the Governor's Son.

"Yes."

"You named her Ava Grace," he said, his voice barely a whisper.

"Yes," she said, her eyes welling with tears as she looked up at him because she knew that he was thinking about the little girl at the Elizabethan Gardens, and it made her desperately sad and stupidly happy at the same time.

Her memories with Erik had no accompanying pictures, or friends who had witnessed their relationship. During these long and lonesome years, there was no one with whom to recall happy days or process the devastation of losing him. There was a certain comfort in someone, no matter who it was, remembering *with* her.

She saw pain cross his features, for sure, followed by an attempt to smile in polite congratulations, but he lost the battle with trying to appear pleased for her and dropped his eyes, staring down at his lap in barely concealed misery.

"So you're married," he whispered, the words tight and gravelly.

"No."

His neck snapped up, his eyes registering surprise, followed briefly by relief and then confusion. "Divorced?"

She clenched her jaw, choosing her words carefully, adding up his meaning: he didn't realize that Ava Grace was his. He hadn't put it together. He didn't know.

For a moment, when he'd whispered her name, Laire was sure it was because he'd put two and two together and realized that she was his daughter, but now she realized that he didn't know, and a wave of relief made her exhale the breath she'd been holding.

He assumed that she'd been married to Ava Grace's father. Good. The less he knew about her and Ava Grace, the better. He couldn't be trusted. He was the worst kind of deceiver, capable of making her believe he truly loved her while he was actually cheating on her every moment they weren't together.

*He doesn't know*, she reassured herself, then decided it would be best to change the subject as quickly as possible, away from their daughter.

"What about you?" she asked.

"What *about* me?"

"I thought . . . I mean, I heard, a while ago, that you were engaged," she said, wishing it didn't hurt her to say these words, but the memory of Mrs. Rexford's revelations bit and stung like they'd happened much more recently than six years ago.

"No," he said softly.

"*What?*"

It was her turn to look up quickly, seizing his eyes to ascertain the truth of these words.

"Never."

Her heart raced as her eyes scanned his. And as far as she could tell, he wasn't lying. His eyes were fraught from their reunion, yes, but open and clear, his face neutral. But wait. How was it possible that he'd never been engaged? She'd *seen* him with Van. He was laughing, his arm around her, a big fat rock on her finger. Laire had seen it with her own eyes. And no, she'd never actually seen a news report that he was married to Van, but she'd always assumed it was just a long engagement. He certainly had been engaged. She'd seen it. She knew it was true—

*Oh, fuck. Laire! He's doing it. Right now. Lying to you. Stop believing everything he says! Whatever else happened or didn't happen, of course he was engaged to Vanessa Osborn at one point in time. He's just playing games with you . . . like he always did.*

His face wasn't to be trusted.

His words weren't to be trusted.

There was no point in even sitting here talking to him, because she had no idea what was truth and what was lies, and she had zero interest in getting sucked back into a toxic, poisonous, cancerous conversation with someone who'd already broken her in half once.

*Fool me once, shame on you; fool me twice, shame on me.*

Gathering her strength, she pushed off from the floor and slid back up the door, holding his eyes as she rose to her full height, staring down at him with disgust.

"If you'll excuse me, I need to go get a copy of my key—"

"Fine. I'll stay here until you get back, and then we can contin—"

"—and then I'm going to bed."

If she wasn't mistaken, her words made his brown eyes darken to black, and suddenly, for the first time since running into him, she realized two things:

One, though she'd always known that there was an uncanny similarity between his eyes and Ava Grace's, now she was struck with the full uniqueness of it. They were the same unusual color. The same deep, dark, soulful brown that turned black when their emotions flared, and for a split second, it made her feel weak to see the resemblance. The man she'd loved so desperately and the child she'd die for had the same eyes. She could get lost in his all over again if she wasn't careful.

And two, Erik Rexford was even hotter at twenty-seven than he'd been at twenty-one. He was built and big, muscular and strong, his jet-black hair as thick as ever, and the way he was looking at her right now made her traitorous body remember how he'd touched her, how he'd loved her, how she'd writhed in his arms, begging for more. She couldn't concentrate on this conversation anymore. She needed to get away from him.

"Please excuse me," she said, though she didn't turn and start walking down the hall. Her booted feet remained rooted, and her cheeks blazed with sudden heat. She stood there in front of her door, staring down at him, wishing that her attraction to him had died with her dreams.

"How long are you stayin'?" he asked, his tongue slipping between his lips to wet them.

She reached up to cover her cheeks, and she dropped his eyes. Fuck him. He knew exactly what he was doing, which somehow gave her the strength not to fall for it. He'd willingly used her for entertainment six years ago. She wasn't available for his amusement anymore.

"None of your business."

He huffed out a breath of air, shaking his head. "You're somethin' else."

"*I'm* something else?" she demanded, hackles raising as

she crossed her arms. "How do you live with yourself?"

He shot up from the floor, suddenly towering over her. "How do I live with myself? Probably because I never did anythin' wrong!"

She scoffed. "Is that what you tell yourself?"

"Did I promise you somethin' that I *didn't* deliver, Laire?"

*Yes! Your honesty! Your respect! Your love! You promised all those things to me, and you didn't fucking deliver! Instead you lied to me, fucked around with another girl behind my back, never really loved me, got me pregnant, got engaged to her, and broke my fucking heart!*

She gasped, her inner monologue so indescribably painful, it knocked the wind from her lungs and left her breathless, gaping at him like a fish on a dock about to die.

*Except I'm not about to die*, she reminded herself, sucking in a big breath of air. *He doesn't have that kind of hold on me anymore.*

"Go fuck yourself," she bit out, hating her eyes for welling with tears, hating him for the unconscionable way he was speaking to her when he'd willfully deceived her and smashed her heart to smithereens.

He flinched, his head snapping back like she'd slapped him. "Real pretty words, Laire."

"You don't . . ." Her voice broke, but she took a deep breath and met his eyes, feeling stronger. "You don't *deserve* any pretty words from me."

His eyes widened as he ran his hands through his hair in frustration.

"What the *fuck* did I ever do to you?"

Behind Laire, she heard the noise of a door unlatching, and when she turned around, Ava Grace was standing in the open doorway in bare feet, a cartoon-princess nightgown thin on her slight body. She looked up at Laire with sleepy eyes, cocking her head to the side and frowning at her mother's tears.

"Are you okay, Mama?" she asked in a small, worried voice. "Are you cryin'?"

"No, baby. Just something in my eye." Laire leaned down and reached for her daughter, lifting her into her arms and pushing Ava Grace's head onto her shoulder. She smoothed out her tangled, dark-red hair and whispered, "I'm fine, baby. I'm sorry we woke you up."

"We?" With her head on Laire's shoulder, Ava Grace gasped and exclaimed, "Oh! It's Oscar! Hi, Oscar!"

"Hey, there, Ava Grace," said Erik, and Laire was grateful to be facing the room, not her onetime true love, because she wouldn't have been able to conceal the riot of emotions on her face as she listened to her daughter greet her father for the very first time.

"You and Mama woke me up."

"Sorry about that, darlin'," said Erik, and Laire shuddered inside, him calling Ava Grace the endearment *darlin'*, which she'd loved so desperately, making her feel a million different things, each more complicated and confusing than the next. She was holding their daughter, and Erik was calling her darlin', the same way he'd called her darlin' an eternity ago.

*Oh, my heart.*

"I gotta go back to bed," Ava Grace told him.

"I guess so," said Erik, his voice gentle and warm, just as it used to be so many years ago, when he was speaking to Laire. She closed her eyes, almost unable to keep more tears from falling, her heart clenching with a longing that she didn't want to feel.

"Wanna have breakfast with me and Mama tomorrow, Oscar?"

*Wait, what?*

"No, Ava Grace!" exclaimed Laire, her eyes popping open. She leaned back to see Ava Grace's face and turned slightly to face Erik too. She flicked her eyes briefly to his, then back to their daughter. "No, baby. We don't have meals with strangers, and besides I'm sure Mr. —"

"Rexford, Mama," said Ava Grace matter-of-factly, reaching up to cradle her mother's face with her tiny hands. "And he's not a stranger. I already met him. His name is Erik Rexford, but Mr. Mopples calls him Oscar because he's a grouch sometimes."

*He's a grouch sometimes.*

From nowhere—*out of nowhere*—Laire felt laughter rise up within her as she looked Ava Grace in the eyes. It was absurd, and yet so perfect, she couldn't contain the wild little giggle that escaped through her lips. She'd been worried that Ava Grace wouldn't be able to hold her own with the Rexfords, yet here she was, with the help of Mr. Mopples, putting him in his place before she even knew who he was.

She chanced a glance at Erik, who was staring down at his boots, his lips turned up as he chuckled softly to himself.

"Is that right?" she asked her daughter.

"Uh-huh," confirmed Ava Grace with a resolute nod. "And you know Mr. Mopples, Mama. When she gets an idea in her head, it's hard to get it out again."

"I know Mr. Mopples." Laire nodded at Ava Grace, kissing her forehead before lowering her to the floor and taking her hand to lead her back to bed.

She might have missed it if she hadn't looked up just then, but Erik's eyes sparkled with humor and tenderness, longing and . . . and . . .

"Time for bed," murmured Laire, swallowing over the lump in her throat.

"Good night, Oscar," said Ava Grace, waving at Erik as Laire pulled her into their room. "See you at breakfast."

"Good night, Ava Grace," said Erik, then added, so softly

that Laire might have imagined it as she closed the door, "Good night, darlin'."

\*\*\*

Erik stood in the hallway, staring at their hotel room door, his feet waiting for the message that they should start moving, but it wasn't forthcoming. He didn't want to go anywhere. He was afraid if he walked away, he'd never see her again, never see *them* again.

Although she wasn't married—news that his heart had received with such profound relief and joy, he hated himself for it—she'd certainly moved on from him fairly quickly. If Ava Grace was four, as he guessed, Laire would have become pregnant with her about a year after she dismissed him in her father's hospital room.

It hurt, desperately, to imagine her with someone else. It hurt worse to imagine her married, for however short a time. It made Erik realize that all these years, he'd still thought of her as his, even though he had no idea where she was, or with whom.

Then again, seeing Laire and Ava Grace together thawed and lifted his heart in a way he never could have guessed. His reunion with Laire on the roof, and the subsequent words they exchanged in the hallway, had been fraught and upsetting, but he still wouldn't trade a moment of it. He'd longed for a glimpse of her for years, and no matter why she'd pushed him away or how badly it had hurt, it fed his soul to see her again. And the moment Ava Grace had appeared, little spitfire that she was, she'd unwittingly defused the insurmountable tension between them.

He grinned, thinking about her sweet, sleepy face as she told her mother that Erik was a grouch. Man, but she was something. A fearless little beauty who should have her daddy wrapped around her finger.

. . . which made him flinch, his lighter mood instantly darkening.

So where the fuck *was* he? A kid like that deserved to have two amazing parents looking after her, raising her, loving her, giving her the best of everything.

*Come to think of it*, he wondered, *how was Laire affording this hotel stay?*

As he started walking back down the hall, he thought about the clothes she was wearing tonight: a designer jacket and jeans, trendy boots, and one of those fur scarves that every woman he knew was wearing this season. Her circumstances had certainly changed from six years ago, but how? Maybe her ex was paying some decent alimony and child support.

*Well, that's the least the fucker can do for abandoning them.*

*Or maybe*, he thought, climbing the stairs to the third floor, *her husband died, leaving her and Ava Grace taken care of, but alone.*

He winced at the thought of Laire losing her husband and Ava Grace losing her father. Although his jealousy toward this unknown man was sharp, he didn't wish that kind of loss and heartbreak for them.

Slipping the old-fashioned key into his door lock, he turned it and stepped into the dark, quiet room, instantly aware of the fact that Laire's room was directly beneath his. He had a sudden, ridiculous urge to lie down on the floor and press his ear to the boards, just to see if he could hear her, to fall asleep feeling connected to her the only way he could.

"Stalker," he whispered, closing the door, crossing the room to the desk and opening a bottle of bourbon he'd pilfered from Utopia Manor. He poured half a tumbler and threw it back, cringing at the burn before filling the glass again.

He turned on the desk lamp, which bathed the room in warm light, and shrugged off his parka, putting it over the back of the desk chair.

Taking his glass to the balcony, he opened the doors and stepped outside onto the icy platform.

*Where has she been all this time? And with whom?*

*Where was Ava Grace's father? Was he still in the picture at all?*

He had so many questions, but as he took another sip of bourbon, they faded, and older questions resumed their place in his mind: *Why did she break up with him? And had she ever loved him at all?*

The final question loomed large and hurt most, and he swallowed back the remainder of the alcohol in his glass as he stared out at the sea, ruminating.

She'd called their epic love affair a summer fling that day in the hospital. She'd practically begged him to leave her alone. And tonight, when he'd said, *You never* wanted *to see me again*, she'd answered simply, *No.*

But he *sensed* it wasn't that simple.

He rested the empty glass on the iron railing, the frigid sea air bracing and welcome.

No. He *knew* it wasn't that simple.

When he'd said to her, *Well, too bad for you, then, because here I am*, she'd sobbed. And when he'd looked at her face, he'd recognized the emotion in her eyes immediately.

"Agony," he whispered into the wind.

He *knew* it because he'd *felt* it every day they'd been apart.

And if Laire felt agony, he reasoned, then things between them hadn't ended clean for her. *In fact*, he thought, remembering his own anguish at losing her, *you didn't feel an emotion that strong unless your heart was broken.*

"But I never broke her heart," he said softly, turning back into the room and closing the French doors behind him. Fuck. He had too many questions and not enough answers.

*Well, I* want *answers*, he thought as he turned off his desk lamp and placed the lowball glass beside the bottle of bourbon, wondering how to get them.

Ava Grace had invited him to join them for breakfast, hadn't she? Well, Erik would go downstairs at seven and wait until nine for them to come down. And when they did, hopefully he and Laire could figure out a time to talk. Because he deserved to understand what the hell had happened between them so many years ago, and this chance meeting might be the last chance he'd ever have to find out.

Sighing with frustration and still reeling from their unexpected meeting, he stripped naked and climbed between the chilly, crisp white sheets, pulling the duvet over his bare chest.

For a moment—just a moment—he allowed himself to remember the flush of her cheeks when she said she was leaving and didn't go. He could feel it between them in that instant: the crackles and currents of attraction that had existed between them since the first day they met. They were still there now, though her suggestion that he go fuck himself made it clear that she wasn't happy about it.

Erik took a deep breath and closed his eyes, drifting off to sleep, dreaming of the days when their attraction had led to love, not hate, and wishing for those days once again.

***

Laire waited until the last-possible moment to go down to breakfast, hoping to avoid seeing Erik. She'd had a terrible time trying to fall asleep last night, her mind swirling with memories and questions. Why had he looked so relieved when she said she wasn't married? Why had he said that he was never engaged when she knew that he was?

But even worse than these unanswered questions was the way he'd made her feel. She'd almost fainted on first seeing him, but he'd been up in a flash, telling her to breathe, holding on to her elbow until she'd regained her composure. She would never have expected such tenderness from him, such instant concern.

And her heart ached from the warm, gentle way he'd spoken to Ava Grace, calling her darlin' and cheerfully tolerating Mr. Mopples's swift and caustic judgment. The way he'd looked at them together—like he'd never seen anything more beautiful in his life . . . She remembered that look from their precious summer together, and it made her long for things that she couldn't have, that she shouldn't want. Not with him, not with the Governor's Son, who was duplicitous, who'd willfully broken her heart.

Finally, at eight fifty, with Ava Grace complaining bitterly that her tummy was "growly," they went downstairs.

And there, sitting in an easy chair in the reception area, facing the stairs, was Erik.

She wasn't as surprised to see him this morning, of course, but it shocked her that her heart lifted effortlessly, practically singing with pleasure to see his dark head bent over his laptop. Her fingers twitched with the sensory memory of those thick strands against her skin. And deep inside, parts of her body that she'd tried to ignore for six long years awoke from their dark, deep sleep, ravenously hungry for the man who'd tricked her and lied to her.

*For shame, Laire, to let a man who hurt you make you feel such things.*

"Oscar!" cried Ava Grace, letting go of Laire's hand and rushing down the remaining stairs. "You waited for us!"

As Erik looked up, his face split into a grin, first at Ava Grace, then at Laire, who held his eyes like seeing them again was a miracle she never thought she'd be granted.

Dear Lord, she still wanted him.

*Gyah, this is bad. This is really bad.*

Suddenly his face changed, and in an instant he'd thrown his laptop on the sofa and was up and running toward them but not fast enough to catch Ava Grace, who had stumbled in her haste to get to him.

She missed the last three steps, flying through the air and landing at the foot of the stairs in a heap. Though Laire cringed at the sound of it, there was a certain relief in the ungodly shriek that followed. As every mother in the world eventually learns, silence is worse.

Rushing down the rest of the stairs, she was no match for Erik, who was already sitting on the floor, gathering Ava Grace into his arms.

Wailing pitifully, she buried her face against his chest, hiccuping and crying all over his pressed, light blue, button-down shirt, the marks of her tears bleeding into wide circles. Erik looked up at Laire, his eyes wide and worried as Laire squatted down beside them.

"Ava Grace, tell Mama what hurts."

"My kn-kn-kneeeee. And m-my elb-b-b-oooooow!"

Erik's face was fraught as he held on to Ava Grace, looking up at Laire for some kind of reassurance.

"You're okay, angel," she said, nodding at Erik, who exhaled a relieved breath and nodded back.

"I'm . . . n-n-nooooot!" she protested, tears still falling.

Laire looked at Ava Grace's elbow, which was red and scratched but not bleeding. And her jeans over her knee weren't ripped, which meant she'd just burned the skin on the denim when she fell.

"You got a few scratches, and I think you got the wind knocked out of you." *And wounded your pride in front of "Oscar."*

"I'm huuuuurt!" she insisted in a howl.

"Come to Mama, baby," said Laire, putting her hands under Ava Grace's shoulders to lift her off Erik's lap, but Ava Grace resisted her, pulling away from her mother to nestle closer to him.

"Hey, little darlin'," said Erik gently, finally finding his voice, "you sure know how to make an entrance."

"What d-does that m-mean?" she asked between sniffles.

"Means that the next time you walk into a room, I'm goin' to be standin' nearby and ready to catch you."

Ava Grace leaned away from his chest, looking up into his eyes. "You w-w-will?"

"Heck, yes," said Erik, grinning at her. "Can't let you take a trip like that again."

"A t-trip?" she asked, sniffling loudly as her tears stopped falling.

"It's a play on words. You tripped . . . so, you 'took a trip,' see?"

A tiny smile tilted up the corners of Ava Grace's mouth as she nodded at him. "I took a trip . . . but not a good one."

"True enough." Erik chuckled softly, reaching up to push a lock of hair from her forehead. "You okay now? Can you stand up?"

"I'm hungry," she said, frowning at him.

"I told Kelsey to save you some pancakes," said Erik, sliding his eyes to Laire. "Just in case you showed."

Ava Grace wriggled off his lap in a flash and stood up. "Thanks, Oscar!"

Laire watched her run to the dining room before returning her glance to Erik. She gulped softly, the word she needed to say sticking in her throat.

"Thanks," she managed softly.

He nodded at her from the floor, then stood up. "Were you avoidin' me?"

"What do you mean?" she asked, though she could feel her goddamn cheeks getting hot because she knew exactly what he meant.

"Comin' down to breakfast late so you wouldn't have to see me?" he asked, raising his eyebrows, his lips on the brink of an old, familiar smile.

Laire took a deep breath, staring down at her boots for a moment before looking up at him. "Yes."

He nodded in understanding, that smile still fighting for life. "Okay."

"Okay what?" she squeaked.

He shrugged. "You're stayin' here. I'm stayin' here. I know where to find you."

"What does *that* mean?"

"It means . . ." He stared at her, his eyes soft and tender, and so familiar, her breath caught with yearning. "I want to talk to you."

"I have n-nothing to say," she answered, hating the waver in her voice.

His eyes, so deep and tender, held hers without flinching, ignoring her words. "Will you meet me later?"

"No."

"Yes."

"No," she said, shaking her head, "I will *not* meet you, Erik. Absolutely not."

"Why? What are you so scared of, Freckles?"

*Freckles. Oh, my heart.*

"Nothing." *Everything.* "*Why* do you want to meet?"

He sighed, and she could see several emotions pass over his face before resignation won. Leaning closer to her ear, there was an urgency to his voice that compelled her to listen.

"I don't understand why you broke up with me that day in the hospital. I've wondered about it every day for six and a half years. And now here you are, and here I am, and it's . . . I feel like it's the only chance I'm ever goin' to get to find out what happened."

She clenched her jaw, remembering that terrible day, a deluge of awful emotions returning in an instant—her desperate fear for her father's life, her tremendous guilt, how she blamed Erik as much as she blamed herself and wanted to hurt him, how she'd bargained with God to save her father in exchange for her happiness with Erik. There were so many reasons she'd pushed him away—fear, spite, immaturity, desperation—and all of them were still painful. What good would it do to rehash it now? Besides, he'd been cheating on her that summer, even though she hadn't known it at the time. Did he really *deserve* an honest answer?

Shaking her head, she started to refuse again, but he reached out and placed his palm on her cheek, his touch so gentle, so surprising, so tender and familiar and unexpected, her breath hitched, and she held it, letting her eyes flutter closed for an instant as she savored the contact.

"Please, Laire," he whispered, his breath kissing her ear as it had so many times before. "You name the time and place. But, please, darlin', I'm beggin' you for this one thing."

Her eyes burned with tears when she opened them and nodded at him.

"The widow's walk. Eight thirty."

"Thank you," he whispered, caressing her cheek as he dropped his hand. "I'll be there."

# Chapter 21

Laire had considered herself in the mirror for the eighteenth time before she heard a knock on the door and answered it.

"Ready for me?" asked Kelsey with a big grin.

Ava Grace hopped down from the bed and rushed to hug Kelsey around the waist. "We're havin' a party tonight!"

"We are?" asked Kelsey.

"Yep! Mama said we could watch a movie and eat popcorn and drink hot cocoa past my bedtime!"

"Wow!" exclaimed Kelsey, giving Ava Grace a loud, smacking kiss on the cheek. "How about you choose the movie while I talk to your mom for two seconds before she goes?"

"Deal!" said Ava Grace, scampering over to her collection of DVDs to choose one.

"You look," Kelsey said, raising her eyebrows at Laire, "pretty hot for workin' downstairs in the salon."

Shoot. Hot? She wasn't going for hot. She was just going for not covered in pizza grease and the dried remnants of Ava Grace's runny nose.

"What do you mean?" asked Laire, pulling her coat out of the closet.

"Skinny jeans, plum velour scoop neck, fur vest," said

Kelsey, nodding in admiration.

Laire turned to her, surprised by her fashion knowledge but playing down her observations. "Skinny jeans are Old Navy. Velour scoop neck was a final project at school. And anyone with access to Walmart.com can make a decent faux-fur vest if she knows her way around a sewing machine."

"Still," said Kelsey, tilting her head with a teasing grin, "looks more like date wear than work wear."

Laire zipped up her ski jacket and sat down to pull on her boots. "I have to meet someone before I go to work."

"Who?" asked Kelsey, eyes sparkling.

Laire flicked a glance to Ava Grace, who was playing eeny, meeny, miny, moe with the *Up, Wall-E,* and *Wreck-It Ralph* DVD boxes, and asked in a low-toned voice, "What would you say if I told you I had some unfinished business with Erik Rexford?"

Kelsey's face registered shock before she schooled it into insouciance and shrugged. "I'd say you could do better."

"Than the governor's son?" asked Laire incredulously.

"He's hot and all," said Kelsey, "but he's not real nice. He barks at people. He's not warm. And you're, I mean, you're *awesome*."

Laire's mind flitted seamlessly to the photos she'd seen of Erik during their years apart, and her observation about his eyes: cold and dead. Kelsey was right—he didn't come off as very warm anymore.

"He wasn't always like that," she said softly, feeling a measure of defensiveness on his behalf. "Once upon a time he was . . ." *My prince.*

"Whatevs," said Kelsey, shrugging again. "Have fun tappin' that because he is seriously hot, Laire. That's for sure."

"I am not *tapping* anything."

"Whatever you say."

*But he is seriously hot. That* is *for sure*, thought Laire, as

Kelsey knelt down beside Ava Grace to break the tie between *Up* and *Wall-E*.

But why *had* his eyes grown so cold over the years? she wondered. She'd never seen a happy picture of him after their breakup, whereas that summer he'd been all smiles, carefree and happy and warm and—

"Well?" asked Kelsey. "*We're* watchin' *Wall-E*. What are *you* waitin' for?"

Laire crossed the room and gave Ava Grace a kiss on the cheek. "Mama loves you."

"I love you too," said Ava Grace.

"Be good for Kelsey?"

"I love Kelsey!"

"I know. But be good. And no spilling cocoa on the bed. Drink it on the floor, okay?"

Ava Grace nodded, and Kelsey said, "*You* be good too," before swatting Laire away with a shit-eating grin and a wave of her hot-pink manicured fingers.

\*\*\*

After finishing up an outstanding legal brief this morning in the reception room of the inn and speaking on the phone with Town & Country Insurance, who said they'd have a rep out in Buxton tomorrow at noon, Erik took a drive to Hatteras, boarding the ferry to Ocracoke and spending a few hours walking around the island before reboarding the ferry and returning to the inn. He was itching to talk to Laire, his mind focused unmercifully on eight thirty, so he figured it was better to get away for a few hours than end up banging on her door, hoping for an earlier meeting.

As he walked around quiet, off-season Ocracoke Island, which was, by all accounts, similar to Corey Island, he wondered about where Laire had been these past five or six years. She'd left Corey, which must have been an incredibly daring and frightening step, but where had she gone? And aside from having Ava Grace, what had she been up to?

She looked good last night. Much more sophisticated than she'd been at eighteen. And, he realized as he bought a bottle of pop at the general store, she'd lost most of her accent. He'd barely heard a trace of it while they spoke on the roof and in the hallway.

On the ferry ride back to Hatteras, he found his mood grow strangely heavy. The time was getting closer when he'd see her again so it didn't really make sense that he was feeling more down as the minutes ticked by.

Except, wondering about Laire had kept him connected to her all these years, and their impending conversation had the potential to break that connection with answers once and for all. Perhaps he was fearful about what she had to say. She seemed to have so much animosity toward him. Had he inadvertently done something to hurt her? Something he'd never known about? He would hate himself if that was the case because losing her had been the greatest misery of his life. If he'd brought it on himself, he didn't know how he'd forgive himself for it.

Arriving at the widow's walk precisely at eight twenty, he had the roof to himself and decided to sit in one of the single chairs facing the fire pit instead of the couch where he'd been sitting last night. He didn't want to watch her eyes choose to sit in a chair alone and not by his side. It would sound stupid if he articulated it, but that's how he felt.

At eight thirty on the nose, the roof door opened, and Laire stepped into the quiet darkness. Erik looked at her over his shoulder, his heart swelling with so much emotion, he wasn't sure how his chest could contain it. Until that moment, he didn't realize how worried he'd been that she wouldn't show up at all.

*You're here. You came.*

She was dressed similarly to last night, except her hair was down and her face seemed softer and brighter somehow. She'd matured so much in the six years they'd been apart, from a girl to a woman, and he was almost speechless now as he beheld her, so beautiful in the moonlight, it hurt to look at her.

"Hey," he whispered.

"Hey," she said, moving toward him, her voice soft, and—if he wasn't mistaken—slightly warmer than it had been yesterday *and* this morning.

She moved around his chair, to the couch across from him, and sat down on the edge. The flames of the small, modern fire pit between them flickered with her movement before stabilizing.

"You're still beautiful," he said, blurting out the words just before remembering how uncomfortable they used to make her.

Her lips twitched, but she didn't smile. "Don't do that."

*Some things don't change.*

He nodded in understanding. "Okay. So, uh, what are you doin' now? I mean, besides bein' a mom?"

Laire relaxed a little, sitting back and looking at him over the fire.

"I went to college. I have a degree in fashion design and merchandising. I work for a European designer in New York City."

Erik stared at her, at a total loss for words, pride making him grin at her like a fool. She'd done it. She'd chased after her dream and made it happen. That's where she'd been all these years, and it gave him a certain amount of satisfaction to learn it.

"You live in New York," he said, his voice filled with awe.

"No," she said, shaking her head. "I still live in North Carolina."

"You work remotely?"

She nodded. "I send up my designs via e-mail."

"Wow. You did it. You're a New York City designer."

Then she did grin, just a little, in conjunction with a modest shrug, and even with her fancy clothes, he recognized his girl in that little movement, and it made him happy.

"I'm workin' for my father's law firm," he said when she didn't ask.

"I know," she said, then quickly cringed, looking away from him and muttering a quiet "Damn it" under her breath.

"You *know*?"

She opened her mouth to speak, then closed it, still looking over the railing at the ocean, blinking her eyes rapidly.

"You kept tabs on me?" he asked, his heart throbbing with this knowledge.

"Not really," she whispered. "Just a little."

"I would've kept tabs on you too, darlin', if I'd only known where to look."

She turned to him, rubbing her eyes with exasperation before nailing him with a glare. "What *is* this?"

"Two friends catchin' up?"

"We're not friends, Erik," she said. "We never were."

"I disagree," he said. "We were lots of things to each other, but I believe we were friends too."

"And is that what you want now?" she snapped. "To suddenly revive an old friendship?"

He clenched his teeth together and swallowed the words he wanted to say: *No, darlin'. I want to jump across this fiery barrier and pull you into my arms. I want to kiss you again the way I've dreamed for six long years. I want you to know that I still love you. I want you to tell me there's still a chance for us. And then I want to carry you downstairs to my bed and make love to you the way we should have made love that night long ago.*

He licked his lips. "I told you. I want to know why you broke up with me."

She leaned all the way back into the cushions, grabbing a shearling blanket from the back of the couch and covering her body with it.

"I went to the hospital to find you, to comfort you," he continued. "But you were so . . . I mean, did I *do* somethin'? Because one minute we were spendin' the night together, and the next minute you hated me. Why?"

She took her time arranging the blanket before looking up at him. "I didn't hate you."

He flinched. "I don't understand."

"When . . .," she started, but her voice broke. She cleared her throat, wetting her lips and pressing them together for a moment before continuing. "When I went home that morning— that morning after we were together—my father was waiting for me on the dock at our house. My sisters were there. My oldest sister, Issy, she'd come by the night before to check on me, and when I didn't come home from work, she radioed my father. He came back early from crabbing, rousing the whole island to search for me."

Her face was shattered as she shared her story, and Erik's heart was gripped in a vise as he waited to hear how things played out. Even without hearing the words, he knew that they'd played out very, very badly.

She swallowed, staring at the fire as she continued. "I docked the boat, and my father followed me inside the house, yelling at me, demanding to know who I'd been with, where I was. I wouldn't tell him. He was getting more and more upset, saying he'd hunt you down and force you to make it right."

"Laire," groaned Erik, leaning forward, wishing he could sit next to her but knowing it probably wouldn't offer her any comfort.

"He was getting more and more upset. And then . . . then . . ."

Tears streamed down her face as she lifted her feet to the couch, clutching her knees to her chest.

"He had a heart attack," finished Erik, all the pieces falling neatly into place. "He had a heart attack, and you blamed yourself for it."

"And *you*!" she cried, raising her head to look at him, her face shattered. "*We* did that to him! We were careless and selfish. *We* caused it. *You*! And *me*! We almost killed my father!"

He winced at her words, letting them imbue the facts with her point of view. She hadn't just blamed herself. She'd blamed him too. That's why . . . that's why . . .

"That's why you pushed me away," he murmured, staring into her eyes. "You held me responsible."

"Yessss," she sobbed. "And me. *Both* of us. We didn't deserve to be happy when he was lyin' there at death's door!"

"Darlin', it wasn't—"

"Our fault? Yes, it was! There's no way around it. I was out all night with you, and he had a heart attack as a result. Those are the facts."

"Laire," he whispered, sitting on the edge of his seat. "I didn't know. I'm so sorry."

"I thought he was going to die," said Laire. "He was in a coma for two weeks. At one point, right before you came to see me, I told God I'd give you up. I'd give up what I loved most if He would spare my father's life."

"So you did," said Erik, unable to keep the bitterness from his voice. "Instead of talkin' to me or lettin' me comfort you, you gave me up. You pushed me away."

"My father was dying and we caused it," she said. "I didn't deserve any comfort, Erik . . . especially not from you."

Her words were harsh, and he reeled from them, sitting back in his seat, though he still stared at her, unable to peel his eyes away. He remembered, easily, the awestruck way she'd spoken of her father that summer, how desperately she'd tried to conceal their relationship from him. She'd lost her beloved mother and had only her father. Erik knew the profound pain it would have caused her to lose her only living parent . . . but to be the *reason* for that loss? It would have been a life-altering sort of horror for her.

He leaned forward again. "I get it."

Her face softened as her head fell to the side, almost resting on her shoulder, tears tracks glistening on her skin. She sniffled. "You do?"

Now he couldn't bear it anymore. He stood up and walked around the fire pit, sitting down on the couch beside her, putting his arm around her shoulders and pulling her against his body. No matter who they were to one another now, they'd loved each other once, and making her talk about this was causing her pain.

To his relief, she didn't push him away. Perhaps she was too tired, or maybe she needed the comfort he offered now, as opposed to then, but she moved her head to his shoulder, resting against him.

*This*, he thought urgently. *Please let me have more of this.*

"I understand," he said gently.

And he *did* understand, but it still hurt.

Because she could have told him. She could have come back at Thanksgiving, once her father was all right, and explained everything. She didn't need to turn her back on him, on them, forever. "I just wish you'd figured out a way to tell me."

"Do you?' she asked, pulling away from his embrace and scooting her body into the corner of the couch. Her voice had changed in an instant—it was cooler, suspicious, and angry.

"Of course."

"Give me a br—"

"You broke my heart that day, Laire."

"Right," she scoffed, rolling her eyes and looking away from him dismissively.

Before he realized what he was doing, his arm had whipped out and he'd grabbed her chin, forcing her to face him.

"That's *right*," he said, fuming at her flippancy. "I was *in love* with you, Laire. I would've done anythin' for you."

She narrowed her eyes, pursing her lips as she jerked her chin from his grasp. "You're a fucking liar."

He flinched like she'd slapped him. "No. I'm not."

She was shaking her head, her face tightening in anger, even as her tears started falling again. "Yes, you are. I know about *Van*, Erik. I *know*."

*** 

"Van?" he asked, leaning away from her, though he still looked at her face, his own increasingly more confused.

"Van," she spat. "Remember *Van*? Your friend *Van*, who Pete was interested in? The gay couple you were friends with?"

"Laire," he said, sitting up straighter and leaning away from her, "there's a reason—"

"What reason?" she demanded. "Oh! So you could date both of us that summer? So you could chase after me every night and and screw her every day?"

"You've got it wrong," he said.

She rebelled against these simple words.

"No, I don't!" she said. "Stop lying! Everyone in the Western world knew that you were with her, kissing her at a party in Raleigh while I was at my sister's wedding!"

"Fuck," he muttered. His eyes shuddered closed, and he bent his head, running his fingers into his hair. "If you calm down, I can explain."

"I don't want to hear it!" she cried, hating him for making her go through this all over again. "I *know* you were with Vanessa that summer! You lied about her being a boy. I *know*, Erik. You were cheating on me all summer."

"I never cheated on you," he said softly, his voice flat, his head down.

"How can you say that? There are *still* pictures of you kissing her on the internet, Erik! Take out your phone. Let's look at them together!"

"I don't need to look at them," he said, looking up at her. He rubbed his mouth with the back of his hand. "But I do need you to calm down so I can explain some things to you."

"Like how her mouth suddenly landed on yours?" she shouted.

"Like how my mother would have hunted you down if she'd known about you!" he yelled back.

*Wait.*

*What?*

Her body was coiled into a tight ball, her knees up against her breasts, her arms around her knees under the shearling blanket, protecting herself or braced to spring.

She searched his face.

She opened her mouth to say something but closed it because his words had shocked her, and at the very least, they sounded like the beginning of an explanation she might actually want to hear.

"I *used* Van that summer. I used her," he said softly, all the fight ebbing from his posture as he leaned forward, resting his elbows on his knees. "I let my mother think I was datin' her so that she wouldn't ask me questions about you. I *pretended* she was my girlfriend so my mother would leave us alone."

"No," said Laire. "No. That's not how it was."

"Fuck," he whispered, exhaling whatever breath he'd been holding. "All this time. All these years. You thought I was cheatin' on you that summer?"

"You *were*," she whispered, but her voice lacked conviction.

"God, you must have hated me," he murmured, staring at her with such profound sorrow, she sobbed, looking away from him, unable to bear his pain.

"I thought . . . I don't understand," she whispered between sobs. "I saw the picture."

Peripherally, she saw him nod. "She was at that party. And yeah, as the photographers started clickin', she leaned over and kissed me. But I didn't kiss her back. I held her at arm's length all weekend, while still tryin' to act convincingly like we were together for my mother's benefit."

"No," she mewled, because the far-reaching ramifications of his words, if they were true, meant that she'd willfully destroyed their chance at happiness, and she could hardly breathe under the weight of what she'd thrown away. "No, Erik."

"Yes, Laire," he said, steel in his voice, waiting to continue until she looked up at him through tears. "I was *never* with her. Never, darlin'. There was *only* you for me."

He leaned back into the couch and sighed, long and hard, his gray breath disappearing into the night sky. And she watched him, scanned his face and observed his body language, and all of it told her the same thing: he was telling her the truth.

"You were *never* with her?"

He shook his head against the back of the couch, then looked over at her, finding her eyes with his. "Never."

She looked away from him quickly, remembering Thanksgiving night at Utopia Manor—the engagement ring, the way he had his arm around Vanessa. Could it have all been an act for his mother's benefit?

"I heard you gave her a ring at some point."

He shook his head again. "Nope."

She blinked, her brows furrowing with confusion. Then what exactly *had* she seen that night?

Suddenly he shifted, reaching into his back pocket and pulling out his phone. She watched as he dialed a number and put the phone to his ear, turning to nail her with his eyes as he spoke.

"Hills? Yeah. It's me. No, no. Listen, I need you to do somethin' for me. I'm goin' to put someone on the phone. She's goin' to ask you some questions. Just answer them honestly, okay? It doesn't matter who it is. I need you to do this for me. Honest answers. No matter what. Okay?" He pulled the phone from his ear and held it out to Laire. "This is my sister. She's my closest friend in the world. Ask her anythin'."

"No, Erik. I don't need to—"

"Yeah, Laire," he said, still holding the phone out to her. "You do."

Gulping, she reached for the phone, taking it in her hands, feeling the warmth from his body stored in the metal. Staring at him desperately, she held the phone up to her ear. "Hello?"

"Hi. This is Hillary. Who's this?" Her voice was cultured but warm, and a little concerned.

"L-Laire," she said. "My name is Laire."

There was a sharp gasp and then a long pause before she heard Hillary say, "Oh, my God."

She reached up and covered the speaker with her hand. "She knows me?"

Erik nodded. "She was the only one I ever told."

"You have, uh, some questions for me?" asked Hillary in her posh Southern accent.

Removing her hand, Laire asked, "Was Erik ever engaged to Vanessa Osborn?"

"What? To *Van*?" asked Hillary. "No! Never! Oh, my God, no."

"I heard . . . I mean, I heard that they were—"

"Oh, honey," said Hillary, "it certainly hasn't been for lack of Van tryin'. But no. She never got her hooks into Erik. Not like that."

"You . . .," she started, then stopped. "You know who I

am?"

"Yeah," said Hillary. "He told me about you. You're the girl from the island who he was in love with."

*Was.*

Her eyes fluttered closed.

Was. *What a horrible word.*

"Um," she said, her voice breaking a little. "Was he . . . was he with anyone else the summer he was with me?"

"Honey," said Hillary, "he's *barely* been with anyone *since* you."

"But—"

"No," said Erik's sister definitively. "He was only with you."

*Oh, God. Oh, God, oh, God, oh, God. What have I done? What a mess. What a terrible mess.*

"Okay," she sobbed. "Thanks, Hillary."

"Laire!"

She hadn't handed the phone back to Erik yet, so she put it back against her ear. "Mm-hm?"

"You gutted him."

"S-sorry?"

"You should be," said Hillary softly, her voice level and even, direct without being threatening. "Don't hurt him again. I mean it."

"I won't," she managed to promise, handing the phone back to Erik and dropping her forehead to her knees as she wept.

\*\*\*

Erik took the phone from her hands, pressing it to his ear. "Hills?"

"What the *hell* is goin' on down there, Erik?"

"I'll call you tomorrow."

"Erik! She is *not* good for you!"

"Hillary, thank you for talkin' to her, but I need to go. I'll call you tomorrow."

His sister started to say something else, but he pulled the phone from his ear and pressed End, then placed it on the couch between himself and Laire.

He could tell, from the way Laire's shoulders were shaking, that she was crying, and it hurt him to see her so undone, but his mind was racing with the knowledge he'd gained tonight. She'd felt responsible for her father's heart attack and held him responsible too. And then, probably just after he'd left for college, she'd found that picture of him and Vanessa online. That's why she hadn't shown up for Thanksgiving—she thought he'd been cheating on her. No wonder she'd been so angry from the moment he'd seen her last night. No wonder she'd treated him with such disdain.

He sighed. "You thought I cheated on you."

"Mm-hm," she sobbed, sniffling softly as she raised her head. "It really looked that way."

He nodded. "I can see that. But didn't you trust me at all, darlin'?"

"I don't . . . I don't know," she said. "I was so young. You were my first . . . everything. We were from such different worlds, and you were going back to college. And then I found out about you and Vanessa . . . and . . ."

"And you assumed the worst."

"You let me think Van was a guy, Erik. On purpose."

"I did. Because, if I recall, you had a jealous streak. I didn't want my friendship with Van to complicate things between us when I didn't feel anythin' for her."

"Well, it did," she said softly, "complicate things."

"You must have thought I was a total piece of shit," he said, rubbing his face, looking over at her, curled into a ball in the corner of the couch, her face tear streaked and shattered.

She sighed, loosening one of her arms from around her knees and reaching out her hand. He took it, of course, because, no matter what he'd believed all these years, the sort of love that Erik Rexford had had for Laire Cornish wasn't the type that died. It was still there, living inside him, dormant but safe, waiting for her all these years, for the opportunity to bloom again.

He threaded his fingers through hers and tugged her hand, pulling her from the corner to his side. She knelt beside him, facing his profile, looking up at his face.

"It hurt," she admitted. "Bad. So fucking bad."

"I can only imagine," he said.

"Mostly because it felt so real to me . . . you and me. I . . . I couldn't understand how you could say the things you said to me . . . act the way you had with me . . . and for there to be another woman in your life the whole time."

"It must have negated everythin' you thought you knew about me," he said, dragging her hand to his mouth and kissing the back of it tenderly.

"It didn't," she said, shaking her head. "I didn't let it. I separated you into two people."

"What do you mean?"

"I think . . . I mean, there was the you who loved me that summer, and then there was the you who betrayed me. Two separate people."

"You mean, in your mind."

"Mm-hm."

"Who were they?"

She gulped, wetting her lips. "My Erik." She paused. "And the Governor's Son."

He stared at her, tracing the lines of her face with his eyes, hating the words "the Governor's Son" as much as he always had, times a hundred.

"I'm sorry," she said, covering their bound hands with her free one.

"Who am I now?" he whispered, capturing her sea-green

eyes with his.

"I don't know for sure," she murmured.

"I do," he said, using his free hand to cup her cheek. "I'm still your Erik. I'll *always* be your Erik. No matter what."

With a gasp and a cry, she released his hand and wrapped her arms around his neck, pulling his face to hers, her lips finding his unerringly, as they always had.

With a growl of arousal, he pulled her onto his lap, cradling her in his arms as he kissed her back. His tongue sought hers, and he reacquainted himself with the pliancy of her pillowy lips, the soft texture of her tongue, the sweet taste of her mouth. Here was his beautiful girl, back in his arms, and his heart thundered with the goodness of it, while another part of him hardened lustily with desperate want.

This woman on his lap, in his arms, had haunted his dreams—asleep and waking—for six long years, and having her back in his life so suddenly was rousing feelings in him that had lain dormant for years. Now awakened, they were hungry and urgent.

He'd never wanted anyone so much in his entire life.

She drew back from him, resting her forehead against his shoulder, panting softly against his neck.

"How does this work?" he asked, wrapping his arms around her as he whispered into her ear.

"What do you mean?"

"I want to see you. I want to catch up, to know you again. I want . . . I want to date you. I want another chance to be with you."

"Erik . . . it's not that simple."

"It's *exactly* that simple," he argued. "I haven't moved on with my life. I've been stuck, waitin' for you. Now you're here." Then something terrible occurred to him, and he leaned away from her, waiting until she looked up at him. He searched her eyes with something close to desperation.

"What is it?" she asked.

"Have you moved on?"

"What do you mean?"

"Are you *with* someone?" he asked her, practically choking on the words.

"No."

"Ava's father?"

Her breath hitched softly. "No . . . He's . . . It's, um, it's complicated . . . But he's not . . ."

"He's alive?"

She clenched her jaw, then nodded.

"Do you still see him?"

She took a deep breath, wriggling off his lap, sliding her body about foot away from his. "He's not in the picture . . . as Ava's father."

"But he is *in* the picture?"

"Not the way . . . I mean . . ." She pursed her lips, then sighed. "I'm not ready to talk about Ava's father, Erik."

The last thing he wanted to do was push her away, but he could see that was what was happening.

"Okay," he said, regrouping quickly, recalibrating his expectations. "I only need to know one thing."

She looked up at him expectantly, her eyes locking with his.

"Are you free, darlin'? If . . . if we wanted to be together again . . . are you free to be with me?"

Whether she intended for it to happen or not, a blinding smile appeared on her face, and she nodded at him as her eyes swelled with fresh tears. "I am."

He reached for her cheeks, cupping them tenderly as he leaned forward, closing the distance between them.

"That's all I need to know," he said, closing his eyes as his lips claimed hers once again.

## Chapter 22

Heaven and hell.

Laire had heard these words said together in contrast at least a few times in her life, but never, before this morning, did she truly, personally understand the chasm that lay between them.

The heaven of it was that her first love—her *only* love—had been suddenly and miraculously restored to her last night. To learn that Erik Rexford—the Governor's Son—was still and had always been *her* Erik made her shake her head with disbelief, even as a smile of bliss spread across her face and tears of gratitude burned her eyes.

He'd never cheated on her.

He'd loved no other but her.

And, reading between the lines, from what he and Hillary had told her, despite everything, he *still* loved her.

Such bounty was foreign to Laire, but when she remembered the fire in his eyes last night, she knew it was true: he still belonged to her if she wanted to claim him.

And she did.

She'd never stopped loving her Erik either, turning down countless dates with fellow students, and even Patrick, the sweetest, kindest man in the world. She hadn't been ready to give up the dream of Erik Rexford, even though he'd eviscerated her heart. Part of her must have still wondered, must have still hoped that one day, someday, he could be hers again.

She grinned, taking a sip of the coffee she'd made in her room and savoring the bitterness as it slipped down her throat. But as she turned her face toward the just-rising sun outside the windows, her buoyancy took a dip.

Heaven *and* hell.

The hell of it was that she had borne his child and kept her hidden from him for six years. Her beautiful, incomparable Ava Grace, who slept like an angel in the bed beside hers, was still a secret from Erik. A secret that *never* should have been kept from him.

She sighed, placing her mug on the bedside table and rolling onto her side. Outside, the colors of the sky lightened steadily from lavender to orange, but her mood remained heavy.

Would he be angry with her for not telling him about Ava Grace? But how could she have? When she'd gone to Utopia Manor to tell him, his mother had misled her and threatened to call the police if Laire didn't leave. What if she told him what had happened with his mother? Would he believe her? Blame her?

Though he was very good with Ava Grace from what she'd seen so far, did he even *want* a child? What if he did? And what if he couldn't forgive Laire for keeping Ava Grace from him? Would he try to take her away? To get custody of her? Laire's circumstances had changed in six years but not enough to win a legal battle against the North Carolina Rexfords.

On the flip side, what if he felt burdened by the sudden responsibility of having a daughter? What if he rejected her claim that Ava Grace was his and washed his hands of both of them?

Obviously he knew that she was a single mother, and he'd

still said, *I want another chance to be with you*, last night. Tears welled in her eyes as she remembered it because it was one of the best and sweetest moments of her entire life. It was exactly what she wanted too: another chance. A second chance to be together. A first chance to be a family.

Were he to withdraw those words, even now, when their reunion was so fresh and new, her heart would surely break all over again.

*I have to tell him about Ava Grace.*

Before things got much further, she owed him the truth about everything: about finding out she was pregnant and how her family would have disowned her were she to have a baby out of wedlock, about going to Utopia Manor that Thanksgiving to tell him, about his mother telling her that he and Van were engaged and threatening to have her arrested if she didn't leave, about being completely out of options. She would tell him that she walked the long way from his house to the Pamlico House to find Judith that terrible, terrible night, and she would tell him that—by the grace of God—Judith had been her guardian angel and taken Laire under her wing. And that she'd turned out to be a surrogate mother to Laire and the very best nana Ava Grace could ever know.

And maybe—*maybe, please maybe*—he would see things through her eyes and understand why she'd kept Ava Grace a secret, and why she would have kept her a secret indefinitely if fate hadn't thrust them back into each other's arms.

Swinging her legs over the side of the bed, she grabbed her cup of coffee as she walked to the window and pulled back the sheer curtains to watch the sunrise over the ocean, desperately hoping for the best.

Biting her lower lip in thought, she winced, reminded that it was bruised from two hours of kissing last night. He'd put a chair in front of the roof door to jam it closed, and when he returned to the couch, Laire straddled his lap, pulling the shearling blanket around them as they kissed. More times than she could count, his wandering hands had plumped her breasts over her shirt or slipped into the crevices of her thighs, touching her intimately over her jeans. Because she was a mother, no doubt he believed she was far more experienced than she was. She'd given birth, but all her sexual experience, without exception, had been with him. And it had been so many years ago that being with him again last night felt scary and new.

Except.

She twitched her nose and took a sip of coffee.

Except not *all* scary and not *all* new.

She wasn't as inexperienced as she'd been the summer they first met. She'd loved Erik that summer—learned about his body, touched him, been touched by him, and lost her virginity to him, even if they'd stopped the act prematurely. In their time apart, she'd read books and met different men, and although she'd never been intimate with any of them, she had matured, and her desires were those of a grown woman, not a coltish teenager.

On one hand, she was scared to move too fast, but on the other, she couldn't bear to keep herself from him physically after missing him so desperately. After years of such poignant and painful loneliness, she wanted the warmth, the heat, of his body on hers.

She reached up to touch her lips and sighed with longing, craving so much more than their deep, passionate kisses from last night. For years, her deepest and hottest dreams had been about Erik finishing what he'd started the night they conceived Ava Grace. And now? Now that her Erik was returned to her? She wanted to make those dreams a reality.

She flicked a glance at the ceiling, whimpering softly, wondering how long she'd have to wait until they were naked in bed together, and—*oh, please*—she hoped it wasn't too long.

As the sun cleared the horizon and made its bright ascent into the sky, she crossed the room and opened her laptop, placing her mug on the desk. As her computer rebooted, she turned to look at the perfection of her baby's sleeping face in repose. Slack pink lips, long dark lashes and ginger-colored hair. Her heart swelled with a love so pure, it took her breath away.

More than anything—*more than anything else in the world*—Laire wanted Ava Grace to have the family she deserved: a mother and a father who loved each other, and loved *her* to the moon and back. And now that that once-unlikely dream felt almost possible, she could only clench her eyes shut and wish, with every fiber of her being, that it would actually come true.

*** 

After their epic make-out session last night on the roof, before they'd said good night, while she was still straddling his lap, Erik had asked Laire if he could spend New Year's Eve, tonight, with her and Ava Grace. She'd accepted with a smile, her lips slick from his attentions, her eyes dilated and dark.

"What did you have in mind?"

He'd chuckled lightly, keeping his hands on her hips, his erection straining his jeans uncomfortably. "Darlin', what I have in mind is impossible with Ava Grace in the same room."

"What if she was asleep . . . and we were in the room next door?" she'd murmured, her heavy-lidded eyes locked with his.

*Fuck.* This was a different Laire.

And part of him was fucking grateful for that, because he wanted her—he wanted her bad, hard, and as soon as possible—but part of him hated it. Who had she been with since him that had given her this new confidence? It slayed him to even wonder.

"I'm sure that could be arranged," he'd said, leaning forward to press a kiss to her chest, just above the edge of her shirt, on the soft, warm skin over her breasts.

"Then arrange it," she'd whispered as her fingers threaded through his hair, keeping his head tilted down and his lips pressed against her skin.

First thing this morning, he'd called down to the front desk and asked for room 206 which was, blessedly, available. He'd be moving as soon as he packed up his belongings. It was only when Kelsey had asked how many nights he'd need the room that a sudden wave of panic washed over him. Today was December 31. He needed to be back at work in Raleigh on January 3. Which meant leaving Laire in two days.

He'd muttered his response to Kelsey, then hung up the phone, his brows knitted, his good mood souring.

First of all, after waiting years to reconnect with Laire, he wasn't interested in leaving her again so soon. Not to mention, he didn't like the message it would send her. For years she had thought him a cheater. He wanted time with her to solidify the fact that he wasn't. Also, he didn't particularly like his job so he wasn't exactly returning to a career he loved. He'd been managing his father's law firm for the past three years, but it was dry, boring public policy work that had never truly interested him. And now? Balanced against spending time with Laire? It felt almost unbearable.

He didn't want to leave her.

But he had fifteen employees—his father's partner, who mostly looked to Erik to run things, three other junior attorneys, paralegals, and office staff—waiting for him to return. He couldn't just ignore that commitment either.

Grumbling with annoyance, he slipped out of bed and stretched, rolling his neck and padding to the bathroom in bare feet. First he was going to shower, then pack, then move downstairs, then meet Laire and Ava Grace for breakfast. He had two more days with them before he had to leave. He wouldn't spoil them ruminating about his job when he'd have to return to

Raleigh soon enough.

An hour later, he was sitting beside Ava Grace in the bright dining room with Laire across from them.

"Ava Grace," asked Erik after Kelsey had taken their order, "what grade are you in?"

"Kindergarten," she answered. "But a different one."

"A different one? What do you mean?" asked Erik, looking up at Laire, who was stirring creamer into her coffee.

"We just moved here," said Ava Grace.

"What?" asked Erik. When he'd checked in, Shaw Leatham had mentioned a mother-daughter pair who had a place in Hatteras. That was Laire and Ava Grace, right? He certainly hadn't seen another mother-daughter pair at the inn. "You live in Hatteras."

"*Now* we do," said Ava Grace. "Or sorta we live *here*. In this hotel. Right, Mama?"

Laire looked up from her coffee. "We just moved here from Boone."

"Boone?" asked Erik, his mouth dropping open.

Boone was on the other side of North Carolina! It was about as far northwest as you could go and still remain in the state. All this time he assumed she'd lived here, in Hatteras, on the Banks, near her family. When had she gone to Boone? And for how long?

"Laire, when did you—"

"Boone." Ava Grace nodded. "That's where Nana lived. Afore she died."

"Nana," said Erik, scrambling to figure out who Nana was. Laire's mother had died when she was a child, so Nana must be the mother of Ava Grace's father.

"Uh-huh."

"Is that where your daddy lives? In Boone?" he asked Ava Grace, shifting in his chair to face the little girl. Since he and Laire had found each other again, she'd been reluctant to talk about Ava Grace's father. Maybe this way he'd get some answers.

"Nope. Boone's where Uncle Pat and Aunt Sam live."

Pat and Sam. Hm. Her father's siblings, maybe?

"My daddy's a prince," said Ava Grace matter-of-factly, pulling her juice to the edge of table and sipping from the straw.

"A prince," he repeated dumbly, shifting his eyes to Laire and waiting until she looked up from her coffee. When she did, her face betrayed nothing. She just stared back at him, her sea-green eyes concealing whatever was going on in her head. *Frustrating.*

"What kind of prince?"

"Dark-haired," said Ava Grace.

"What else?"

She shrugged. "I dunno."

"Sure you do. He's your dad," said Erik.

"That's enough," said Laire, her voice holding a warning.

"Nope." Ava Grace shook her head. "I never seen him. But since he's a prince, I'm a princess. That's for sure. Right, Mr. Mopples?"

Wait. Ava Grace didn't know her father? So who *was* her father? A one-night stand? His heart cracked a little at the thought of his modest girl giving herself away so cheaply. Had she even *known* this guy? Or was he some unknown sperm donor? Had he been kind to her? Gentle with her? Loving? He hadn't used protection, that's for damn sure. Had he stuck around long enough to help her during her pregnancy? Had he been there when she gave birth, holding her hand, telling her that everything was going to be okay?

*Fuck.* If Erik ever got his hands on him, he'd—

"Here we go!" said Kelsey, arriving with pancakes and bacon for Ava Grace, oatmeal for Laire, and two eggs over medium for Erik.

He stared at the plate but couldn't eat. His appetite was gone.

"Erik," said Laire, her voice soft as Ava Grace spoke animatedly to Mr. Mopples about "the best pancakes in the universe."

He looked up, his expression surely shattered by his train of thought, by what she'd gone through alone—all because she'd believed that Vanessa was his girlfriend. How he wished he could go back in time and take his chances in telling his mother the truth. How he hated that his deception, meant to protect Laire, had hurt her instead.

He focused on her eyes and found them soft and gentle, almost as though she knew what he was thinking and wouldn't let him blame himself. "It's okay, Erik."

"It's not," he bit out.

Laire reached across the table and took his hand, lacing her fingers through hers. "It is now."

He could see it in her face, in her expression, that she was at peace with whatever had happened. And if she, who had gone through it, could bear it, he would bear it too.

"I'm sorry," he mouthed.

"It's not your fault," she said. Her glance flicked to Ava Grace, and her eyes softened further. "I wouldn't change anything."

He tightened his grip on her fingers, his heart throbbing with love for her.

"Mr. Mopples," said Ava Grace with a giggle. "Mama and Oscar are holdin' hands."

And suddenly whatever sad spell had overcome him was broken, and he pulled Laire's fingers to his lips, kissing them as he grinned at Ava Grace over the back of her mother's hand.

"You okay with that, little miss?"

She shoved a forkful of pancakes in her mouth and nodded.

"Yup."

He looked back at Laire, who was watching them thoughtfully, her lips turned up, her eyes sparkling with unshed tears.

"Me too," she whispered.

\*\*\*

After breakfast, Erik headed out to Utopia Manor to meet his parents' insurance adjuster while Laire and Ava Grace took a ride to Judith's condo. Because it was on the second floor, it hadn't suffered any water damage during the storm, and the last Laire heard, the power would be restored by the third. Just three days. She and Ava Grace would be able to move in—move *home*—soon.

They moved some boxes from the back of the Jeep up the stairs, placing their small pile of belongings in the living room so they'd be ready to unpack once the power was back on. While Laire checked e-mails on the complex's functioning Wi-Fi, Ava Grace and Mr. Mopples visited with her other stuffed animals. Then Laire locked up their new home and drove them back to the Pamlico House to get ready for New Year's Eve.

Erik was joining them at five o'clock for pizza, cupcakes, Champagne, and apple juice, and by the time he arrived, knocking on the interior door that separated their adjoining rooms, mother and daughter were ready to welcome him.

They sat on the floor, having a picnic—Erik and Ava Grace picking the pepperoni off their slices while Laire took their extra pieces and heaped them on her own. This morning, when Erik was asking about Ava Grace's father, she was tempted, for just a moment, to tell him. To give him a look or slide him a note across the table that simply read, *She's yours*, but no matter how wonderful he was with Ava Grace, she still didn't know how he would react to finding out that she was his. She couldn't risk telling him in front of her. After their daughter was asleep tonight, Laire would tell him . . . and he'd either embrace the idea of them in his life, or not. Her stomach swarmed with butterflies as the minutes ticked by.

Finally, at six thirty, after too much pizza and a cupcake each, they all snuggled on Laire's bed together—Laire and Erik side by side against the headboard, and Ava Grace in the triangle of space between their legs, her head on Laire's lap—watching *Up*.

Certain that Erik had never seen it before, Laire surreptitiously watched his face in the beginning. She'd never been able to watch the first ten minutes of *Up* without crying. The story of a man and a woman who'd been very much in love had always hit home with her, and when the wife, Ellie, died, leaving the man alone, she couldn't help the waterworks. To her immense satisfaction, Erik sniffled once, tightening his jaw when Ellie miscarried and again when she passed away.

Halfway through the movie, Ava Grace was fast asleep, snoring softly, and Erik turned to Laire.

"Want to watch the rest?" he whispered.

She shook her head. "I've seen it a million times."

"You could've warned me about the beginnin'."

She grinned. "Sad, huh?"

"So sad. Lovin' only one girl and losin' her." He paused. "I know how that feels, Laire."

"Pretty awful," she murmured.

"Agony."

Ava Grace stirred between them, and he looked down at her. "She's wonderful. You're an amazin' mom."

Judith and Patrick had always been forthcoming with supportive comments about Laire's parenting, but after losing Judith and moving away from Patrick and Samantha, she felt the loss of that support. She was grateful for it from Erik.

"Thank you."

"Do you want more?" he asked. "Kids?"

She nodded. "Someday."

He smiled at her, a little sadly maybe, then looked back down at Ava Grace. "Should I carry her to her bed?"

"That would be great. She's getting so heavy. We have more Champagne. Maybe we could . . ."

". . . take it to *my* room?" he suggested, his dark eyes blackening.

She felt the sudden warmth in her cheeks and nodded. "I'd like that."

"Me too," he said, sliding off the bed, then reaching down for Ava Grace. He picked her up easily, cradling her in his arms as he walked around Laire's bed.

Laire pulled back the sheets on Ava Grace's bed, and Erik bent to kiss her forehead before placing her gently on the sheets. And Laire, who watched this gentle, beautiful gesture with her heart in her throat, couldn't keep her eyes from watering. *Please want us. Please, please, please want us. Please understand why I kept her from you. And please want us anyway.*

He drew the covers back up over her sleeping form and turned off the bedside light, turning to Laire. "Ready?"

*Now or never.*

She nodded. "I am."

\*\*\*

Spending time with Ava Grace had been wonderful, and watching a movie, snuggled up on Laire's bed like a little family, had been warm and cozy . . . but his body was on fire for her, and he was relieved when they decided to cut the movie short and spend some time alone.

Just as they approached the door to his room, she asked him for a minute so he went back to his room and lit the candles he'd borrowed from Utopia Manor today, then sat down on the edge of the high, Colonial-style bed to wait for her.

He didn't know what was going to happen tonight, but he

was wild with want and knew what he hoped for: one, to be buried cock deep in Laire's sweet body five times before sunrise, and two, to hear her say that there was still a chance for love to grow between them—still a chance for them to be together.

He tried to temper his expectations and hunger with reality—they'd only *just* reconnected. It could take a while—days, weeks, months even (*please, God, not months*)—until they were comfortable enough to share themselves with each other again.

That said, if there had ever been a decision for Erik to make, about whether or not he would pursue Laire for the long haul, there wasn't a shred of ambiguity in his mind now. In the space of two days, every ounce of love he'd kept on ice for six and a half years had thawed out completely until he burned for her. He was every bit as much in love with her now, today, as he'd been the day he arrived at the hospital to see her. They'd hurt each other, yes, but not on purpose, not with malicious intent. She'd been a frightened girl, scared of losing her only parent, lashing out at him for his share of the blame. And he'd been a foolish boy who lied to his mother instead of just telling her the truth and dealing with the consequences.

Now they were adults. All grown up and, he hoped, ready for forever together because he didn't intend to live his life without Laire ever again. He'd already tried that, and it had been an unparalleled misery. There was life with her, or there was hell.

The door squeaked open, and he looked up to see that she'd changed from jeans and a T-shirt into a simple black cotton dress. It had a plunging neckline and hugged her slight curves—the swells of her breasts, the little belly and slighter wider hips that were new to him, probably left over from her pregnancy. She'd taken down her hair, which she'd worn in a ponytail during dinner, and it trailed, strawberry red and straight, down her back as she approached him.

He spread his legs so she could walk right up to him, into him, eye to eye, breast to chest, sex to sex. He held out his arms as she invaded his space, pressing her body against his, and he wound his arms around her, enveloping her in a strong embrace.

"I love you," he whispered, the words rushing forth uninhibited. "I never stopped."

Her cheek rested on his chest, over his heart, under the throbbing pulse in his throat, and he heard her breath shudder, felt it hitch in a soft gasp.

"I love you too," she murmured, her voice breathless but certain. "Even when I hated you, I still loved you."

Drawing back, she looked into his eyes, then dropped her glance to his lips, leaning forward until their mouths met, hungry but sweet, sealing their words with a kiss. He swiped his tongue along the soft seam of her lips, and she opened for him like a flower, letting him taste her, explore her, claim her as his once again. Sliding his hands down to the hem of her dress, he slipped his hands to the bare skin of her thighs, then to her silk-covered ass, which he cupped, lifting her onto his lap. Winding her arms around his neck, she used the leverage to slide herself forward, flush against his body, arching her back to crush her breasts against his chest as he loved her mouth with his. His fingers continued their journey upward, under her dress, finally resting on her waist, the skin soft and warm under her dress.

"Erik," she whispered, pulling away to suck his earlobe between her lips, loving the soft pocket of skin, then using her teeth to raze it before letting it go.

"What, baby?"

"We have all night," she said, grinning up at him. Her lips were slick and delicious, and he wanted so much more. "Isn't that strange?"

"Why?" he panted softly, grinning at her in the candlelight.

"Because it was so hard to find time alone that summer?"

"We only had that one night," she said softly, the light in her eyes dimming at little, "and it ended in disaster."

He nodded. "I wish I'd known what happened with your dad. I wish . . . I wish you'd come to see me that Thanksgivin'. I know you thought I was with Vanessa. But . . . did you ever consider showin'?"

She tensed in his arms, reaching for his hands and dragging them from her waist, withdrawing them from under her dress before replying in a grave tone, "We need to talk."

*Oh, fuck.* That didn't sound good.

She paused, climbing off his lap and crossing to a small sitting area with two chairs. She sat down in one and gestured to the other, looking at him meaningfully.

"Let's sit for a bit, okay? There's a lot you don't know, Erik, and before we go any further, you need to know everything."

*** 

Laire watched him stand and cross the room like a man being led to his execution, but she didn't comfort him or try to soften the blow of everything she was about to say. What he was about to hear was going to change the entire course of his life in the space of a few minutes—it would be dishonest to minimize it with platitudes before she even started talking.

She pointed to a bottle of bourbon on the desk. "You want a glass?"

He furrowed his brows. "Do I need it?"

"Maybe," she answered honestly, and the lines on his face grew deeper.

He picked up the bottle and uncapped it. "Do you want some?"

"I don't drink bourbon."

"There's Champagne," he reminded her.

She shook her head no. If, after she'd told him everything,

he didn't throw her out of his room and threaten to call Child Protective Services, she would have a glass then.

He poured himself a glass of the amber liquid, then sat down across from her, his eyes worried, his posture stiff.

Laire took a deep breath.

"I haven't been with many men," she blurted out.

"Um . . ." His glass was halfway to his mouth, and it froze in midair as he stared at her. Slowly, he lowered it. "Okay . . ."

"I mean . . . at all."

"Great! That's great to . . . I mean . . ." The worry lines on his face lightened as he nodded. "Can't say I'm sorry to hear it, darlin'."

Her heart was racing as she rubbed her forehead with her thumb and index finger. *Tell him. Just tell him.*

"So," he said, "just me and . . . Ava Grace's father?"

"Well . . ."

*It's time*, thrummed her heart with every beat, and she gulped over the lump in her throat. *Do it. Tell him now.*

"Just you," she said, holding his eyes with hers.

"Right. Just me and Ava's—"

"Erik," she said gently, scooting to the edge of her chair and looking into his eyes with all the love that hadn't died inside her and all the love that had been so recently reborn in her heart. "Just. You."

She watched his face as he made sense of her words, as he figured them out and added them up.

"I don't . . . What are you sayin'?"

It took courage—so much courage—for Laire to share her baby with Erik, but he'd never cheated on her with Vanessa. He'd been true to her, and her heart ached with longing for him and for the years they'd missed together. Erik was a good man, worthy of their child, and it was time for him to know the truth. She lifted her chin.

"I've *only* been with you. You're the only man I've ever been with. Ever." She stood up abruptly, plucked the glass of bourbon from his hands, took a long swig, then offered it to him again.

"Wait," he said, his eyes searching hers wildly as she sat back down. "Laire, are you sayin' . . . that . . . that Ava Grace is . . ." He shook his head, faster and faster. "No. That's impossible."

But she could see it—the way he was putting the pieces together:

The strange coincidence of her name.

That her hair color was a perfect mixture of theirs.

That her eyes were mirror images of his.

That her father was a "dark-haired prince."

That he'd fallen hard—head over heels—for Ava Grace, when he met her only a few days ago, almost like his heart knew her heart, knew that the blood coursing through her veins belonged, in part, to him.

"Well, actually," she said gently, "if you do the math, you'll see that it isn't impossible at all. She was born on May 10."

"She looks like she's about four."

"She'll be six this coming year."

"Wait," he said, lifting the bourbon to his lips and finishing what Laire hadn't. "No. This can't be possible."

"She's just petite," said Laire, her voice breaking. She couldn't read his face. She couldn't read his voice. She couldn't figure out what he was feeling. All she could see was stark disbelief, and she was starting to get scared.

He ran a hand through his thick hair, holding on to the back of his neck as he stared at her with wide eyes. "But we didn't—"

"We did enough."

"You're sayin' . . . Oh, my God, Laire." He stared at her, the truth finally becoming clear to him. "You're sayin' she's my

. . ."

"She's *yours*, Erik," she gasped, her heart racing so fast, she wondered if she might faint. "Yours and mine. We're her parents. Just . . . just look at her. You're her father."

"I'm her father," he whispered, tears welling in his eyes, which he blinked away, staring down at the empty tumbler in his hands. "I'm her . . . *father*."

"Yes." Laire dropped to her knees, taking the glass from his hands and threading her fingers through his. "I swear I'm telling the truth."

"Ava Grace is my daughter," he said, looking up at her, a fierce, wild look in his eyes.

"Yes," she confirmed, ignoring the tears that streamed down her face and down his.

He snatched his hands away from her and leaned back in his chair, his face contorting with anger, his nose flaring and his lips tightening.

"She's almost six years old, Laire."

Laire nodded, sitting back on her haunches, feeling wary.

"Six. Years," he growled softly, his eyes furious.

"Yes," she whispered, her heart in her throat as she knelt at his feet.

He pressed a hand to his chest, staring at her through watery eyes, his face a mask of anguish. "*Why didn't you tell me*?"

"I tried," she sobbed, her shoulders starting to shake with the force of her tears.

"What the fuck do you mean, you *tried*?" he demanded, lurching forward in his seat. "Here are the facts, Laire: I didn't know because you didn't tell me. So you sure as shit didn't try hard enou—"

"I was there!" she cried. "On Thanksgiving. I was there, Erik."

"No." Erik stared at her, his chest rising and falling rapidly with each shallow breath. He shook his head, holding his hand up in refusal. "No. No, you weren't. You didn't come. Your boat wasn't there. You didn't—"

"I did," she said, her voice breaking as more tears slid down her cheeks and she sat back on her bottom, raising her knees and clutching them against her chest. "My brother-in-law drove me over. Your mother . . ." She sobbed, then took a deep breath. "Your mother intercepted me by the pool, and we . . ." She raised her chin and nailed him with her eyes, unable to keep the bitterness from her voice when she remembered that terrible night, "talked."

He narrowed his eyes, scanning her face as his attack posture relaxed, and she knew what he was doing: desperately trying to figure out if she was telling the truth.

Finally he flinched, holding his breath like breathing would hurt.

"Tell me what happened, Laire." His voice was a mix of gravel and thunder, his eyes flinty—as dark and dangerous as she could ever remember them. "Tell me what my mother did."

# Chapter 23

"I have to start earlier," she said, still sitting in a ball at his feet. She sniffled, then reached up and wiped away her tears. "But . . . can you calm down? A-and listen to me and not yell at me? Because I'm feeling very emotional and . . ."

Inside, he was in turmoil, but he nodded. "Fine."

"I'm just going to get a cup of water. I'll be right back," she said, standing up and walking over to his bathroom.

He heard her run the water and forced himself to take a huge breath of air before she started talking again. Leaning his head on the back of the chair, he closed his eyes for a moment, clasping his shaking hands together in his lap.

In the past five minutes, he'd learned that he had a daughter—that *he and Laire* had a daughter.

Part of him was in shock.

Part of him was raging with fury.

Part of him was trying to keep a massive wave of protectiveness and gratitude and excitement at bay until he had all the details. He actively fought the overwhelming urge to race into the adjacent bedroom, pick up Ava Grace's sleeping body, and hold it against his for hours, staring at her face and listening to her breathe.

Only one emotion was completely salient and undivided within him: the pure, unadulterated, deep, forever-love he suddenly felt for Ava Grace. In fact, if he hadn't actually been experiencing the instinctive and instant love that was presently overtaking every cell of his body, he wouldn't have believed it was possible to love another human being so completely, so profoundly, so eternally, in the space of a few minutes. But there it was inside him: so much love for that little girl, he didn't know how his heart could possibly contain it.

She was *his* baby, *his* child, *his* daughter—

Laire cleared her throat as she stepped back into the room, and Erik opened his eyes, focusing them on his daughter's mother.

—and they had been *deliberately* kept apart for six agonizing years.

He desperately hoped that she had a good reason for this because if she didn't, it was unconscionable that she would do such a thing to Ava Grace . . . and to him.

She sat down in her chair and took a deep breath.

"I thought I had cancer," she said softly. "By November, I was tired all the time, and gaining weight. Smells that had never bothered me suddenly made me nauseous. When I put my symptoms into Google, pregnancy wasn't even a suggested diagnosis, but hypothyroidism was."

She turned to look at him, her eyes so sad, he had to force himself to stay seated and not reach for her and pull her into his arms. "My mother died of thyroid cancer, so I was certain that's what I had. I even . . ."

Her voice broke for a moment, and she bit her bottom lip until she was composed enough to speak. "Erik, I was so messed up at that point, I actually thought it could be a *good* thing if I had cancer. My father and sisters would have to forgive me for being with you that night if I was that sick. They'd have to stop looking at me sideways, like I was a dirty girl, a bad seed.

They'd have to love me again."

She took a deep breath and exhaled on an "ohhhh" sound, clenching her jaw before continuing. "Kyrstin brought me to the clinic here in Hatteras, and they did a urine test. That's how I found out I was pregnant . . . the week before Thanksgiving."

Erik stared at her, his chest hurting as he tried to take a deep breath and failed. He couldn't imagine how frightened she'd been, or how alone she'd felt. Hating himself for not being there for her, he somehow managed to nod, urging her to continue.

"Kyrstin said that I should choose an island boy and seduce him." She chuckled ruefully, wiping a tear away. "Crazy, right? But you have to understand where she was coming from—being away for a night with you had sent my father into a coronary. Telling him I was having a baby out of wedlock? It would have killed him. Kyrstin actually thought she was helping by making that suggestion. She said that I should choose one of the boys we'd grown up with, get him drunk, sleep with him, get married to him, and let everyone on Corey believe it was *his* baby."

She shook her head. "I couldn't do it. I still . . . I still loved you. I still believed in you. I insisted to Kyrstin that if I told you, you'd make it right. And the timing? It almost felt like a miracle. I knew how to find you, exactly where you'd be. If I could just get to Utopia Manor on Thanksgiving and talk to you, it would all be okay."

"But it wasn't okay, was it?" he asked, his voice thick with emotion.

She shook her head, dropping his eyes to stare down at her lap in misery.

And it was that small, vulnerable gesture that made him leap from his chair and stand before hers. Without asking her permission, he leaned down and gathered her body into his arms. She looped her arms around his neck, staring into his eyes with such grief, he understood that their chance for happiness—their chance to be a family six years ago—had been stolen from them. And it wasn't Laire's fault. And it wasn't his.

"I love you," he murmured.

"I . . . I was s-so s-scared," she sobbed. "S-so alone . . ."

Her face crumpled, and she hid it in the curve of his neck, her body shaking from the force of her sobs. Warm, wet tears landed on his collarbone, rolling down his chest, wetting his undershirt. Holding her carefully, he crossed the room and laid her gently on his bed. Then he walked around and climbed in beside her, drawing her into his arms, her back to his front, his arms under her breasts as she wept.

"No matter what," he whispered, pressing his lips to the back of her neck, "I love you forever. I love Ava Grace forever. Tell me the rest when you're ready, baby. I'm here now. I'm here."

After a few minutes, her sobs turned into deep, ragged breaths, and she turned in his arms, her face tear streaked in the candlelight. Pushing her hair from her forehead he stared into her eyes. "You okay, darlin'?"

She sniffled, mumbled "no," and half chuckled, half sobbed as she bent her elbow, slid it under her head and looked at him thoughtfully. "D-did you mean it?"

"What?"

"About . . . l-loving us?"

"With every cell in my body," he promised.

Her eyes closed and she nodded. "Th-thank you. I needed to hear that so b-badly."

"Six years too late," he said, everything inside him hurting.

"It wasn't your fault," she managed in a thready voice.

"It kills me that you went through this alone, that I missed six years with you, that I missed the first five and a half years of my daughter's life." He stopped because his heart was racing so fast, he felt dizzy. *Calm down. Calm down, Erik.* He swallowed over the massive lump in his gullet. "I need to know what happened. Tell me the rest."

She exhaled carefully, nodding. "Okay." She took another deep breath, like what she was about to say was going to hurt very much, and Erik braced himself. He'd seen Fancy in action since he was a very little boy—he knew that when her claws came out, blood was spilled, and she was always the one left standing. He didn't know what was coming, but he knew it was going to be bad.

"Okay. Let's see . . .," she said. "I had Thanksgiving at Kyrstin's and then her husband, Remy, drove me up the coast from Corey to Utopia Manor. I was so scared, but I wanted to see you again. I mean, I knew I was young to be pregnant and we weren't married, but I still loved you. I felt like we could make it work if I could just get to you."

"Wait," he said. "What about Vanessa? I would have thought you hated me by then."

"I didn't know yet," she said softly.

"But I thought you saw the pict—"

"No." She shook her head. "I hadn't seen it yet. I saw it much later. I didn't know yet . . . about you and Vanessa. I still thought Van was just a male friend."

"You loved me?"

She nodded. "Madly. I was going to ask your forgiveness for how I treated you in the hospital. My father was okay. Whether we planned it or not, I was expecting your baby. I wanted a fresh start with you . . . f-for us, you know, to be a family."

"Oh, my God," he whispered, blinking at her through a fresh burn of tears, these revelations more and more painful and frustrating. "You still loved me, and you were pregnant with my child, and you were comin' to tell me."

She bit her bottom lip again, her eyes answering his

question before she said, "Yes."

"And my mother?"

"She was outside."

"Smokin'? By the pool?"

She nodded. "Yes."

"You told her that you were pregnant?"

"Not at first. I told her I needed to speak to you. I told her I was invited." She looked down at the small space of white sheet beneath them, tracing a small circle with her finger. "She didn't believe that I knew you. I insisted I did. That's when I told her that I was expectin'."

"She threw you out?"

Laire's sigh was ragged and shaky, and Erik could tell the memory hurt.

"She called me a liar and an opportunist. She thought I wanted to extort money from your family. She said it was . . . a clever plan. And then she threatened to call the police."

Laire stopped for a minute, clenching her jaw, her face a mask of misery when she finally looked up at him. "But that wasn't the worst of it."

"Vanessa," he said, the name bitter on his tongue. "She made you think that we were . . ."

She nodded. "She told me to look through the sliding glass doors, and there you were, next to her with . . . with your arm around her shoulders . . ."

Her voice broke, and a tear splashed into her little circle. "I recognized her from the photos on your piano. She was wearing a ring that night—a really huge, beautiful ring—and your mother said that you were engaged to her, that you'd been together all summer, that you'd been in love forever, and that's how she knew that I was lying about being with you because you'd never cheat on Van."

"Enough."

Something inside Erik ripped apart, and he whimpered in

pain, rolling onto his back and staring up at the ceiling as tears of fierce, sanity-stealing frustration rolled from the corners of his eyes and into his hair.

Contemptible. Reprehensible. And unforgivable.

She'd come to him. Laire had come back to him to tell him that she loved him and was having their baby, and his mother—his despicable *fucking* mother—had sabotaged his happiness. He'd lost six years of his life, and five and a half years of his daughter's life, because of that night. He'd lost his faith in women and his trust in love. He'd lost hope. He'd lost himself. And it was so devastating to learn that it had been at his mother's willful hands, he almost couldn't breathe.

He threw his arm over his eyes, hiding his tears from her—from Laire, who must have been so scared and alone that night. She'd had no family, no money, no plan . . . and his mother, Ava Grace's *grandmother*, had threatened to have her arrested, so she'd run away. How the hell had she survived? How had she and Ava Grace made it?

"Laire," he ground out, still lying on his back. "Who helped you?"

"Who do you think?" she asked softly.

Erik took a deep breath, thinking back to those days: she'd had her family, right? But they wouldn't have helped her. The moment they found out she was pregnant, they would have washed their hands of her.

So who else? Who else? Her whole life was Corey Island, except for the nights she spent at the Pamlico House.

"The Pamlico House," he murmured, lowering his arm. "Your boss . . . Mrs . . . Ms. . . ."

"Sebastian," she said softly with a sad smile.

*Boone. That's where Nana lived. Afore she died.*

"Nana," he said, rolling onto his side, mirroring Laire, watching her eyes soften as they spoke of her benefactor.

She nodded. "Nana."

"She took you in?"

"She adopted me, for all intents and purposes. She was moving to Boone to be closer to her son, and she took me with her. She was next to me when I gave birth to Ava Grace, coaching me through my breathing. She gave us a place to live. She watched my baby while I went to college. Her son, Patrick, was an uncle to Ava Grace. We were . . . Erik, we were surrounded with love." She was still crying, but her face wasn't as heartbreaking as it had been when she was talking about his mother. "She saved our lives."

"The condo here?"

"Was hers," said Laire. "She left it to me when she died last summer."

"I'm sorry," he said, wincing at her loss. He reached for her hip, pulling her closer. When their foreheads were touching, he closed his eyes and took a deep breath. "I'm so sorry you lost her."

"I'm so grateful I had her," she whispered back.

"Am I all caught up, darlin'?"

"Yes," she said, her sweet breath kissing his lips as the tension drained from their bodies. "Wait. No."

"No?" he asked, cracking open an eye.

"By chance," she said softly, "I ran into the love of my life at the inn where she hired me to work so long ago. And I just . . . maybe this sounds crazy, but I feel like that was Judith's—Ms. Sebastian's—final gift to me: giving me a condo here so that I'd have to come back and find you."

*You don't have any business with an island girl, now, do you?*

He pictured Judith Sebastian's stern face with a wave of gratitude that almost leveled him. She'd always wanted what was best for Laire, and maybe, finally, at the end of her life, she'd decided that was him. He'd always respected her—it comforted him to believe that Ms. Sebastian had put Laire in a position to find him again.

"Doesn't sound crazy at all," he said, tenderly kissing the bridge of her nose. "Sounds like she wanted you to be happy."

"We'll be happy if we're with you," she murmured, nuzzling him.

Erik drew her so close that their hearts were touching and their legs intertwined. "I want that more than anythin', darlin'."

"Good." She snuggled closer, melting into him with a sigh. "This is so nice."

He rubbed her back, pressing his lips to hers.

"Mmmm," she sighed, her eyes closed, her body languid against him. "Would it be okay if we slept for a little while? I feel like I've been running for years. I'm so . . . tired."

"Of course, baby," he said, clasping her body tightly to his. "I've got you now. You sleep."

"You too," she murmured.

"Sure," he said, kissing her forehead. "Me too."

It took only a minute or two for her breathing to become deep and even, but there was no way Erik was going to sleep. His mind was racing, bouncing between the four most important women in his life and trying to make sense out of where they each fit into his after this epic conversation with Laire.

Hillary was easy. He was desperate to talk to her—to explain everything and to introduce her to Laire and Ava Grace. He imagined Hillary and Laire becoming good friends and Hillary being an amazing aunt to her niece. He couldn't wait to tell her everything.

The revelation about Ava Grace's parentage had finally sunk into his consciousness, and he accepted it without a shred of doubt: he had a daughter, and, yes, he had a lot to learn, but he was going to be the best damn father the earth had ever known. There would be time to make up for, and time to celebrate, and the next time he and Laire had a child together, he fully intended to be there from the very beginning.

Leaning forward a little, he pressed his lips to Laire's forehead again, resting them against her soft skin as she slept.

As soon as possible, he intended to have a ring on her finger and a date to meet her at the altar. It was as though he'd awakened, over the past couple of days, from a years-long nightmare, and he knew, beyond a shadow of a doubt, that Laire was the key to his happiness. He had missed out on enough time with her—he wanted her to be his wife, and he wanted it now. She was the missing piece of his heart, the joy of his soul, the very lifeblood of his being, and the mother of his daughter. As soon as she said yes, he would bind his life to hers forever and thank God for the gift of her love every day of his life.

Taking a deep breath, he clenched his jaw and shut his eyes for a moment before opening them again.

As for his mother.

As for Ursula "Fancy" Rexford.

He would confront her only to disown her.

He would make her take responsibility for what she willfully stole from him.

And then he would wash his hands of her forever.

Drawing his sweetheart as close to him as possible, he pulled the comforter over them both. Then, seeking and matching the rhythm of her beating heart with his own, he closed his eyes and joined her in sleep.

\*\*\*

"A sleepover, huh? 'Cause that's what it's called when you sleep over with someone else. And Mama and Oscar are still sleepin' so this is definitely a sleepover."

There was a pause in Ava Grace's monologue as Laire's eyes fluttered open to find Erik's room flooded with sunlight, his arms still tightly around her.

"No, Mr. Mopples. That's a very naughty suggestion.

We're not goin' to wake them up until—Mama! You're awake!"

Laire blinked as she rolled onto her back. She was still in her clothes. *Oh, Lord*, she thought, rolling her eyes internally. *Our first night together with no one to judge or interrupt or interfere, and we wasted it by falling asleep.*

Ava Grace knelt on the bed, holding Mr. Mopples in her lap.

"Mornin', baby," Laire murmured through a yawn.

"Mama, you and Oscar had a sleepover."

Reversing her previous thoughts and thanking God that they were both fully dressed, she smiled and nodded. "Yes, we did."

"Why did you have a sleepover?"

Erik's arm was thrown over Laire's chest, but she moved it just enough to sit up.

"Oh. Well . . ." She and Erik hadn't discussed when they'd tell Ava Grace that he was her father, but she hoped that they would agree to tell her today. Laire was sick and tired of secrets. She wanted Ava Grace to know that she had a father who loved her, who had missed her, and who intended to stick around. "We had some things to talk about. And I guess we fell asleep."

"What things?"

"Well," she said, smiling gently at her daughter, "I knew Oscar, um, *Erik*, a long time ago . . . before I had you. He was really important to me."

"Like your best friend?"

"Yeah. Even more than that."

"Do you like him a lot, Mama?"

"I do, baby. In fact, I love him a lot."

"As much as you love me?"

"Mm-hm," answered Laire, grinning at her daughter. "But in a different way."

"Like a mommy loves a daddy?" whispered Ava Grace,

like her words were sacred.

"Would that be okay?" asked Laire.

Ava Grace looked at Erik, resting her eyes on his face. "I have the same eyes as he does, Mama."

Laire's chest constricted, but she kept her voice even. "Yes, baby. You do."

Under the covers, Erik's fingers found hers, threading them together and holding on tight. He wasn't sleeping anymore; he was listening.

"If you love him like a mommy loves a daddy . . ." Ava Grace pressed her lips together, still staring at Erik.

"What, honey?"

"He's dark-haired like a prince. Maybe he could be *my* daddy."

She heard his breath catch as his fingers squeezed the life from her hand.

"Would you like that?"

Ava Grace nodded.

She knew he was unable to bear not knowing her answer when he opened his eyes, pretending to wake up. "Mornin', girls."

"Mornin'," they answered in unison.

Erik rubbed his eyes and yawned, sitting up against the back of the bed beside Laire, then scooting away from her a touch to make room between them.

"Want to get in with us?" he asked his daughter.

Ava Grace's face broke into a huge smile, and she nodded happily, crawling up the bed and snuggling in between them.

Erik looked at Laire over their daughter's head, mouthing the words, *Can I tell her?*

Tears sprang into Laire's eyes as she nodded.

"Hey, Ava Grace," said Erik. "I gotta ask you somethin', darlin'."

"What?"

"Well, I thought I heard you sayin' somethin' about me maybe bein' your daddy just now while I was wakin' up."

"I thought you were sleepin'."

"Nope." Erik put his hands under her shoulders and transferred her to his lap, facing him. "What if the dark-haired prince got all mixed up in the sea witch's evil plan for a few years? What if it took him a while to escape, to find you and your mama?"

Laire shifted her eyes from Erik's face to Ava Grace's, watching as she absorbed this new chapter of the story.

With wide eyes, Ava Grace looked up at her father. "Is that what happened to you?"

"Somethin' like that."

To Laire's surprise, huge tears swelled in her daughter's eyes as she stared up at her father. "But that would mean . . . that would mean you're my *real* daddy."

"That's right. That's exactly who I am, baby," he said, trying to smile, though Laire could see him fighting back tears. "Your *real* daddy. And now that I've found you and your mama, I'm never goin' away again."

Ava Grace launched herself into his arms with a sob, and Erik gripped her close as she rested her cheek on his shoulder.

"You're my real daddy?" she asked again as she clung to him, as though it was too amazing to be true.

"I sure am," said Erik, releasing Ava Grace on one side to pull Laire into their embrace. She was a mess at this point, tears streaming down her face as Erik and Ava Grace sorted out their place in each other's life. Laire laid her head on Erik's shoulder, leaning into him as he held his girls close.

"Then I'm gonna call you Daddy instead of Oscar," said Ava Grace, her small arms looped tightly around his neck. "Is that okay?"

"Better'n okay," he said, his voice gravelly with emotion

as he tightened his arms around his family. "That'd be perfect, baby."

# Chapter 24

Since the morning, Ava Grace had probably called Erik Daddy about a hundred times, even managing to insert it three times into a single sentence. The truth? He didn't think he'd ever get weary of hearing her little voice say it.

Tucking her into bed that night, they rehashed the fun day they'd had together: running on the beach, eating hot dogs at a café in Hatteras, visiting Laire and Ava Grace's new condo, checking out her new elementary school, and dining on grilled cheese sandwiches for dinner, courtesy of Kelsey.

With Laire on one side of her and Erik on the other, they read a bedtime story together, watching as their daughter drifted off to sleep. They kissed her good night, then tiptoed to Erik's room, leaving the door to Ava Grace's room cracked open just enough to hear her call out if she needed them.

Holding Laire's hand, and with an alacrity that should have surprised him but didn't, he switched gears entirely as he stepped into his dimly lit, quiet room.

As much as he'd loved every minute he'd spent with Laire and Ava Grace today as a family, his body now had a separate agenda altogether. He'd waited a long, long time to be alone with his woman again, and with no more lies and secrets between them, he was finished waiting.

He wanted her.

He needed her.

And he intended to have her in as many ways as she'd let him before morning.

He sat down on the bed, holding her hand, looking up at Laire, who stood before him. She wore a slight smile on her face as she raised her free hand. It was fisted, but as she opened her fingers one by one he recognized the necklace he'd bought her so long ago at the Elizabethan Gardens.

"You kept it," he said, taking it from her hand and staring at the intricate design of overlapping hearts.

"I was tempted to throw it in the fireplace many times, but . . . I couldn't." Her eyes were dark and languid as she dropped his hand, lifted her hair off the back of her neck and turned around. "Put it on me?"

His heart sped up at the sight of her swanlike neck bared to him, at the quick mental image of making love to her while she wore nothing except this necklace. Standing up on suddenly shaky knees, he leaned his arms over her shoulders, each half of the clasp between his fingers, and fastened the necklace around her throat.

Before she could let her hair fall back, he bent his head quickly and pressed his lips to her soft, warm skin, closing his eyes as she gasped quietly. She leaned her head to the side, giving him better access, and he wrapped his arms around her, pulling her back against his chest and inhaling the sweet womanly smell of her.

"I missed you," he murmured, sliding his lips along her throat, behind her ear, stopping to kiss and nibble, and reveling in the feeling of Laire back in his arms.

"Me too," she sighed, covering his hands with hers.

"Last night," he started, pausing, not wanting to jeopardize the moment with indelicacy. "You said you hadn't been with anyone . . . but me."

"That's right," she whispered, her fingers tightening over his.

He kissed her shoulder, then leaned his head up, turning her around in his arms.

Her face tilted up, her clear green eyes searching his.

"Only you," she said, licking her sweet lips nervously, then braving a little grin as she lifted her chin.

He nodded at her, the rush of love in his heart so pure and strong, it warmed his body like a blanket. "Only me."

"I didn't want to be with someone unless I loved them as much I loved you." She looked down for a second, then raised her head and nailed him with her eyes. "So I waited."

The truth bubbled up inside him like an unstoppable force. "Me too."

At first she gasped, then she flinched, her brow knitting as she stared at him in disbelief. He could tell that she was holding her breath because her breasts pushed against his chest without drawing away.

"Breathe," he whispered.

Huge tears welled in her eyes as she sucked in a ragged breath, still staring up at him in shock. "W-what?"

Suddenly his eyes burned and he blinked at her, every moment he'd tried to force himself to bed another woman rushing back to him. He'd failed. Every time. And part of him had wondered if he'd ever be capable of an intimate relationship again . . . or if Laire had ruined him for every other woman in creation.

He shrugged, still holding her tightly in his arms. "No one was you."

"You haven't been with . . . *anyone*?"

He gulped over the lump in his throat and shook his head. "Got close a few times but . . . couldn't."

Her face crumpled and she leaned forward, resting her forehead on his chest, under his chin. "Are y-you . . . l-lying?"

"No, baby," he said gently, rubbing her back as she cried. "I didn't just love you as a kid or as a summer fling or as anything that was temporary. Don't you see? I loved you as a man, in every season, forever. And when I lost you, I lost . . . everythin'. There was a hole inside me the size of a crater. And . . ." He paused, flinching as he recalled the depths of his agony before reminding himself that now, *here and now*, the woman of his dreams was back in his arms. ". . . and nothin', *nothin' on God's earth*, could have filled it but you."

"I'm so sorry," she sobbed. "I'm so sorry I hurt you like that, E-Erik."

"Hey, hey," he said, leaning away just enough to reach for her cheeks. He clutched them tenderly, turning her tear-streaked face to his. "We hurt each other. We didn't love like kids, but we *were* kids. We made mistakes."

She nodded, sniffling softly. "Big ones."

"Bad ones."

"Terrible ones."

He chuckled softly, shaking his head slowly. His voice was intense with need and awe when he told her, "*I love you.*"

"I love you too," she responded on a sigh, her lips tilting up into a brilliant, glorious smile. "I love you forever."

Leaning his head down, he pressed his lips to hers, surprised—in the best possible way—to feel her fingers reach for the buttons on his shirt and start unfastening them. He followed her lead, slipping his hands under her sweater and pushing it over her belly, skimming his palms over her breasts, and leaning away from their kiss as he slipped it over her head. He shrugged out of his unbuttoned shirt and pulled his T-shirt over his head. Laire reached behind her back and unfastened her bra, then straightened her arms, letting it glide down to the floor in a whisper.

His eyes dropped to her perfect breasts, and he sucked in a sharp breath. Just as perfect as they were when she was his girlfriend, they were fuller now, no doubt from her pregnancy. Glancing up for permission, she nodded as he reached for them, cupping the soft mounds of warm flesh from the sides, plumping them together, and sighing from the sight.

"You're . . . beautiful," he murmured, looking up at her for a moment before sucking one pert nipple between his lips.

She whimpered, a low "unh" sound, as she plunged her hands into his hair, pulling him closer and arching her back as he skimmed his lips between the valley of her breasts to kiss the peak of the other.

"Erik," she moaned, breathless with need.

He knew that if he slipped his fingers into her panties, they'd be damp, and his cock, already rock-hard, pulsed, swelling impossibly bigger.

It had been a long, long time since he'd had sex, and even then, he'd come on Laire's stomach, not inside her. When he'd dreamed of tonight, he'd imagined going slow—treating her gently and with reverence, and drawing out every possible moment between them. But her response to him was just as hungry as his was to her—and suddenly he felt himself changing gears. Fuck slow. They could go slow later. What they needed— what they both really needed right now—was to *be* together in the most intimate way that a man and a woman could share themselves.

"I wanted to go slow," muttered Erik, nuzzling her taut nipple before kissing it again.

"I don't need slow," said Laire, forcing him to look up at her. "I just need you."

He nodded, reaching for her jeans, which he unbuttoned and unzipped. He slipped his thumbs into the waistband of her panties and yanked, pulling every shred of clothing over her hips and exposing her to him in the most vulnerable possible way.

In response, she smiled at him, her eyes dark as she leaned down and stepped out of her pants, walking around to the side of the bed, climbing on top of the comforter and kneeling in the middle.

His shaking fingers unbuckled his belt, and he shoved his pants over his hips without unbuttoning them, wincing at the burn of denim over skin, but hopping frantically to get his clothes the fuck off so he could be as naked as she was.

From the bed, she giggled softly, her small shoulders bunching as he cursed at his jeans, one side catching on his ankle. "Fuck!"

"That's the idea," she said. "You need help?"

Leaning down, he pulled the offending cotton from his body and chucked them across the room. "No, ma'am."

When he looked up, her eyes were wide, focused, with a bit of trepidation, on his cock. It was veined and swollen, standing straight up, the cap purple and slick. Deprived of a woman for so many years, it was more than ready to make up for lost time.

Licking her lips, Laire raised her dark eyes to his as he stood beside the bed, his thighs pressed against the comforter.

"I'm . . .," she started, dropping her eyes to his sex again and blinking.

Scared? Worried? Fuck. He should have made sure the lights were all out. Did she want to back out? Did she want more time? He couldn't help the small groan of deep longing that released from his throat as he watched her eyes trail back up his body.

". . . ready," she whispered, locking her eyes with his.

*Thank fuck.* He let go of the breath he'd been holding.

Climbing on the bed and spreading his legs into a V, he opened his arms to her. "Come over here, darlin'."

Still on her knees, she crawled forward until she was kneeling at the apex of his legs, his straining cock standing tall between them.

"Are you on birth control?"

She shook her head. He reached for the bedside table, reaching inside the drawer for the box of condoms he'd picked up earlier in the day. Grabbing one and ripping it open with his teeth, he pinched the end and rolled it over his throbbing sex before meeting her eyes.

"You sure you want this?"

"I want this," she said, licking her lips, "but I don't know what the hell I'm doing."

\*\*\*

"I do," he said, his face reverent and tender as he nodded. "Kneel on either side of my hips."

She followed his directions, never looking away from his steadfast gaze, grateful for his patience and for the loving way he watched her. Kneeling over his erection, she could feel the tip brush against her as she positioned herself and it made her shiver with the enormity of what they were about to do. But no part of her, not one cell, questioned if this was the right decision for her and her life. She'd dreamed of this moment for six long years.

"When you're ready," he said, his voice pure gravel, "reach down and guide it inside."

"Like . . . sit on it?" she asked.

He nodded, his jaw tight, like he was in a little bit of pain.

"Okay," she said, her voice breathless in her ears.

She tilted her ass up which made her breasts rub against his chest, tightening her already rigid nipples. Biting on her lower lip, she reached between their bodies, her fingers wrapping around the velvet-covered steel of his erection. It pulsed in her palm, alive and eager, and made her mouth water with anticipation. Her body, deprived of his for so long, was slick and wet with want as she lined up the tip of his sex at the opening of hers.

Her breathing was shallow and ragged as she released him, holding his eyes with hers as she rested both hands on his shoulders and slowly—so slowly that she could feel the ridges of his cock massage every inch of her—she lowered herself onto him until her ass rested on his upper thighs, and he was embedded as deeply within her as possible.

"Ahhh!" he cried, the sound a mix of a growl and a groan as he reached for her hips, his hands landing on them gently but firmly as he thrust upward.

It was her turn to moan, her head falling back as her shoulders clenched and her eyes rolled back in her head. He was so big, so thick, filling her completely, stretching parts of her that hadn't been touched since their daughter was born years before.

"Am I . . . oh, baby," he asked, groaning as his hands guided the movements of their bodies, moving hers up and down on his. "Am I hurtin' you?"

"Noooo," she sighed, leaning her head up and opening her eyes. "It feels so . . . *good.*"

"It does," he said, taking one hand from her hip to plump her breast and suck the nipple into his mouth. He laved it with his hot, wet tongue, making her whimper in pleasure-pain, his cock still driving up into her body with increased speed.

She reached for his jaw, lifting his head and kissing him, their tongues seeking each other with urgency as he continued sliding into her. A swirling had started in her belly when he'd first touched her tonight, and now it had color and sound. It was brighter and brighter whenever she closed her eyes, and her heartbeat was louder and louder in her ears as heat radiated out from the place where they were joined, inviting her entire body to experience the climax that was coming.

Her fingers curled into his cheeks as she kissed him, and he leaned back against the pillows, flat on his back. Laire tipped her body forward, still impaled on his thickness, her palms flattening over his erect nipples as she rode him, meeting each of his upward thrusts. His hands slid from her waist to the backs of her thighs, pushing her forward with faster, tighter movements inside her.

Her breathing was as ragged and shallow as his when she felt the contractions start deep within, changing quickly into lightning-fast muscle shudders, her body fisting around his cock as her head fell back and her body convulsed with a cry that came from the depth of her soul.

He jackknifed into a sitting position, wrapping his arms around her.

"I love you. I love you. IloveyouIloveyouIloveyou . . .," she murmured blindly, looping her arms around his neck and letting her sweaty forehead fall to his shoulder as her body shattered and shook, coming apart and fitting back together in his arms.

He thrust upward with a guttural groan of pleasure.

"Laire!" he cried, his arms tightening as his cock strained, pulsing wildly within her. "Laire. Laire. Laire. My darlin' . . . you're mine . . ."

His forehead fell limply against her shoulder, and that's how they remained. Entwined in each other's arms, finally sated, finally whole, their hearts beating madly against each other, love found, love made, love requited.

***

It was torture to leave her.

*Torture.*

As he pulled out of the Pamlico House driveway at the crack of dawn, he looked up to see Laire, wrapped in a sheet, waving from the second-floor window. Her eyes were soft, and her lips tilted upward in a sad smile. She pressed her fingers to her lips then flattened her palm and blew. *I love you.*

*I love you too*, he mouthed, rolling down his window and

blowing a kiss back before pulling away.

Turning onto Route 12, he sighed, letting himself relive a little of last night's splendor. They'd made love four or five more times, reaching for each other ceaselessly, showering in the early hours of morning, only to crawl into bed and make love again. Finally giving up on sleep, they opted instead to cuddle together in Erik's bed with Laire telling him stories about Ava Grace until the first strains of sunlight forced him from her arms.

He resented the sunlight. He hated it.

"I don't want to leave you," he muttered. "But I have to go now to come back for good."

"What's the plan?"

He shrugged. "Tie up loose ends."

"Your parents?" she asked, her eyes conflicted.

He nodded. "Yes. I need to confront them. I need to make it clear that you and Ava Grace are off-limits. Forever."

He was lying on his back, naked, with Laire's head on his chest. Holding her close with one arm, he stroked her hair with his free hand.

"What about . . . the future?"

"You mean us?" he asked.

"Mm-hm."

"Well, I want you and Ava Grace in my life, but I don't like the idea of you havin' to see my parents on a regular basis. I don't trust them. So that makes Raleigh a bad idea for us. I think I'll relocate here for now."

"To the Banks?" she asked, propping herself up to look into his face. "Are you sure?"

He pressed a swift kiss to her lips. "We need to be together. You're here. I don't want you there. So . . . yeah. The Banks. For now."

"You'd do that for me?"

"Baby," he said, "I'd do anything for you. Don't you know that by now?"

She leaned up and kissed him passionately, though their lips were bruised and swollen from so much loving, and she'd winced as she pulled away.

"When will you be back?"

He sighed. He needed to speak to his parents, wrap things up at his job, figure out what to do with his apartment. But when he looked into her green eyes, he knew that more than three days away from her would be anguish. "Thursday."

She nodded and smiled, lying back down on his chest. "Okay. Did I tell you my condo's ready tomorrow? Mr. McGillicutty said the power would be back on by then."

"Then that's where I'll go, darlin'. I'll come straight home to you."

Now, as he sped away from Laire and their daughter, it took all of his strength to stay the course and not turn the rental around. He didn't want to leave them. Damn it, but he wished he could stay.

Seeking levelheaded counsel, he dialed Hillary's number, letting it ring seven times before she picked up with a very groggy, "'lo?"

"Hills?"

"Erik?" She was instantly more alert. "Are you okay?"

"Yeah," he said. "Drivin' back to the city now."

She sighed, long and low. "Let me go to the other room. I don't want to wake up Pete." He heard some rustling and shuffling, and then Hillary's voice again. "What happened? The last time I talked to you, you put *that woman* on the phone, and I didn't—"

"I love her, Hills. I love her and she loves me too, and she's goin' to be in my life, so don't call her 'that woman'—call her Laire."

"Well," she said, sighing again. "I think you better tell me everythin'."

386

An hour later, on Route 64 headed west, he wrapped up the story, pulling into the Speedway just west of Roper to gas up and grab a cup of coffee. Lots of sex and no sleep meant that his body was running on fumes.

"I can't believe it," Hillary was saying, as she'd probably said twenty-five times during his retelling of the past few days. "You have a *daughter*, Erik?"

"Yes, I do."

"Are you *sure* you believe her?"

"A hundred percent positive. You'll know when you see her. She's my spitting image, Hills. Same eyes."

"And Fancy . . . my God, I just . . . I can't believe that she'd just—"

"Believe it. She did."

His sister paused, and Erik stared out the windshield, wondering what she was gearing up to say.

"Will you hate me if I play devil's advocate for a second?"

Erik unbuckled his seat belt. "The word *devil* is right enough."

"You *did* lie to her. You let her believe that you and Van were an item that summer."

"She still should have come and found me. She should have at least *checked* with me before throwin' Laire out on her ass."

He opened the car door, stepped over to the pump, and swiped his credit card.

"But, Erik, think about what you're doin'—pickin' a fight with them. I mean, Daddy's awful powerful, and—"

He started the pump. "You're on their side?!"

"No! No, of course not. I mean, I'm just worried about this. For you."

"Well, don't be," he said. "I don't intend to say much. Just to make it clear that they're not welcome near me or my family."

"Your . . . *family*?"

"Laire and Ava Grace."

"Right, right. Oh, my God. I think it's startin' to sink in. You're a daddy now."

"And nothin's goin' to hurt my baby," he said, opening the door to the convenience store and stepping inside. He beelined for the coffee counter and chose the largest cup.

Hillary was quiet for a long while before saying, "I wouldn't trust her either. Fancy."

"So you get it."

"I do," she said, though her voice was sad. "Call me? After it's done?"

"I will," he said. "I promise."

"And Erik!" she called, just as he was about to press End. "Yeah?"

Her voice was excited. "I can't wait to meet her. Ava Grace. I want to get some presents for you to take back to her from her Aunt Hillary, okay? I'm thinkin' five-year-olds like stuffed animals, right? Any idea which would be her favorite?"

An image of Mr. Mopples appeared front and center in Erik's head, and he chuckled softly. "I think I have a pretty good idea."

***

Ava Grace had a big smile on her face as Laire dropped her off at school for her first day, refusing to let her mother walk her to class, and opting to hold the principal's hand instead.

*She's tough*, thought Laire, feeling proud of her daughter as she drove back to the Pamlico House, where a boat rental was waiting for her.

Kindergarten was three and a half hours long, which meant that Laire had an hour to get to Corey, an hour to visit with her father and sisters, and an hour to get back. She parked her car in the space that Erik had vacated that morning, then walked inside the Pamlico House to grab the keys that Mr. Leatham promised to have waiting for her. After school, she and Ava Grace would pack their things and settle the bill before moving into their new home.

Twenty minutes later, with the cold wind biting her cheeks, she passed Utopia Manor on the portside, a chill running through her as she recalled the last time she'd walked up to the house, only to be called a liar and an opportunist and to be turned away.

She'd been so young, a child. A scared little girl with a baby on the way and no plan, no real means, no support. Looking away from the grand mansion, a vision of Judith's kindly face entered her mind and soothed her heart. *Thank God for you, Judith.*

Laire had called Kyrstin this morning and asked if she could come and see her, Issy, and their father this morning. Kyrstin said that, since their father and Issy worked at King Triton on Tuesdays, it would be easy to catch them in one place, and Kyrstin promised to stop by the shop at ten o'clock, right around the time Laire would be docking.

"Goin' t'be quite the reunion, li'l Laire."

"Does he still hate me, Kyrs?" she'd asked.

Her sister had sighed into the phone. "I don't know, Laire. We barely speak of you. I know you hurt him bad when you pulled that stunt with the governor's son, stayin' out all night. And he knows why you left. 'Cause of . . . the baby." She sighed again. "I hope this isn't a mistake, you comin' here."

"He's still my father. And you're still my sisters. I just want to see you. I want peace between us. Someday I'd like you to know my daughter."

As she always did, Kyrstin ignored Laire's reference to her illegitimate child. "You don't even sound like an islander anymore, Laire."

"See you at ten?" she asked.

"All right," said Kyrstin. "At ten."

Laire hung up quickly because she had to get Ava Grace

ready for school, but also because she didn't want Kyrstin to change her mind.

Now, as she neared the dock owned by King Triton Seafood, her heart clenched, and a mass of butterflies appeared in her stomach out of nowhere. Would her father reject her? Would Issy refuse to speak to her?

Laire had learned how to live away from Corey, and, as she'd always suspected, she preferred it. She had no interest in ever going back to island life, but still, this had been her home for eighteen years, and she desperately wanted peace with her family, no matter what hurts they'd heaped on one another once upon a time.

As she pulled up smoothly to the dock, she threw the two buoys over the side, cut the engine, and leaped from the boat with the stern line in hand, securing it to the waiting cleat with a practiced flick of her wrists. She grabbed the bow line and did the same, quietly marveling that, after six years, she still had the skills.

*I'll always have them, I guess. Corey will always be a part of me.*

Taking a deep breath, she looked up the gangplank to the little blue, shack-style storefront that read "KING TRITON SEAFOOD," her heart racing.

*Breathe.*

She heard Erik's voice in her head, and reached inside her shirt for the necklace she'd worn last night. It was warm from her skin, and it comforted her as she walked slowly up the planking, closer and closer to where her father and sisters waited.

Each step was loud in her ears as her boots scraped over the metal walkway. When she got to the end, she stared down at the ground, afraid to move forward, frightened that she'd do more damage than good by coming here. She froze, rethinking her decision, wondering if she should leave things be and turn around.

Suddenly she heard the tinkling sound of a bell and raised her eyes to the source. And there, standing just outside the little shop, was her father. Hook Cornish. Not quite as big. Much more gray. One side of his face sagged, but otherwise, it was just as tan and craggy as ever.

She raised her eyes to his, staring at the father she hadn't seen in six long years.

"Well, if it isn't our li'l Laire, finally come home."

Still uncertain, she stood stock-still, watching his face . . . and that's when she noticed: his blue eyes sparkled as his uneven lips fought to smile. He nodded at her in welcome and opened up his arms.

With a sob of relief, Laire sprinted into them.

\*\*\*

Erik considered going to his apartment and getting some sleep first. Truly he did. But as he grew closer and closer to the city of Raleigh, he found his temper flaring, his anger rising, and instead he turned off the highway and pointed his car toward the Governor's Mansion.

Uncertain whether or not his parents would be in at ten o'clock on a Tuesday morning, he realized it didn't really matter. He'd sit in the front parlor until they returned. Tomorrow and Thursday he'd deal with his job and apartment. Today, he needed to take care of the most pressing business at hand: confronting his parents—*his mother*—about what she'd done to Laire.

He pressed the code into the keypad to open the gates, but as he pulled into the circular driveway and cut the car engine, he realized he felt like a stranger at the house he'd called home for much of his teen years, and opted for ringing the doorbell instead of using his key on the front door.

"Why, Erik!" exclaimed Esme, the maid who'd been with

his family for years. "You didn't tell us you were comin'!"

"Mornin', Esme," he said, stepping into the front vestibule. "How are you?"

"Just fine! Your folks got in late last night from Vermont. Took breakfast in their room. You want coffee?"

"No, thanks," he said. "You said they're in their bedroom?"

"Yes, sir."

"I'll find them there," he said, nodding at Esme as he crossed the huge hallway to the grand staircase. He took the marble steps two at a time, turning left at the landing and climbing another set of stairs to the second floor. At the balustrade, he turned right, walking down the carpeted hallway to his parents' suite.

His heart pounded as he knocked on their door—not out of any misgivings or fear but because he was eager to confront them and get this over with so his life could finally start moving forward again.

"Come in," called his mother's voice.

He stepped inside, closing the door behind him before turning to his parents, who sat at their breakfast table in front of a big-screen TV tuned to Fox News.

"Sweetheart!" cried his mother, placing her teacup back on its saucer and beaming at him. "Here to welcome us home? What a darlin' son!"

"'lo, son," said his father, glancing up from his newspaper. "Happy New Year."

He stared at them, at the privileged domesticity of their midmorning breakfast, at the steam that rose from his father's coffee mug, at the bright orange of the fresh-squeezed juice in their goblets. He had a fleeting thought that never again would he be welcomed so warmly, without suspicion or baggage, into his parents' home. Everything was about to change.

"I need to talk to you," he said.

"Oh?" asked his mother. She turned to the table, found the remote, and muted the TV before turning to her husband. "Put the paper down, Brady. This might be serious."

His father grumbled, but complied, placing the newspaper by a budvase on the white tablecloth, and looking up at his son. "Well?"

Erik locked eyes with his mother. "About six years ago, while we were celebratin' Thanksgivin', a girl showed up who wanted to speak to me. Do you remember her?"

"What?" His mother laughed softly, shrugging her shoulders. "I have no—"

"Do. You. Remember. Her?" he growled, enunciating each word with a bite.

"Why, Erik . . . what are you talkin' about?"

"A girl, mother. A girl showed up at Utopia Manor. Six years ago Thanksgivin'. She had red hair and green eyes. She was on her way to speak to me but ran into you by the pool. She spoke to you instead. Do you remember her?"

His mother's smile slipped. "Well, now, I don't know if—"

"Her name was Laire, and she was pregnant." He stared at her, into her, willing her to give him a good excuse for what she did. "She was pregnant with my baby. Do you remember her?"

Her eyes flared with fury, and she flinched, turning away from her son. Picking up her teacup deliberately, she took a sip, then turned to him, her smile plastic but in place. "Yes. I believe I do remember some cheap piece of white trash comin' to my house on a holiday and claimin' that she was pregnant with my son's bastard. Yes, indeed. I do remember her. I remember her hightailin' it off my property when I threatened to call the police."

"Fancy!" gasped the governor, and for the first time since Erik started speaking, his eyes darted to his father.

"Did *you* know?" he asked, searching his father's deep blue eyes for answers.

His father shook his head slowly, as though in shock. "No, son. I did not."

Finished with him, Erik slid his gaze back to Fancy, who didn't look a bit sorry for what she'd done. She shrugged. "There was no way to know if she was tellin' the truth! If she spread her legs for you, then surely she could have spread them for—"

"Shut up!" he yelled. "I *loved* her! I got her pregnant, and when she came to tell me, you called her a liar. You threatened her. You made her leave."

"Yes, I did," she said. "And I *protected* you from the scandal she would have caused!"

"*Protected* me?" he demanded, feeling sick.

Fancy's lips were pursed as she stared back at Erik with his eyes. With Ava Grace's eyes.

"You were out every night fuckin' some little island tramp, and then you expected me to welcome her with open arms into our esteemed famil—"

"Wait!" he said, holding up his palm. A puzzle piece—a very important puzzle piece—wasn't fitting together, and he scrambled to figure out what it was.

"She would have ruined your future! She was some little piece of ass that you—"

"Wait. Did . . . did you know she was tellin' the truth?"

Fancy sniffed the air, then looked away, picking a nonexistent piece of lint off her satin robe.

"You called her a liar. You said that she made it all up. You told her that I was with Vanessa all summer and it was impossible that the child could be mine."

His mother lifted her chin. "Whatever I did, it was for you."

"Don't say that. Don't *fuckin'* say that!" growled Erik,

advancing on his mother. One step. Two. He halted, forcing himself to stop, fisting his hands at his sides, not trusting himself to get closer.

"Did you know I wasn't with Van?"

"Of course I knew you weren't *with* Van," she said, her voice lethal, her eyes cold. "Vanessa went to England for a month that summer, but you were still out every night."

"You used my own lie to chase her away," he murmured, his voice breathless, his brain finally understanding the truth: his mother had known that he and Van weren't together. She'd also known, staring into Laire's helpless eyes that night, that she was probably telling the truth.

"It was convenient," said Fancy, sipping her tea like they *weren't* in the middle of a conversation that was destroying their relationship forever.

"You knew I wasn't with Van. You knew Laire was tellin' the truth," he said, surprised by how much the words hurt, surprised that there was anything left of his heart for her to break.

He thought he'd hated her when he walked into her bedroom this morning, but part of him still felt guilty that he'd deceived her that summer, and he wondered about his share of blame for her sending Laire away. He'd let her believe that he and Van were together; he'd willfully misled her.

Except he hadn't. She'd known all along that he and Van were a sham.

"How did you know that I was lyin' about bein' with Van?"

"I knew you were spendin' a lot of time that summer with someone else. I'm not a moron, Erik. You were out every night. You raced back to the Banks when the house was empty. You had a spring in your step every Sunday, and you'd be gone for hours and hours on end. Yes, I knew you had a piece of ass on the side. Wouldn't be the first Rexford to find someone else to fill your . . . needs." She took a deep breath, placing her teacup back on her saucer and looking at her husband meaningfully before turning back to her son. "Boys will be boys, I suppose. Their peckers get a workout. But *my* boy wasn't goin' to be saddled for life with some little tramp."

"All you cared about was your goddamned social status. About avoidin' a scandal."

"And what's wrong with that?" she sniped, her eyes narrow and mean. "You'd have me welcome some fish-smellin' piece of white trash into our family because you knocked her up?" She hooted. "Think again! I didn't raise us to this level only to have your wanderin' cock destroy us!"

"Fancy!" cried Erik's father.

Erik blinked at her, shock and fury mixing inside until he felt his stomach roll over. "You're a fuckin' monster."

"Here, now!" cried his father, slapping his palm on the table and making the china rattle. "You will *not* speak to your mother that way!"

He turned to his father, nailing him with a wild gaze. "My pregnant girlfriend showed up at Thanksgivin' to tell me she was expectin' our child, to ask for my help. And *she*—" Spittle flew from his mouth as he pointed at his mother. "—turned her away. Into the night. With nothin'!" His father stared back at him, expressionless. "Your *grandchild*, Father!"

His father took a deep breath, then dropped his eyes to the tablecloth, running his fingers along a crisp seam in the cloth.

"Well, it's in the past now, isn't it?" he asked rhetorically.

"No," said Erik, picturing Laire and Ava Grace in his mind, feeling them in his heart, knowing the strength of his love for them and the certainty of what he wanted in his life. "It's not in the past. I found them. I found her—Laire—and Ava Grace, my almost six-year-old daughter."

Fancy gasped, her face furious. "Ha! I hope you have a

good specialist on retainer to do the DNA test becau—"

"She has my eyes," he snarled. "*Your* eyes, Mother."

His mother blinked at him, swallowing before looking away.

"I'm about to leave this house, but before I go, I need to be very clear with you both, so listen carefully.

I will be resignin' from my job at Rexford & Rexford today. I will be tyin' up loose ends and packin' up my desk tomorrow and Thursday. I will not be back to work. Ever.

I will be sellin' or rentin' my apartment. I will be leavin' Raleigh to be with my daughter and her mother. I will not be back. I wouldn't condemn them to the humiliation of livin' in the same city as you."

"Now, Erik—" started his father.

"Shut up," he said, shifting his eyes to Fancy, holding her dark eyes in a cold, unwavering gaze. "You are not welcome, in any way, shape, or form, around my daughter or her mother. You are not to contact me. You are not to try to reach out to them or me. As long as you leave us alone, you can tell the press anythin' you want to about my resignation and move, and I won't say a peep. If, however, you decide to contact my daughter or her mother, I will publish a full and unabridged account of the way my daughter and her mother were treated by Fancy Rexford. I will tell the world about the time my daughter's mother came to *my* mother for help, and how she was turned away, into the dark night, with nothin'. I will tell them that is the reason I was kicked off the Devils and almost became an alcoholic. I will tell them that's why I have looked dead for the past six years. I will tell them everythin' you did to me . . . and to them."

"Erik," said Fancy, her posture changing from angry to worried. "I think you need to—"

He ignored her, turning to his father. "Have I made myself clear, sir?"

His father's face was filled with shock and regret, but he nodded before staring back down at the table.

"Ma'am?" he prompted. "Are we clear?"

His mother's nostrils flared as she stood up, throwing her napkin on the table. "How dare you! All I ever wanted was to keep you safe, and this is how you—"

"ARE. WE. CLEAR?" he bellowed.

Ursula "Fancy" Rexford's lip wobbled as she stared back at Erik. "Son, you can't mean this. I was only tryin' to protect you! We're your—"

"No, ma'am," he said softly, his voice biting, cutting like a whip. "You are *not* my parents anymore. You are *not* my family. I do *not* forgive you." He paused, letting his words sink in, watching as his mother gasped, her eyes filling with tears. "Are we clear?"

Without answering, she burst into tears, screaming at her husband "to make Erik come back and listen to reason" as he turned on his heel, walked out of their room, and closed the door behind him.

## Chapter 25

*I'm almost home*, thought Erik as he drove across the Croatan Sound, sped through Roanoke Island, and crossed the Washington Baum Bridge to the Banks. Turning right onto Route 12 at Nags Head, he felt a rush of anticipation. He was only an hour from Laire and Ava Grace now. *Thank God.*

He hadn't spoken to his parents since the conversation in their room on Tuesday morning. They were taking his threat seriously and keeping their distance.

As promised, he'd resigned his position at Rexford & Rexford, LLC quietly, without causing a stir of any kind. For now, for the foreseeable future, he wanted nothing whatsoever to do with his parents. He didn't trust them around Laire or Ava Grace, especially in light of the fact that his mother had manipulated the situation that night even worse than he'd imagined. He'd always known that she was dangerous, but some part of her *knew* that Laire was carrying her grandchild, and she'd still turned her away.

He couldn't imagine a situation in which he'd welcome his parents back into his life or ever regard them as his family again. He'd made his choice: he chose his daughter and her mother without exception.

But while disowning his parents had given him a freedom

that felt right, saying good-bye to Hillary felt far less victorious. She'd visited his office this afternoon as he packed up the last of his belongings.

"Hey, you," she said, knocking softly on his open door, "gettin' ready to go?"

He nodded. "Yep."

"I, uh, I heard from Daddy today."

"That right?"

"He didn't know, Erik. I swear to you, he didn't know that Laire came by that Thanksgivin'. Didn't know that she was pregnant. Fancy never told him."

He remembered the shock on his father's face. "I believe you. But they're a package deal, Hills, and you know it. Always have been. The fabulous Governor and Mrs. Rexford. If I let him back in my life, she'll figure out a way to weasel in too, and I can't have it."

"I get it, Erik. I do," she said, closing the door to afford them some privacy. "I get why you don't want Fancy in your life." She sat down on the couch, looking up at him. "But Daddy? He didn't do anythin'."

"Exactly. He *never* did anythin'," said Erik. "No matter what she did, he never checked her, never called her out, just turned a blind eye no matter who she hurt." He sighed. "I don't know, Hills. Maybe . . . maybe someday down the line, Daddy and I can talk again. I just need some space right now. I need to keep my girls safe."

"Right," she said. "But quittin' your job? Leavin' Raleigh? It's rash, Erik. This is your home."

"No, Hills." He looked up from packing some manila file folders into a cardboard box. "Laire and Ava Grace are my home."

"Couldn't they move here? To Raleigh?"

"How are you not gettin' this?" he snapped. "I don't *want*

them in Raleigh. I don't want them *near* here."

"I *do* get it," she said miserably. "What about your apartment?"

"The buildin' had a waiting list a mile long. They already found me a tenant."

"Need help packin' up?"

"Hired people. Everythin' will be put in storage tomorrow until I figure out what comes next."

"What *does* come next?"

"I'll get a job once we're settled somewhere."

"*Where*? On the Outer Banks?" she demanded, her voice shrieking a little on the word *Banks*."

Erik stopped what he was doing and looked at her closely—at the red spots in her cheeks and the glistening of her eyes. He stepped around his desk and sat down next to her on the couch.

"Maybe," he said slowly. "Or maybe I'll live off my trust for a while."

"Won't last forever," she said.

"Yeah, it will," he said gently.

Hillary, who had the same trust of five million dollars gifted from their maternal grandfather, had nodded. "Yeah. It will."

"Laire's a designer," he said. "She has a job in New York. I'm guessin' . . . I mean, maybe we'll head North."

"You're *not* goin' to New York, Erik!" she exclaimed, her face aghast. "We're Southerners."

"Things change," he said. "If that's where she needs to be, that's where I need to be too."

"And what exactly will *you* do in New York?

"Pass the bar. Practice law. Get married. Have more kids. Be happy."

"Just like that?"

He nodded, pulling her into a hug. "Just like that, little

sister. Stop worryin'.' "

"I *do* worry." She drew away, looking up at him with glistening eyes. "I worry so much. Erik . . . We'll never see each other."

"That's not true," he said. "We'll make sure that's not true. I want you to know Laire—to love her as much as I do. And Hills, you're an aunt! My daughter needs family, and you're all I've got to share with her. Promise me we'll make this work? No matter where we are."

She inhaled deeply, wiping away her tears as she embraced her brother again. "I promise, Erik. We'll figure it out." She sniffled, offering him an enormous plastic bag. "There's about two dozen penguins in here. Every single one I could get my hands on. You tell her they're *all* from Aunt Hillary. No takin' credit. Promise?"

He kissed her cheek and smiled. "I promise."

His heart clenched for a brief moment as he thought of stepping into the elevator and waving good-bye to his sister. But once he'd gotten into his car, which was full of several boxes and suitcases, and headed for Hatteras, any remaining apprehension over his decision to leave his life in Raleigh had quickly faded.

His conversation with his parents had been horrible, and he still didn't know if reconciliation would ever be in the cards. Forgiving his mother for what she'd done would take years—maybe a lifetime. And protecting his new family from his birth family felt like an absolute necessity at this point in time.

Leaving his job, vacating his apartment, and leasing it to a new tenant had led to mountains of paperwork, and saying good-bye to Hillary had been wrenching.

But as he crossed the bridge to the Outer Banks, all he felt was freedom and hope. Freedom to follow his dream and create the family he longed for with Laire and Ava Grace. And hope—

so much hope that after six years of cold, aching loneliness, a life full of warmth and love with his girls awaited.

He stepped on the gas, cracking the window and inhaling the cold, brackish air, closer, with every mile, to those he loved most in the world.

*** 

Ava Grace had fallen asleep an hour ago, even though she'd tried hard to stay awake to see her dad. Curled up on the couch, with a homemade "Welcome Home!" card in her lap, she'd finally succumbed to sleep, and Laire had carried her into her bedroom and closed the door. She placed the card on Ava Grace's bedside table. It would keep until the morning.

Erik texted two hours ago that he'd get dinner on the road so she didn't prepare anything for them, but she had a bottle of Champagne on ice, and the condo was immaculate for his arrival, except for Ava Grace's dinner dishes, which she decided to tackle now.

Her body, deprived of his for three long days, was ravenously hungry for their reunion, and she kept looking out the kitchen window over the sink, hoping to see his headlights as he pulled into the parking lot.

She knew that things had not gone well with his parents. His mother had admitted to using Vanessa as a way to keep Erik and Laire apart, and also to knowing that Laire was likely telling the truth about being pregnant with his child. In response, Erik had essentially disowned them, forbidding them to ever reach out to him or to try to know their granddaughter.

It was a terrible thing that Fancy Rexford had done to her son and granddaughter, but Laire, as a mother of her own precious child, had split feelings about her actions. Did she forgive Fancy for threatening and frightening a pregnant eighteen-year-old? No. But she understood that inherent, visceral need of a mother to protect her child from evil or danger, no matter what.

Still, she grieved that Erik wouldn't have a relationship with his parents. She hoped that, over time, maybe he would learn to forgive them, and perhaps—if they were *truly* penitent and eager to know their granddaughter in a real and loving way—he'd be able to find a place for his parents, however controlled, in their life.

Mending family relationships didn't happen overnight. It had taken Laire six years to return to Corey, after all. Sometimes it took years. Sometimes a lifetime. And sometimes that healing was simply impossible.

As she thought back to her reunion with her father and sisters on Tuesday, she knew that their relationships with one another would never be close again. Her father had welcomed her home, but after a brief reunion filled with hugs and kisses and tears, it turned out that they didn't really have that much to say to each other.

Her father filled her in on the fishing industry, and her sisters complained about motherhood and their husbands. They had six children between them and Kyrstin was due with her third any day now. They kept Pop-Pop busy, and—if her father's grins were any indication—happy too.

Laire's plan to live in New York and spend summers at her condo in Hatteras was met with blank stares. Any reference to Ava Grace led to averted eyes and awkward silence. It hurt Laire that no one asked about Ava Grace, though she'd sent her father and sisters pictures of her daughter every Christmas. At one point, Issy looked meaningfully at Laire's empty ring finger and asked if Laire would ever move back to Corey. When she said that she wouldn't, Issy seemed relieved.

Laire received the message loud and clear: she was an outsider now.

For all intents and purposes, she was probably worse than a dingbatter.

She had transformed into someone worldly, someone who'd turned her back on their island ways and chosen the wicked, wider world over a good and simple life on Corey Island. And though she was grateful for the hugs hello and waves good-bye—she finally felt a certain sense of peace where her father, Isolde, and Kyrstin were concerned—there was an inevitable feeling of disappointment as well. Gone were her dreams of summer weeks spent with her sisters and their kids, her father bouncing Ava Grace on his knee.

It's not that they wished her harm. They just wished her away.

Whoever said "You can't go back" had been right. But lucky for Laire, the only real direction she was interested in moving was forward.

As she washed the last of the dishes, she was blinded by the bright headlights of an incoming car, and she blinked, quickly rinsing a soapy *Frozen* cup and plate, and tearing the rubber gloves from her hands.

*He's here. He's here. He's finally home.*

When she heard his key in the lock, her throbbing heart burst with joy. She whipped open the door, giggling with glee as he stepped inside and grabbed her around the waist. She clutched his cheeks, drawing his lips to hers before they even exchanged hellos.

His tongue swept into her mouth as he pushed her against the door, slamming it shut with their bodies, his lips hot on her face, sliding down her neck, landing on the valley between her breasts. Panting as he looked up at her, he started unfastening the buttons of her blouse, cupping her flesh through the lace of her bra as he paused in his work to kiss her again.

She reached for the buttons and finished them, shrugging the shirt from her shoulders, then reaching for his, pulling it from his waistband and sliding her hands underneath. She sighed as she touched the warm, taut skin of his stomach, her breath hitching, her heart skipping.

His lips, brushing gently over the swells of her breasts, paused.

"Ava Grace?" he whispered.

She slid her hands out of his shirt and reached up to thread them through his thick, black hair, looking into his fierce, black eyes. "Asleep."

"Fuck, I missed you, darlin'."

"Me too."

She whimpered with need, pulling his face down to hers as he slid his hands under her ass and lifted her easily. With her back against the door and her core flush with his, she could feel his erection pushing urgently through the tented gabardine of his charcoal trousers, and she arched her back to position his length of muscle as close to her clit as possible. But it wasn't close enough. All she found was frustration, and she bit his lip gently in retaliation.

"Take me to bed," she panted.

"My pleasure," he muttered, turning away from the door to walk through the living room and down the narrow hallway. He passed by Ava Grace's room and beelined into the master bedroom, kicking the door shut behind him.

"Shhhh!" she hissed against his lips. "You'll wake her up!"

"Sorry," he said, chuckling as he deposited her on the bed. He reached behind his neck, grabbed his T-shirt and dress shirt, and pulled both over his head, revealing his ridiculously beautiful abdomen.

"You know," said Laire, standing up and reaching behind her back to unclasp her bra as she approached him. It slid down her arms and whooshed softly to the floor, leaving her torso as bare as his. Reveling in the hiss of appreciation that issued from his lips, she reached out and placed her fingers on the ridges of muscle before her, tracing the contours slowly, with reverence.

"I've been around men all my life—bare-chested men who fish for a living."

She leaned forward, kissing his skin as his hands reached up to cover her breasts, her nipples instantly tightening against his palms. "They haul up full nets from the sea. They work against the weather and the tides. They exert themselves all day, every day."

He rolled her nipples between his thumb and forefinger, the sensitive buds throbbing from the attention and making her moan. "Ah. E-Erik."

He leaned his head forward and replaced his fingers with his lips, sucking first from one distended nub, and then the other. "But none of them," she continued, panting and whimpering, "were ever as beautiful as you."

His teeth razed her flesh, and she cried out, her fingers landing on the button of his pants and pulling down the zipper. Her hand reached inside the warm fabric, under the waistband of his boxers to find his swollen, rigid cock standing straight up. Her breath hitched as he reached for his pants and yanked them down. Placing one hand on his chest, she forced him to sit on the edge of the bed, then dropped to her knees and took him into her mouth.

"Laire!" he cried, as her lips slid effortlessly down the silken shaft of throbbing muscle, her tongue swirling around the precum-covered tip, her fingers curling into his hips as she held on to him.

She sucked on him as their daughter had once suckled from her, thrilling in the grunts and groans above her, the way his hand wound through her hair, fisting it into a ponytail and guiding her as he saw fit. As he worked his cock in and out of her mouth, she looked up at him, watching the play of emotions on his beautiful face—lips pursed in deep desire, soft cries of lust, a flinch of pain-filled pleasure. She tracked his face as his erection throbbed between her lips, pulsing against her licking, swirling tongue.

"Laire . . . baby, I got a little worked up in the car. I'm goin' to . . . You have to . . ."

She slid her lips from the base of his shaft to the head, releasing it from her lips with a soft *pop* and looking up at him.

"Fuuuuck," he groaned, grinning down at her, putting his hands under her arms, and pulling her up to a standing position. His fingers quickly unbuttoned and unzipped her jeans, jerking them down over her hips. She toed them off and stood naked before him.

"I need you," he said, his voice ragged with need as he pushed his own pants off completely, leaving both in a pile on the floor.

His hands landed on her ass, and he pulled her forward, lifting her onto his lap. With a sigh of deep, deep pleasure, she lowered herself onto his slick, pulsating member, bracing her feet on either side of his hips as he clasped his arms around her.

Once fully impaled, she looked into his eyes, which were dilated to black.

"I love you," she whispered, wrapping her arms around his neck, rubbing her breasts against his chest. "I choose you. I choose us. Forever."

Gently, with a reverence that make tears prick her eyes, he thrust upward, palming her cheeks and forcing her to look at him. "We make our own rules."

"Yes," she panted, moving rhythmically with him, the rasp of his chest against her nipples heightening the sensations between her legs, where his cock massaged the inner walls of her sex.

"We belong together," he whispered near her ear, biting on her lobe, his fingers digging into the soft flesh of her hips as he directed their movements.

"Yes," she whimpered, feeling the gathering, the

quickening, the throbbing sweetness of her climax close, so close.

"Forever!" he cried, his cock swelling, then releasing, within her, his thick, hot cum coating her womb, the vibrations of his orgasm compelling her own.

She screamed his name, letting her head fall limply to his shoulder as she rode out the waves of bliss, feeling her muscles contract and relax around him again and again, the action that made the words real and bound them to each other forever.

*Forever.*

***

They slept tangled in each other's arms, but when Erik awoke at six o'clock, he jolted upright and ran naked to the front door, where they'd started undressing. He gathered together their cast-off clothes and took them back to the master bedroom, wondering if he should pull on his boxers and T-shirt, just in case Ava Grace wandered into their room.

"Erik?" Laire murmured. "Everything okay?"

He let the boxers in his hand drop to the floor and slipped back into bed bedside her, pulling her back against his chest and kissing her warm neck. "Mm-hm."

"Where'd you go?"

"I didn't want Ava Grace to find your blouse on the floor in front of the door."

She sighed contentedly. "What a good daddy."

Her deep, raspy, sleepy voice had the effect of making him hard all over again, and he held her closer, letting his growing erection press against her back just in case she was up for round two.

"I'm goin' to be the best I can be."

"I know," she said. "Speaking of . . . we had sex last night. Without protection."

For a split second, he froze, letting the ramifications of her words sink in, but just as quickly, his cock pulsed and swelled, the idea of making another baby with Laire better than porn any day.

"You'd be okay with that?" he asked, placing his palm on her flat stomach. "If you were . . . I mean, if I got you—"

"Mm-hm," she murmured, her voice dreamy as the rising sun began to lift the gray of night. "I'd be okay with that."

Reaching for her leg, he lifted it a little, leaning forward to guide himself into the warm, wet heaven of her sex. As he slid forward, she gasped, covering his hand with hers, moaning as he started moving within her.

"I want to see you pregnant with my child," said Erik, groaning into her ear as he clutched her thigh, keeping her legs open, his lips sliding blindly over the skin of her shoulder as he drove deeply inside, faster and faster. "I want to know that I made you that way."

"Erik," she moaned, pushing her body rhythmically against his.

"I want to be there when the baby comes. I want to be there . . . for everythin'," he panted, his teeth biting gently on her shoulder.

"Yes," she sighed, her voice thick and breathless.

He raised her leg slightly higher. Then, withdrawing from her completely, he thrust back inside her to the hilt. She whimpered, arching against him, but he stilled, his eyes rolling back in his head as the walls of her sex tightened like a glove around him. "Tell me . . . you want it . . . too, Laire."

"I . . . oh, God, please . . . I want it too!" she cried.

He thrust forward twice more—so deep, he swore his cock kissed her womb—and as she shook and shuddered, her muscles milking the cum from his cock, he prayed that their wish would come true.

Letting his head fall forward onto her neck, he panted in ragged breaths against her skin.

"Fuck," he muttered, gently releasing her thigh and wrapping his arms around her. "That was hot."

She sighed, turning in his arms to face him, her eyes dilated but soft. "How many do you want?"

"How many do you want to have?" he asked.

"Four," she said, grinning at him.

"*What? Four?*" he asked, smiling back at her, surprised she had an answer ready.

She giggled softly, leaning forward to kiss his lips. "I hated being one of three. I always wished the number had been even."

"You felt ganged up on?"

She shook her head. "Not really. But I was the odd man out."

"Not anymore," he said, nuzzling her nose with his. "You've got me."

She nodded. "Yes, I do."

"I leased my apartment and quit my job, baby," he said. "I'm all yours now."

"I have to tell you something." She reached up and tousled his dark hair. "I heard from Madame Scalzo yesterday. She doesn't feel like my working remotely is, well, *working*. She asked how I'd feel about relocating to New York to work in-house."

"What'd you say?" he asked.

"I said . . ." She searched his eyes. "I want to go, Erik . . . but I don't want to go without you."

"Why would you go without me?" he asked.

She gasped softly, her eyes filling with tears. "Your whole life is here in North Carolina."

"No," he said, sliding his hand from her back to her hip, then placing it flat, between her breasts, over her heart. "My whole life . . . is *here*."

A tear slipped from her eyes, plopping onto his arm. "You'll come with me? With us? To New York?"

"Can't think of a better place to practice sports and entertainment law, darlin'."

Her smile was so bright, he didn't understand how she could still be crying, but he tasted her tears as she captured his lips with hers.

"I wasn't sure," she said, sniffling as she nestled under his chin, her hands flat on his bare chest.

"Laire, my darlin'," he said, "wherever you go, I go. Wherever you are, I'm home. And whatever happens, we'll handle it together. Our rules. Deal?"

She nodded, her strawberry blonde hair tickling his throat as she pressed her lips to his skin and whispered, "Deal."

\*\*\*

They spent the morning in bed, planning their move to New York, and decided that they'd fly up to the city on Saturday to start looking at apartments. Laire e-mailed Madame Scalzo to say she'd be available to start work in two weeks, and her boss replied that they'd get a drafting table ready for their newest in-house designer.

Ava Grace ran into their room around seven thirty, jumping into bed with them—thank God they'd pulled on some clothes a few minutes earlier—and handing her "Welcome Home!" card to Erik. And he was perfect—commenting on every carefully drawn detail and declaring it the best card he'd ever gotten.

Laire made them scrambled eggs and toast, pleased when Erik stepped up beside her to dry the dishes she washed, the small gesture all the dearer to her because she doubted that he'd ever washed or dried a dish in his entire life.

She took Ava Grace to school, then returned home to find the condo empty. Erik had left a note that read, *Wanted to research some NYC law offices and would be way too distracted by you if I stayed here. Went to the coffee shop at Hatteras Landing. Will pick up Ava Grace at school and be back later.*

*Kelsey's coming to babysit so I can take you out to dinner. Wear something sexy. I love you. —E*

She grinned at the note, setting it beside her laptop on the kitchen table as she reviewed e-mails and made some changes on the sketches she'd sent to Madame Scalzo last week.

Her thoughts wandered as she was sketching, as she considered how drastically her life was changing—finding Erik, sharing the secret about him fathering Ava Grace, moving to New York, working in a couture design studio based in London. It was almost too much to believe, and yet it was all hers, within her grasp: li'l Laire from Corey Island, pop. 886, daughter of a fisherman, wife of a—

She blinked at the waiting cursor, pushing away from the kitchen table.

Wait. Wife?

*Slow down, Laire*, she told herself. *Erik didn't say anything about getting married.*

He wanted to be with her and wanted to have kids with her, and yes, he wanted to move to New York and start a life with her there, but marriage? He'd never actually mentioned it. And yet, from the sudden throb in her heart, she knew how badly she wanted it: to be Erik Rexford's wife.

Oh, she didn't doubt his love for her and Ava Grace—that was plain. And she knew he wanted to build a future with her. But deep in her heart, where she could still hear her mother's voice, she felt the word *husband*, and she wanted Erik to own that role in her life.

Standing, she walked to the fridge and pulled out a pitcher of sweet tea, filling a glass and leaning against the counter as she sipped it.

He'd ask her, wouldn't he? When the time was right? When he was ready? Maybe after they'd been in New York for a while, when they were settled in and life had resumed a steady beat. Maybe then he'd ask her.

*Or*, she thought, sitting back down at her computer, *maybe he wouldn't. Maybe he never would.*

They already had a daughter together and could very well have another on the way. They'd be bohemian, living in one of the biggest cities in the world with their kids, unmarried, bound to one another solely by love. That could work, couldn't it?

"Of course that could work," she said aloud, with false conviction. More quietly, she added, "Love is what matters. Nothing else."

Her brow knitted, she went back to work on her designs, hoping that the words would become her truth sooner than later, and hating that the traditional part of her would never truly believe them.

***

After school, Erik took Ava Grace for ice cream, then to Utopia Manor. The water had been drained from the house, the carpets had been removed for repair and cleaning, and work had already started on the hardwood floors.

He didn't know when he'd ever set foot in the house again, but he wanted his daughter to see it—to see where he and Laire had met so many years ago, to see where their love story was born. She oohed and aahed as they walked through the mansion together, her little hand tightly clasped in his, her other hand holding Mr. Mopples's flipper. He showed her pictures of him as a child and a teen, and pictures of her Aunt Hillary, whom he promised she would meet soon.

At four thirty, he texted Kelsey to confirm that he'd be picking her up at five, and when he turned around, Ava Grace was staring at the large portrait of Erik's mother, hung over the fireplace in the living room.

"Is she a queen?" asked Ava Grace solemnly.

Erik squatted down beside her, hating like hell that the woman holding his daughter so rapt was the same woman who had kept them separated for the first five and a half years of her life.

"Nope. That's my mother."

Ava Grace turned to him. "My grandma?"

Erik took a deep breath, tilting his head to the side, wishing that things were different and he had a warm, loving, wonderful family to share with his little girl. "I guess so."

"And will I meet her when I meet Aunt Hilnary?"

He grinned. After receiving two dozen penguins this morning, Hillary had achieved legendary status, which was reflected in the way Ava Grace said her name.

"*Hill*ary." Then, recalling her question, he quickly stopped grinning. "And no. You won't meet . . . your grandma."

"She's dead like Nana?"

"No, baby," he said, sighing as he stood up and looked at the regal face of Fancy Rexford, which made him grimace. "She's just . . . far, far away."

"And she can't go to New York ever?" asked Ava Grace, slipping her hand into his.

"Not right now," he said. "Maybe . . ." He flinched but forced himself to say the words for his daughter's sake. "Maybe someday."

She looked up at him, smiling happily. "Someday's good enough as long as I got you and Mama."

"You definitely have me and Mama," said Erik, reaching down to pick her up so he could look into her eyes, marveling, as he did every time, how much they looked like his own. "In fact . . ."

Leaning forward, he whispered something into her ear, then drew away to look at her face. "Would that be okay?"

Her small face spread with an ear-to-ear grin, she giggled and nodded, clasping him around the neck as he squeezed her tight, his heart bursting with happiness.

\*\*\*

By five o'clock, Laire was showered and dressed, wearing her favorite winter dress: a House of Scalzo original wrap dress in a zebra print with an oversize belt, three-quarter sleeves, and a plunging neckline. At a street fair in Paris, she'd picked up a chunky jet necklace, which she clasped around her neck, and she tugged on her black suede Roger Vivier boots, on which she'd splurged when Madame Scalzo had offered her a job. She darkened her eyes with kohl and dark brown mascara, and brightened her lips with coral gloss.

Checking herself out in the mirror, she grinned. Runway ready? Not quite. But sexy for a girl from the Outer Banks? Hell, yes.

As she closed her closet door, Ava Grace scampered into her room, telling her all about the castle on the beach called Utopia Manor, and she looked up to find Erik in the doorway.

She watched his eyes as they traveled slowly down her body, darkening with desire.

"Laire," he breathed, "you look . . ."

She smiled at him. "Thanks."

"I mean, damn, woman!"

"Erik!" she exclaimed, her eyes widening as she looked down at their daughter.

Chastened, he chuckled. "Your mama looks like dynamite tonight, Ava Grace."

"Yeah, she's pretty." Then she jumped up and down. "Mama! Kelsey's here! She brought pizza, and we're goin' to watch a movie!"

She raced from the room, dark red braids flying straight back and Mr. Mopples holding on for dear life.

Erik stalked her. "Who are you?"

Her heart flipped over. "Laire Cornish."

Erik took another step toward her, shaking his head. "No way. I know Laire Cornish. I met her six years ago at my parents' summer house. She had pinkish-gold hair and was wearing jeans and boots and a black shirt. She told me she had crabs, then ran away."

Laire giggled, her stomach fluttering as he took another step closer. "You don't like this look?"

"You're so sexy, baby, I don't want to leave this room."

He was so close now, she could smell the sea air on his skin. "You took her to your house?"

His hands landed on her hips, and he pulled her against his chest. "I wanted her to see it before we moved."

"You don't think she'll ever have another chance?"

He shrugged, his face hardening. "Not for a while, darlin'."

Laire sighed, looping her arms around his neck and resting her cheek on his shoulder. She didn't want to spoil the mood by asking about his family. "So, tell me, where are we going tonight?"

"Not a chance. You'll see when we get there. You ready?"

She drew back from him and nodded, happy that his flirty mood seemed to be restored. Backing out of his arms, she grabbed her black silk clutch. "I'll go say hi to Kelsey."

He nodded. "Just give me a minute to change."

\*\*\*

Erik pulled into the Pamlico House parking lot, as he had hundreds of times before—as he had all that summer when he and Laire were first dating, as he had a little over a week ago, when he came out to the Banks to check on his parents' house. But tonight his hands sweat and his stomach was alight with butterflies. Yes, he had already gotten Ava Grace's permission in the living room at Utopia Manor, but would Laire say yes? Or would she ask for some time? They'd only just been reunited, he reminded himself. If she needed a little time, it wasn't a no; it was just a pause. Right? Right.

Opening her car door, he took her hand as they walked up the steps to the reception area.

"The dining room's not open for dinner yet, is it?" asked Laire.

Erik held open the door. "We're not goin' to the dinin' room. We're goin' upstairs."

Laire turned and looked at him. "Up to the widow's walk?"

He nodded. "Is that okay?"

"I thought we were having dinner."

"We are," he said, leaning down to press his lips to hers. "Now, no more questions."

He'd arranged it all with Kelsey, calling her from Raleigh two days ago, after he'd purchased the ring at Sidney Thomas, and asking if it was possible for her to arrange a private dinner for two under the stars on Friday night. After some pretty impressive haggling, Kelsey had agreed to set up everything, her excitement taking over as she told Erik to let her handle everything. Now, as he ascended the stairs with Laire, he hoped that "everything" would be perfect.

Opening the door to the roof, he held it for her, watching over her shoulder as she stopped beside the candlelit table, feeling the satisfaction of her surprised gasp and silently promising to give Kelsey a hundred dollar tip when they got home tonight.

A small table, covered with a long white tablecloth, had been set for two with china plates and gleaming silver. Ice water sparkled in two goblets, and a bottle of Champagne shifted in its icy bath. On the table was a low arrangement of red roses, surrounded by flickering candles, and in a heater beside the table, Erik knew he would find fresh catch plated with sautéed vegetables and warm rolls.

But the most important part of the night was going to happen right now. Erik dropped to one knee as Laire turned around to face him.

She gasped again, the tears in her eyes spilling onto her

cheeks as she covered her mouth, her sea-green eyes so wide, he couldn't help but smile.

"Darlin', can I have your hand?"

Shaking like a leaf, she dropped her hands from her face and offered one to him.

"Erik," she murmured through a soft sob, shaking her head. "You didn't have to do this for me."

"Of course I did," he said, taking her hand firmly in his. "We dated in secret. You had our child all alone. But this, baby? This time I'm goin' to do it right."

She smiled at him, sniffling softly as she wiped the tears from under her eyes.

Reaching into his pocket with his free hand, he withdrew a black velvet box and flipped it open. She inhaled sharply, staring at it for a moment before shifting her eyes to his, more tears following the others.

"Laire. Darlin'.

Wait. First, I want you to know: this afternoon at Utopia Manor, I got permission from Ava Grace to ask her mama to marry me so I don't want you to think she's not on board. She is. And Mr. Mopples is too, bless her heart."

Laire chuckled softly, her shoulders shaking as she nodded at him to continue.

"Darlin', I have loved you since the first moment I saw you. My feelin's only grew deeper that summer, until the only future I could imagine included you. I was destroyed for any other woman."

His hand squeezed hers.

"Even when I lost you, I didn't stop lovin' you, Laire. All it took was a glimpse of your face for every feelin' I ever had to come rushin' back so fast, I could hardly bear to let you out of my sight."

Tears cascaded down her face, and she nodded at him, her smile so true and so lovely, it took his breath away.

"I don't want to live another day without you. I don't want this life if you're not in it. I want to wake up next to you every mornin' and make love to you every night. And every moment in between, I want to know that you're mine and I'm yours and we're the only family we'll ever need."

A small sob squeaked through her lips as she nodded.

"And if you need time, darlin', that's okay. Because we've always followed our own rules. And I'm not goin' anywhere ever again, unless you're goin' with me."

Her hand was shaking, but damn, she looked so beautiful, part of him wished he had more to say, just so he could kneel at her feet a while longer, looking up at his mermaid, the freckled, red-haired girl who had captured his heart so long ago.

"You ready?" he asked, grinning up at her, hoping against hope that their happy ending was just within reach.

She nodded and kept nodding as he asked, "Will you marry me, darlin'?"

She had started nodding halfway through his proposal, but now she managed, through tears and laughter, to answer, "Yes."

Smiling up at her, Erik took the ring from its pillow and slipped it onto her finger, the two-karat diamond, flanked by two emerald-cut sapphires, catching the moonlight as she wiggled her fingers experimentally. "Ahhh, Erik. It's *so* beautiful."

Reaching for her other hand, he stood up, looking down at her face, lit by the moon and the stars, yes, but also lit by the spirit of this amazing woman who was the mother of his child and his future bride, on earth and into eternity.

"Yes," he said, cupping her sweet face and leaning down to claim her lips with his, "it is."

# EPILOGUE

### Valentine's Day

Finding an apartment in New York City wasn't quite as simple as Laire had planned.

She had always imagined that she and Ava Grace would live in a simple walk-up not too far from Madame Scalzo's midtown offices, and she'd drop Ava Grace off at school each day on her way to work. But Erik was accustomed to a different way of life altogether, and his trust fund, combined with the salary he'd be making at Dryer & Wolverton, LLC, the premier entertainment law firm of New York, meant that they could set their sights a little higher.

Though it felt like an undue extravagance to Laire, they'd finally agreed on a three-bedroom, three-bathroom, two-floor apartment in the Atria, a luxury doorman building in the Murray Hill neighborhood. Erik liked the fitness center, Ava Grace liked the indoor children's playground, and Laire liked the rooftop garden, where she could see the East River when she was feeling homesick for the sea. When Erik tried to insist on private school, however, Laire put her foot down, telling him that the local public school—one of the newest in New York City—was the right choice for Ava Grace. It was going to be hard enough convincing their daughter that she *wasn't* a princess after the way Erik and Hillary had showered her with gifts. Laire needed to make *some* decisions to keep Ava Grace grounded.

Then again, she thought, covering her stomach lovingly with her palm, there were other factors that would make sure Ava Grace wasn't too badly spoiled—sharing her parents, for example, would be good for her.

But for now, just until tonight, when she would share her good news with Erik as a wedding gift, the sweet secret of her pregnancy was hers and hers alone, and she savored it.

The door creaked open, and Laire looked up as Patrick's wife, Samantha, entered the church's small bride's room with two glasses of Champagne, holding one out to her.

"How are the natives?" asked Laire, placing the glass on the dressing table without taking a sip.

"Restless," said Samantha with a grin. "But thank God Jude's still asleep. Patrick looks terrified that he'll wake up any second raise Cain."

"Any sign of Hillary and Pete yet?"

Samantha shook her head. "Nope. I asked Erik, and he said that their plane got in half an hour ago. I guess they're in a cab?"

"Probably in traffic," said Laire, holding out the necklace from the Elizabethan Gardens to her friend. "Can you fasten it around my neck?"

"Mm-hm," said Samantha, smiling at Laire in the mirror. "I wish Judith could've been here today."

Laire thought wistfully about her two mothers—the mother she'd lost as a child, and dear Judith, who'd been so good to her as a struggling teen and young mother. She wished they were here today too.

Samantha caught Laire's eyes in the mirror. "I didn't know if I should ask or not, but . . . your family couldn't make it?"

The truth? Laire had told her father and sisters about her wedding, but they hadn't offered to come up and she hadn't asked them to. Not out of any meanness, but because they would have had to figure out a way to say no. For people who wanted nothing more than to live and die on the same tiny island, a trip to New York City wasn't the stuff of excitement or adventure, but terror. And asking them wouldn't be an act of inclusion, but selfishness.

Laire would always love her father and her sisters, and every summer, when she returned to the Banks with her husband and children, she would visit them. But she had chosen a very different path for her life, and part of respecting her unique upbringing was not forcing her family to embrace the changes she'd decided to make in her own journey.

"*You're* my family," said Laire. "You and Pat. Jude. Erik and Ava Grace. And Hillary and Pete, if they'd just get here already!"

On cue, the door to the little room burst open, and Hillary rushed in, looking frazzled. "Sorry we're late! I brought my dress!"

Laire jumped up to hug Erik's sister and introduced Hillary and Samantha before the latter hurried off to find another glass of Champagne to calm Hillary's nerves, and grab Ava Grace for the processional.

"Goddamned cabdriver!" yelled Hillary, throwing her blouse on the floor and unzipping her skirt. "Took every possible goddamned detour!"

In the month and a half since Laire and Erik had reunited, Hillary had become one of her dearest friends. They spoke on the phone or over e-mail every day, and when Pete had finally proposed to Hillary, two weeks ago, Erik and Laire were the first people she'd called. She understood why Erik loved his straight-shooting sister so much, and Laire was relieved to have an ally in the Rexford camp.

At Erik's insistence, they had not invited his parents to the wedding, but Laire still hoped that, over time, he would thaw.

They would never be close to the senior Rexfords, but for the sake of their children, Laire would always work toward achieving peace.

"I'm glad you're here, Hills."

"Me too!" she said, pulling up her bridesmaid dress and turning around so that Laire could zip it.

"Now show me the bling!" insisted Laire, taking Hillary's hand to look at the mammoth engagement ring Pete had given her: a two-and-a-quarter-karat princess-cut diamond solitaire. She sighed in appreciation. "It's gorgeous."

"Just as gorgeous as yours," said Hillary with a grin, hugging Laire close. "You make him so happy."

"He makes me happy," said Laire, blinking back tears as she held on to Hillary.

The door opened again, and Samantha stepped inside, handing Hillary a glass of Champagne as Ava Grace ran over to her mother.

"Are you ready, Mama?"

Dressed in a pale pink flower girl dress with little pink satin rosebuds and a matching crown with ribbons that trailed down her back, Ava Grace was utterly beautiful.

"Yes, baby."

"Daddy's real nervous," she said. "So I let him borrow Mr. Mopples."

She snorted softly. "You did?"

Ava Grace nodded. "She's sitting on the church steps, next to Daddy's feet."

"That's perfect, honey."

"You look beautiful, Mama."

"You too, Ava Grace. Say hi to Aunt Hillary."

"Hi, Aunt Hillary! Did you bring me a present?"

"Yes, I did, rock star, but let's get your mama and daddy married first, huh?"

Samantha took Ava Grace's hand in hers and smiled down at her former ballet student. "Are we ready, little miss?"

"Uh-huh."

Laire reached down for her bouquet—a mix of white roses and freesia—and nodded. "We're ready."

Samantha, Ava Grace, and Hillary preceded her into the church's vestibule.

The wedding planner, who had worked at Mach speed since their move to New York the second week in January, opened the doors to the small sanctuary just as the organist started playing Pachelbel's Canon in D.

Ava Grace and Samantha started down the aisle first, then Hillary, which left Laire alone, lifting her eyes to the altar, where her handsome prince waited, his dark eyes focused, with profound depths of love, on hers.

As she took her first step toward him, she felt it in her bones and in her blood, in every nook and cranny of her heart, as though God was showing her a preview of her life, a promise for her future: there would be more babies to love and more days on the beach to share, a life in New York and summers on the Banks. There would be good days and bad, of course—moments of joy and moments of despair. Life is a cornucopia and nothing less.

But throughout it all, the ups and downs, the highs and lows, until the end of their days, Laire and Erik would never again be apart. There was a rare gift in having experienced the wild loneliness of separation: for as long as they lived, they would never, ever take their togetherness for granted.

"Hi," she whispered as she reached the altar.

He offered her his hand and she took it.

"Hi," he said, lacing his fingers through hers as she stepped up beside him.

There was so much more to say, of course, but there was a lifetime ahead to say it. Bound by their hands, they faced forward as the minister addressed them, starting the ceremony that would officially *marry* them . . . though they were, already, a family.

We are each born into a family, it's true, but Laire, who was born of the sea, and Erik, who was born of the land, had taken their destinies into their own hands, and, with their own rules, they had secured each other's forever.

And that's how they lived . . .

Happily ever after.

THE END

## A LETTER TO MY READERS

Dear Reader,

Thank you for reading my latest modern fairytale, *Don't Speak.* I hope you loved reading Laire and Erik's story as much as I loved writing it.

I am the mother of two children, and they are the lights of my life, but I cannot imagine the work it would have taken to have them alone or raise them on my own. I admire single mothers more than I can say because I know how much work it takes to raise a child and I had a great partner.

In *Don't Speak*, Laire struggles for a plan to have and raise Ava Grace on her own after she finds herself alone and expecting. Luckily, Judith Sebastian becomes a sort of surrogate mother and guardian angel, helping with room, board, and childcare as Laire pursues a college education, which changes her life. This is such a wonderful example of a woman selflessly helping another woman make her dreams come true—a mission near and dear to my heart.

I want a portion of the proceeds from *Don't Speak* to help women in need pursue a college education, so I am donating 15% of the gross royalties of its sales for February and March 2017 to P.E.O. International, an organization of which I am a proud member. P.E.O. sponsors no fewer than six international projects designed to assist women with their educational goals.

From the website: *P.E.O. is clearly making a difference in the lives of women all over the world. Almost 99,000 women have benefited from our organization's educational grants, loans, awards, special projects and stewardship of Cottey College. To date, P.E.O. has awarded Educational Loan Fund dollars totaling more than $172 million, International Peace Scholarships are more than $34* *million, Program for Continuing Education grants are more than $49 million, Scholar Awards are more than $21 million and P.E.O. STAR Scholarships are more than $5 million. In addition, 8,875 women have graduated from Cottey College.*

I am honored to help other women achieve their educational goals and hope you will take pride in your purchase of this modern fairytale, owning *your* part in empowering women to be the best that they can be.

Love,
Katy

a   m o d e r n   f a i r y t a l e
*beloved fairy tales ♥ modern love stories*

### The Vixen and the Vet
*2015 RITA® Finalist*
*2015 Winner, The Kindle Book Awards*
(inspired by Beauty & the Beast)

### Never Let You Go
(inspired by Hansel & Gretel)

### Ginger's Heart
(inspired by Little Red Riding Hood)

### Dark Sexy Knight
(inspired by Camelot)

### Don't Speak
(inspired by The Little Mermaid)

### Swan Song
(inspired by The Ugly Duckling)
Coming 2018

For announcements about upcoming
a   m o d e r n   f a i r y t a l e
releases, be sure to sign up for Katy's newsletter at
**http://www.katyregnery.com**!

DON'T *Speak*

**THE ROUSSEAUS**
**(Blueberry Lane Books #12–14)**

*Jonquils for Jax*
*Marry Me Mad*
*J.C. and the Bijoux Jolis*

**THE STORY SISTERS**
**(Blueberry Lane Books #15–18)**

*The Bohemian and the Businessman*
*The Director and Don Juan*
*The Flirt and the Fox*
*The Saint and the Scoundrel*

**THE AMBLERS**
**(Blueberry Lane Books #19–20)**
*(Coming 2018)*

*Belonging to Bree*
*Surrendering to Sloane*
*Merry Matrimony*

**THE ATWELLS**
**(Blueberry Lane Books #21–24)**
*(Coming 2019)*

*Four books to be named*

**STAND-ALONE BOOKS:**

*After We Break*
*(a stand-alone second-chance romance)*

*Frosted*
*(a romance novella for mature readers)*

*Four Weddings and a Fiasco: The Wedding Date*
*(a Kindle Worlds novella)*

# ACKNOWLEDGMENTS

First and foremost, I owe so much to my Mia, who held my hand every step of the way with this novel. With daily texts and voice messages of mutual encouragement, we wrote *Don't Speak* and *Preston's Honor* together, and I will always think of these two books as kindred spirits in my heart. I love you very much, sweet Mia, and I am so grateful for your friendship.

To Amy, Heidi, Leylah, Toni, Amy, Karen, Mikey, Laura, Robyn, Ilsa, Beth, Becca, Penny, Pam, Kelly, Melody, Aleatha, Aly, Corinne, Tia, Jennie, Molly, Christi, Carey, Kristen, Kirby, Vi, P, Skye, Marquita, Kally, Annika, Violet, and all the girls going on KWK17 and participating in THIS IS INDIE/THIS IS ROMANCE, **you** are my tribe. I'm in awe of you and grateful for you and love watching as each of you makes your dreams come true in this sometimes-maddening world of indie publishing.

To Chris, Nik, Tanner, and Tyler, thank you. You four are the best trainers in the world, and I am so lucky to work out with you four times a week. A special thanks to Tanner, who trained me on a day when I'd lost a significant amount of writing on this book. He listened as I spent an hour re-creating the plotline, offering helpful suggestions to replace the work I'd lost.

To Samantha Shafer and her Patrick, thank you for letting me borrow your names for Judith's daughter-in-law and son and for being my #FBBFF. And to my readers, Madelyn and Karen, both of whom gave me names (Kyrstin and Remy) to use in *Don't Speak*, I am grateful for your contributions.

To my friends in Katy's Ladies, many of whom have been cheering me on since the very beginning, I am incredibly blessed to have all of you in my life and on my team. Thank you for loving my books and being the most amazing audience an author could wish for. I appreciate each and every one of you.

To my production team: Chris and Melissa (line and copy edits), Tessa (developmental edits), Marianne (cover design and graphics), Tanya (graphics), Tina (trailer), Cassie Mae (formatting), Julie (proofreading) and Heather (PR)—I do not merely flatter you when I say I have the best team in the entire world. I'm just telling it like it is. I am grateful for **every one** of you. Your talent is immeasurable, and I depend on you more than you can ever know. Thank you for coming through for me time and time again. I hope you're proud of the work we do together. I know that I am!

To my parents, Diane and George, for being the guiding lights of my life. You encourage and inspire, support and celebrate. Thank you from the bottom of my heart for your unconditional love. I am the luckiest daughter in the whole world.

And finally . . . to George, Henry, and Callie. You are my dearly beloved, my heart, my soul, my whole life, and everything worth living for. The most important thing is kindness, and I love each one of you all the much.

# ABOUT THE AUTHOR

***New York Times*** **and** ***USA Today*** **bestselling author Katy Regnery** started her writing career by enrolling in a short story class in January 2012. One year later, she signed her first contract, and Katy's first novel was published in September 2013.

Twenty-five books later, Katy claims authorship of the multititled *New York Times* and *USA Today* bestselling Blueberry Lane Series, which follows the English, Winslow, Rousseau, Story, and Ambler families of Philadelphia; the six-book, bestselling ~a modern fairytale~ series; and several other stand-alone novels and novellas.

Katy's first modern fairytale romance, *The Vixen and the Vet*, was nominated for a RITA® in 2015 and won the 2015 Kindle Book Award for romance. Katy's boxed set, *The English Brothers Boxed Set*, Books #1–4, hit the *USA Today* bestseller list in 2015, and her Christmas story, *Marrying Mr. English*, appeared on the list a week later. In May 2016, Katy's Blueberry Lane collection, *The Winslow Brothers Boxed Set*, Books #1–4, became a *New York Times* e-book bestseller.

In 2016 Katy signed a print-only agreement with Spencer Hill Press. As a result, her Blueberry Lane paperback books will now be distributed to brick-and-mortar bookstores all over the United States.

Katy lives in the relative wilds of northern Fairfield County, Connecticut, where her writing room looks out at the woods, and her husband, two young children, two dogs, and one Blue Tonkinese kitten create just enough cheerful chaos to remind her that the very best love stories begin at home.

DON'T *Speak*

Sign up for Katy's newsletter today: **www.katyregnery.com**!

Made in the USA
Middletown, DE
26 April 2017